Ike

Ike

A novel by
Ron McAdow

GMB
Great Meadows Books
Lincoln, Massachusetts

ISBN 978-0-9906084-1-7

Library of Congress Control Number: 2015900765

Great Meadows Books
an imprint of Personal History Press

59 South Great Road
Lincoln, Massachusetts 01773

Life, at its best, is a flowing, changing process in which nothing is fixed.

Carl Rogers

Chapter 1

How do people decide about marriage? Perhaps I allowed myself to be influenced by factors that should not have been considered. I envy those who are sure they took such an important step for the right reasons, at the right time. Maybe I was too susceptible, too hungry to be needed. Maybe it was my best move. I really don't know. I seem to have drifted into it.

Helen and I met at a reception. I had only been doing my talk show, *Hubcaps*, for a year. At that point I felt like a bright young star of the Boston media scene, with my future before me and no limit on how far I could go. I had been dating an actress and was just starting to think that maybe I loved her when she announced that she had a new agent and was moving to Los Angeles. The agent had convinced her that she needed to be out there, *where the work was*. She made it clear that our relationship ended with her move. I am imbued with the notion that when a woman opens herself to physical intimacy with a man— especially if he is a gentle and cheerful kind of guy—she becomes, as a natural consequence, emotionally involved and thinks about making a life with him. My girlfriend's unhesitant departure was not the first refutation of my sentimental theory. Although contrary experience seems unable to dislodge my belief, it has taught me that I cherish known falsehoods and often behave as though they were true.

The reception was at a new museum of modern art. Our WIVB program manager, Doug Conant, wanted what he called his *talent* in attendance, to see and be seen by the city's movers and shakers. For me it was an opportunity to meet prospective *Hubcaps* guests. I didn't go to this party with the expectation of having a high profile—but as it turned out I was made much of. This was partly because our audience was growing but mostly because Doug steered me to various movers, then interrupted those conversations with introductions to shakers. "Ike, here's someone I want you to meet," he said, as though he hadn't used the same line six times earlier in the evening; as though this was the one person in the room he most wanted to connect me with. "Say hello to Helen Marsh," was his command, but before I could obey he continued, "This young lady has done wonders with my house. She chose all our colors and carpets and helped us find outstanding works of art."

A lovely dark-haired woman looked up at me through bright blue eyes. "Hello, Helen," I said.

"Hello Mr. Martin. I enjoy your show. I don't see it every time, but when I do, I admire your way with your guests."

"Thank you. Please call me Ike."

"We're in a brainy town so we need a brainy guy like Ike to chat 'em up," Doug said over his shoulder as he stepped away.

"Are you his interior decorator?" I asked.

"You could call me that, although I've been doing less and less about anything but art. I want to be done with window treatments."

"Do the Conants have a good art collection?"

"It's good for them. It would not be good for everyone. He and Jill hang edgy stuff that would turn some couples off."

"You don't judge—"

"I feel smart about art and what works in what households. I wish I were smarter about people. You are wise that way, aren't you? It comes across on your show."

"I don't know about the wise part but I certainly find people interesting. Don't you?"

"In theory, yes, but in practice they are usually predictable."

"Predictable? I suppose so. What would you predict about me?"

"I predict you'll succeed."

Would she have predicted that I would end up asking her to lunch? Probably she knew exactly how guys responded to her. I would not have predicted that she'd accept my invitation, but she did and we met at a restaurant a few days later.

I tried not to notice how many glances were stolen in our direction. Did people wonder, *Have I seen that guy on television?* Or did Helen literally turn heads? What made her so unusually attractive? A rapid flow of changes animated her face in response to what she was hearing or, when she was speaking, adding to her expression. The twinkle of her earrings drew your eyes. Her complexion and her hair were smooth and soft-looking. Her figure was slender but feminine. She seemed perfectly at ease, as though she were free of insecurity. Her lack of self-consciousness included acknowledging her weaknesses. "I can make a client believe in me," she claimed, but then she brought me up short by adding, "On the other hand, I leave a lot to be desired in the motherhood department."

"You have a child?"

She nodded. "Two boys."

It was surprising to find out she was a mom. She looked about my age—I was twenty-eight. I tend to jump to the conclusion that people who are the same age as me have about the same amount of life experience. I had never before been attracted in a boy-girl way to a known mother. It felt a little inappropriate and somewhat interesting.

"Where did you grow up?" she asked, as though to change the subject. I told her about Ithaca and my professor father and my politically active mother. I described my older brother, the steady one, and my younger brother, the intelligent-with-learning-disabilities enigma, and mentioned that I had a sister who, I claimed, defied description. Then I asked about her.

She was an only child. She'd grown up in New Jersey. After college at Wellesley she'd married a guy named Greg. A year ago Greg had moved his startup to the Bay Area because his backers thought there was a better chance for the company if he was based in Silicon Valley. The plan had been for Helen and their sons to follow him west at the end of the school year. But, as spring progressed and it was time to put their house on the market, Helen had decided that she was not a California girl after all. I eventually learned she'd had more tangible reasons to stay in the East. They had legally separated and were in the process of getting a divorce.

Helen was thirty-three, five years my senior, but she had really good skin. Her sons were ten and seven. "I shouldn't have had them so young," she told me. "But Greg wanted to launch his company and his family at the same time and grow them together. Little did I know his priority would be the company and that I was expected to do the family pretty much by myself, never mind that I had my own career. Why did he consider my work less important than his? We had au pairs when the boys were little, and that helped, although usually they were high-maintenance. Now my guys are both in school and they go to camp in the summer so we get along with just Auntie Fiona, my sitter."

When this lunch date began I still thought of myself as a carefree young bachelor enjoying extended adolescence, uninitiated into the serious adult life of child rearing and home ownership. As the conversation went along I felt myself peeking into that realm with a certain interest. When Helen said, "I'd like you to meet my sons. Would you come on a picnic with us?" I couldn't think of any reason to say no. "Their names are Sean and Denver," she told me. "I think you'll like them."

Maybe I would or maybe I wouldn't. When the day arrived, and Helen picked me up in her big sport utility vehicle, with her sons belted into the back, I was ready to do the best I could at what was, for me, an entirely novel challenge. As I sat down in the front passenger seat, before Helen could introduce me, a young voice asked, "Why are we picking him up at Starbucks?"

"Because—"

"Doesn't he live anywhere? Is he a homeless person?" It was the larger of the two boys who was speaking.

"Ike," Helen said, "Sean would like to know where you slept last night."

"Hello guys," I said. "Do you mean, like, what park bench was I on? I have a favorite not too far from Fenway. Last night when I got there a really big ugly guy had already taken it. He was snoring."

Helen darted her eyes my way. "Life is full of disappointments."

"Yes. It just wasn't his night. The poor guy got pushed off and had to go find himself another bench."

"Did you push him off?" Denver asked.

"He's kidding, idiot," Sean said.

"Are you?" Denver asked.

"Yeah, I'm kidding." I looked over my shoulder at Denver, who gazed back with earnest concern. "I share a place with some guys but I needed to work for a while this morning and that's why I asked your mother if we could meet here."

"If he was a homeless guy the car would be stinking by now," Sean said.

"Where are we going for our picnic?" I asked Sean.

"Holt Hill," Helen answered. "Ever been there?"

"I don't think so."

"Mom said you worked on TV."

"Yeah, at WIVB," I said. "Channel Four. The station's a couple blocks from Starbucks."

"Why didn't we pick you up there?"

"Security. They don't let people drive in unless you work there."

"Ike has his own show," Helen said.

"We wouldn't know," Sean grumbled. "We're not allowed to watch. Auntie Fiona only lets us watch one hour a day."

"How do you spend your hour?" I asked.

Denver said, "Sean makes us watch *Boy Meets World.*"

"You like it, too," Sean argued. "When we go to Dad's we can watch all we want. Are you on in California?"

"Not yet," I said. "I'm just on around here. Maybe someday."

We left the car in the reservation's small parking lot and carried a picnic basket up the trail, along with two kites and my daypack. At the top of the hill was a large open area. There were no picnic tables—this was conservation land, not a park. "We came here once before, to fly Sean's kite," Helen said, "and it seemed like it would be a good place to have lunch. But there's nothing to sit on." Her white shorts would have fared poorly on the grass. Although the morning sun had taken up the dew, recent rain left the ground quite damp. I had a nylon poncho in my pack, which, spread out like a blanket, allowed us to keep our pants dry.

As Sean started preparing his kite he asked, without looking at anyone, "Is this a date? Are you guys on a date?"

I expected an instant denial from Helen but it didn't come. I said, "It looks like a family picnic to me."

"Then what are you doing here?"

That was Sean. Denver added, "You're not in our family."

"Can't a family take along a friend?" their mother parried.

"Oh, I see, he's our friend even though we never heard of him before," Sean said.

"Go fly a kite," Helen said.

Which Sean did. After two false starts, it rose steadily. Its blue and white wings became smaller as it climbed.

When Denver held up his red kite, Sean objected, "You're way too close." Denver moved a few steps to the side. "No! They'll get tangled." Sean pointed to the other side of the open area. "Go over there."

Helen sat on the poncho, watching her sons. I stood a careful distance away—a friend-of-the-family sort of distance, as I calculated it. "Want some help?" I called to Denver.

"No," was his firm reply. He moved fifty yards off. When he lifted the kite over his head, the wind took it. The mowed area was surrounded by mature forest, and I thought Denver had gone too near the trees. The wind stopped and his kite fell to the ground.

"When the wind drops you have to run backwards," Sean coached, and to my surprise Denver was able to make good use of this advice. After a few more tries his kite was climbing. Just as I began to hope that he could match his brother's success the unreliable air flow shifted; the kite zoomed sideways toward the trees, then dived straight down. It snagged a branch and stopped short. The string went limp. Denver looked toward his brother as though he expected humiliation and reproach, but all Sean said was, "Too bad, but there was nothing you could do."

I walked past Denver to the tree and looked up. The kite was well out of reach. It didn't appear to be damaged but it was entangled in oak twigs and leaves. "If you take up some string, maybe you can tug it loose," I suggested.

Denver patiently wrapped string around the spool. I glanced over at Sean, who was reeling in his kite. When Denver's line was taut, he gave it a pull. The kite didn't come loose.

Sean left his kite with Helen and joined us. "Try a different angle," he suggested. Denver walked in an arc down the hill, keeping tension on the string. The kite remained caught. "Go back the other way." Denver reversed his arc and swung up the grade. As he neared the trees, the kite moved. "Pull it again," Sean said. Denver obeyed. The kite popped loose. I caught it before it hit the ground.

Denver walked toward me, winding string as he came. When he reached me I handed him the kite.

"Thank you," he said.

We went up the hill and sat down. Helen distributed sandwiches. "What's this thing we're on?" Sean asked.

"It's a poncho I carry in my daypack," I said. "In case it rains."

"Can I wear it?" Denver asked.

"You can't wear it," his mother told him. "We're sitting on it."

"Anyway it's not raining," Sean added. He pointed at my pack. "What else is in there?"

"Let's see." I reached in. The first thing my hand touched was a bag of marbles—my childhood marbles pouch. I'd brought it along on a whim. As I lifted it from the pack, it clicked as marbles knocked into each other. Just then my cell phone rang. I looked at its screen. "It's my producer," I said. "Please excuse me." I poured the marbles onto the poncho, accepted the call, walked off, and had a brief conversation with Anna. When I turned back toward my companions, Denver and Sean were playing with the marbles.

"What do you do with them?" Sean asked. I showed him the difference between shooters and the others and explained the basics of the game. But a poncho spread over grass on a hillside is not satisfactory for marbles. Sean pointed out a flat place under a pine tree. Helen said she was too old for marbles and would stay where she was with her book. Denver asked to see my phone. With some misgivings, I handed it to him.

Sean and I went to the tree and brushed away the pine needles, revealing moist black earth. I marked out a circle and we tried to start a game. It was too muddy. Sean lost interest and announced he was going for a hike. Denver joined us and handed back my phone. He tried a shot. His crisp expulsion of the shooter was surprising for such a young boy.

Sean said, "Let's go for a hike."

"Go ahead," Denver said.

"Denver you know we have to go together," Sean complained.

"I'm playing marbles."

"It's too muddy."

I offered to lend the marbles to Denver and said I thought hiking was a good idea. We did go for a walk and Helen went too, but it felt awkward or boring or we were just too anxious. We hadn't gone far before Denver relieved us all by asking to go home. They took me to my car and, with little ceremony, we parted.

I'd been back at my place for an hour when my phone rang. It was Helen. "Ike, they liked you," she told me.

"Who did?" I asked, stupidly.

"Sean and Denver. Are you busy tonight?"

"I was going to—well, no, I'm not busy."

"Because Auntie Fiona is coming over after supper so I'm free and I could stop by if you want. For a glass of wine or whatever. Because we didn't really get a chance to talk today."

I said that would be fine. One of my roommates was traveling and the other was at his girlfriend's. I had the place to myself. I picked up my roommates' junk and threw it into their rooms, did the dishes, showered, and was ready to receive company by the time she said she would come. A half hour after that, she rang the bell. She handed me a bottle of cold white wine and came in the door complimenting me for having had "that thing we could sit on" and letting Denver take her picture with my phone and helping the boys with their kites—which I had not—and giving them the marbles, which she said Denver had been playing with when she'd left the house. I did not correct her mistaken impression that I had given, rather than lent, my marbles.

I opened the wine and we sat on the sofa. Helen offered no conventional remarks about my apartment—a compassionate suspension of professional judgment. She said she was glad that we could get together because next week she was headed to New York on business. Her babysitter, the unrelated woman they called Auntie Fiona, would get the boys to and from day camp and mind them in the evenings. Sean had his first sleep-away camp coming up later in the summer. She repeated that they liked me. I said I liked them, too.

Helen asked me questions and I gave long answers. It was nice to talk to her about myself and it was comfortable on that couch. After the hours outdoors with her guys, we felt relaxed and friendly, and the wine made us more so, and before long we were kissing. That went well and she kept getting more of herself closer and closer to more and more of me, so I started feeling her body with my hands which led to opening her blouse and kissing her breasts and the friendly relaxedness became displaced by a distinct and positive desire. When I ventured a fumbling effort to unfasten her pants, she put her hand on my hand and whispered "Maybe this is as far as we should go on our first date."

"It's our fourth," I countered.

"If being introduced by Doug was one and after that a lunch and then a family picnic today. You count those as three dates?"

"That's how I do the math."

"It's not as though we're teenagers." She unhooked her shorts and kissed me. Soon we were naked in my bed. We made love comprehensively and repeatedly. When I was exhausted Helen put on her clothes and went home to relieve Auntie Fiona.

The events of that day and evening made my head spin. I felt that beginning a friendship with the two little boys had used all the intelligence, of a certain kind, I had to offer. It felt good to have penetrated their shield of suspicion. I was drawn to them. There must have been something in me that was ready to be a dad.

As for their mother, I had never seen anything like her. How flattered was I that such an extra-good looking and sophisticated woman would want a relationship with me? And the sex! How soon could we do that again? But . . . was there a but? It was so sudden. Was this lady too fast? Too far along in life? Why had she called me after the picnic? Why hadn't she let things develop more slowly? Eventually I needled her about having invited herself to my place that night. She explained that she had liked how I was with her boys and the way my butt looked in my jeans. "Did you think I was a bad girl?" she teased. "Too easy? I'm not easy. I'm impossible, unless I want something. I know what I need and I want all of that right now and nothing else ever."

If she had called me the day after the picnic and the sex, I think it would have turned me off. When she did not call me that day or the day after that I decided to call her. I reached the babysitter, who said she was supposed to tell me that Helen was in New York and to give me her cell number. I called it but there was no answer, so I left a message: "Hello. It's Ike. When will I see you again?"

She returned my call a few hours later and we agreed on an evening the next weekend. When I picked her up, Denver answered the door. "This time is it a date?"

"I guess so."

He came outside and looked at my car. "A Toyota?"

"Yeah."

He went back into the front hall and shouted, "Sean, it's a Toyota." He looked up at me and said, "My dad has a Lexus."

"Is that better?"

"I don't know," he said, and he disappeared.

Over supper Helen and I entered the *we've made love, now what?* phase of our relationship. She told me that she'd never wanted to live in the suburbs but that Greg, her soon to be ex-husband, had insisted that suburban life was better for families. So they had bought the place in Westforest and now she was stuck, because Greg was right about the schools being good, and the boys had friends. She told me about growing up in New Jersey. She described her mother as a helpless person whose default expression was *deer-in-the-headlights*. Her father was a cold fish and probably drank more than he should. Now that they'd moved to Florida she did not see them often. They occasionally talked on the phone.

Helen asked about my interests. When I said I liked to ride my bike, she said that was something we could do together. That clued me in that she was picturing future togetherness. When I asked if she had a bike, she said, no, but she could get one. I told her I had always liked animals and I thought it was fun to go to the zoo even though it was sad that the animals were captive.

"Most of them were born in captivity," she assured me. "That's all they've ever known."

After I didn't argue, she said, "I haven't been to a zoo in years. We could all go." Which we did. We had a good afternoon at a small zoo a half hour from Westforest. Denver took pictures of a jaguar with my phone. My courtship of Helen became a mixture of family outings, traditional dates, and bedroom sessions at my place. I liked her, and her kids, and we had fun.

A few weeks after the picnic Helen called me on my cell. "Ike, I have a problem."

"What's that?" Thus far she hadn't asked me to fix anything or lift anything heavy and I was ready to be a solution to something.

"I'm in New York." Although her clientele was at that time in and around Boston, they believed and Helen believed that the real art scene was in New York. Helen occasionally spent time there, talking to dealers and meeting artists. "Auntie Fiona's sick and here I am in Manhattan."

"Uh oh."

"I have a teenager I could call but I thought of you first."

"How would the boys respond to that?"

"They'd like it."

So I packed an overnight bag, drove out to Helen's house, and rang the doorbell. Sean greeted me with, "What are you doing here?"

"Auntie Fiona's benched. Coach sent me in."

He walked away without saying anything—but he left the door open. I went in, sat down in the living room, and waited.

Five minutes later, Denver appeared. "Sean says you're moving in."

"No such luck. I'm just filling in for Auntie Fiona."

"Want to play marbles?"

Denver had become remarkably adept at shooting marbles. He beat me easily. Next, we played checkers. I could hold my own at that. Then we talked homework. Sean's was done. Denver didn't have any—so he said. It was too late to cook, so we had pizza from the freezer and watched the show they liked on television.

I decided to sleep on the couch in my clothes so it wouldn't look like I was moving in. Lying there I wondered, was I going to fall in love with Helen? Maybe I already was. We had flown right by the crush phase. It felt like I had become attached to both her and her sons. I didn't have anything else going on in the romance department and this was rich and interesting. It wasn't what I had expected; it wasn't classic boy-meets-girl but why did I have to be like everybody else?

I let myself go with it.

When Helen came back from New York, we went to Boston's puppet theater, and to the Aquarium, and to the Museum of Science. In those days Helen only visited New York every five or six weeks and Auntie Fiona usually stayed with the boys. In September Helen asked me if I could look after them for a few nights because of some complication for her sitter. I knew she had just been to New York, so I asked where she was going.

"To Maine."

"Maine?"

"Yeah. They've got artists there, too. Especially on Monhegan."

"Monhegan?"

"The island. Some clients love that Monhegan connection."

I said okay. It was the weekend in the middle of the Australian Olympics. The weather was awful—the fringe of Hurricane Emma was wet and windy. I suspended Auntie Fiona's television budget and we watched the Olympics more or less continuously. Sean brought out the laptop from his room and made a spreadsheet to record data—times, scores, the medal count. After a few hours he was a better source of information than the commentators.

Denver watched Sean with interest and peered at his computer screen. He found paper and a pencil. Every time there was a medal ceremony, he wrote down a score for the gold medalist's national anthem, on a scale of one to five, like the gymnastics judges used. He let us vote. When Denver found that this amused his brother and me, he extended it to commercials, which stimulated a long intermittent conversation about what qualities, in the commercials, we were rating. Appeal to macho men was a parameter we settled on for beer and pickup truck ads. For others, we scored grossness of the product. Denver wrote it all down, "so I can tell it to Mom," as though it was all very serious. He was a funny kid.

After that weekend, when I wasn't with Denver and Sean, I missed them.

There came a time the following summer when the boys were visiting Greg in California and Helen and I were driving out to the Berkshires for the weekend, to hear music at Tanglewood and to see dance at Jacob's Pillow and theater at The Mount. I said, "You know what?"

"What?"

"The picnic was a year ago today."

"Which picnic?"

"Our first one. When I met Sean and Denver."

"Oh." About half a mile farther west on the Massachusetts Turnpike, she added, "It's been a great year."

"Yeah."

"I think you should move in."

"You do? Just like that?"

"I love you. The boys love you. Don't you want to be with us?"

"I do want to be with you," I said. Which was true. After the boys returned, we told them the plan and gave them a month to get used to the idea. My roommates found someone to replace me in the house, and I moved to Westforest.

Living together was an adjustment for all of us. Helen had given her sitter notice, as far as regular weeknight assistance was concerned. We were on our own. I soon came to realize that the family's daily routine had been provided by Auntie Fiona. Helen didn't see the value of it. If our family was to have that kind of structure it was going to come from me. When I asked Helen what time she thought we ought to sit down to supper, she looked blank and said, "Whenever. Does it always have to be the same time?"

"No, but it's good to know when to start cooking. So you can plan." I checked in with Sean. "What time did Auntie Fiona serve supper?"

"I don't know."

I thought there must have been something confusing about the way I'd worded the question. "What time did you usually eat?"

"I don't know," he said.

Neither did Denver.

I gave up on finding out about *when* and shifted my inquiry to *what*.

"Food," was all Sean could tell me about Auntie Fiona's cuisine.

I asked the boys what they liked.

"Meatloaf," Sean said.

"Mac and cheese," Denver added.

On those foundational entrees I gradually raised a system of suppertime expectations that included collaborative cooking and cleanup and acceptable behavior at the table. It was easier to proscribe Denver's comic books than to keep Helen from bringing her laptop into the dining room—but I was persistent.

Having forbidden distracting media, I had to generate civilized conversation. Probably that would have been easier if we'd had girls, because on the whole they seem more talkative. Our boys might not have been intentionally secretive about their lives but their reticence made it seem so. I, a professional talk show host, had to learn new tricks to get them to tell us about their days. I thought it was important and I kept after it.

Helen sometimes lost patience with my structure-making. She characterized it as middle-class—which was, to her, an aspersion meaning shallow and empty. Our lifestyle *was* middle class, obviously. So what? I argued that family time around meals and holidays had nothing to do with social status. I said it was good for kids at any income level. She laughed but for the most part she played along and she never undercut me in front of the boys.

So we functioned as a family. We were typical in that we were one woman, one man, and two children. We were not typical in that the mother did the business travel, the man had the stronger instincts for domesticity, and he was not the biological father. In the first decade of the new century, it was fairly normal for a family to be abnormal. No doubt Sean and Denver envied schoolmates whose parents were still together—but they knew plenty of kids who were dealing with divorce or other variations on the traditional two-parent theme.

Although there was no way, being ourselves, to make our little family entirely conventional, there was one action we could take— by getting married we could convert me from live-in boyfriend to stepfather. Helen and I didn't need that to cement our relationship. But I wanted Sean and Denver to be able to describe me as their stepfather and I thought it would be good to put my own parents into a step-grandparent relation to the boys. So I asked Helen to marry me.

"Sure," she replied. "If you want to. Why?"

I explained.

"Do you think it really matters?"

"Yes, but if you don't, we shouldn't."

"No, I'll do it." She gave me a little hug. "Then I would be your wife."

"I already feel like your house-husband. A wedding would make an honest man of me." I wasn't truly a house-husband; I remained fully employed. *Hubcaps* continued, with me as its host. Doug Conant had stopped lionizing me at parties. Our audience had leveled off and my ambitions had calmed. Now that people were relying on me at home, jumping to a larger market would have been a major disruption. I stopped watching for opportunities. The heavy-hitters of Los Angeles and New York could have discovered my talent—but they hadn't called. I enjoyed my work—and being somebody in Greater Boston— and it left me a reasonable amount of time to attend to my new family.

The plan to legalize my family status required a wedding. Helen and Greg—beautiful young first-time-for-marriage couple that they were—had had the whole nine yards, financed by her father. Helen had no wish to go through that again and I didn't need a big production. Because I wanted my folks to be on hand, Helen invited her parents. Mine drove from Ithaca the day before and Helen's flew up from Florida the morning of the ceremony. My to-do list included picking them up at the airport.

I had met the Marshes once before, but had not spent much time with them. Their plane was a little late. We managed our rendezvous by cell phone. As Helen's father settled into the front passenger seat, I held the rear door open for her mother, who said, "I wish Helen would call more often." This struck me as an odd opening remark.

"Why should she?" her husband rebutted. "You didn't have anything to say to each other before. Why would you now?" He continued as I pulled away from the curb. "What do you want to talk about with her? You don't know anything about art." He turned to me and confided, "Helen has never been close to her mother—"

"We never fight!"

"It takes two to fight. You can't stand up to her."

"She would have minded you," Mrs. Marsh said, "but you were never around. Ike, your future wife didn't have a real father. He was away from home too much."

"I was the provider, for God's sake. Businessmen travel. That's just the way it is."

"Half the time you were at golf tournaments—"

"That was business, too. Those relationships were the key to my success. I wasn't Helen's problem. Helen's problem was that you couldn't control her. And neither could Greg, apparently. I wish you luck, young man."

"His name is Ike," Mrs. Marsh reminded him.

"I know his name is Ike, for Christ's sake," he snapped. "I'm not the one with the neurological issues. Ike, I'm sorry you had to come get us. You had better things to do than pick us up. We should have taken a cab."

"Helen and I thought it would give us a chance to get better acquainted," said Mrs. Marsh.

Her husband growled.

After that, the car was quiet until I dropped them off at the hotel where in three hours I was to become their daughter's second husband. I reflected, after they were out of my car, on *control*. I hadn't been hearing people use that word to describe the discipline of kids. I suppose when they say, *you have to set limits*, or, *no is a love-word*, they mean the same thing, sort of—but *control* sounded farther-reaching and more authoritarian. For the most part Sean and Denver were well-behaved—but that wasn't because anybody controlled them. It's just how they were. Helen's dad had said that her first husband had failed to control her. I didn't dream of controlling Helen—I just wanted to do a good job of holding up my end of the relationship.

Later, when I was alone with my own parents, I mentioned my new father-in-law's use of *control* in the context of raising children. My mother waved her hand as though to brush aside nonsense. There was little similarity between Helen's family and mine.

When, at the supper table, I maneuvered to get people to talk with each other, was that controlling? Manipulative? Or was I just being a good dad? I worked at it year in and year out and it always seemed worth the effort. For example, one evening while Sean was in high school I used one of my prized open-ended questions to get things going. That was, "Did anything funny happen today?"

"Yes," Denver responded, with mischievous promptness. "Sean invited Emily Bingham to the prom."

Sean had a lively social life. He hung out with a group of boys and girls, chatted online and via text, and took phone calls from girls who lately have become shamelessly forward with boys at the cute end of the spectrum. For all that, Sean had not yet gone on a date in the traditional sense of the word. The combination of Denver outing his big brother and the topic he was outed about captured our full attention.

"Smidge fling, Denver," said Sean, deploying an encoded expletive they had developed after I forbade profanity in the house.

Denver smirked.

"And what was Emily's response?" Helen asked, falsely implying that she knew who Emily was.

Sean ignored her invasive query but Denver answered brightly. "She said she's going with Josh Stiner."

"I didn't realize that Sean kept you so well informed," Helen said.

"I don't," Sean said.

"He doesn't," Denver had said at the same time.

"Do you make him wear a wire?" Helen asked Denver.

"I have sources," Denver said.

"Yeah he has lunch every day with Ashley Tanner," Sean said in an accusatory tone.

"I don't have lunch with her. I sit at a particular table and she's one of the other people who sits there."

"He hears all the girl gossip," Sean said.

"No way."

"Way."

"Ashley's sister is Emily's best friend and, you know, they text a lot."

"That doesn't mean you have to blab about it," Sean complained. "And you think it's funny? How weird is that?"

"I didn't get to the funny part yet."

"What was the funny part?" Helen asked.

"The funny part is that Emily likes Sean," Denver said. "But he doesn't have a car."

It was true. Sean is a disciplined person who applies logic with more rigor than most of us. If he wanted a car he borrowed mine, or used his mother's if she was out of town. He got rides from friends. And he went to school on the big yellow bus, which he treated as a handy amenity the town provided for free, whereas other kids acted as though being seen on a school bus proved your family relied on food stamps.

"Do you want a car?" Helen asked Sean. She generally cut to the chase.

"They are too expensive," Sean said. "I don't need one."

He didn't think he needed one but Helen thought otherwise. One of her art-and-interior design clients owned a string of auto dealerships. She called him that night and also called Greg and the next day when Sean got home from school there on the driveway was an automobile. "Your father leased it for you until you leave for college," Helen explained. While not over-the-top ostentatious, the vehicle proclaimed by its make and lines the desirable social status of the teenager who drove it to school.

Emily approved. She rode to and from the prom in Sean's car. Which shows how families benefit from good conversational leadership. Denver wanted to tell his story but he needed a place to start. I provided one. Sean with a car gave Emily Bingham the complete high school boyfriend package she had hoped for.

Chapter 2

Sean had gone off to college when things started changing at my job. *Hubcaps* continued, but it had begun to feel like public interest programming. We weren't selling that much commercial time. My guests were a mixture of touring authors, Boston-area intellectual, political, and religious leaders, and second- or third-tier show business personalities. Doug encouraged us to emphasize celebrities—even if they were fading—but Anna, my producer, preferred substance to fluff, and so did I. We tried to keep to the high road. At one of our planning meetings, Anna said, "Ike, here's an idea. Bill Trippy. Know him?"

"Bill Trippy . . ." I searched my hazy memory for associations. "MIT?"

"Yup. He was a big deal in the moon shot. A go-to guy for electronics back in the day."

She filled me in and we agreed that Bill Trippy looked at least as good as our average prospect. She invited him and he accepted. Doug didn't like it. "I see on the schedule you are having Bill Trippy."

"Yes," I replied.

"He's booked so go ahead. But he's old and he's a nerd. You and Anna ought to keep in mind that the *Hubcaps* numbers are better when you have Stephen Stills or Bette Midler or someone of that caliber."

He's booked so go ahead. That's what trouble sounds like, but I didn't recognize it.

The day of the show Bill walked into the studio, sat down on my set, and told me to ask him about global warming.

"How about the Apollo Program?"

"They've heard all that," Bill said. "I want to talk about climate change."

They counted us down, we went on the air, and I introduced Dr. William Trippy, Professor Emeritus of Applied Physics at the Massachusetts Institute of Technology and one of the reasons Americans have journeyed to the moon. "If you will, Dr. Trippy, take us back—"

"Bill, please. Doctors are for chest pains. I'm an engineer."

"Bill, it's the early sixties, and the Russians—the Soviet Union, it was then—"

"Yeah but we still called them Russians—"

"Had orbited a satellite—"

"And every baby boomer out there," he said, looking straight into the camera, "knows the name of that useless little tin garbage can they sent up."

"Sputnik?"

"Yes. It drove people crazy that they—the Russians—could have something flying over our heads, day and night. We glorify that era— the '50s and early '60s—and paint it all nostalgic but it was not a pleasant time. Everyone was paranoid."

"Bill, how would you compare that fear of the Russians to the current fear of global warming?"

"Every era has its concerns." Bill said. "I'm glad you mentioned climate change because we need to clarify our thinking. People have been led to believe that there are only two ways we can respond to global warming. We can deny that it's happening or we can wring our hands." He made an exaggerated helpless worried face and took his left fingers in his right hand.

"The environmentalists don't just wring their hands," I objected. "They want us to change our behavior."

"They might be doing more harm than good."

"How so?"

"By persuading leaders that reduced fossil fuel consumption should be public policy."

"Wouldn't that be a good thing?"

"The problem is, that's not going to happen. People aren't going to change their lifestyles. Even if they would it would be too little, too late. And where's the equity? People in developing countries want to live like we do. What do we say to them? 'Sorry, the First World got there ahead of you and had a great time burning coal and oil but you mustn't because if you do, climate change will accelerate and there will be inconvenience and expense.' Whose inconvenience? Ours, of course."

When Bill pronounced *inconvenience* he broke his rhythm to linger on and emphasize each syllable. Our camera slowly zoomed in on his face. It was great television—a strong character with a novel take on a big issue, first scorning the general public's selfish uninformed apathy and then dismissing the prevailing wisdom of the educated elite.

I lobbed the obvious softball. "What approach do you recommend?"

"Was it Buckminster Fuller who referred to Earth as our spaceship? That's the correct image. We're riding this blue and green ball through the void, the barren black desert of space—"

"As the environmentalists remind us—"

"They are correct. And we have to manage the climate control system."

"Ah. Take control. Adjust the thermostat."

"That's right but you say it sarcastically because to you and to most liberals *control* is a bad word. Especially where nature is concerned. We're supposed to let nature take care of everything without interference from us."

"You are putting those words into the environmentalists' mouths."

"I'm not putting anything into their mouths—that's exactly what they say. But I'm an engineer and, to an engineer, control is a good word. The human species cannot stop causing change. We're too big and there are too many of us. We have to take control."

Bill stated his opinions as facts. I try to express my opinions as opinions. Bill's approach is less humble and sounds stronger. It *is* stronger, and probably more entertaining, but it wasn't entertaining enough. I glanced at Anna in the booth and saw on her face what I myself was feeling. This interview with Bill Trippy was exactly what *Hubcaps* was supposed to be like. We were discussing a serious topic with a telegenic genius who spoke intelligible unscripted sentences. In response, viewers were lifting their remotes to see what else was on. Our success would fail. Doug Conant was right.

"Have you ever heard of Bill Trippy?" I asked Helen that evening.

"Yes," she said. She seemed a bit startled. "Why do you ask?"

"We had him on the show and he did a good job."

"He was charismatic?"

"Yes, for an egghead. Do you know him?"

"I met him. We talked. At a party or an opening or something."

"You do get around."

"Yeah," she agreed. "Always did."

I thought that Bill was one of the most interesting guests we had had on the show—and apparently I had impressed him, too, because a week later he called and asked if I would have lunch with him, to hear a proposition. We made an appointment to meet at the Black Horse Tavern in Cambridge. I was waiting in a booth there, just beginning to get that stood-up feeling, when in came a guy about my age looking around as you look around when you are searching for someone who matches the description you were given and who appears to be waiting for somebody. That all worked and he found me. He was a skinny guy a little younger than I and a couple inches taller. His straight black hair was pulled behind his head into a short ponytail.

"Ike?" he looked at me "Are you Ike?"

"Yes."

"Hey. I'm Stephen. I have a message for you from Bill Trippy."

"What's that?"

"He's on his way but he'll be late. His flight was delayed. His granddaughter's picking him up at Logan. He's sorry to keep you waiting."

"Okay—"

"I'm to keep you entertained until he gets here."

"Oh, that's really not—"

"Quite all right, my friend, I have to wait for the lady—the granddaughter—so you can amuse me at the same time. I hear you are in television."

"I'm sorry, it's just—"

"Don't apologize, my friend, never apologize," he said. " I, too, am in showbiz," he continued.

"Are you?"

"I am a magician." He looked the part, with his tall, slender build, dark hair and moustache.

"A magician. Professionally or by avocation?"

"I am a dedicated professional," he declared. "I transform one thing into another."

"An alchemist."

"Correct. I change falsehood into truth, guilt into innocence, and everything into money."

"You're a lawyer."

"Cooper, Waters. I try cases."

"A litigator," I said. "I've had trial lawyers on my show from time to time. They seemed to want to get the best of me."

"We have to win. We are creatures of the jungle and its law is the real law. I have no way of knowing whether you are friend or enemy and I want to be sitting on your chest when I find out."

"Ah."

"I've just finished a tasty tort. *Lawn Care v. Starbucks*. For plaintiff. Tragic circumstance."

"Oh?"

"You might have read of Bernie the Blower Basher. Of the fateful autumn afternoon Starbucks served him after he was already over-caffeinated."

"Oh come on."

"He was buzzing and twitching but they gave him more. Their breach of responsibility caused Bernie to go berserk. He went from one neighborhood to another following the roar of leaf blowers. With a sledgehammer he smashed them."

"And the workers?"

"He assured the operators they were safe, but they didn't speak English and were frightened. Legally that's assault. We nailed Starbucks for negligence and brought home a big award."

"Are you kidding me?"

"Sadly, the workers had left the country before the settlement was paid. Irregularities in their documentation. The dough went to the bosses. And to Cooper, Waters, of course."

Bill Trippy came through the door followed by a young woman. When they reached our booth Bill said, "I see Stephen found you." The woman had a warm smile and brown hair to her collar-bone.

"Yes, he's telling me about his law practice."

The woman looked surprised, then she said, "Oh. That's from his play. He has a lawyer in his play."

Stephen grinned.

"Have you been trying out a character on Mr. Martin?" the woman asked.

Stephen put on the expression of self-indulgent contrition worn by a scamp who is confident of his charm.

"Ike, this is my granddaughter, Marjory Trippy," Bill said.

"Hello Mr. Martin," she said.

"Ike. Please. Ike."

"And everyone calls me Marjie. I'm sorry that I can't stay for lunch. I have to get to school."

"Do you teach?"

"Yes, and school starts next week and my classroom is not ready."

"She picked me up in my car," Bill explained, "Stephen has to take her to her school."

"Back to the salt mines for me, too." Stephen said.

I looked at him. "You are not a litigator after all."

He shrugged.

"An actor?"

"Playwright. I've got a lawyer and I need to understand the part. Thanks for helping me out."

"Happy to oblige," I lied.

"He's going to think you are a weirdo, Stephen," Marjie said, taking his arm.

Stephen looked as though that was okay with him.

"He's not always weird," she assured me. As they walked away I thought that she seemed grounded and nice and I thought she was too good for him.

When they were gone Bill said, "Stephen was one of my son's graduate students."

"What does your son teach?"

"Reading. At Tufts. Everett knows all about reading."

"A complex subject," I said.

"Yes. Ev is a big shot in the reading world. This guy," he said, jerking his thumb, "This guy Stephen, he's not. He changed course. He thinks he's creative."

"You're not so sure?"

"Who knows? Marjie seems to like him. And I like Marjie so that's that."

We ordered lunch. Between bites of his salmon burger Bill told me about growing up in North Dakota and Texas and being a little too young for World War II and coming to MIT and getting involved in defense work and then in the space program. He looked at me and said, "I could use some help with my autobiography."

"What makes you think I can write?"

"You can listen," he said. "That's what I need. We can always find an editor to tune up the prose." Bill laid out some next steps, if I chose to accept his offer. And he invited me and my wife if I had one to a party at his place on Cape Cod. "We'll drink a toast to Marjie and Stephen; to their life-long happiness."

"They're engaged?"

"So they tell me."

Although I had full time employment, I didn't turn Bill down. I said I'd think about it. I was not too confident about my job security. My worry was well-justified. Three days after that lunch at the Black Horse, Doug Conant summoned me to his office and handed me a letter signed by the station manager.

> Dear Mr. Martin,
> Thank you for all the creativity and effort you put into *Hubcaps* over the years. Your work has enriched the cultural life of Boston and its metropolitan area. Unfortunately circumstances prevent WIVB from entering into a tenth season—

We were cancelled. They had a job for Anna but not for me. I called Bill and accepted.

When *Hubcaps* went off the air, Denver was about to become a high school senior. As teenage boys go he had been a pleasant lad, but as his last year of high school began his shoulders slumped and his head bowed as though to avoid dampening his hair in the clouds just above it. This did not surprise me—it would have been odd if he had sailed through high school in a rosy frame of mind. But it was hard to see him down, and somewhat lonely for me when he was withdrawn, because we often had the house to ourselves. Helen's business kept her more and more in New York because, as she put it, the art and the artists were there.

I wondered whether perhaps his mother's frequent absences had put him in the dumps. He didn't complain of that and there were other possibilities. He was an adolescent. That flood of hormones is capable of derailing the steadiest disposition. He didn't have a girlfriend—whereas his brother always did. Next year this time he'd be leaving home for college—maybe he imagined that and shrank from the difficult transition, which he wasn't ready for—why should he be? It was still a year away. Maybe my career interruption bothered him. He probably saw me as a capable adult and here I was suddenly out of a job. If the world didn't need me, how could he be confident that it would need him?

I hoped that a tour of colleges would cheer him up. He still planned to go to MIT, but he knew there was a chance he wouldn't get in, even though he had excellent test scores. I wanted to put images of viable alternatives into his head. We planned to leave the day after his birthday, which was on a Saturday in mid-September. Because Helen usually spent weekends at home, Denver and I assumed that we would have our traditional celebration: a cookout followed by ice cream and miniature golf. Denver had loved miniature golf as a kid; over the years it had become a comic ritual birthday activity. The Thursday before his birthday, Denver was sitting at the kitchen table doing his homework. He had been on the phone with his dad. Having passed beyond the levels of math and science I understood, Denver had begun turning to Greg when he needed a homework consultant in those subjects.

My cell phone rang. It was Helen. "Ike, the Siemands thing is delayed until Saturday so I have to stay over."

I could tell she'd forgotten Denver's birthday. Most moms don't forget their children's birthdays but Helen wasn't most moms. I hoped that Denver hadn't heard what she said and tried to decide whether it would be worse to leave the room or to stay put. I made the wrong choice; I could have needed to step out to discuss his gift. It was one of those rare situations in which acting sneaky was not a give-away. I missed that chance and said, "That's okay, he and I can come there for his birthday party."

Usually Helen's response to being exposed in an error would be an emphatic "Fuck!" Then without pause she would denigrate the importance of the oversight and excuse herself from culpability. This time, though, she was ashamed. She pretended she had known all along. She accepted my offer to bring Denver to New York City.

We re-ordered the sequence of campus visits based on waking up in the Big Apple on Sunday. Denver had figured out what happened with his mom and he was hurt and mad but trying to hide it. Saturday afternoon we walked in Central Park and then went for drinks even though the guest of honor was under age. In the hotel bar Helen greeted a man she had invited to meet us there. "Julian," she said, "these handsome fellows are Denver and Ike."

In most parts of the world Denver and I would have been identified as her son and husband, but not in big-city art culture where allusions to family sound corny and middle-American. Julian would not have looked out of place in Iowa—on Halloween. Was that really an ascot? Was magenta chosen for its relationship to the blue silk shirt? Were his trousers white linen? Denver, whose exposure to his mother's world was limited, had never seen anything like him.

"Julian and I often work together," Helen explained, "so I wanted him to meet the two of you."

Julian offered his hand and an extremely complicated smile. His grasp was, I thought, calibrated to be just barely too firm to be limp but far too weak to imply heartiness. Your handshake should not be at odds with your shirt, and Julian's shirt was not flannel. "How do you do?" Julian whispered. "Welcome to the Village." He referred, of course, to Greenwich Village which this hotel was not technically within, but Julian probably felt that the Village travelled with him as his aura. I put his age at around sixty. "Are you from Boston?" he asked, which was a little strange if he was such a pal of Helen's but then of course any status she held in Julian's world had been won in New York on New York terms without reference to personal affiliations she might have elsewhere. Boston was marginally less nowhere than, say, Cleveland, or Houston—but there's only one New York.

"Outside Boston, actually," Denver answered. "In the suburbs."

"A nice leafy one, I hope," said Julian, putting on a rapt and appreciative expression. He looked at Helen as he added, "That phrase works so well, doesn't it? Leafy suburb? The image is apt." He beamed at all of us. "I have visited leafy suburbs. In fact, I store my automobile in such a place. I've not yet lived in one."

"It's boring," Denver said.

Julian's expression changed to display sympathy, which struck me as patronizing and off base. When a teenage boy uses the word *boring* he just means in the last thirty seconds nothing has blown up and no one's head has been chopped off because unfortunately real life is not a video game. Denver didn't deserve sympathy; only a roll of the eyes. Julian couldn't know this because he had never seen a video game. I reflected that, had we been at home, we'd be playing miniature golf right now. I wondered how much Julian knew about that sophisticated entertainment. What was this character doing in the middle of our birthday party? He made us sullen. Helen rescued the social situation by posing as Denver's and my biggest fan. We listened to her praise us. She built up Denver's youthful achievements and boasted of my stellar success with *Hubcaps*. This got us through my first glass of wine, after which I was able to mutter, "Rumors of my success are greatly exaggerated," and, faking a better attitude, I showed some courtesy to Julian.

We survived our encounter with the ascotted-one and adjourned to supper without him. Helen filled us in about Julian and his supposed sovereignty amongst art consultants and appraisers. Then, after what I imagine to have been an internal pep talk, Helen launched an effort to make amends for other lapses by demonstrating interest in her younger son. She did a good job and Denver's posture improved for the rest of the time he was with her. When we said goodbye to head for the campuses, his body language lost its tone. He resented being alone in the car with his stepfather. He kept buds in his ears, listening to music on his phone. What was playing? Kids might like show tunes or other corny stuff without telling us. Anyway, he shut me out with the earbuds and by staring at the phone. Sometimes he made a flurry of two-thumbed keystrokes.

"What are you typing?"

He ignored me.

I tapped his shoulder.

Without looking up, he removed one earbud.

"What are you typing?" I feigned patience.

"A text," he mumbled.

"Who to?"

"My dad," Then he replaced the earbud.

Ten minutes later we had an identical exchange except he identified his correspondent as "my brother."

There was one chink in his armor. The game that we had begun during the Australian Olympics had continued and branched out. We ranked tennis players by their grunts and during football season we rated touchdown celebrations. We scored food samples handed out at the supermarket and outrageous U-turns made by Helen. Denver kept notes about her history of aggressive driving and its consequences, such as whether she received a warning or an actual citation. She got extra credit if she wept real tears while expressing fake remorse to the cop.

Denver recorded it all. Whenever we felt like annoying Helen or Sean we reported our findings at length, with exhaustive commentary, which they rewarded with groans, commands to stop, and other satisfying protests. During our college visits it was natural for us to score campuses based on irrelevant criteria such as the percentage of students with visible tattoos, comprehensiveness of the magnetic-striped ID card system, and the estimated IQ of our student guide. Denver categorized our fellow student visitors by the brands of their clothing. He had to do this on his own; I couldn't tell the difference.

As long as we were on a campus we were friends, but back in the car the weather changed. On a highway in Maine he remarked, "Cars are funny."

"How so?"

"They're like these little capsules stuffed with people. Like they're bacteria and we're viruses riding around in them and at the same time we're their DNA. And planes are just larger capsules that go faster."

"And trains?"

"Trains are different. Because they're on tracks. Nothing on tracks is like a car."

"People do love cars."

"I wonder what my first car will be? A used Toyota? Yuck. Maybe my dad will buy me something cool and hot and I'll drive it across the country to see him."

The phrase *cool and hot* didn't sound like any version of Denver I knew. That should have been a caution. I ought to have shut up but instead I said, "It's great that you're more in touch with him now."

"You don't have to approve, you know."

"No, I just mean—"

"You mean it's good that my real dad loves me."

"Okay . . . "

"Don't you want to have your own kids?"

"Hadn't thought about it."

"Ah. The Great Wall of Ike. Semi-permeable membrane. All ask and no tell."

"I guess it would mean something to me to have my own biological kids but I love you guys and your mom."

"She's too old for you."

"I don't think five years is that big a deal. Are you upset about something?"

"No. I just think it's too bad that you need to act like my dad when I have a dad who's more like me than you are and the whole thing is keeping you from having kids of your own. And why do you always have to be such a psychiatrist?"

"Who's being the psychiatrist?"

"I can't wait until this trip is over."

"Do you want to skip the last two schools?"

"No I don't want to skip the last two schools. What would be the point of that?" In went his earbuds.

I felt numb for an hour and left him alone. Then, after a pit stop, I attempted to rebuild solidarity by requesting the results of our campus comparison survey.

"It's stupid," he said. "Mom forgot my birthday, didn't she? Do you think Mom would rather hang out with her New York friends than with you?"

"Maybe so. I'm pretty mild fare."

"Oh, God, Ike, when you say stuff like that it's like you have no balls whatsoever. I mean, I'm sorry, but that's how it sounds. No wonder she'd rather be in New York."

I took a deep breath and kept the car in its lane. I wasn't his therapist; I was only his step-dad; and it was hard to take this pounding. I recognized that *Mom forgot my birthday* was an olive branch, an acknowledgement of the source of this storm, but then he followed with the knife, uttering a thought I had no need to have pointed out to me and no wish to hear spoken. I was a house-husband in the suburb while Denver's mom traded witticisms and flirtatious glances with Julian and his ilk on the island of Manhattan.

Five minutes after questioning my manhood Denver said, "I'm sorry. Are you mad at me?"

"No, not really," I said. "You make some good points."

"I wish she was different."

"She may inhabit a leafy town but she's not boring."

There was tension in Denver's laugh, but it signaled a standing-down from hostilities. He pulled a little spiral-bound notebook from the pocket of his fleece jacket. "So I know you're waiting to hear," he said, and he gave me a detailed wrap-up of our campus comparisons.

It began to rain. I made a mental note to replace my wiper blades before winter.

Chapter 3

Marjie's engagement party was on a Saturday not long after Denver and I had returned from our college tour. It was a midday clambake at the Trippy summer place on Cape Cod. Helen and I parked our cars on a quiet, narrow, dead-end street. Dark rhododendrons hid the house. A small sign with an arrow directed us along the low wall to a wooden gate that clicked as I unlatched it. We followed an old brick walk beneath a pergola. Beyond one final rhododendron we turned toward the house, a mass of brown wooden shingles with dark green trim. The path split; the left fork, which led to the house, was barricaded by a chair and a sign that read *Perfect weather! Party on the beach!* The right fork took us across a lawn past a bird bath. A blue jay protested our interruption. We continued under mid-sized oaks descending toward the shine of sky and surf, hearing party sounds. At the bottom we emerged into September light, warm not hot; bright not blinding.

We were greeted by a short-haired woman who identified herself as Marjie's aunt. Behind her came the bride-to-be, looking uncertain and a little trapped, as though today whatever she did she necessarily neglected something else, and wherever she was she was conscious of where she was not. They led us to the sand, where several dozen guests stood in knots or chased frisbees. At the back of the beach a catering crew was busy making steam. I took off my shoes and joined the frisbee tossers.

It was pleasant. I enjoyed the sound and smell of the sea and the feel of my feet running on the sand. We strangers traded praise for good throws and deft receptions. After frisbee, chatter came easily because our connections to Marjie or Stephen-the-ponytailed-fiancé gave us places to begin. Lunch was New England seafood—clams and lobsters with local sweet corn, eaten on low-slung beach chairs. If a party is supposed to make you feel relaxed and glad to be there, this one was succeeding with me.

The chairs had begun the day in a row facing the ocean, but their line was breaking into C-shaped clusters. I carried my clams and lobster from one to the next until I found Helen, who had only steamers and an ear of corn. She treated carbohydrates as if they were toxic; that's how she kept her belly flat and her thighs girlish. Sweet corn, in season, she allowed herself. She disliked lobster—no picking through that rosy carapace for her. She was seated between two women who took turns talking at her.

As I dismembered my lobster, I listened and observed. They were telling Helen about the exhibit one of them was curating for a suburban museum. I knew the place; it had been the estate of deceased wealthy art lovers. For their sins their grounds have been filled with sculpture that might be fragments randomly extracted from train wrecks.

Apparently these ladies had become aware of Helen's standing in the art world. Although they wanted to impress her with their sophistication, it was uphill because their eyes kept darting to their children—they each had one, at play near the water—and their customary topic was kids. They understood that Helen's were grown up and they tried to situate themselves in her urbane post-mom consciousness.

Helen had skipped the mom mentality even when her boys were young. She winked at me and made the face of one who pretends to suffer while she is being deferred to and courted. Her snobbery could be fueled by admiration or it could feed itself. It was a perpetual motion machine.

I was still working little blades of meat out of the fins of my lobster's tail when the kids announced their need for a bathroom. The moms invited Helen and me to accompany them to the house, to see Bill's collection of Inuit art. I pleaded *still at lunch*. Behind their backs, Helen grimaced, but she allowed herself to be led.

I had not yet dunked my last steamed clam in drawn butter when a tallish bearded man sat down beside me. His plate held a slice of watermelon rocking on its rind and he was at pains to keep it from slipping off. "They should develop hexagonal watermelons," I suggested.

"That's too good an idea not to have been tried somewhere," he replied. "California, maybe."

"Probably. We Yankees are suspicious of change."

"We cause change, though. There's this contradictory thing where we invent change and resist it at the same time."

"I'm Ike," I said. "Do you think there will be any speeches?"

"Yes, I believe there will be because I'm on the hook to give one myself, being the father of the bride."

"Our gracious host!"

"Not really; this is my father's place. I've spent plenty of time here, though, over the years."

"You must be Everett. I just signed on to help your dad with his autobiography."

"Oh, you're that guy. Yes, I'm Ev."

"The reading expert."

Marjie's aunt, the woman who had welcomed us to the party, arrived in time to hear me say that. As she lowered herself into the chair next to his, she said "He's an expert about everything. The difference with reading is he gets paid. On other matters he gives expertise away for free."

"It runs in the family," Ev said. "This is my sister. Sister Trippy. The Unitarian nun. Rainbow order."

"Georgia," she said. "He calls me a Unitarian nun because he's rude and I'm his lesbian sister."

"Ah," said I, disarmed by the alacrity of this disclosure. "Me, I'm a straight white guy without religious affiliation. What does that make me?"

"It makes you a younger member of my demographic," Ev replied. To Georgia he said, "This is the guy Dad hired instead of Stephen."

"Ah. Dad's new amanuensis. To enshrine the paternal majesty and give his memory eternal life," Georgia said.

"Is that the goal?" I asked.

"Could be," she said. "Self-effacing people don't get around to making notes for their grandchildren, let alone hiring someone to play Boswell to their Dr. Johnson."

"Is he a worthy Doctor Johnson?" I asked.

"He absolutely is," Georgia declared, "although you have to figure that any famous person benefitted from being in the right place at the right time."

"Which Dad absolutely did," Ev said.

"Where is he?" I asked. Bill wasn't in my field of view. I wanted to know whether he was listening.

"He's down the beach talking to a lady," Georgia said. "Isn't that the gal you came with? Cute!"

"That's my wife," I said.

Georgia waggled her eyebrows.

"Watch out," Ev warned me.

"I don't know that she's got anything on Lee," Georgia said, as she aimed an admiring gaze at her pretty partner.

"Your trophy wife," Ev smirked.

"Fuck off," Georgia said, smiling. "I wish."

"It was chance that manned space flight happened in Dad's era," Ev resumed. "Without that, no celebrity."

"He'd still be rich," Georgia said.

"Ev, I'm interested in all the research about reading," I said, returning to an earlier thread. "Has it paid off in teaching?"

"Wouldn't you think?" Georgia complained. "How many studies? How many conferences? Professors professing night and day! For all that, are kids reading better or worse?"

"We understand a whole lot more about what brains do when people read," Ev said. "Does that translate into a miraculous pedagogy that overcomes all other impediments? Maybe a little, just around the edges. We don't claim to be magicians."

"Stephen did," I said. The repetition of magician in the Trippy family context caused me to blurt out this irrelevant statement. Ev and Georgia waited for me to explain. "When he introduced himself to me he said he was a magician then it turned out he meant lawyer because he could turn falsehood into money or something like that and—sorry—nothing to do with anything . . ."

"That would be Stephen," Georgia said.

"And you?" Ev asked. "Are you an expert? Necessarily you are. Where lies your expertise?"

"Yeah—you look like an expert." Georgia said. "Tell us about yourself."

"I used to host a talk show. If I'm an expert about anything I guess it would be talk."

"Talk!" Ev said. "Second cousin to reading aloud. Remarkably little is known about their relationship."

I asked what his own research was about.

"Lexical cognition," he said. "I started using technology to analyze eye-movement. And for the past few decades we've been looking at the information brains get through those jerky little gaze-hops we make when we are reading."

"He started way back with the computer," Georgia said. "He is his father's son. He has those quantitative chops."

"At first it was the university mainframe," Ev said. "And wasn't it great when I could have my own? I was saved by the personal computer!"

"He's still got it," Georgia said.

"Got what?" I asked. "Quantitative chops?"

"The computer—his old Commodore," Georgia said. "He's never thrown one away. Not a CPU, not a hard drive."

"I have thinned out my floppies, though," Ev said.

"You started early," I said.

"Yeah," Ev said. "I was punching those cards in college and letting other guys run my jobs. When they came out with personal computers I died and went to heaven."

"All this to do with reading?"

"Yup. I got data-driven before my brethren in education."

"About twenty years before," Georgia said.

"What generates the data?" I asked.

"Anything you can measure," Ev said. "Eye movements. Brain waves. All that good stuff. I think it's time for the speeches."

We gathered around Bill, who used his height and his big voice to focus our attention. "I've had many fortunate experiences," he said, "but watching a granddaughter grow up trumps everything. You can be in the thick of exciting work—that's great—you can visit exotic places, meet famous and interesting people, receive prestigious awards—it all pales in comparison to what Marjie has meant to me."

Bill had called attention to his big-dealness while expressing his feeling for Marjie. He had his arm around her. I looked at Helen, who whispered, "What an attractive guy she's got. He's after her grandfather's money."

Ev proposed an earnest, workman-like toast to them as a couple. After other family members added pleasantries and good wishes, Marjie thanked everyone for being there and said she supposed that they were now expected to hold an actual wedding. She said they would but they weren't setting a date just yet. And she wanted people to know that it wasn't Stephen's fault that she didn't have a ring. She didn't really like diamonds and didn't need people at school to be talking, at least not until their plans were clear.

Everyone clapped and her friends called out "Good luck! We love you, Marjie."

"She should have taken the ring and put it in a drawer," Helen whispered.

As the audience dissolved, Stephen turned our way.

"Helen, did you meet Stephen?" I asked. "The fortunate groom-to-be?"

"I don't believe I have," Helen said.

"Hello," Stephen said.

"Stephen is it?" Helen said.

"I've never answered to Steve. I'd like to say that you could call me what they called me at school. But that's not a privilege I'd wish to offer everyone so it would be awkward to go further at present."

This was flirtation. Although I did not enjoy such productions I was accustomed to them. Helen radiated something that made men unduly forward. How did it happen? The set of her shoulders? A certain fore-thrusting of her ribs?

"What did they call you at school?" she asked.

"Stuff," he said. "Stuff."

Helen smiled. "Hello, Stuff."

He looked at me. "It's still Stephen to you."

"Stephen, heartiest congratulations to you and Marjie," I said. When you're eating the host's lobster and drinking his refreshing beverages you have to be polite despite all irritations.

"Any advice?" he asked.

"Don't have kids unless one of you wants to spend all your time on them," Helen warned.

Inwardly, I winced.

"Marjie's got plenty of kids," Stephen said. "A first grade class of them."

"Maybe she'll want some of her own," I suggested. Why did I say that? It was too personal.

"Could be," he said, and added, to Helen, "You remind me of a character in my play."

"Your play?" She took the bait.

Discovering that I'd prefer to find a glass of wine than to hear more about Stephen's play, I went to the cooler at the back of the beach, took a plastic glass from a polyethylene sleeve, and poured myself some Riesling. Georgia walked up and held out her own glass. As I filled it she said, "I'm realizing I've seen your show."

"It was fun while it lasted," I said.

"On to the next chapter, I guess," she said.

I nodded. "We talked about your brother but I don't know much about you. Are you an expert, too?"

"I'm an expert about an uninteresting but absolutely necessary aspect of running an insurance company that's complicated and subtle enough to be worth a good salary."

"How long have you and your partner been together?

"Lee and I have been a couple for two years." We both looked at her girlfriend, who was at that moment talking to a guy.

Georgia pointed toward the house. "Dad built a little lawn between his garden and the beach. I've set up the wickets and stakes for croquet. Are you game?"

"Is sending permitted?"

It was. Georgia recruited more players, took a full bottle of red and another of white, and led the way to the court. Croquet entertained me until Helen came to say goodbye. She had driven her own car because she was going on to New York. I walked her to the wooden gate.

"Nice party," I said.

"Nice weather," she said, which meant she begged to differ. To her a party was good if she could advance her art business by expanding either supply or demand. She needed to meet a saleable artist or a prospective client. Having fun wasn't a strength of Helen's. I liked making random new acquaintances and chasing frisbees on the sand and winning and losing on the croquet court, but I had an advantage: parties weren't part of my job.

Back on the beach, I talked with Georgia and her girlfriend, whose aura of innocence complemented Georgia's worldliness. And with Stephen, who told me that he was an ace cyclist who thought nothing of riding fifty miles before breakfast. To atone for having flirted with my wife, he made a point of being friendly to me—talking about himself was how he conceived of friendliness.

The afternoon passed from mid to late; the sun made longer shadows and yellower highlights. I sat in a beach chair next to Bill, who described how he and his late wife happened to have been able to acquire this property and how much she had loved it. It was never easy to keep her in Cambridge; she had wished to be here at all seasons. He praised the uniqueness of its location and recalled the distinguished guests he had entertained here. When he paused, I, on the mellow trailing curve of my wine buzz, found myself choosing not to prompt Bill to go on about his enviable beach house. I was out of energy to humor his grandeur. Into my empty mind came the recollection of my boast to Ev and Georgia about being a talk expert. I thought, why not write about it? I laughed at myself, at this grandeur of my own. Famous author.

That train of thought was interrupted by Marjie. "Everybody's gone," she said to her grandfather. Her uncertain air had departed with the guests. "Except Mom and Dad and they're almost finished cleaning up. Want to have our shore stroll?" She was wearing one of those bathing suit wraps to reduce the explicit presentation of her physical self. Her hair did not quite reach her shoulders.

"And leave Ike here sitting by himself?"

"He could join us."

"I didn't realize the party was over," I said. "I've stayed too long!"

Bill said, "I usually escort my granddaughter down the beach but I'm thinking I'd better not, today, because I'm feeling just a little vertigo. I'm going to act my age and go sit on the sofa. Why don't you fill in for me so Marjie can have her shore stroll?"

"That's what we always call it," Marjie explained. "Are you okay, Granddad?"

Bill leaned forward, got his center of gravity over his long legs, and stood up. "I'm fine," he said. "Just couch-ready."

Marjie took his elbow. "We'll go up with you." As we escorted the old man from the beach to the house, our three heights corresponded to the inner fingers on a hand, with Marjie as index, Bill as the middle finger, and me as ring.

"Keep an eye out for plovers," Bill instructed.

"Okay, Granddad," Marjie said. As Bill crossed the porch, Marjie and I turned back toward the beach. Before we started down the steps she said, "Ike, I do feel like walking but you don't need to come with me if you want to head home."

"No hurry on my end. My wife is on her way to New York and my stepson is at his friend's house ostensibly doing homework but more likely playing video games." She kept looking at me with a patient stillness I found pleasant and unusual. A beat went by until I added, "And it would be a privilege to walk with you. To join your shore stroll."

Marjie started down. I took advantage of the moment in which she couldn't see me to say, "Allow me to congratulate you on your engagement."

"Thank you. Is it funny to get engaged when we're not setting a date?"

"You're allowed to do it however you want."

"Did you and your wife—what's your wife's name?"

"Helen."

"Did you and Helen have a long engagement?"

"No. We skipped that phase. I walked into a family that had an opening for an East Coast dad."

"An East Coast dad? Instead of, like, a Midwest dad?"

"Her ex had moved to California. He's a prince of Silicon Valley. One of them. So the actual dad, the West Coast dad, does his part well enough but Helen's maternal instincts called for a local stand-in." As I heard myself speak I regretted having taken this tone. "I guess it wasn't a storybook romance, but it's worked for us."

"She is gorgeous," Marjie said. "How old are the children?" We turned onto the firm moist band between the foaming wave-tails and the loose dry sand.

"Sean is twenty. He's in college. Denver's seventeen and he's applying."

"You don't look old enough to have a son in college."

"I'm thirty-eight so that does put me young as college parents go. There have been times that I felt more like a big brother. It's been great. This time next year, though, empty nest."

"Nests begin and end the same way. Vacant. I don't think my mom is over it, even after all these years."

"Maybe you and Stephen will give her some new chicks."

"I don't think so. Stephen's not interested. He has too many hobbies. I should call them interests I guess. Hobbies sounds kind of demeaning."

"He writes plays," I said.

"And he rides his bike and he kayaks. He's a busy guy."

"But he has time to be your husband?" Where in the world was I going with that?

"He's been my boyfriend for a long time."

Aren't you afraid you're settling? I wanted to ask but I didn't. *Of course she is settling,* I thought. That's what it means to get engaged. That's why you need a bribe of diamonds or reliable sex or family money to do it. Because you are letting go of your quest for the fantasied ideal and accepting someone real—and limited. "I guess we all think life is going to be a fairy tale."

"Like at just the right age you'll meet just the right person and you'll live happily ever after."

Happily ever after. Perpetual satisfaction and fidelity. Healthy children. Money enough. Lives to the full span, and good feelings and respectful offspring throughout.

We took a few steps in silence before I said, "Georgia's your aunt, right?"

"Yes."

"I like her."

"She's great. I loved her as a kid because, you know, a childless aunt gives the best presents. As a grownup I appreciate her as a person."

"It's fun to watch her interact with your dad."

"The Ev and Georgia Show is always good for a laugh."

"Dangerous for innocent bystanders, though," I said.

"And for uppity young girls like I was sometimes. I guess they trained it out of me."

"Is your family hard to live up to?"

"Sure. How about yours? Is your family full of hard chargers?"

"Just middling," I said. "My father's a retired professor and Mom's into politics."

"Do you have brothers and sisters? Or are you an only child like me?"

"I'm the second of four. Two brothers and a sister."

"Do you spend much time with them?"

"Not too much. Only one of them is local—my sister Kate. She's into yoga."

"I might be, too, if I had time."

"You must enjoy your summers. I guess that's what everyone says to teachers."

"Yes. My favorite summer thing is to go to my patch of community garden and work for a while and then sit down in the middle of it and read. I take my carafe of coffee and an extra chair and if Mrs. Lu comes along she sits with me and we have one of our talks."

"Mrs. Lu?"

"Mrs. Lu is about a million years old and we are friends."

"What is she like?"

"She's wise . . . and sort of loopy." Marjie laughed. "And she doesn't think I should get engaged."

"What's her objection?" I was too nosy. I should have changed the subject.

There was a pause while she suppressed disclosures she didn't wish to make. "She has her own take on everything. That's why I love her. She listens to me rattle and then she makes observations and predictions. She's my personal oracle. My aged Chinese oracle."

"Some people have personal fitness trainers. Much better to have a personal oracle!" We stopped to watch a tribe of tiny quick-footed sandpipers chase the ocean into its bed, then flee as water pushed back up the beach. "That's a nice image, you reading in your garden. Talking with your friend."

When we resumed our intermittent progress down the beach, Marjie said, "What about you, Ike? Is there a picture like that for you?"

"I picture me jogging."

"By yourself?"

"Yes. Or with my brother, when I'm back home in Ithaca. And I have good images of me and the boys—Sean and Denver. We played touch football with other fathers and sons. Then we had donuts and hot chocolate on the way home. That was a good picture—them with red cheeks and cocoa moustaches. That was good."

"Past tense? No more?"

"Sean grew up very self-sufficient. Denver is needier, but he's in a challenging phase and he's reaching out to his biological father."

"Do you wish that you and Helen had a child of your own together?"

"That's the kind of thing Denver's been saying. 'Don't you wish you had kids of your own?' Helen's past that."

"She doesn't look old."

"She was completely finished with reproduction before I came along. She's not exactly the family type. She was young when she married Greg and got pregnant and I don't think she even knew who she was yet. Like she had to try being a mom on for size and, surprise, there were permanent side-effects."

"The boys."

"Right."

"Well, it sounds like you have been a godsend to them and to Helen, too."

I didn't know what to say to that.

"And I know you'll do great for Granddad. I have to admit I was annoyed that he picked some stranger when Stephen could have used the work."

"Ah."

"But I think I'm starting to get it," she said.

"Because I ask too many questions. I'm sorry. Do you ever call him Steve?"

"No. No, he's Stephen. No ambiguity about that."

"It's nice when things are clear."

"Yes, clarity is good when you can get it," Marjie said. "I wish I had more of it."

I thought of being in Marjie's garden, listening to an old lady express opinions in accented English. Wondering if it was time to start harvesting Brussels sprouts. I was surprised to realize how natural it would have felt to take Marjie's hand. But our long shadows preceded us, as we walked back toward the house. It was easy to see they never touched.

Chapter 4

My adopted state of Massachusetts had passed from the darkening green of September through bright high-autumn colors to gray November and whispers of snow. Thanksgiving is the holiday native to our Commonwealth and Helen loved it. Each year she announced, "I'm A.D.D." It was her Annual Day of Domesticity, she explained, and she was barefoot in the kitchen but not pregnant to the best of her knowledge and belief. She ordered a turkey from the preferred farm stand, pies from the local bakery, and made her grandmother's stuffing and cranberry sauce. The odors of her cooking had drifted up the stairs to me at my computer when I heard a *thunk thunk* of closing car doors. Helen called, "Sean and the fall's fair lady have arrived."

I found them in the kitchen. "Hey," I said.

"Hey Ike," Sean said. He already had a deviled egg in one hand and spiced nuts in the other.

"Ike this is Cindy," Helen said.

"Susan," the girl corrected. "Susan Speeks."

"Hello," I said, trying not to let my eyes linger on the tattoos that crept from beneath her sleeves onto the backs of her hands.

"Thank you for having me."

"The more the merrier," Helen said. "Besides, we need help with the annual Thanksgiving jigsaw puzzle. Some families do football; we do a puzzle."

"With five thousand pieces." Sean added.

"Never more than a thousand," Helen said. "So far."

Sean mimed playing a violin. "They try to make it seem interesting with boring music."

"You know you like the music," Helen argued.

"A puzzle's something to look at while we talk," I said.

"Instead of each other," Sean said, with his mouth full of deviled egg.

"We want to hear all about everything," Helen said. "Or I should say, the part that's family-friendly."

"Thanks for the helpful guidelines, Mom," Sean said. "Where's Denver?"

"What could I do to help?" Susan asked.

Helen answered Sean by pointing in the direction of Denver's room. "What a nice offer," she said, turning to Susan. "Would you be willing to cube the bread?"

The kitchen opened to the family room. I went to the table where the puzzle had been dumped in a heap and began to turn pieces picture-side up.

"We're glad you can be with us," I heard Helen say, "but maybe you're sorry you can't be at your own home. Does your family have Thanksgiving traditions?"

"Dad spends the day with his Indian friends," Susan said. "I know you say Native American here back East but I'm from the West and everybody says Indian. He spends Thanksgiving with them for solidarity because he says, like, the Pilgrims were double-crossing exploiters. So he goes off with the Apaches to a football game and barbeque or something and Mom and I go to her sister's."

"So you can hang with your cousins. Where do they live?" Helen asked.

"I'm from Tucson but my aunt and uncle are over in Arizona City. They are, like, born-again, you know, and somehow my cousins caught it, too—I'm sorry; are you born-again?"

"Not to worry."

"I didn't think so. So my cousins are not totally on my case but I always feel like they are trying to be polite—"

"We'll try to be polite too, but we'll be coming from a different angle."

"I'm good with being here," Susan said. "It would have been okay with me to stay at school and work in the studio but Sean invited me so here I am."

"He says you're an art major."

"Yes, studio. I've always had to make things. I watch my hands do their thing. Sean says you are in the arts but you don't, like, make art."

"I'm kind of at the other end. I help collectors get what they want, object-wise. And sometimes I help artists in various ways."

"Modeling? You have a great body."

"Well, no. It's more, really, if I had to describe it, more like marketing."

"Oh."

Helen laughed. "I haven't undressed in front of an artist in a long time." I wondered where she would go from there. "What would you have been doing in your studio?" she asked.

"Painting. Bug faces. I've got this friend who has a binocular microscope and she's always looking at all kinds of things through it—did you ever do that?—it's so wild what like ordinary things look like—and she showed me a bug. I couldn't believe its face; it was a grasshopper I think or no it might have been a beetle anyway its jaws went sideways and it has, they all have, those wild multiple eyes so that's what I'm painting. Some are from sketches that I made through my friend's microscope and some are just made up with those eyes and sideways jaws and antennae for God's sake."

"I'd love to see them."

"They're too strange. I don't think you'd like them."

"Try me."

"Well okay I could email you some pictures."

"That would be great." Helen now felt the ice was sufficiently broken for her to pry. "How long have you been seeing Sean?"

"Isn't that funny how people say *seeing* that way, like when you said *it's been a long time since*—not exactly but you know how the seeing sort of has a double meaning about nudity privileges. Temporary and mutual you know. Not that it's any great treat to see me naked but you know what I mean, how seeing means the same as *going out with*—"

"And both of them mean *sleeping with* but we don't say it that way—"

"Right right right and they don't really mean about the sleep and it turns out that when you read books or see movies all people are interested in is the part between when they first, like, notice each other or meet or whatever and when they start waking up together and getting to know each other's bathroom smells because at that point it's like who cares from here on, good luck, neither one of you was all that good looking to begin with and now you'll just be eating corn chips together and getting enormous. I hope you don't mind the weird stuff I say; Sean's dad isn't . . . oh my god he's right there and I'm so obscene—"

"He's not paying any attention to us," Helen told her, knowing better. "Kitchen chatter is just white noise to a man with his Thanksgiving jigsaw puzzle. And he's not Sean's father by the way."

"Oh that's right his father is in California, sorry, but he's his stepfather, right?"

"Yes and he's up for a Pulitzer Prize and a genius grant for stepfathering—are you listening, Ike?"

I waved without looking toward them, as though I'd heard my name but was too preoccupied to have tuned in to anything else.

Susan said, "The bread is for the stuffing, right? Are you using a recipe?"

"Yes," Helen said. "Did you know they used to call them *receipts* here in New England?

My thoughts went to the Thanksgiving party in Arizona. It sounded interesting, hanging out with real Apaches, going to a football game, partying afterwards. I wondered what they drank. Bad beer? Bud Lite or something, by the case, I supposed. What did they talk about? What were their jokes? Was Susan's dad educated? I imagined sitting on aluminum stands in Arizona, watching high school boys play football. Fast Indian kids racing down a bright green field of plastic turf. The band's brass instruments flashing. The drums would sound different there in clear air far from forests, echoing from treeless ridges. It would be all those kids had known and they would have the same concerns as other kids, amounting to *how will I fit into life?*

"Ike." Helen called me back. "Go ask the boys if they want some quesadillas."

Rising to perform this errand, I looked into the kitchen to check out the guest. She was tall, a little taller than Sean. She had a determined-looking face and dark hair, oddly cut. Her clothing was used, from sports and the military.

After our traditional Thanksgiving brunch of quesadillas Sean and I set up the ping-pong table in the garage. "How's school?" I asked.

"Oh you know just classes and studying mostly," he said.

That was all I could get. So, to make him feel at home I played the gabby cheerful holiday parent. The conversational equivalent of overstuffed furniture. I described Denver's college tour. I did not report his petulance but I did mention that he'd been more in touch with their dad than formerly.

"Yeah, me too," Sean said. "We're both going out there for Christmas."

"But you'll be here some, too, right?" I said. "As per usual?"

"Ah, no, I think we'll be out there the whole time this year."

Ouch. I was trying to find an expression that showed the correct measure of disappointment when Denver and Susan emerged from the house. We played doubles. There wasn't enough space so we had continual comical arguments about which team was unfairly cramped. Then we traded ends and argued the opposite points of view. We bounced candy-colored balls off the ceiling and pursued them behind and under the storage boxes that lined the walls. When the kids were called to set the table, I opened the fireplace flue and built a fire and poured wine and we were ready for the feast.

As I carved and served I said, "I hope I'm going to get plenty of help with that puzzle after the meal." Denver looked at Susan and made a face to indicate that I need not be taken seriously.

Helen said that she would pitch in after they'd cleaned up although she had a few things to do online first.

Sean said, on behalf of his generation, that they were disappointed to be unable to tackle the puzzle but, "We have to meet some friends. We'll do it tomorrow. Can we look at the picture this year?"

"You may always look at the picture," I replied.

"He lets you look at the picture once," Denver told Susan. "The picture on the box. When you first start working on the puzzle. After that you aren't allowed to see it again until the puzzle is finished."

"That's if you follow his rule," Helen said. "I believe there have been occasions in which his authority was ignored."

"Disregarded," Sean added.

"Denied," Denver said.

"Everyone makes their own choices," I told them.

After the meal the three kids slunk out the door. Sean called, "See you later" to the accompaniment of tittering that suggested *much later indeed if at all don't wait up.*

When the kitchen had been set to rights I settled in to assemble the border of the puzzle. Football players ran across the television screen but the only sound was a string quartet from my iPod. Although we sometimes watched football plays and replays, we didn't like to hear commercials or announcers. Helen sat on the couch with her laptop.

I thought, so much for the famous tradition of working puzzles. It was something we said we did but didn't really get around to. We must have finished puzzles some years; maybe even last year. Or had it become just a family legend? Something we had done long before that was now honored by allusion and ritual but no longer actually happened.

Helen typed rapidly on her keyboard.

"Did you ever enjoy doing puzzles?" I asked.

"I'll help with it later."

The phone rang. It was Georgia Trippy. "Ike, we wanted you to know. Dad's in the hospital. It appears he's had a stroke."

"Where is he?"

"Mount Auburn."

"Are you there?"

"Yes."

"How serious is it?"

"Serious."

"Would it be okay if I came down?"

"Oh, thanks, Ike, but you shouldn't interrupt your holiday. We just wanted you to know."

"I'd like to stop by."

"He's in intensive care and we can't be with him. We're all in the waiting room. There's nothing we can do. But, sure, if you'd like to look in."

I invited Helen to go with me.

"I'll stay here," she said, "in case the kids come back."

Half an hour later I entered the waiting room. Ev was on his cell phone. The woman beside him said, "I'm Kathy, Ev's wife. He's talking to our daughter. Georgia's in with their dad. They're allowing one member of his family at a time."

"I'm Ike," I whispered. I had seen her at the beach party, but we hadn't been introduced.

"I know who you are," she said.

"I'm sorry to meet you under upsetting circumstances."

We both eavesdropped as Ev said into his phone, "The doctor thinks he might have stabilized. There's still danger but he has a decent chance."

"He's talking to Marjie," Kathy explained. "She and Stephen are driving back from his parents' house on Long Island."

"The important thing is for you to drive carefully," Ev continued. "Why isn't Stephen driving?"

"Stephen's her fiancé," Kathy explained.

"Yes, they say there's likely to be some injury but it's impossible to know how much," Ev continued. "There's nothing we can do about any of that so there's no point in worrying. Just drive safely and we'll see you in a few hours. Boswell's here," he added, looking at me. "Yes, *Ike*, right. I'll call you back if there's any change. Let's hang up now." He lowered the phone from his ear and poked the screen of his phone to end the call.

"Why did you want her to hang up?" Kathy asked.

"Because she doesn't have the car charger for her phone," Ev said. "I don't know how she can be well enough organized to run that classroom and yet be in chaos everywhere else." He turned his scowl to me. "Hello Ike. No need to have interrupted your holiday."

"We were finished and the kids had taken off and I am concerned."

"He'd old but he's strong."

"We were all at Georgia's," Kathy said, "when Dad suddenly seemed disoriented."

"That's a polite way of putting it," Ev said.

"That's the accurate way," Kathy said.

Georgia came out of the unit. She looked drawn and worried. "How's he doing?" Ev asked.

"No change," she said. "Your turn."

Ev nodded and headed toward the patient rooms.

Georgia looked at me. "Hello, croquet-master."

"Hello, Georgia. Is he aware of what's going on?"

"You can't tell. I don't think so. He's sedated because of the intubation and who knows what all. Poor old Dad." Her eyes were moist.

"Could I do anything for you? Bring you something from the cafeteria?"

"No, Ike, really, we're all set."

"I am grateful that you let me know about this," I said.

It was a difficult situation. It was strange that Ev had referred to me as Boswell instead of my name. I supposed that he was still annoyed that Bill hired me for the autobiography.

I thought about Bill. I had interviewed him every week since the party on the Cape. From what he told me, and from my own research,

I had become increasingly impressed with how much he had affected fateful world events during the 1950s and '60s. The buildup I'd given him on *Hubcaps* was an understatement. As a young MIT graduate student he had become involved in the problem of how to make computers small enough to be useful in military weapons. At first I expected the story to be just a tale of electrical engineering whizzes defining technical goals and systematically figuring out how to achieve them. There was that, but there was plenty of intrigue that went with it. Once it was proven to non-engineers that electronics could do what had seemed impossible, they tended to jump to the belief that everything was possible, and to be disappointed when it wasn't. Personal loyalties and irrational perceptions could push funding decisions in irrational directions. Success for Bill's lab included figuring out not just how to get it done but also how to convince the bigwigs that they had the right approach. The stakes were high. Benign deception was part of the process and the young Bill Trippy, who had proven to be a brilliant engineer, also showed an aptitude for persuading powerful people. He was tall, athletic, and confident—and his team got results.

Compared to Bill, the celebrity of sports stars or big-name actors was vacant and silly. Relative to what he had done, Bill's self-respect was humble. If you think it mattered who won the Cold War. Whose values were backed up with accurate weapons and who could move people back and forth from Earth to the moon with the whole world as witness, ready and willing to watch America crash and burn. Driving away from the hospital I reflected that the mind that had given deft intelligence to U.S. projectiles was having its own circuitry compromised.

When I got home I found Helen reading in bed. "How's he doing?" she asked.

"Not too well."

She puckered her lips and furrowed her brow, which I read as concern for my feelings in the matter.

"He's old," I said. "He might make it. Are the kids back?"

"They trooped in a little while ago."

"What did you do about sleeping arrangements?" I asked.

"The same as last spring with that other one. I offered the guest room. This one said 'It's not necessary,' and I said, 'Okay. Whatever.'"

In bed, I hinted at amorous interest. Helen ignored me so I took a more direct approach. "Oh, Ike. Not tonight." She didn't sound like her usual self. "My little teenagers are turning into young adults. It makes me feel old."

Early the next morning I went downstairs and started coffee. Hearing something on the porch, I opened the door. There was Susan, smoking and shivering. She was barefoot in jeans and a t-shirt. She tossed her cigarette butt and said, "Hello."

I held open the door for her and she came into the hall. I handed her a fleece jacket and she folded herself into it.

"Coffee?"

She nodded.

"Sleep okay?"

"As well as ever. I don't sleep much."

Neither of us spoke again for several minutes. When we had each benefited from half of our mugs of coffee Susan said, "It was funny yesterday when your wife said she was A.D.D. and she meant temporarily domestic or whatever because I really am A.D.D."

"Did you feel like she made a joke of it?"

"No no I don't care. But that's why I don't sleep."

"Medication. It's speed, right?"

"Yeah and then I drink coffee on top of that," Susan said. "But at least I can concentrate sometimes which is more than I used to be able to. Sean's so different. I don't know what he sees in me. He's almost like a straight arrow. He's good, and look at me. Weird. But I'm interesting and I like interesting. Motorcycles are interesting and craziness is interesting while good might be sane but it might be boring. Not that Sean is boring."

"But safe bores you?"

"Like, is *good* too safe and do I get off on risk?"

"Risk is sexy for most people I should think." I watched her eyes. I was curious about her tattoos but they were hidden by the fleece. How strange, to decorate your body so permanently.

"Risk is kind of tame if you really want to get hurt," she said to provoke me.

"Whoa…"

"That sounds crazy to you because you have a nice life and a pretty wife and a house and everything."

"Boring, huh? But why wish to get hurt?"

"What else means anything?"

"What does?"

"You're old and wise, you tell me. I'm just sitting here in this funny-looking body with a bad report card, on the whole, you know, permanent-record-wise, just ask my relatives. What's life all about? *Family*—" she recoiled as she said it. "*People*? Give me a break."

"Relationships can be challenging."

"I read a book once where some lady dumped the ashes of her dead relative through the hole of an outhouse she used every day."

"Strong image. Read much?"

"Not really."

"What about *service*?" I asked.

"What about it?"

"As a candidate for meaning?"

"Oh, like Girl Scouts or something. Yeah, I was a great Girl Scout would you believe? I was working away on those badges and serving, serving, serving. I'm kind of past that."

"Maybe it's something you'll go back to."

"Go back, I don't think so. Happening is going forward."

"But after you traipse around you might figure out what life is all about for you and going back might seem a good choice after all. If you figure something out. Service to the planet or to humanity or whatever."

"Yeah, well . . . maybe that's more for you than for me." She took out her cigarettes. "I'm an artist," she said, and she returned to the porch.

I wasn't sure service was for me, either. Sometimes I take a line of argument just to hear how it sounds when I say it. This one sounded prissy. I like to see how people respond.

When they finally got out of bed, Sean and Denver made pancakes. Helen never came down; Denver took her a plate. When I went up I noticed she had not eaten her pancake. She sat staring at her laptop.

"Susan says she was a Girl Scout," I informed her.

"Yeah, me too."

"She's out smoking on the porch. That's what she was doing when I got up."

"Wouldn't Sean let her smoke in his room?"

"He knows no one smokes in this house."

"Rules are made to be broken," she said, looking up, closing her computer.

"You hate the smell of cigarette smoke."

"I'm getting over it."

I thought, *that's because of your New York friends.* I said, "I'm headed over to the hospital."

When I arrived at the intensive care unit's waiting room, I found Marjie and Georgia holding hands. When they looked up, I could see that their eyes were red and swollen. My heart sank.

"Ike, good news," Georgia said. "He's going to make it."

I crossed the room and took each of their free hands in mine. We had a giggly three-way embrace.

"The doctor said it was a near thing last night," Georgia said.

"He bulled his way through," Marjie said. "Too stubborn to die."

"The neuro doc told us his signs were all over the place which is terribly dangerous and then about two a.m. he seemed to assert his will and one by one his numbers improved," Georgia said. "It looks like we'll have old Bill to boss us around for another decade or two."

"That's great," I said. "How relieved you must be. What a Thanksgiving you had!"

"It's been a strange one," Georgia said. "Sit down and tell us about your family. How was your Thanksgiving?"

"Yes," Marjie said. "Are the boys home?"

"The younger guy still lives here. The older one's home from college. He brought a friend."

"Male or female?" Georgia asked.

"She is a young woman, an artist, and she's kind of out there in an entertaining way." I was mentally organizing a narrative about Susan when I noticed that interest had already faded from their faces. The drama of the past twenty-four hours, the intensity and sleep deprivation, had consumed their power to listen. I stopped talking and just looked at the two of them, Bill's daughter and granddaughter, the aunt and the niece.

Would I have seen Georgia differently if she had not identified herself as lesbian? Was there a certain masculinity in the set of her jaw? What did I mean, anyway, by that word *masculinity*? It didn't seem politically correct to think of it. But something in Georgia's expression and eye movements were firm and determined rather than pretty and coy. Was the lens of my perception distorted by bias? I had no other lens and no choice but to peer through this one and try to sort

out what it showed. I wanted to be open to impression, objective, free
of interference from prejudice or well-intentioned filters. In Georgia
I saw a handsome woman entering the late summer of her adulthood
with vigor and sturdy self-respect.

I looked also at Marjie. I watched the rapid movements of her
hazel eyes, her fluctuating expression, the flash of earrings as she
turned from her aunt toward the doorway then to the art on the wall and
back to me. She remained alert despite the weariness of her overnight
vigil. She seemed reflective, intensely aware of her surroundings, a bit
uncertain. Feminine.

A nurse invited the two women to see their patient. Marjie
promised to come back with an update, then followed her aunt.

A man held the door for them, then entered and sat down. His
face was weary. He was older than Ev but younger than Bill—about
seventy. Because he didn't offer eye contact, I didn't speak. He
withdrew as you would if you had been through trying hours and
expected more of the same and needed to reorganize your emotions
while you had an interval alone.

I wondered what his story was. I speculated that the patient was his
spouse, his partner over many years and the mother of his children. If
they had children, why was he here alone? Perhaps they had no kids or
the kids were far away or maybe they had been here earlier and would
return. What was he feeling? His sick wife was human grist within this
high-tech mill, in the hands of medical people at work on their jobs,
whose efforts had two outcomes—their patients lived on, or stopped
living.

I supposed he contemplated his wife's demise. If she died, what
did he stand to lose? In the privacy of his secret heart, what bubbled
up? Perhaps she was the dearest intimate companion of his life, whose
temperament and body were as familiar as his own. A sweet reciprocal
protectiveness was central to their lives and had been their daily
blessing. Without her he would enter a scary, unfamiliar solitude.

Or perhaps their two selves had always been distinct, vaguely
competitive, engaged together in the business of life but not
emotionally tight. His loss of her would fracture for a time his
accustomed normalcy but, so he imagined, would open later into
new possibilities. Or perhaps she had been a harridan, feeding him a

constant diet of correction—and perhaps he needed that and would be at sea without it.

The man rose and went out into the corridor.

I allowed myself to be moved by an impulse. I entered a space off the waiting area, a room labeled FOR FAMILY CONFERENCES that could also be used for sleeping. It had a table with a drawer and in the drawer was stationery. I took out a sheet and wrote:

> Dear Marjie,
> Ever since our walk on the beach I have
> carried a feeling toward you that I should
> let you know about. Seeing you in this
> crisis, I want to tell you, in case it might
> be a support. I would describe it as a
> crush. What would your oracle think?

When Marjie came back to the waiting room, I said, "There's mail for you," and offered her the note.

With a puzzled face, she unfolded the paper and read what I had written. Without looking up she said, "May I use your pen?" She took it and went into the little room, closing the door behind her. Through the glass I could see her writing on the back of the stationery. When she came out she handed it to me, still avoiding eye contact, and disappeared into the hall.

She had written:

> Ike, I am sorry that you feel this way and even
> sorrier that you mentioned it. At a time like this,
> or ever. You are married! And I am engaged.
> Perhaps I had hoped that we could be friends,
> but your note certainly discourages that. I do
> believe that you are sincerely concerned with
> Grandfather's condition. I will ask Aunt Geor-
> gia to give you updates by email. I hope you
> can see that it is not appropriate for you to stay
> any longer—please don't be here when I return.

Chapter 5

I left the hospital and walked. Why had Marjie reacted that way? Should I have foreseen that she would? I hadn't meant anything bad. Or had I? What if she had written back, *I feel the same way?* What would I have wanted to do? Did I think I was going to have an affair with a not-too-confident young woman who had just become engaged? No. I wasn't looking for anything like that. I just wanted the feeling of crush and crush returned. I love that feeling. It didn't have to be serious.

Marjie's note was a rejection. I had looked for a *she-likes-me* buzz; what I got was humiliation and anxiety. Marjie's father had disliked me to begin with—he referred to me as Boswell—and now I had offended her. She'd tell, and they'd all hate me.

I had brought it on myself by writing her that note. On impulse. I knew that precipitous actions can lead to mistakes. But how can you be spontaneous if you always hang back? If you never take a chance? In this case, though, I wished I'd been more circumspect.

I took the note out of my pocket and tore it up, distributing pieces in multiple litter receptacles as you would if you thought you were under investigation and someone was following you and delving into your private business and correspondence. As though if I made it too easy someone would puzzle out my torn-up note and tape the pieces together and be in possession of strong evidence of how poor my judgment was and how firmly I had been shut down.

Feeling bruised, I wanted to take care of myself—that's why I was walking, which was good but not good enough so I decided to enjoy a comforting cappuccino at the first coffee shop I found.

I observed the young person who took my order and my money. He directed his eyes and inflected his voice as a person does when cognizant of dealing with a fellow human being. Was he being psychologically present because he was serious about the coffee business? Perhaps he was an ambitious barista, hoping to rise through the ranks, to open and close the shop and train newcomers and be himself trained in the art of roasting coffee, committed to this enterprise.

Or maybe not. Maybe he had no interest whatsoever in coffee or the business of running a coffee shop but he was intensely curious about the human condition and gathered data everywhere he went. Each customer was another face, a complexion, a head of hair, a voice, eyes that sought his or did not, posture, awareness of surroundings, anxiety, vulnerability, wellness and vigor—or exhaustion—confidence or timidity, a mode of dress projecting self respect or its absence, humility or narcissism. Perhaps this kid absorbed impressions all day long.

Watching the young man make change, I pictured him ten years earlier as he chose a crayon from a box. To color a map. Black lines on white paper. He was earnest; how seriously he took this choice of color. I rolled him forward into his future, to his wedding. The bride might be a woman already known to him, perhaps another worker in this coffee shop. He will offer her a ring much as, in the present, he hands me coins.

While I drank my cappuccino I thought about getting fired. Marjie would tell her father and her aunt that I'd been inappropriate and they would tell Bill. I'd be finished with him. Marjie would not report my behavior to Helen but she'd mention it to Stephen, who would, without delay, inform my wife. She was probably reading his email even then. *By the way, thought you'd be interested, your husband has a crush on my fiancée; he told her so an hour ago.*

The young barista. I reflected on his mental presence—he seemed completely there, today—an ordinary work day at a low paying job. How will it be at his wedding? Will he have that same impressive focus? Transition and drama! Today his father enjoys good health, but it won't last. In the flickering final hours, will the son be with him as completely as he is here today? Is it not an aspect of our condition that our limited attention sometimes goes astray?

I returned to my own distress. *Gosh Marjie,* I thought, *does it have to be a crime to like you? That you attract me even though I'm married? I'm over it already.* And when I get back home Helen will be mad and hurt and righteous and make a scene right in front of the kids—or maybe she won't but the house will be full of tension and strangeness obvious to everyone. Our both-boys-home weekend will be ruined. According to Sean they would spend Christmas vacation in California! Thanksgiving was going to be my whole holiday season with the boys and now this to mess it up—because I had yielded to my appetite for closeness.

But nothing happened.

I went home. The kids were out. Helen and I did some yard work, nibbled cold turkey, dressed for Symphony, and went to hear the music.

When we returned we were greeted at the door by the odor of cigarette smoke. We found Sean, Denver, and Susan seated around the puzzle table. The boys were assembling pieces. Susan was applying a black ink marker to areas of the puzzle that were done. To the flowers and fountains in the Italian garden she had added strange insects. Some were perched or in flight. One struggled to emerge from its larval skin. Others were dead-eyed and flat, as though they were fossilized. Two had faces that resembled Sean and Denver. The annoyance of discovering someone drawing on the puzzle I had purchased combined with admiration for her wit and talent to stun me into silence.

"How was the concert?" Sean asked.

"Good. How were the cigarettes?" Helen replied.

"Sorry," Susan said, without looking up. "I'll be gone tomorrow."

"You are leaving us a souvenir," I said.

"Hope you don't mind," Susan replied, still without raising her eyes.

"I told her you liked originality," Sean said.

"True enough," I said.

"You want to help?" Sean asked. "We can make room."

"Nah," I said. "I'm for bed."

"G'night," they mumbled.

When I came down in the morning, I half-expected Susan to be smoking on the porch, but all I found was the puzzle, adorned with her drawings. A bug in the center held a sign that said *Good morning* next to a sleepy grasshopper whose high forehead and glasses made me feel caricatured. The grasshopper dozed while three wide-awake ants marched by carrying puzzle-pieces. One ant was tattooed. Now that I was past the surprise of the unauthorized defacement, Susan's additions seemed funny.

An hour later Sean and Susan came down stairs carrying their luggage.

"Is Mom up?" Sean asked.

"She has not yet appeared," I said. "You guys headed back so early?"

"Yeah," Sean said.

"I have to finish some stuff in the studio," Susan explained.

Helen descended in her robe. "Good morning, Youth of America. Want Ike to make you breakfast?"

"We need to get going," Sean said.

"Thank you for having me," Susan said. "I had a good time."

I was surprised that she would choose such conventional formulaic expressions of courtesy.

"Our pleasure," Helen said. "Come again, if, if you, you know . . ."

"Thanks Mom," Sean said, trying to prevent her from clarifying her meaning.

"If what?" Susan asked. "You mean if Sean doesn't . . ." but she decided, on this occasion, to abandon her habitual frankness. She got into the car, rolled down the window, smiled, and said, "Bye."

It was the first time I had seen her smile.

Later that morning I stuck my head into Denver's room to remind him to work on essays for his college applications. He was in a video conversation with his father, being coached in some kind of math they do after calculus. I withdrew and went to our bedroom, where Helen was packing.

"I might go down this afternoon, if you don't mind," she said. "That would give me a jump start on my Monday. I have a big week."

Denver used my car to drop his mom at the airport bus. After that he had planned to take his ice skates to be sharpened. He liked to play hockey; he hoped the ponds would be frozen soon. He'd been gone about an hour when he called my cell. "I hit a tree," he told me. "I hit a guy on a bike. He's down."

"Where are you?"

He named a street a mile away.

"Are you okay?"

"Yeah."

"Call 911," I said.

"I did."

"I'll be right there."

By the time I found Helen's car keys and remembered how to start her car and actually got there, a cop was directing traffic and an ambulance crew was hunched over a guy beside the road. The front end of my car was wrapped around a tree. Denver stood beside the car looking frightened and forlorn—but intact.

A second officer was asking Denver if he needed medical attention. "I'm his dad," I said. I pointed to the cyclist. "How bad is he hurt?"

The policeman shook his head and shrugged. To Denver he said, "Please wait here." He crossed the street to some onlookers. I supposed they had witnessed the accident.

"Are you okay?" I asked again.

"Yes," he said. "The airbag went off."

"Wow."

"He rode out in front of me," Denver said, pointing across the road to a driveway.

"Is that why you hit the tree?"

"Yeah or I would have smashed him," Denver said. "I'm sorry about your car."

I looked at the car, peering into the place the passenger window had been. There were the limp sacks of the air bags. Turning to Denver I asked, "Did it hurt you? The airbag?"

"I don't know," Denver said. "I can't remember."

We looked toward the clustered emergency medical technicians. Their patient wore high-visibility yellow trimmed with black. They slid a back board under him.

I delved into my glove compartment and found the registration, which I handed to Denver. "We'll need this," I told him. "Do you have your license?" It seemed unlikely that he would because he never carried a wallet. Any money or cards were loose in various random pants pockets. But when the officer returned Denver was able to hand him his license.

The policeman made a series of notes from the car's registration. Another of our town's cruisers raced up, followed by a third, from the next town over. Blue lights whirled in all directions. Every side of the ambulance flashed red. A flat-bed tow truck arrived but hung back under its amber dome. The time had not arrived for the wrecker to haul away the damaged car. My car. My kid. We'd fallen into a theatrical event. We were principals at the scene of an accident, objects of interest and scrutiny to passers-by. A victim lay on the pavement. The perpetrator was—of course!—a teenage boy. My car was no longer a vehicle, like a shot-gunned duck is no longer a bird. It was a shapeless immobile carcass, broken bits, rubies and diamonds on the pavement.

There stood the immovable tree and the frightened boy telling the cop what had happened.

"I came over the hill," Denver said, "and this guy came out of there," Denver pointed to a driveway across the street, "like, whizzing, like he didn't see me, so I just reflexively jerked, you know, away, to keep from hitting him, trying not to hit him, braking, and I hit the tree."

After he'd made more notes, the policeman went to the driver's side of the car. How fast had Denver been going? I supposed they could calculate that—if you knew what you were doing the front end of the car would tell you its speed when it reached the tree. And the skid marks would say how much it had slowed down so you could back into his original speed. I followed the cop and looked at the side of the car. You could see where something had dented and scratched the driver's door. From where it lay, it appeared that the bike had collided with the side of my car and bounced away.

The policeman took photographs. I went to the ambulance. As they removed the cyclist's helmet, I said, "Good luck." Just then the attendant pulled back, giving me a view of the patient's face. It was Marjie's boyfriend! "Stephen!"

Without moving his head, he waved. The ambulance doors closed and it pulled away. The policeman had returned to Denver. "How fast were you going?" he asked.

"I don't know," Denver said. "Not very fast."

"What's your best guess?"

Telepathically, desperately, silently, I tried to persuade Denver to say he didn't know.

"About thirty, I suppose," he said.

He was standing next to a twenty-five-miles-per-hour speed limit sign.

The policeman made another note. Then he pointed to the curb cut Denver had indicated. It wasn't the driveway of a house—it was rear access to a strip mall. "The bike came out of there?"

"Yes," Denver said. "He was coming straight in front of me, not slowing down or anything, like he didn't see me. I just tried to miss him."

"But you didn't miss that tree. I asked you before, but I'll ask again, do you need medical attention?"

"No."

"Repeatedly declined medical attention," the cop said, as he made another note. "Air bags are a good thing." He looked at me. "I'd keep an eye on him. He's young. But he hit that bag pretty hard. If it was you or me we'd probably have cracked ribs or worse. You could have him checked out."

"Okay, officer. Thank you." His name badge said *Decker*. Of course I wanted to know whether Denver was in trouble. Again it seemed that an oblique inquiry was preferable. "Can you tell what happened?" What I meant was, *Do you infer fault from what you see here?*

Officer Decker said, "The bike hit the driver's door."

"By some strange coincidence, I think I know the cyclist," I blurted. "I think he's a friend of a friend. I hope he's okay."

The cop looked at Denver. "I'm not going to cite you at this time," he said. "Where there's personal injury I have more work to do here at the scene, and then we'll get your car out of here. Tell the guy where you want him to take it. Come down to the station later on and fill out a report and we'll see where we are." He took out a tape measure and turned toward the black marks on the pavement.

I looked at my car. Sometimes it takes an expert to decide whether the cost to repair exceeds the value of the car—but this was not one of those times. My car was totalled.

"Sorry, Ike," Denver said.

"That's okay," I said. "How do you feel?"

"I'm okay."

"Let's see what's in the car," I said, but when I reached in the cop waved me off.

"Later," he said.

"Can I get my skates?" Denver asked.

The cop shrugged. "Okay."

Denver grabbed his skates. As the wrecker backed up toward my demolished car, we got into Helen's. I considered having Denver drive, to show confidence, and so I could call his mother. I thought better of it, and that was good, because as soon as he was in the passenger seat and had closed the door he began to shake. He needed hugging by his mom or even by me but under the circumstances that would have required a big production. I decided to give him an interval of invisibility. He was of a gender and an age when talking about his feelings—well, we had gone there only a couple months before, on the college trip, in the car he had just wrecked. The painful memory of the conversation in Maine made me cautious. But this was no time to say nothing. Adopting a tone I thought would sound reassuring, I said, "That must have been a frightening experience. The airbag. Wow."

"Yeah," he said. The shaking abated.

"Are you recalling any more of what happened?"

He shook his head. "I just remember the bike suddenly appearing and then there's the tree trunk right in front of me and the smell of gun smoke."

"Whew. The cop said it had worked. The airbag."

"Yeah."

"Are you feeling okay? What do you need?"

"Nothing," he said.

But as we were about to turn into our driveway he said, "I'm hungry," so I passed our house and drove on to his favorite fast-food restaurant. I gave Denver my order and my wallet and left him in line. "I'll call your mother."

Her face was on the screen of my phone. I touched it with my finger and prepared for the tricky challenge of unspooling bad news in a way that spares the listener a fright but brings her quickly to an understanding of the situation. "Helen, hi, we've had a strange incident here but everything's okay. We're still sorting it out, but Denver seems okay."

"What happened?" she asked.

"Denver encountered a cyclist while driving. After dropping you off. He tried to avoid him and hit a tree."

"Hard?"

"Hard enough for the airbag to fire," I said. "And we know the cyclist! It was that guy Stephen. I think it was he. So strange. I'm almost sure it was. Marjory Trippy's fiancé."

"Is he okay?"

"I don't know. They took him away in the ambulance. They put him on a back-board and all that."

"Blood?"

"Not that I could see."

"Denver's okay?"

"Yes, basically. He seems stiff. The cop mentioned having him checked out."

"You will, right?"

"Okay."

"Was it Denver's fault?"

"I'm not sure. I think maybe not. Maybe he was going a little faster than he should have been."

"Who doesn't?"

"It's like the cyclist actually ran into him while they were both braking. Here comes Denver. Want to talk to him?"

"Sure."

Denver put the tray with our food down on the table between us. I handed him my phone. "I'm okay," he said. He ate steadily as he talked to his mother.

"Taking my skates.

"After I dropped you off.

"I don't know he just suddenly appeared.

"It's pretty messed up.

"Yeah.

"Okay." He returned the phone to me.

"How bad's your Camry?" Helen asked.

"It's a goner," I said.

"Well. You can get a new one."

"Yeah. Do they give car loans to unemployed guys?"

"It'll work out. Take him to the emergency room."

"Okay. Bye for now."

"Bye," she said. "Should I come home?"

"I think we're okay."

"Okay. Tell Denver I love him."

"Want to tell him yourself?"

"Okay."

I handed Denver the phone.

He listened.

"Okay, you too, bye," he said to Helen, and closed the call. "She said she loves you, too," he told me.

We went from the restaurant to the hospital. Not to the big-time urban hospital that was treating Bill's stroke, but to the decent suburban hospital next town over. At the admitting desk they asked Denver how much pain he was in, on a scale of one to eight. He replied, "I'm a little sore. I dunno. Two maybe. One?" The nurse directed us to the adjacent waiting room.

It seemed to me that Denver was fine. I was still worried about the other guy, who I was pretty sure was Stephen. I supposed the privacy rules were so strict that there was really no point in even asking. Who wants to volunteer to be shut down by petty functionaries like the admitting nurse? Wouldn't she enjoy exercising her powers of indignation on me! I could hear her sanctimonious tone as she rejected my impertinent invasive inquiry. My curiosity arm-wrestled my reluctance to expose my dignity to censure. Curiosity won. I left Denver and returned to the admitting desk.

"My son was in a collision," I said. My tactic was to relate my forthcoming question to the scruffy skinny lad.

The woman looked neutral. I couldn't read whether she was going to be sympathetic or hostile.

"A cyclist was also involved," I ventured. "He was transported from the scene. I suppose they would have brought him here."

"Was he dressed in bright yellow?" she asked.

"That's him."

"Yes, they did bring him here," she volunteered.

"How's he doing?"

"Okay I guess. He's gone."

"Up to a room?"

"No. Home. We gave him some Tylenol and sent him home."

"Excellent."

"I heard him tell his wife he'd have to get a new helmet."

"His wife?"

"His girlfriend, whatever. Some of these bicyclers aren't so lucky as this one."

At that point they were ready to see Denver. He was getting stiffer and starting to show bruises from the seat belt and the air bag. The doctor looked bored. He told me to take him home and bring him back if he developed any symptoms.

In the car with Denver I asked, "What's your homework situation?"

"All set," he said. "We can finish the puzzle."

When we got home we turned on the television to football, with the sound off as usual, and put music on. Denver chose a playlist of mine that featured Louis Armstrong and Ella Fitzgerald. From my chair I could watch the television or I could look down at the puzzle. Susan's drawings were upside down. "What did you think of our artist?" I asked Denver.

"She was cool. I'm sorry about your car."

"I'm happier that the car got crunched than if that guy had been hurt. You did the right thing." I listened to myself. Throughout our years together I had tried to catch him being good, as the psychologists recommended. Was he onto me? Had these affirmations, intended to reassure, become a mannerism—trite, transparent, empty?

If so, he didn't call me on it. He just said, "Thanks."

I persevered. "You didn't have long to think. Good instincts."

"Thanks."

"So, now, the fun of a new car. Or at least a different car."

"What will you get?"

"I don't know. Maybe a used hybrid. Time for a hybrid!"

"Used?"

"Yeah."

"You got the Camry new, didn't you?"

"Yeah. But I had a job then."

"Oh. Did you know that guy?" Denver had his iPad on the table so we could score touchdown celebrations.

"You are knocking pieces off."

He bent down to pick them up. Slowly. "Want some Tylenol?"

"No."

"I think the guy was the boyfriend of Bill Trippy's granddaughter."

"Oh."

"I can't say he'd made that great an impression on me," I said. "He pretended to be somebody he wasn't. But I wouldn't have asked you to run him down."

Denver grinned.

"It might have come to that, if I knew him better. I might have put you up to it. If it had occurred to me that you would do it. Life is full of surprises."

"I could be your hit man."

"A pro," I said. "Cool and deadly."

"You don't like 'em; I kill 'em. Want to see what Sean and I did?"

"Sure."

Denver pressed the screen of his tablet. Somehow he could change the television through it—something to do with a box we got to watch internet movies on. Without getting up, Denver changed the television picture. Suddenly we were in a war zone. At first it looked real, but soon I realized it was a computer animation. "Is this a video game?" I asked.

"Demo."

"Of a video game?"

"Yeah."

A black-masked figure with an assault rifle shot at us. A gun barrel appeared in the foreground, as if held by the viewer. It fired, blasting the shooter and painting the background wall with his blood.

"Score that," Denver ordered. "Guys getting killed. One to five."

"Three," I said, to be cooperative.

My cell rang. It was Georgia Trippy.

"Georgia?" I said.

Denver turned off the music.

"Hi Ike," she said. "Stephen says you waved at him in the ambulance."

"It *was* him!"

"Yeah. Did you know the kid in the car?"

"Yes. It was my son. Denver. My stepson. Is Stephen all right?"

"Yeah, he's okay. How's your kid?"

"He's okay, too. The airbag saved him. He's sore."

The picture on the television changed to an Oz-like world, a fantasy landscape through which small blue guys were being chased and devoured by a long-armed demon.

"Was it your car?" Georgia asked.

"Yes."

"That's what Stephen thought. I think he feels kind of bad. He didn't exactly say so but when he described what happened you could read between the lines. He was a little sheepish."

"Denver says he had to choose between killing him and hitting the tree."

Georgia received that information in silence.

"The main thing is they're both okay," I said.

"Right. Well the reason I called is because we were pretty sure it was your car and we have an extra."

"An extra car?"

"Yeah. It was Bill's and it's not really a car, it's a van. Bill was going to sell it but it's old. I don't think it's worth anything. You could use it, or you could just have it. Or anyway it could be something to drive until you get the car you want."

I glanced at the television. It showed two people skiing. One smashed into a tree.

"Guys getting killed, one to five." Denver said, looking at me. "Denver, four; Ike—"

I held up three fingers.

"That's a nice offer, Georgia." I told her I didn't think my insurance would pay for a rental and I'd be happy to use Bill's van while I got my transportation situation sorted out. The TV screen switched again, back to the war zone. An armored vehicle crept along. It exploded.

"Things blowing up," Denver said. "One to five?"

"It's old, but low mileage," Georgia said.

I held up two fingers. It hadn't been that great an explosion.

"I have power of attorney," Georgia said. "Dad planned to sell it. We didn't even know he had it." She told me where to find the van, in a garage at MIT. I wrote down the phone number of the administrative assistant who had the keys.

On the television, a guy and a girl were in a dance contest. I thanked Georgia, hung up, and held up three to Denver.

"We don't score dancing," he said. He turned the music back on— but not to my playlist.

"What the hell is this?" I asked.

"Dubstep," he said.

"What are we watching?" I asked, trying to ignore the nightmarish music.

"Sean and I ripped game demos off the web and we made an app that randomizes scenes."

"Oh, man. You guys are too much. Do you think we can finish this puzzle tonight?"

"Yeah," Denver said. He pressed his tablet again. The music went off. Football reappeared on the television.

"Good news," I said. "The guy you hit, or who hit you, or whatever—it *was* the guy I know. And he is okay. If we're going to kill him, we'll have to try harder."

"I'm a failure as a hit man."

"Nobody starts at the top," I said. "Oops. We forgot to go to the police station."

"Why do we have to go there?"

"The policeman told us to. You have to fill out an accident report. We'll do it in the morning. Before you take me to pick up my new car."

"What car?"

"My new old car. Bill Trippy has an extra and they are going to let me use it."

"Will you drive it or Mom's car?"

"You can drive Mom's car."

"Excellent."

"What a lucky kid."

"Want some pie? I think I'll have some pie."

Chapter 6

I can't remember what I dreamed but I woke up worried. They still, you know, do have capital punishment. Lying there, I suffered. Judgment is passed; you're scheduled for the rope, the bullets, fire, a needle, whatever. You've got it coming. *I've* got it coming, but no, I'm safe, comfortable, and guilty, in a warm bed, between flannel sheets. Remembering Denver's accident, I see the tree headed fast for my windshield. I rewind to the bright yellow cyclist zooming from the left and there's the tree, the instant crumple-crash against the unyielding trunk. *Blam* goes the airbag. Oak leaves sixty feet over head tremble briefly, diffusing the shock into the unfeeling air.

The improbably quick balloon helped the seat belt save the kid as he heaved toward the steering wheel and windshield. Spared a crushing blow, he released his belt, stepped outside the now-shapeless car, and used his phone, his still-working cell phone, to call for help, to summon those who manage small disasters for a living.

So Denver was okay. But I'd found my own tree when I wrote that note to Marjie. Why did it matter? I'd admitted to a little crush.

In grade school you might confide *I like you*—did my note amount
to more than that? But it brought reproach from the person it was
intended to flatter as though by acknowledging fondness I had become
adulterous.

I remembered Georgia's phone call. I listened in memory to her
voice. She had not sounded righteous or resentful. Maybe Marjie had
not mentioned my note or perhaps Georgia didn't care. Maybe she
thought Marjie had over-reacted and had told her so. *Lighten up girl.
Life is too short not to take a sweet crushy feeling where you find it.
He's a nice guy, don't you think?*

A nice guy? Yes, and what does that get you? If you want to cause
excitement you'd better be a bad boy—nice guys bore 'em—we're
like sleepy grasshoppers with glasses. The flannel sheets felt great. As
I awakened, the firing squad faded into the fog of the passing night.
Maybe Marjie'd kept the whole thing to herself. I wondered what she
was thinking. It was impossible to guess.

Finally came the heart-sinking recollection that the boys would be
in California for Christmas.

I got up and made coffee.

In the shower I thought about that video Denver had shown me.
Random scenes from game demos. What an odd thing to have spent
time on. Thanksgiving entertainment for him and his brother—making
pointless software with comical content. Denver had played it from his
iPad. Is that where the file was? Where was it written?

I asked him as we drove to the police station. Not that I cared
much, really, but it was a way to show interest. "Where did you and
Sean write that file?"

"Huh?"

"The scrambled game demos? What disk is it on?"

"I don't know," Denver said, in a tone that implied that my
question was as random as their project.

"Wasn't it a file?"

"Sure I guess."

"It had to have been," I persisted.

"Yeah I guess."

"So where was it written?"

"Written?"

"On what disk?"

"I don't know. I'm not sure it was local," he said, trying to be patient with my strange line of inquiry. "Sean might have put it in the cloud. What difference does it make?"

"I don't know. I was just wondering."

In normal life you don't go around expecting serious physical trouble. In the police world, it's different. They have bars and guns and bullet-proof vests. Morning after morning the rest of us wake up in what Helen's New York friend called a *leafy suburb* where everyone you encounter is either friendly or taken up with their own concerns and nobody steals your property or hurts you. You know that a few people around town must be fairly crazy but they hide it, they are on meds, they don't go wild in public, and you are allowed to function as though everyone's a steady citizen. When you go to the police station you're aware that somewhere in the building is a cage they could lock you into. The desk officer is behind bulletproof glass because violent behavior can happen here and because force is deployed to subdue it you encounter a police officer wearing a real gun, just like what kills people on the news. Police expect trouble. I entered the door of the police world followed by my nervous teenage stepson who will be late for school.

But today the strong arm of the law only forced us to fill out a form. An accident report. Under my watchfully supportive eye Denver did a thorough job, in a reasonably legible hand, and after twenty minutes he handed it through the opening to the uniformed woman behind the glass. I asked, "Is Officer Decker here this morning?"

"No," she said." She glanced at the form, then looked at the kid. "Are you Denver Shields?"

He nodded.

She scanned the log in front of her. "Sergeant Decker said to tell you," then she paused while she located the note, "that he finds no basis for you to be cited but reminds you to drive carefully and observe all speed limits."

"Okay," Denver said.

"Thank you," I said.

"Holding up the accident report she said, "You need to send one copy of this to your insurance company. Would you like a copy for your files?"

"Yes, please," I said.

"I'll make two copies." When she handed them to me she said, "Have a nice day."

"Thank you," I said.

We drove to Cambridge. Denver drove. The traffic was awful. It took forever to get to MIT. He dropped me off at the building where Georgia had told me to pick up the keys for Bill's van.

"What if you can't get it?" Denver asked.

"I don't know," I said. "I'll take the train or something."

"I could wait."

"No. You should get to school as fast as you can. Safely."

"Yeah, yeah." He drove off.

I went in the front door of the building, waited in line at security, made out a visitor badge, and was directed to the office of the lady who had the keys.

I identified myself to the receptionist and explained why I was there. She said, "Oh right," and went to a cabinet. She rummaged for a few minutes then returned with the keys in an envelope. "Been no call for these for a long time."

"Thank you," I said, taking the envelope. "Where is the vehicle?"

"It's in the MIT Garage."

"I'm sorry, I don't know where that is."

She took the envelope from me and wrote *454 Everett* on it.

"Thank you. Which way is that?"

"Hmm. Up toward Porter Square, I think." She turned to a woman passing through the office and asked "Do you know how to get to the garage? On Everett?"

"What garage?"

"The MIT garage."

"Didn't know we had one."

"Where Professor Trippy keeps his research van."

"Research van?"

"Yes. That's what it says on the key tag."

"I'm sorry. I don't know anything about it," the woman said, and continued on her way.

The receptionist turned back to me and said, "Well you've got the address. I guess that's all I can give you right now."

Out on the street I took out my phone, opened the map application, entered the address, and selected navigation on foot. After a minute the device determined my location and told me to walk north for five hundred feet. I followed those and subsequent instructions until they brought me around the corner to the rim of a deep broad pit, a construction site protected by a formidable chain-link fence.

I headed back the other way. Instead of helping me skirt this obstacle the navigation voice said, "Turn around when possible." I ignored it. The phone rang.

It was Denver. "You have to sign me in."

"Sign you in?"

"Yeah."

"Why?"

"Because I was late."

"Ugh. Couldn't I just talk to them?"

"They say that my parent has to come to the school and sign me in."

"Why haven't I ever had to do that before?"

The phone said, "In fifty feet, turn right."

Denver said, "I was never late before."

He was a senior. How could he have never been late before? "Okay," I said. "I'll pick up the van and be there in twenty-twenty-five minutes."

"More like thirty-five or forty," Denver said.

"I'll hurry," I said.

"Drive carefully," he said. I guess he had not liked my parting admonition.

My destination turned out to be a drug store. I went in. "I thought this was a garage," I told the clerk.

The South Asian man at the cash register said, "No, no, I'm sorry, it is very confusing, this is Everett *Street*, you see."

"Yes."

"The garage is on Everett *Place*."

"Okay. Where's that?"

He gestured the way I had come. "About three blocks. And on the other side."

I hurried. I found the garage. It had a tired, timeless office. No one was at the desk. I could hear television talk from an adjacent room. There was a bell. When I tapped it, the television fell quiet and a heavy

African American woman appeared. I told her I was there to pick up a vehicle.

"I'll have to go down there and open the door for you. Drive your car up to the top of the ramp and honk your horn."

"I've never been here before. How do I get to the car?"

She pointed to a dark stairway. "Down there. Light's on the right."

I flipped the switch. A compact fluorescent bulb glowed dimly.

"He'll brighten up in a minute," the woman predicted.

I descended.

At the bottom of the narrow stairway I entered a dimly-lit low-ceiled space ranked with large objects at rest on the concrete floor, silent in the airless dusk. There were antique and sports cars, a tractor, and some wheeled machines that might have been air compressors but probably had arcane functions understood by people at MIT but not by me. Maybe they were prototypes of military devices that we were well off not knowing about. To help me read license plates I turned on the flashlight of my phone. The first thing it illuminated was a crazy pile of pieces of what could only have been a carnival ride, a Whirl-a-thon or something, perhaps an artifact of the MIT tradition of practical jokes.

Eventually I found a dusty Dodge van. The plate matched the number I had been given and the key opened the door and fit in the ignition but when I turned it, nothing happened. I pulled out my wallet and called the automobile association. I dialed in my member number. Eventually the computer connected me to a person, who promised to send help and asked, "Will you be with the vehicle, sir?"

"Yes—hold on—" I went upstairs and found the lady.

"My car won't start."

She said, "I'm sorry that's not really something I can help you with," while the phone said, "Yes, sir, I'm going to have someone there as soon as possible."

I said to the phone, "Yes I'm trying to find out where to meet your truck." I asked the lady, "What side of the building is the garage door on?"

"It's at the back. Or is it the side?" she wondered out loud.

"What street is it on?"

"Hmmm. Maybe that's Blackwell. Blackwell, I think. Or Thornton."

"Okay," I said into the phone. "Tell the driver I'll meet him in front of the office at 454 Everett Place—that's *Place*, not *Street*."

"Yes sir. He should be there in fifteen minutes to an hour."

"I'll be waiting."

"Yes sir."

I called Denver.

"They are yelling at me for using my phone," was his greeting.

"Sorry," I said. "The van didn't start. I'm waiting for triple-A."

"It would be good if you could get here."

"I know. Let me talk to them."

"There's nobody here right now."

"Okay. I'll hurry. See you." I put the phone in my pocket. I told the lady, "I'll just give it another try." I went back downstairs, relocated the van, and turned the key in the ignition. Nothing happened.

My phone rang. "Is this Mr. Martin?"

"Yes."

"This is the roadside assistance driver."

"Are you already here?"

"Where are you? Because Cambridge has an Everett *Street* and an Everett *Place* and Somerville has an Everett *Court* and I need to know which you are at."

"I told her. *Place*. I emphasized that."

"You're at Everett *Place*?"

"Yes."

"That's down by MIT, isn't it?"

"That's right. It's the MIT garage."

"Okay. I should be there in ten minutes."

"I'll meet you in front of the office and take you to the vehicle," I promised.

As I waited on the sidewalk it began to snow. The truck pulled up. I stuck my head into the office and said, "He's here. Could you please open the garage door?"

"Yes sir. Let me just find that key." She began to search.

After a minute I went out to the truck. When the driver rolled down the window, I said, "She's looking for the key to the door."

He nodded. The window went back up.

As snow melted in my hair, I wished I had a hat. The woman came out the office door putting on her coat. She led me along the sidewalk.

The truck followed me at a crawl. Our guide turned at the corner. I could see the garage door halfway down the long building.

The driver honked. I looked at him. He pointed to a DO NOT ENTER sign. I pointed to the garage door. He nodded and set off to penetrate a labyrinth of one-way streets and dead-ends to reach that door.

The lady unlocked and raised the door. "Just close it behind you when you come out if you don't mind," she said.

"Okay," I said. "Thank you."

"Where's that truck?"

"One-way," I said.

"Oh yes. Sure is. He has to go around or they'll give him a big fat ticket. Um-hmm. Good luck. Merry Christmas."

"Merry Christmas to you."

She trudged up the slope toward the front of the building. I took out my phone and dialed Denver. "Darn. Denver's missed your call," said his recorded greeting. "Do whatever you want."

"Denver," I said, "The truck's here. But it's snowing pretty hard. I'll get there as fast as I can."

The truck came around the corner and up the hill to the entrance. It barely fit under the door, but he inched through. His headlights shone on a Stanley Steamer. When he reached the van he said, "Okay, go ahead and pop the engine cover."

"I don't know how."

He gave me a look at once questioning, superior, and patient. He used his flashlight to find the release.

"It isn't my van," I explained. "I'm just borrowing it."

"Okay," he said. He hooked up his battery charging device. "Been a while since this engine ran. Long while. When it gets going you better let it idle for fifteen-twenty minutes to let that oil circulate."

"How long?"

"Fifteen-twenty minutes would be good. That will charge the battery at the same time."

"What about carbon monoxide?"

"Better take her outside I guess."

He started the engine.

When he left I eased out of the parking place. The tires, out of round, thumped the concrete. I wondered where I could get air.

I pulled into daylight and turned right. Snow blurred the windshield. I turned on the wipers, which were stiff. At the end of the block a police car pulled out in front of me with its lights flashing. The policeman came to my window.

"This is a one-way street," he told me.

"I'm sorry, officer."

"This vehicle's registration is expired."

"I'm just taking it out of storage."

"You'll have to get it right back off the road until it's registered and inspected."

"Yes sir."

"Okay." He got back into his car, turned off the blue lights, and drove on. I pulled around the corner into a DELIVERIES ONLY place on the curb. Leaving the engine running, I yanked the emergency brake, got out, and hurried to the open garage door. When it was closed I skated back down the slippery sidewalk to the van. I tried to call Denver. "Darn. Denver's missed your call." I hung up and pressed the gas pedal. The emergency brake held and killed the engine. I supposed it wouldn't start and I'd have to call AAA again. But it caught. I drove off through the snow, struggling to see the road.

An hour later I pulled up in front of the high school. In the mirrors I could see bright blue lights behind me, reflecting in every direction on mid-air snowflakes. The cop named Decker appeared at my window. I noticed that his badge said *Sergeant*. "Your registration and inspection are expired."

"Yes sir. Remember me from yesterday? The car the kid hit the tree trying not to hit the bike? I borrowed this van. The smashed car, mine, and they won't let Denver go to class. The kid. I have to sign him in then I'll be right back. Okay?"

He just looked at me.

I rushed toward the school. The snow was over the tops of my shoes. I stopped and called back, "Thank you for not ticketing the kid."

"Your tires are low," Sergeant Decker replied.

I hurried into the school office.

"I'm Ike Martin," I told the woman at the counter.

"Yes?" she said.

"I want to sign my student in. Denver Shields."

"Denver? He's in class."

"Oh. I thought I had to rush over here to sign him in."

"Yes, you were supposed to but he said you were in Cambridge and he'd totalled your car and your new car wouldn't start so Mr. Kelly declared amnesty."

"That was decent of him. I wish . . ."

"Yes?"

"Never mind. Thanks."

Sergeant Decker and his cruiser were gone. It had stopped snowing. I drove home and parked the van in the driveway.

The house was empty and silent. The completed puzzle was on the table in the family room. There was the lush Italian garden, with fountains, grottoes, flowers, a goddess with a dozen breasts, and Susan's drawings over all. Out the window the afternoon was dusky. In late fall New England days end early. On the empty lawn, gardening equipment, coiled hoses, and a cart, reproached me from beneath the snow. They shouldn't have been left out. I went out to the woodpile, brought in firewood, and laid but did not light a fire. I started to break up the puzzle, then changed my mind and put it back together.

I took a photo album off the shelf. I looked at the pictures my dad had taken of me and my brothers and sisters at different ages. One showed all four of us. It was captioned, *Adam, Ike, Henry, and Kate at Disney World.* I was the only one in glasses.

I poured a glass of wine. I lit the fire and watched it catch and take on a flickering life. Success. Something I did could work out. The flames multiplied and offered warm yellow light to the dim room.

I noticed that the bird feeder was empty. Leaving a screen in front of the fire, I went out. I filled the plastic tube with sunflower seeds and put it back in place. A chickadee scolded me, "Dee dee dee!" before it advanced to the feeder and took a seed.

The snow was melting. It was dark, wet, and chilly. It was that time of year. No frozen ground. No deep long-lasting snow. It was the season to be tired. Tired of darkness. Tired of how long it was until summer. Tired of my situation. Tired of myself.

I went back inside and sat down in front of the fire with my laptop. The screen showed that Georgia was available to chat. I clicked her name and typed *Georgia?*

In a moment she replied, *Hey Ike.*

I picked up the van.

Good.
It needs to be registered.
?
Registration's expired.
Oh right.
And inspected.
I ought to have realized that.
I drove it home anyway.
Did you get stopped?
Only twice.
Why don't I give you the title and you can get it registered to yourself?

I considered her offer. *I'd pay you something for it.*
Dad doesn't need the money and you might have to get it fixed.
Could I ask you something?
Sure.
Could I visit your dad?
Why not?
Is he up to it?
He's still doped up but I think he likes someone to sit with him. I'll meet you there with the papers for the van.

We set a time to rendezvous the next morning in Bill's room.

As Denver and I cooked supper I told him about the amazing garage. In bed, ready for sleep, I imagined that the machines in storage had been designed to spray invisibility, to vaporize bullets, to neutralize gravity. I wondered about the man who had come from the AAA to start the van. Was he happier than I was? I supposed he had kids of his own.

There was still no evidence that Georgia knew about my exchange of notes with Marjie.

The next morning, in Helen's car, I dropped Denver at school ten minutes early and drove to the hospital. I parked in the garage and threaded my way through corridors and elevators to intensive care. The unit had its staff area in the middle and patient rooms around the circumference. Even though I wasn't a family member no one questioned my right to enter. There was intense commotion in a room three doors down—a crisis. Instructions were being given in voices loud and sharp. Bright light spilled from the room. I was arrested by that drama for a moment before I went into Bill's room. Georgia wasn't there. Bill was asleep. He had a tube in his arm. That's one way for strangers to control you. They don't have to ask you to take a pill or breathe gas because they just drop whatever they want through that tube. You try to trust them.

Bill was wired for heartbeat and blood pressure and blood oxygen, all reported on the screen over his head and no doubt out to the nurses and doctors and—who knows?—maybe it was on the Internet so that some lady doctor could read all about it on her smartphone while she was in line for the lady's room at Symphony Hall. Maybe she knew who Bill was, or maybe her grandfather had known him at MIT and she paid him extra attention without compromising her quality of life.

There lay Bill, unconscious, alone with me. A nurse looked in. "We have a code," she told me, pointing at the room with the crisis. "He should be okay for now," she said, meaning Bill. She hurried off to do her part to see if they could pull someone back to the Massachusetts side of the River Styx. I had the thought, *I bet it's silent over there.* The world we know is full of clatter and chatter, back-up beeps, honks of Canada geese and impatient drivers, talk about food and movies and games and complaints about bosses and co-workers and family members but over there it's really, really, quiet. That's probably how you know you're dead.

Georgia walked in. "How's he doing?" she asked.

"He hasn't stirred."

"Dad, can you hear me?"

Bill's breathing didn't change.

Georgia took an envelope from her bag and handed it to me. "Let me give you this before I forget about it. Dad, I'm giving Ike your van. You are giving him your van," she informed the sleeping man. "Don't worry, you still have your Porsche and your SUV." Then, to me, she said, "He really knew, knows, how to enjoy being rich. I wonder what he'll be like when we get him back."

"Do they think he will be different?"

"The doctors don't know or aren't saying but Wikipedia says people do recover, even from serious damage, to varying degrees. So, we'll see."

"Has he talked much yet?"

"No and we can't wait to hear him talk because what he said on Thanksgiving was the first sign that something was wrong."

"He became incoherent?"

"No, he was perfectly coherent and perfectly inappropriate." She laughed. "He saw me using Mom's old electric mixer—it still works and it's the only one I have—and he said, 'I made your mother's whipped cream with that mixer.' We all knew he never prepared meals. He always did clean-up. He said, 'After you were asleep. How your mother's eyes would sparkle when she saw me take out that heavy cream.' The room got quiet and I said, 'Dad I'm thinking maybe we've got a little TMI here, don't we?' but that didn't slow him down and we got *way* too much information accompanied by gestures and Ev noticed that one arm wasn't working and called the ambulance."

She looked down at her father. "Are you hearing this, Dad? I'm not trying to embarrass you or anything but that's what happened. It won't go into your autobiography." Bill didn't move or open his eyes. Georgia turned back to me. "So when he wakes up God only knows what else he's going to say. I have to go to work."

"I sure appreciate you letting me use the van—"

"Oh you're welcome—no sense in it just sitting there."

"It comes in handy because—"

"Ike, really, don't mention it, and you know we feel bad because of Stephen and hitting the tree and your show cancelled and now Dad's project probably winding down or, you know, going on hold for a while or whatever—it can't be an easy time for you."

"Oh, as for his project I could—"

"Sorry—I've got to run—you'll have to discuss that with Ev—I'm afraid I've spoken out of turn—he has strong views—whatever is okay with me." She bent over and kissed Bill. "See you later, Dad. Bye, Ike," and she left.

Well. That didn't sound good. I thought I'd just be moving right along with the book and billing my hours like I had been and getting along okay while Bill recovered. But this made it sound like the van was a severance gift.

During Georgia's visit the nearby commotion had ended. A gurney went by with a motionless passenger.

Bill opened his eyes. "Hey Bill. It's Ike Martin. Your daughter was just here but she had to go to work."

Bill made a hoarse growl. Even here in the hospital, old and beaten up by this illness, he looked big and not without power. Semiconscious and damaged as he was.

"You okay, Bill?"

He nodded.

"Need anything?"

He said, "No," then closed his eyes and went back to sleep.

The nurse came in. "Was he awake?"

"Briefly."

"We've got him pretty drugged," she explained.

"How long will that last?"

"The attending will decide."

I watched her leave. She showed an excellent knack for walking away from a fellow. I wondered what it was like to sleep with a nurse. That's a stupid way to put it because there are thousands and thousands of nurses but nurses and doctors have such a different relationship to the human body than the rest of us. They have social permission to see and touch the bodies of strangers. What would that mean in bed? Even women who were not nurses didn't seem particularly surprised or impressed by my body and its responses, not like I was by theirs. Every lover's body has been mysterious to me, and interesting, but I guess that's a peculiarity of mine. Maybe it's a boy-girl difference. Or maybe it's just me. I think I've always been a bit wide-eyed about women and their bodies. As though the planet weren't full of them; as though there were something unusual in their anatomical departments.

Stephen and Marjie came in the door.

"How's the patient?" Stephen asked.

"He opened his eyes a little while ago," I said. "But he didn't make any speeches. Stephen, are you okay?" I was unprepared for this encounter.

"Still thrilled by my first ride in an ambulance."

"You're okay though? Is he okay, Marjie?"

"He seems to be fine," she said. "And your son? How is he? I hear he smashed into a tree."

"He's okay. The airbag and seatbelt saved him." I looked at Stephen. "What saved you?"

"Being a lightweight," he said. "I can't hit anything hard enough to do damage. Or at least, to damage beyond what my chiropractor can repair. He took some kinks out of me yesterday."

I was all ears for the tones of their voices. Was Marjie still mad? Had she mentioned my note? It seemed probable that if the answer to those questions was *yes* an involuntary edge would have been audible as we exchanged our greetings. I didn't hear it.

"This is the guy who got hurt," Stephen said, looking at Bill. "He got smashed from the inside, out. Your car, on the other hand, took it from the outside, in."

"Yeah, my Toyota's finished but Bill seems to be hanging in there."

"I guess he's coming along," Marjie said. "Dad says they think he'll be in a regular room in another day or two and in rehab not long after that."

"He's tough," I said.

"I'm glad your kid's okay," Stephen said. "Sorry about your car. Really. I think sometimes when I ride I'm too preoccupied. Like all that oxygen makes me high or something."

"I'm glad both of you came out okay."

"And Georgia's fixed you up with a car, right?" Stephen asked.

"Yeah. My next stop is the registry."

"Granddad's research-mobile," said Marjie, half stating, half questioning.

"Is that what it is?" I said. "It's a van. It seems more like a camper. I haven't figured out about the research part."

"It's odd," Marjie said. "I don't think we knew he even had it. Until the other day, when Dad and Aunt Georgia went into his papers for the health proxy and came upon the title and the note about where it was parked. I hope it helps you."

She didn't sound mad. She looked nice. It was possible to imagine that she was glad to see me.

Chapter 7

"How's your play coming along?" I asked Stephen.

"Great. Or, not so great," he said. "I'm a little stuck. In fact, I was out on my bike to get clear on the next step when I had that encounter with the young man in your car. The whole thing is a pair of conversations. Remember the lawyer? Picture the kid who becomes the lawyer, that litigator I told you about before—he had been hitchhiking thirty years earlier and was picked up by a rabbi and they have this deep philosophical dialogue—"

"Stephen, he was just being polite," Marjie said.

"No, I'm interested," I said, in partial truth.

"Thirty years later that talk between strangers is repeated in another car. But this time the successful egotistical litigator debates a young divinity student. My anti-protagonist has become non-reflective and worldly; his clients include planet-raping cheap-labor-exploiting Republican-financing corporations and now the moral voice is a kid."

"Nice," I said.

"You see the problem. Is the lawyer played by one actor or two? Does the same guy have the nineteen-seventies dialogue in one direction, then turn the other way to be in the two thousands? Or are they played by different guys? Or should I leave that to whoever does the staging?"

The nurse came in. "Could we keep it down a little in here? Indoor voices, please," she added, as though she knew that Marjie was a teacher.

"Sorry," Stephen said.

"He's theatrical," Marjie explained. The nurse left.

"I've got to go anyway." Stephen checked his phone. "I'm supposed to be having office hours right now. But nobody's texted me."

"They, the students, are supposed to text him in advance if they are coming to his office," Marjie told me.

"Yeah because why sit around like a store clerk waiting for somebody to show up in this day and age when you don't have to? When nobody's coming anyway because if they had a question they'd just email. The whole office-hours thing is a medieval holdover. So long, Bill," he said to the sleeping patient. "Glad to hear these good reports, be well, see you around." He turned to Marjie. "Your mother's your ride, right?"

She nodded.

Moving to the door Stephen looked back to me. "Until we meet again." His voice was still too loud. The nurse chided him with a gesture. With his thumb and index finger, he sealed his lips while giving us, with the other hand, thumbs up.

When he was gone, I said, "Marjie, I'm afraid I was rude to you last time we were here."

"It was the stress, Ike," she said. "We were both under stress and you meant well. I can't remember what I wrote but I think I overreacted."

"I had it coming; I was off base; but anyway—"

"We don't need to say more about it. It was the stress. Granddad's recovering and that's all that matters."

The room felt like a better place than it had been. When it was time to resume talking I asked Marjie about her teaching.

She said she had taken today as a personal day because of her grandfather, but was about to prepare for parent conferences. She asked, "Did you have a good Thanksgiving?"

I told her about Sean's girlfriend Susan and how she'd taken a black ink marker to the jig-saw puzzle.

"She hadn't asked you if was okay?"

"Neither Helen nor I was home. Sean told her we liked originality. Which is true."

"She could have been just as original on a nice pad of drawing paper."

"The idea of marking up the puzzle was the original part," I said. "Plus, she related her drawings to the puzzle image and to our family and to her bug art. All at the same time."

"I don't see it being okay without permission."

"She had permission from Sean."

"Were you mad at him?"

"I was surprised and annoyed when I first saw it. But with teenagers in the house you have to stay loose, you know. Roll with stuff."

Ev came in scowling. He had barely greeted us before he informed Marjie that she and her mother hadn't thought things out very well because if they gave her a ride who would be there with Dad? When a knot of doctors arrived I slipped out to the waiting room so they could confer with family. I reflected on Marjie's reaction to Susan's treatment of the puzzle. I supposed it showed that she was more conventional than Helen. In my fantasies, life with Marjie featured more tenderness than I could expect from Helen. Maybe Marjie wasn't as sweet in real life as she was in my imagination?

Five minutes later Marjie came out and asked if I would be willing to give her a ride home. On the way to my car she told me that the doctors continued to be pleased with her grandfather's progress. They were going to take him off sedation. She said she had used a personal day so she could be at the hospital. Her car was in the shop and Stephen had to work so everything was a little mixed up. And her dad was acting crabby.

When we reached her neighborhood, as we passed a large open area, Marjie asked if I wanted to see her garden. I said yes.

Walking down the aisle among the garden plots the word *sere* came to mind. I thought it meant shades of brown but I looked it up. It means *dry, withered*. Not the first time I'd found a right word for a wrong reason. The post-Thanksgiving gardens were uniformly brown and withered except for some gaudy purple cabbage. And Marjie had one plant that remained a grayish green. "I love Brussels sprouts," she said. "They keep getting better all fall." While we picked the remainder of her crop, an aged Asian person appeared in the enclosure.

"Mrs. Lu!" Marjie said.

"Hello Marjory," the woman said.

"Mrs. Lu, I want you to meet a friend of mine. This is Ike Martin. You might remember him from his television program."

She offered her hand but gave no sign of recognition. She was small. She wore a bright red wool coat and a hat, like an oversized pink beret, made of synthetic fleece. I tried not to notice the painful clash between her hat and her coat. Remembering Marjie's mention of her oracle, I ventured, "Are you the person who sits with Marjie in fine weather?"

The old lady smiled.

Marjie said, "Yes, Mrs. Lu is my protector and advisor."

Marjie's oracle had a certain aura, which led me to a conversational challenge that affects the inquisitive. I wanted to hear all about her.

Occasionally on dates I've had good luck signaling interest and giving attention by going straight at it. *Please tell me the story of your life* can work in situations where you hope to get acquainted really fast. But in most contexts it's no good. *How do you do? Please narrate the drama of your life for my pleasure, edification, and curiosity.* Wouldn't it be a better world if we could cut to the chase and discover what we have to learn from each other?

I was as direct as I felt was socially acceptable. I said, "I think you must be a person who has acquired wisdom."

She looked at me harder. No doubt there are persons who do not like the sound of themselves being complimented but they are scarce and Mrs. Lu wasn't one of them. "Wisdom, no. Wisdom is too hard for me," she said. "I have tried to profit from experience."

"Were you born in this country?"

"No. I was born in Shenzhen. China. Long ago. I have been in this country fifty years."

"Are you glad you came here?" Marjie asked.

"It is good here. And also in China," Mrs. Lu said. "All countries have some good, some bad. I like all countries."

"You have profited from your experience," I said.

"I have tried to do so. That's all I can say."

"You succeeded, Mrs. Lu," Marjie said. "I'm sure you did."

Then, unexpectedly, my sister appeared. "Kate!"

"Ike! Did you know I had a plot here?" Her greeting-smile faded into the serious expression that I associated with her, that she had worn her whole life. I was eight when she was born; I remember her as a tiny kid. She's always had that intense straight-ahead focus. It's just an appearance, though. She never really gets much done.

"No. You have a garden here?" I introduced her to Marjie and Mrs. Lu. Kate was polite but quickly brought her eyes back to me. Marjie picked up on that and said, "Ike, go catch up with your sister. I can walk home from here."

Kate said, "Yes, Ike, let's have coffee."

"Okay," I said. "Mrs. Lu, I hope we can talk longer next time." I said goodbye to Marjie and walked away with Kate.

"They're an odd couple," she remarked, without sounding interested in how I happened to be there with them or what they were to me. That was like Kate.

"Marjie's my client's granddaughter," I said, but that didn't seem interesting even to me and there was no evidence that Kate cared, so I let it go. She showed me her garden plot, which featured three statues of Buddha, two enamel foo dogs, and lots of weeds. "How were your crops?" I asked.

"Not too good," she said. "I got some peas and a few beans. My sunflowers looked nice but birds got all the seeds."

We walked on toward a coffee shop. "How is Steve?"

"He's fine. Jones, Jones, Jones . . ." she added, which I understood to have a funny double meaning. Kate's husband was named Steve Jones. She always called him Jones. And he did have a major jones, in the slang sense of an obsessive interest. It was sports. He watched games and watched more games. If possible he watched them as they happened; if not, he recorded them and watched them later.

"His job's okay, though?"

"Yeah, oh yeah, he's doing great. I don't know why they think he's worth so much. But you, your job, not so good?"

"No. Not so good. My show's over. I've been helping the grandfather of that woman you just met. A famous guy. I was supposed to research and co-author his autobiography. But he had a stroke."

"But your wife makes plenty—"

"I'm not sure how much she makes but between whatever it is and what she gets in child support we don't seem to have a problem."

"Ha, Ike, we're both kept. Kept spouses. Pretty good deal for us, huh?"

"How have you been spending your time, Kate?"

"The usual. Yoga. Teaching some yoga. Taking care of Fievel. I can't believe you found me at the park without Fievel because it's usually him and me at the park." She took out her phone and displayed a picture of a small gray dog with curly fur. "Isn't he cute? Why don't you get a dog?"

People want to show you pictures of their pets and grandchildren. Why? I don't get it. Food for thought. After we ordered coffee, I replied, "We have a teenage boy. That's close enough. He's all the pets we need."

"Isn't he in college yet?"

"One of them is and the other's a senior. He's applying."

"We missed you at home for Thanksgiving."

"But Helen and I always stay at our own place with our guys at Thanksgiving."

"Yeah, and we always miss you in Ithaca. What about Christmas?"

"Both of the boys are spending Christmas in California with their dad. Maybe Helen and I could make it."

"You should come. Have you talked to Dad? I really think he's slipping."

"He sounds okay to me."

"Mom and Dad ought to get a dog."

"They are busy volunteering and doing politics."

"A dog would be good for them. And meditation. I shouldn't talk, though. I ought to meditate more. I've been skimping."

As we drank our coffee Kate told me about yoga. It was hard for her to realize how little I knew about it. I wanted to be interested because she was my sister and I *was* interested because it's always good to learn. When she wound down about yoga she asked about my life. I began by telling her that Denver was in the middle of college applications and ended there, too, because the thought of colleges reminded her of something about yoga which somehow led to dogs. While she described one way Fievel demonstrated his intelligence her phone made a noise and she glanced at it. "Okay, well, great to catch up. I've got to head to the studio."

"Studio?"

"Yoga. I'm leading. My phone reminded me. Jones and I should have you and Helen over."

She left. I wondered if they'd really have us over. Once they had invited us to dinner, when they first got married, and we reciprocated but we didn't have all that much to say to each other and Jones, as I am trying to learn to call him, would clearly have preferred to be watching athletes do their thing. And Kate had been Kate. Helen thought they were both shallow and made little effort to disguise her sense of superiority. The result was that even though we lived not far from each other, Kate and I seldom talked.

I wondered if Kate would ever have kids. Not the kind of thing you bring up. And she never mentioned it.

At the Registry of Motor Vehicles I transferred ownership of the van to myself. Then I picked up Denver at school. He took his mother's car and headed to a friend's. I had my first look at the van's interior. It was a camper. Its windows were deeply tinted. You could see out but no one could see in. There were no back seats, only a bed and some storage space that was empty except for half a bottle of Jack Daniels. What kind of research did Bill do? If he had been a naturalist, like an ornithologist on the hunt for the last ivory-billed woodpecker, this could have been his mobile base. But for an engineer and physicist it was hard to figure. I drove my new wheels to a service station that did state safety inspections. After replacement of a signal light, I got a sticker and was good to go.

That night I emailed Helen. I suggested that since Sean and Denver would be with Greg for Christmas, I'd like us to go to my parents' house.

That would be fine, she responded.

So I sent my mother a message asking if it would be okay. In the morning she had answered, *Of course. Stay as long as you like.*

I decided to visit Bill. This was motivated not just by friendly concern. I thought maybe once he was off the meds it would be possible to go back to work on his book. Georgia had told me that I should talk to Ev. I could have called him but it seemed better to wait until we knew how intact Bill was. I was trying, for once in my life, to be strategic.

Bill was awake when I went in. "Ugh," he said.

"Hey Bill. What's doing?"

"Humph," he replied. I took that to mean *okay I guess considering the circumstances.*

"I stopped by before but I think you were distracted or something."

"Yeah," he said. "Maybe so." He was hoarse, and the words came slowly, but they were words.

"Happy Thanksgiving. And all that."

"It was Thanksgiving I took ill?" Half statement, half question.

"That's right. You've had a few tough days since then."

"Well. I'm still here."

"Good job."

He felt his throat.

"They had you on a tube for a while," I said. "No picnic."

"Ugh."

"Need anything?" I asked, gesturing over my shoulder toward the door, the nurses, the free-living world outside.

"Nah." He paused. "Coffee. Next time."

"You got it."

I sat there. Neither of us spoke. Finally I asked, "Are you ready for a nap?" I was offering to leave.

"Nah," he said. "If I'd kicked the bucket, the service would have been wrong."

"You haven't planned it out?"

"Guess I better."

"You made it through."

"This time."

We were silent in the room together. The room in which he had rallied and lived. The room in which I had learned that Marjie had forgiven me, or had not been too offended, or whatever, or at least was not telling everyone she knew that I, a married man, had come on to her.

Because I was thinking of Marjie it startled me to hear Bill say, "Do you love them?"

"Love who?"

"Women."

"Oh. Women."

"God I love them. The beautiful ones."

"Yes," I agreed. "I love them too."

"They are great," he said. "I'll sleep." He closed his eyes.

"Okay, Bill. You're doing fine. See you soon."

He grunted.

Leaving, passing through the waiting room, I met Ev coming in. When I told him that Bill was resting he suggested that we talk, if I had time. We sat down.

"Georgia and I have discussed the situation," Ev said. "This seems like a natural transition point. You've done a good job—we don't question that. But as you know Stephen will be joining the family and his adjunct teaching position is really just part time, so we think the co-authoring role with Dad will be a good fit for him."

I just sat there.

"Sorry."

"Bill hired *me*."

"Yeah, well, the situation has changed. You seem like a reasonable person so I think you will understand how things are."

That was true. I did understand. Teaching paid little and Stephen was unlikely to make anything writing plays. Then Ev dropped the other shoe.

"So, as for you hanging out here at the hospital visiting Dad, probably you ought to wind that down."

"Wind it down?"

"Yeah, you know, give it a rest."

There was a long pause. Ev and I looked at each other with neither sympathy nor hostility. Finally, I said, "Okay, I hear you."

"I like you and we all like you and we think you've done a good job."

"Thanks," I said. "One thing is that I have a relationship with Bill. He's become a friend of mine."

"Okay, right," Ev said. "We have to recognize that and honor it. And you have to consider what's best for Dad under the circumstances." He stood up. "Meanwhile you should assume that Stephen will be needing your notes and whatnot."

"Yes." As far as the business relationship was concerned, I'd been on a work-for-hire basis. Bill owned everything I'd done. "He wants visitors to bring him coffee."

Ev nodded, and I went home.

There was commotion in the kitchen. It was Helen. I hadn't expected her back from New York for another day. Everything was pulled apart. The counters were covered by the contents of drawers and cabinets. Helen had a new haircut and looked excellent. "What are you doing?" I asked.

"Changing the shelf paper."

"We didn't expect you today."

"I came back early. It's a fluid situation, a lot going on, lots of balls in the air. But I could slip back so I did."

"I'm glad to see you. Denver will be, too."

"I'll make him something. What would he like?"

"I think we're running low on spiced nuts. Why are you changing the shelf paper?"

"Somebody's got to, from time to time," she said. "I don't know. I just felt like it."

"Well. I'm just from seeing Bill. Bad news—"

"Is he getting worse?"

"No, he's getting better but Ev wants to replace me with Stephen."

"Who's Stephen?"

"He's the future son-in-law. The guy who made Denver run into the tree."

"Well if he's joining the family you can see the logic."

"Yeah. And I bumped into Kate."

"Oh oh. Did you say we'd have them over?"

"No. She said she'd have us. The ball's in her court. Pretty haircut."

"Like it?"

"Yes. You say it's logical they want Stephen. But that was, for the time being, that was my job."

"Not a great job. Maybe you should go to law school."

"Really?"

"You're not too old."

"Don't you think there are already enough unhappy lawyers out there? Not to mention they are under-employed."

"Maybe you'd be one of the happy fully-employed ones."

Setting aside that strange notion I said, "Not only am I not supposed to ghost for Bill, I'm not even supposed to go see him."

"Why would you want to go see him?"

"I like him. We're friends. We have a relationship. They gave me his car, for crying out loud."

"That old van parked in the driveway?"

"Yes. He had it stored in the strangest place. Like out of a movie."

She had left off with the shelf paper and was clinking ice into a glass. "Can I make you a drink?"

"Sure." She had her back to me. It wasn't just her haircut that looked good. When I noticed the liquor bottle I became confused. "Is that from the van?"

"Huh?" She screwed the cap back on the Jack Daniels as I realized that of course we had a bottle of our own.

"Never mind."

She started to say something, stopped, and handed me a glass. I swirled the ice in the copper-colored fluid and smelled it. Usually I had beer or wine.

"So what do you want to do next?" she asked.

"One guess," I said, raising my eyebrows.

92

"Okay. But I meant, for work."

"We could sit by the fire to discuss it."

"We don't have a fire."

"I'll make one," I said.

"How long until Denver gets home?"

"Not long enough."

By the time the fire was going the whiskey had me. Helen repeated, "What do you want to do next?" I kissed her and put my hand between her legs. She didn't resist, but didn't throw herself in, either. I whispered, "When Denver's gone to college, we can get naked right here."

She didn't say anything but squeezed my arm in a not-turned-on sort of way. "I have to tell you something I don't think you are going to like."

I felt my body shift from *get-it-on* to *uh-oh*.

"It's about Christmas," she said. "I have to go to France."

"France?"

"Paris. Of course you can go, too, if you want, but I'll be working. We can go to your parents' house," she continued. "We can drive there together, but I have to fly out the twenty-third."

"Why?"

"It turns out that in Paris, which is, you know, civilized, on Christmas Day the artists have informal shows. In parks. On sidewalks. And they open their studios. I've been hired to collect objects for a show that's to travel. The Teller Museum in the city—it's their project. They have a sort of art for the masses shtick. Can we go upstairs now?"

We took second drinks to our bedroom. Helen rubbed my shoulders and did everything she knew I liked and by the time Denver tapped on our door I had become accustomed to the idea that she would be in Paris on Christmas.

"Are you in there?" Denver asked.

"Yes," I said.

"Why is the kitchen messed up?"

"Your mother's home."

"I'm changing the shelf paper," Helen said.

"Hi Mom," Denver said through the door.

"Hi honey. I'll be right out."

We worked together in the kitchen. Denver and I restored order. Helen made spiced nuts and asked about Denver's accident. She worked on her laptop while Denver and I made supper.

That night I got an email from Stephen—Marjie's Stephen, not my brother-in-law who we're supposed to call Jones. Stephen asked me to send my notes for Bill's book, as I had told Ev I would do. He closed with *I hope you're okay with all this.*

In the morning I sent Stephen the files from my work with Bill. He replied with thanks and asked if he could buy me lunch and pick my brains. I don't see any point to going through life feeling alienated and angry. I took a deep breath, decided I could deal with it, and agreed. But due to his teaching schedule and my dentist appointment we did not get together until the following week. We met at the Black Horse Pub.

As was becoming my habit, my easy opening, I asked about his play.

"It's right where you left it," he said, "stuck on the problem of one player at both ages or one at each age."

"Have you written the actual dialogue?"

"No. Not yet. I want to have the picture of what the audience sees on the stage clear in my mind."

"But you have some of the text?"

"No. But what do you think of my premise?"

"I have a soft spot for philosophical discussion. I like the way you've set it up. An intelligent guy at different ages. How does he sort out his ethics? Versus his self-interest? How does his thinking change as he goes from a kid to mid-life?"

"Maybe you should write my play."

"Think you can afford me? I could use the dough."

"I'll see what I can do."

"How's Bill?" I asked.

"Oh, man. He's obsessed."

"With?"

"Women. On what's left of his mind, he's got women."

"So you've been to see him?"

"I thought I'd jump right in, pick up where you left off. On his genius-ness and world-changing-ness and so on."

"He could talk okay?"

"Yah, he talks just fine but only about his affairs and stuff."

"He wants to tell his future grandson-in-law about his affairs?"

"Yeah, too weird, but I guess the family kind of knows that monogamy wasn't his thing; that his dear departed spouse was never his one and only female attachment. Although he talks about her, too, and their various enjoyments. It's like the stroke knocked off his privacy filter."

"Did you tell him he was being inappropriate?"

"I let him talk. He solved the mystery of your so-called research van. It seems your new vehicle was acquired to facilitate carnal research with his last girlfriend."

"Really?"

"Yeah."

"It's an old van."

"He's an old guy. He said she was so beautiful he wanted to quit while he was ahead. They had one long last weekend at Monhegan and then let it go. Her friend had a house out there."

"Monhegan?"

"Yeah. That island for artists. On the Maine coast. For people who think they're creative. Cars not allowed. They watched Hurricane Emma from bed."

I was alone with the boys during Emma. Helen was off somewhere . . .

Stephen continued, "He said he loved that woman but she had a family. He said she was so young and lovely he hoped he'd be remembering her when he died. Then he said, get this, 'Don't tell my kids.' What a character."

"So, go back a sec," I said, trying to steady myself. "He got the van for her?"

"Not for her to drive, but yes, in the sense that it was kind of a mobile motel room for them to screw in. After the farewell trip to Monhegan he barely used that van and that was ten years ago. I don't know why he didn't sell it. Maybe he hoped for a resurgence."

While I tried not to think what I was thinking, my mouth kept talking. "He's a handsome man. He probably cut a wide swath."

"No. At least he said not. He said he only had a few affairs and they were real relationships. He says he couldn't be a playboy because he usually fell in love with his lovers."

It wasn't easy but I kept trying to sound normal. "It's funny how the stroke affected him. He never talked to me about that stuff," I said.

"He talked to you about stuff you could actually tell his family and put in his book. I need more of that." Stephen made me earn my lunch by clarifying the contexts of, and connections among, the anecdotes he'd found in my notes. And by examining the thinking behind the outline I had sent. It was hard to concentrate because it seemed like maybe Helen had been Bill's lover. I hoped I'd gotten the wrong idea. I try not to be paranoid. I answered his questions.

After Stephen had paid the check he looked at me and said, "Marjie likes you, you know. I don't mind you, myself. We should have you and your wife over sometime. What's your wife's name?"

"Helen."

"Ah. Well, thanks for your time today."

Chapter 8

When I got home, Helen was staring at her laptop. That was predictable. I suppose she was different in New York. Probably she could be there in person.

"I need to talk with you," I said.

"Okay."

"I just drove home in Bill's old van."

"Yeah?"

"Were you ever involved with Bill Trippy?"

"Why do you ask?"

"Were you?"

"Way back when I was with Greg. And Greg had withdrawn from me. I felt that he had withdrawn. Yeah."

"You had an affair with Bill?"

"Yes."

"Were you still seeing him when you met me?"

"Let me think—"

"Oh, Helen."

"We were tapering off by then. Because of you."

"Why didn't you marry Bill?

"I never considered it. He was too old. And it wasn't like a match made in heaven or anything."

"Were you with Bill at Monhegan?"

"What?"

"At Monhegan. During Hurricane Emma."

"Oh. I guess Bill's been reminiscing. That was a long time ago."

"We were already a couple."

"Only just. It was farewell. It was goodbye."

"God damn it."

Her eyes were wet. From shame? Sympathy with me? Sadness from missing Bill? Or perhaps these tears were theatrical, to divert my anger, as, after she announced she was going to Paris for Christmas, she had distracted me with sex.

"How embarrassing for me to find out after all this that you and Bill . . . and what about the van?"

"We didn't use it all that much," she said. She embraced me.

But I didn't hug her back. I said, "Sometimes I wonder if you've ever really loved me at all."

"Of course I do. You have been father to my kids—and you are great. I know I'm a strange person. I'm not the kind of wife you wanted."

I resisted this invitation to her point of view and offered myself to anger. I noticed myself thinking and tried not to; this was no time to be objective. I heard her words in my memory: *It was a long time ago. It was goodbye.* Outrage wouldn't come.

I put my arms around her. We wept a little. I was sad not because it was true that a man and a woman could live together and share every intimacy and yet be strangers, but because this truth applied to me and my marriage. Aren't there couples who are each other's constant joy? There must be such. Did I know any? As far as I could tell my married friends and relations did their best to make their lives together comfortable and happy but it was work, with good days and less good days and times they tried to forget. That's how it looked to me.

That same day I traded the van for a used Toyota. I put some money into the deal, from my savings, and bought a car that as far as

I knew my wife had never had sex in. I drove that car to the zoo and parked and went in.

It was a small suburban zoo. They didn't have an elephant. Because it was December in New England most of the animals were indoors. Before I went into any of the buildings I made a circuit of the grounds, walking fast to clear my head. I wanted to shake off self-pity and forget the weirdness of Helen and Bill and the van. That was a long time ago and it was about them, not about me. Nothing had changed. Except that the boys were growing up and my career had faltered while Helen's blossomed. I reflected on my marriage. How would I answer Helen's question about whether or not she was the kind of wife I wanted? Was my expectation trapped in a forever-after fairytale? Maybe so—but what rules did Helen play by? Was her thing with Bill an exception? Did she fool around in New York? There had to be temptations. Her looks still turned heads and she was self-assured, worldly, and clever. And her husband? Nurturing, yes, but unemployed, over-sensitive, and too intellectual. Not a powerful and decisive manly man. Not rich. No trophy, I, not for my glamorous spouse.

The zoo seemed empty. Few animals were visible outdoors. I saw their tired coyote—a captive at home in the Boston suburbs, which had plenty of wild ones. Clouds dimmed the afternoon. Darkness would come early. I began to notice signs that told you where you were and which lane would take you to what destination. They were bright and cheery, designed for visitors on a sunny summer afternoon. I pictured people planning those signs, arguing over words and fonts. They put on this zoo as others would put on a show or a party. They wanted you to learn and to have fun and to speak well of their zoo and to make it one of your charities. When I realized that my brain had gone down that road, I thought, *This is good; I've stopped feeling sorry for myself.*

I entered the next building I came to. It had that strong zoo smell. There were more visitors indoors than out. The tamarins had attracted a small crowd. My eyes were drawn to a big pink head on a small person. Then I noticed her red coat. *The oracle—what's her name?* For once, it came to me.

"Hello Mrs. Lu," I said. "Remember me?"

"Oh. Hello. Yes. Marjory's friend."

"I am Ike. Ike Martin."

"Yes. Have you been here long?"

"No, I just arrived."

"I am surprised to see you."

"Why?"

"I have never seen you here before."

"I have only been here a few times. I come when I am having a bad day. I don't know why."

"Because of the animals."

"The animals," I agreed.

Mrs. Lu said, "It is already time for me to go."

"It was nice to see you again."

"Yes. Goodbye."

I turned to the tamarins. Two sat while one dashed around. *Mrs. Lu at the zoo had much to do won't stay with you.* My thoughts returned to zoo-as-project. The managers, on good days, considered the big picture. For underlings the zoo was a series of tasks, minor friends, minor enemies, a place to work, but the animals made it exotic. Everyone wanted to put on a good zoo; they liked to think of theirs as one of the excellent small zoos. I thought back past the current designers and planners to their predecessors, whose application of capital to land had created these brick-and-mortar boxes, antiquated, antithetical to present zoo philosophy and taste. Unnatural.

As I moved from the tamarins to their neighbors the crested porcupines, I wondered why my mind occupied itself with the absent zoo-authors. Why did I go so meta so often? Wouldn't it be better to stay in the moment?

There wasn't much to see and I didn't stay long. Leaving the building, there was Marjie, coming straight toward me.

"Hello Ike!"

"Marjie! Aren't you teaching today?"

"Yes, I taught. School's out. I've got work for tonight but I had time to stop by."

"It's so odd to come upon you because I saw Mrs. Lu a while ago."

"Yes, I was talking to her on her cell and she said you'd had a bad day so I thought I'd pop over. I'm not far from my house."

Did Mrs. Lu call her on purpose to tell her I was here?

It was getting dark. The zoo was closing. Marjie accepted my invitation for a glass of wine. As we walked she mentioned Stephen getting my job and how she wasn't sure it was a great idea, maybe not a good fit for him, but she was in an awkward position. She was glad I'd been nice about it and I was going to meet with Stephen.

I told her I already had.

Marjie thought because I was so famous from television I wouldn't have much trouble landing another television program or whatever else I wanted to do. She predicted that I would be an excellent teacher if that appealed to me.

I told her I had an idea for a book and an idea for a television series. I thought I'd see if a publisher would be interested in my book concept but the publishing world was in disarray due to the Internet so maybe it would just end up as a blog or whatever. We reached our destination before I could describe my ideas, and gave our attention to finding a table and ordering drinks.

"I wanted to let you know," Marjie said, "that I told Aunt Georgia about that jigsaw puzzle, how that girl, your houseguest, drew on it and everything. Aunt Georgia thought that was great and I have to admit it sounded amusing to me, too."

"Hearing yourself talk about it changed your reaction?"

"Yeah. And like why am I so straight-laced about stuff like that to begin with? So alert for bad behavior? Is it from teaching?"

"Georgia thought it was funny?"

"Yes but even before that I had changed about it. It's like my first reaction is from a goody-good girl and then after a while I can kind of be a normal person."

No sense letting her wander into self-disclosure by herself. "At least you have a clear reaction that you can recognize as yours."

"Yeah. Like the way I reacted to your note."

"Me, I can't tell what my reaction is half the time. It's like I'm an observer who just watches and doesn't react. Like I have to work to figure out my take, what I think, what I'll take title to."

"I should be more like that," Marjie said. "Like, with your note, I was mean when you were being nice."

"Too nice for the circumstances—"

"When I thought about it I realized, okay, he was just being sweet. He couldn't have a serious crush on me when his wife is everyone's ideal. Such a knockout."

"Well I can't really—"

"I don't mean I think I look horrible or anything; it's just, you know, I just look like me. So it's not just that I'm engaged and you're married; well yes it is about that; they have rules for a reason but I was in no place to be self-righteous because—did I sound self-righteous?"

"I guess I heard something like that in the tone."

"Did you keep the note?"

"No."

"Well I shouldn't have been self-righteous because I like you, too, and value our friendship and, you know, under other circumstances, I could imagine there being more to it than that."

Her left hand was at rest on the table. I put two fingers of my right hand lightly on top of her little finger. Without moving that hand, she said, "I think for some reason my friend Mrs. Lu wanted to set up a chance for me to speak to you. So I've said that and it's true but that doesn't make it a great thing to say or a great thing to feel." She withdrew her hand from under my fingers. But she didn't pull away; perhaps the rest of her leaned a centimeter closer.

"Just because she called you," I said, "you didn't have to come find me."

Marjie didn't say anything. She just looked at the table.

"I really appreciate that you did."

She lifted her shoulders and said, "It's all happening at the zoo."

"I do believe it. I do believe it's true."

Veering from danger, we talked about Paul Simon. And emperor tamarins—little monkeys with white moustaches. I described my train of thought about the people whose project the zoo was. I didn't see any reason to disguise myself; what did I have to lose by letting her in on the peculiar me I actually inhabit? Driving home, I felt happy about the encounter. Marjie had, more or less, said 'I like you, too,' which obviously felt good. Way better than disdain and ridicule. But of course there wasn't really anywhere to go with such a friendship.

At home, Helen was making supper. She had bought a seafood casserole at an evolved farm stand of the kind that flourishes in upscale areas around Boston. Ours is on a real farm but it's also a gourmet grocery store, deli, and bakery. Their kitchen produces prepared meals for the benefit of working couples. Helen planned to serve the creamy seafood over rice she herself had actually cooked. She had rolls for Denver who hated rice but loved bread. She asked me to deal with the green beans, flown in from who-knows-where, that she'd purchased at the same place.

As I trimmed the beans, Helen announced that it would be a good idea for us to have a house sitter over Christmas because none of us would be there and, according to her, I was always so worried about the pipes freezing. It had come to Helen's attention that Sean's friend Susan and her artist-roommate were not going home over the holidays because their families were too strange or because they themselves were too *out there* for their families. Helen guessed that singing carols around the piano just wasn't part of their style this year. They were on a roll with their art and needed a place to live and work over Christmas. Helen had already told Sean that they could stay at our place.

I thought that all sounded fine but wondered how long they would be there.

"Until classes start again, whenever that is," she said. "Sometime in January, I guess."

"It might get crowded."

"I'm not sure when I'll be back from Europe and when I am I'll have things to catch up on in the City."

"I guess the house can't expect much guarding from you. But Denver and I—"

"Yes but your mother invited you for as long as—"

"She invited *us*."

"And Denver, it turns out, might stay in California."

"What?"

"He's got all those winter independent study weeks coming up and Greg's at the center of the nerd universe so he's thinking about doing that work with his father."

Having heard his mother's remark, Denver came into the kitchen looking at me. "I'm not sure, though. It just sounds like a good idea, maybe, but I haven't decided."

The question of how long the young artists would be under foot was dwarfed by the prospect of Denver spending so long in California. It made my heart sink—but it would be good for him to have some time with his dad.

Helen went back to New York. The days became shorter and shorter as the time approached for Denver and Sean to go to California. Sean would fly from Maine to meet Denver in Chicago and they would travel together from there.

It wasn't a good time for me. The word *depression* crept into my thoughts. I needed more to occupy me than the gym and keeping the bird feeder full. I decided to get in touch with my former colleague Anna to talk about my television concept. And I planned to make an early start on Christmas riddles.

Accompanying your Christmas gifts with riddles in verse was a tradition from Mom's family. The riddle gave clues to what the present was. Good ones also made fun of the recipient, who had to read it aloud before opening the gift. The best ones, which were Mom's, alluded to family events from the past year and teased everyone in clever rhymes while staying related to the gift. We suspected that she worked on them all year. Her riddles were the only way you could know how funny she was. Dad's were short, nonsensical, and loved for what they were because they said *I'm a good sport and comfortable being silly.* Adam, ever the dutiful elder brother, offered one good one every year. I set my sights to out-do Adam.

Before I could start writing I had to find some presents. I went to craft fairs and museum shops and import stores. I was shopping for my parents, my siblings, and their kids, trying to make a good guess as to what they'd like. Hunting for stuff that would please them and have some useful function and be within the four corners of my style.

Shopping for Helen, Sean, and Denver was quite different— brokered online by an app Sean had written. He called it Getters and Givers. You set up an account and listed what you wanted. You could put in a link to exactly what you had in mind. That's what you did as a getter. Givers looked at your wishes and reserved what they wanted to give you. The app generated a list for you as a giver and let you mark the status of each of your presents: *ordered, received, wrapped,* and *under the tree.* Sean included a field for *where hidden* because his mother once forgot where she had put his most-wanted present, which he didn't get until she found it by accident in February.

In this system, getters are never surprised, neither for better nor for worse. You don't get anything you didn't want and you don't get something you would have wanted if you had known about it and somebody who knew you made the right guess.

Denver helped me shop for my family. We went to malls together. Our rate-everything game was changing. Our patter was the same, just more facetious, but we didn't actually make notes the way we used to. Over the years, mall Santas and mall representations of the North Pole had been subjected to detailed critical analysis from us. We ought to have gone public with our comparisons. Lately the puberty-ridden Denver had branched out to scoring the bodies of Santa's female elves. When he was little he wouldn't sit on Santa's lap, but now he had his picture taken with every Santa he could find. He added captions in which he supposedly was asking Santa to leave some particular actress or super-model in his stocking and posted the pictures to Facebook. I didn't see them myself, but Denver was 'friends' with my brother Henry, who kept me informed.

Gradually my shopping paid off and I began to accumulate gifts to take to Ithaca. That meant it was time to start writing witty riddles. I wished that Sean had an app for rhyme and rhythm and cleverness. Every time I sat down I spun my poetic wheels until I decided to pay bills or run the vacuum cleaner. Or read and comment on the writing Denver was preparing to send to institutions of higher learning. Although college deadlines were after the holiday, I insisted that his applications be in the mail before Denver left for California.

December went by, his applications went out, and the day came for Denver to fly west. Helen, the boys, and I exchanged gifts that morning. Sean's presents had been shipped to us by their vendors, as had ours to him. He was with us on Skype from his dorm room. Something Sean said to Denver made it possible to infer that he had received cell-phone pictures of selected mall-elves. Which Denver must have taken when I wasn't looking.

After our traditional Christmas breakfast of bacon and waffles I took Denver to the airport. When we reached the departures curb Denver said he had one more present for me that he had left in the back seat.

"Should I open it today or on Christmas?"

"Whenever."

I gave him a half-salute, half-wave, which he returned, and he started to walk away. "Hey," I called after him. I was going to pursue him for a hug, but considered his teen-aged pride, changed my mind, and just waved.

"See you online," he said, and he was gone.

When I got home I carried my present inside. It was wrapped, like all of Denver's presents, with brown paper that had been a grocery bag. This was Denver's re-use, re-cycle program. He had added ribbon and a bow with a red crayon.

"What's that?" Helen asked.

"Denver gave me another present."

"Oh? He didn't think the purple beret was enough? He wanted to do more damage?"

"Apparently so."

"Next time you ask for a garment you better specify the color."

"I guess you're right." The box was about the right size and shape for a shirt or a sweater, but when the lid was off, there lay a vest. A many-pocketed vest like a fisherman's but without a patch of fleece for trout flies. And it was green, dark green, not khaki.

I put it on.

"Very nice," Helen said. "What will you put in the pockets?"

I opened the first pocket my hand came to. It was small, with a velcro closure. It had a slip of paper in it—a list of the names of candy bars, in a childish hand, with a numeral beside each. At the bottom it said, *Captain Hook*, in Denver's grade-school handwriting. I realized what it was: his tally of trick-or-treat results. He had made one every year; this specimen was from the Halloween he'd dressed as Captain Hook. I handed it to Helen.

In a zippered pocket I found a photograph I had taken on a camping trip. Denver and Sean's faces were illuminated by a campfire in front of them. I showed it to Helen and returned it to its pocket.

The third pocket I looked in held a letter-sized paper, folded. It was densely printed with a table of names, dates, and scores. It was our cumulative multi-year ratings of football touchdown celebrations. Asterisks meant that the celebrants had been penalized for excess. In a place of honor, highlighted, was the time the guy had reached under the goal-post padding, extracted a cell phone he had hidden there, and called his mother.

I kept looking in pockets. Each of them contained something. One little pocket had an agate shooter I had given Denver when I taught him to play marbles. Another was the actual note from Emily to Sean: *Cool car.* At that point I had to stop opening pockets because my eyes felt full and I didn't want to prove to Helen that I was as overly sentimental as she thought I was.

Too late. "What's the matter?" she said. "What's all this stuff?"

"Stuff of Denver's," I mumbled. "Stuff he kept."

When everything was back in its proper pocket I refolded the vest.

"What's the matter?" Helen asked again.

"Hard to say goodbye," I said.

"He'll be back," she said. "You can Skype."

That day, the day Denver left for California, was the shortest day of the year. The solstice. I texted Denver, *Hey, great vest, amazing.* I hesitated, then added, *Love from me.*

The next day I met Anna for lunch. She updated me on WIVB. It hadn't been that long; little had changed. I gave her my meager news and my idea of a book about conversation. Then I said that I had a concept for a television program I wanted to run by her.

"What is it?" she asked.

"I've been thinking what a good team you and I always made."

"We usually agreed about what to do and how to go about it."

"I am interested in doing a new show, writing a proposal, for, say, public broadcasting, or the Discovery Channel or whatever. But I'd be a lot more excited about it if I could put you down as a collaborator."

"Ike, that's flattering," she said, "but I can't just walk away from my job. No matter how good the idea is."

"I'm not asking you to. I'd just be looking for you to discuss the proposal, to help shape it, and then I'd try to sell it, and if it did get funded then you could decide whether to take it on or whether you'd be better off where you are."

"It would be great to do something more creative," she said. "What have you got in mind? The conversation thing? Something about that?"

"No, I think of that as a book. The series concept is about work. What people's jobs are like. How their day really goes."

She didn't look impressed. "Where's the tension that carries you through? The reality shows have conflict and competition. Even the nature shows create drama."

"What about people's natural curiosity?"

"I have bad news for you," she said. "People don't have much of that. Mostly they want to be entertained. If they learn along the way, that's okay. But they have to be grabbed by a story."

"Well—"

"Your idea reminded me of that show where they take the big boss and put him, incognito, among his workers, as a new guy. That sets up mistaken identity and the tension of waiting to see what awkwardness will arise. I think you have to have something like that. You can't just say, here's what it means to have this job at Intel or to run your bed-and-breakfast or whatever."

"Okay. I'll think about that."

"I like the conversation thing, though," she said. "Series name: *Talking the Talk*."

"How is that an improvement?"

"Because you could put in different kinds of drama. Arguments. Flirtations."

"Confessions."

"Criticism."

"Interesting! Would fair use cover scenes from movies?"

"Huh?"

"How much of a movie can you excerpt without infringing on the copyright?"

"You can show a clip in a review."

"Then we could borrow dialogues from movies. Great conversational moments."

"Oh. Like Elizabeth Bennett and Lady Catherine."

"You'll have to remind me," I said.

"In *Pride and Prejudice*. The aging aristocrat orders the young woman not to marry her nephew. But Elizabeth shows backbone."

"And Shakespeare? Too high-brow?"

"The comedies are okay."

"*Much Ado About Nothing* has the angriest falling in love."

"Okay, right. And you balance Shakespeare with television. *All in the Family*. Archie argued with everybody."

"And classic movies. *It Happened One Night*."

"Which part?"

"I can't remember. There were lively scenes."

"Okay," Anna said, "If you wake up in the morning and this still seems as good as it does over a glass of wine, then start writing."

"Okay," I agreed. "What's up with you? Seeing anybody?"

"Yeah, there's a guy," she said. "Nothing serious, but I don't have to stay home alone."

"How'd you meet him?"

"Online," she said. "Such social life as I have, I owe to the Internet. How's Helen?"

"She's okay. Her business seems to be doing well. She's in New York a lot."

"Big city. Exciting."

"If you had your druthers would you move down there and work in the major leagues?"

"Maybe at one time. I think I'm past that. I like it here."

"Do you think we can dream up a project to do together?"

"Maybe," she said. "But I have to focus mostly on my job."

"But if I can find funding. Will you produce?"

"I don't know. That's a huge *if.* I wouldn't rule it out."

"Not enthusiastic."

"I'm sorry if it sounds like that but I have to support myself. No spouse, no trust fund. It would be great to work with you again on some cool project but it would have to be pretty solid for me to leave IVB."

I told her that I'd be at my parents' house and have some time and see what I could come up with. I still liked the jobs idea but I'd think about the conversation thing, too.

I bought groceries, went to the gym, and got home to an empty bird feeder. The new *New Yorker* was in the mailbox. I sat down with that. I put on music. My blues playlist. I checked my email—all from computers; none from people. I picked up the magazine and put it back down. I went to my room and took Denver's gift off the shelf in my closet. I opened a wide pocket from which I pulled out a piece of shingle, cedar shingle, decorated and inscribed with woodburning tools. He had given it to me for Father's Day five years before but he knew where I kept it and he stole it back to put in the vest. I read, once again, what Denver had burned into the blonde wood.

> Stepfathers
> Ike - 100
> Others - 0

Life was kind of up and down. It would be nice to see my parents.

Chapter 9

My parents? A pair of well-intentioned persons who lived up to those intentions more often than the average person is able to do. They raised four kids—a large brood for their generation. They had devoted themselves to our upbringing but when we reached adulthood they focused on other interests. Mom went in for local politics. She was on the Democratic committee and on the city's Board of Public Works. In season, she campaigned, and she attended many meetings. At home she did political emails and watched Cable News Network. Dad had no time for that stuff. He hoped never to sit through another meeting. He volunteered for Meals on Wheels and Habitat for Humanity. He played sports in old-guy leagues. He loved softball and plants. He grew flowers and he studied ferns.

Neither of my parents seemed impatient for grandchildren. I had brought two half-grown step-grandsons into the family. I was in no position to do more, but Adam, with his wife's assistance, had given them one biological grandchild. Kate—married; no kids. Henry hadn't married and seldom dated. We weren't very fertile, but if either Mom or Dad cared, they didn't show it.

I phoned from the road when we were about an hour away, to let them know when we would arrive. No one answered. When we got there the house seemed empty. In the basement, Henry had a sign on his door. One side said *Come In*. The other side, currently on display, said *Sleeping*. Henry worked at a bakery. He had an alternative lifestyle.

Mom and Dad were nowhere to be seen. I looked for a note explaining their whereabouts, but they had not left one. The Christmas tree was partially decorated. It had some lights but the ornaments were still in their red plastic storage boxes. I wasn't sure which room Mom wanted us to sleep in. No beds were made up in any of the guest rooms. We sat down in the living room to wait. Helen opened her laptop. She might have worked or read magazines or played solitaire; you couldn't tell from her expression whether she was being entertained or composing a message to her most important client. She locked her gaze on the screen and withdrew into her own space.

I looked at my dad's aquarium. He had ordinary tropical fish: neon tetras, black mollies, and swordtails. And one angelfish. The aquarium had been a regular feature of my childhood, too familiar for interest, but now it drew my attention. Each fish was as self-contained as Helen and her computer. They were weightless and autonomous. I took a picture of the fish with my cell phone to send to Denver— but then decided this was a good subject for video. I kept starting, stopping, and trying again, centering on the angelfish, trying to get a clip with other species swimming by. Finally I had one I liked. I was about to send it when Mom walked in.

"Hello! Here already?"

"Yes," I said, "right on schedule."

"Your mother has better things to do," Helen informed me, "than to study our travel schedule."

"Here you are and I don't have the stockings up," Mom said.

"Ike can put them up," Helen said.

"I knew you'd be coming and it didn't matter when," Mom said. "Adam's crowd has the third floor, of course, and you two and Kate are on the second, sharing the bathroom. That's considered a hardship these days, so I'm told. You're here first so you get your pick of bedrooms but if you take the one with the television poor Jones will have to spend the holiday at Sports and Spirits."

"Would we be able to tell the difference?" Helen said. "Sorry. I'm getting catty in my old age."

"Anyway I don't think they are coming until the twenty-fourth or maybe even Christmas Day, I can't remember. They're going to his family before us. Take your pick, the beds are all made up."

"They didn't seem to be," I said.

"Then the sheets are in the drier, help yourself," Mom said. It always surprised me, when I visited, to be reminded of how done she was with domesticity. To the extent she had ever been a homemaker, she had retired. It made me a little proud but it had its inconveniences. Meals could be an adventure. For tonight, now that there were five of us, she decided we'd go out because it would be more festive and no one would have to do dishes.

I went up to make the bed in the room without the television. Henry appeared in the door and said, "Bro."

"Hey."

"Run?"

"Sure. Did Mom and Dad fire the servants?"

"No, they quit. They found out that serfdom was over. As soon as they got the news, Mom registered them as Democrats and Dad built them a house."

"Too bad," I said.

Henry helped me finish the bed. I put on my cold weather jogging outfit and off we went, in intermittent sleet. Henry slowed his pace for me. "How's the world treating you?" I asked.

"Fine!" he said.

Henry held to a strict routine. He got home from work mid-mornings and slept until supper. He ate with Mom and Dad, watched TV with them for a while, and then went to his room and played games, role-playing games, online, for the rest of the night, taking breaks to do email and Facebook, until it was time for him to leave, on his bicycle, for work.

For a few years Denver had considered his uncle the most admirable guy he knew, and wanted to be like him when he grew up. This distressed Helen, who imagined both of her sons becoming successful high-tech geeks like their father. That was her ideal of American manhood. Denver got over his desire to emulate Henry—but Helen hadn't forgiven my brother for having temporarily influenced her adolescent son. She usually admired unconventional people. Behind their backs, she was snotty and superior toward anyone she saw as a middle-class conformist, whereas she took odd-ball-ness as a sign of intelligence or personal strength. Henry, though, was in her books as an unambitious schlump.

"Are you giving Denver any of those chicks for Christmas?" he asked. Henry had previously informed me, by email, of the girl-gifts Denver had requested on Facebook.

"Maybe Dad will," I said. "Shouldn't those items come from the grandfather?"

"What did you get him?"

"From his list, I gave him some particular sunglasses."

"Cool shades. Denver the Cool."

"I didn't know they could be so expensive," I said. The sleet changed to drizzle. "Terrible weather."

"Welcome to Ithaca. We love it, though."

"Also I went off-list and got him a book about the Central Pacific Railroad."

"Is he a buff?"

"No, but I thought it might be interesting to him since he's going to be out there. He might do independent study with his Dad for the next few months. And it's good to remind our contemporary geeks that there were technologies before digital."

"Out west all winter?" Henry said. "Well, it doesn't matter to me; I only see him on Facebook anyway."

"Yeah."

"Not so great for you, though."

"I'll get over it. It will be good for him to have time with his dad."

We kept running. It was dark. Ithaca had sidewalks. So did the Cornell campus, where Dad had been a professor.

"What's new with you?" I asked Henry.

"FIOS," he said.

"What?"

"FIOS. We got fiber optic broadband. Snappy Internet. Life improves!"

"Better gaming?"

"Sure. At work, I've got trouble. They tried to promote me again. They just don't understand that a guy who takes pride in craftsmanship doesn't want to be a manager."

"They think everyone wants a raise."

"Yeah."

"Don't you?"

"Why would I? What haven't I got?"

He didn't have anything. He rode his bike or took the bus to work. He paid rent to Mom and Dad. He never travelled.

While I was still befuddled about whether to treat his question as rhetorical, or to say something in response, he asked, "What are you doing for work these days?"

"I seem to be between engagements."

"Should I see if they can put you on my shift? Lots of orders this time of year. Of course you couldn't do the fun stuff right off, but you learn fast."

"Thanks. Could we slow down a little?"

"You got it, old folks. Is your wife still mad at me?"

"No."

"She sure is cute."

"Too old for you," I said.

"Too everything for me."

"For me, too, maybe."

"Nah. You've got the right stuff, Bro. You're the man."

"Please slow down, Henry." He slackened the pace a little. When I had enough wind I asked, "Wouldn't you ever like to travel?"

"Not really."

"You could at least come to Boston."

"I travel online. Go everywhere. Real places and unreal. Sleep in my own bed. It's all good."

After supper everyone played Hearts. We debated whether or not to use the Jack of Diamonds rule. Dad always wanted to, and the rest of us grudgingly agreed. He won the game. After cards, Henry adjourned to his private downstairs world, Mom and Dad went to bed, and Helen found a movie on television that she wanted to see.

I sent Denver the fish video. I thought I'd start an outline of my conversation book, but then I remembered my riddle-writing ambition. I hadn't gotten anywhere yet, and the clock was ticking. My gift for Mom was *Team of Rivals*, a political biography of Lincoln. Dad didn't think Mom had read it. The author lived a town away from us. Helen and I had seen her twice at a restaurant. I pushed myself to get started on composing a riddle. I listed words for rhymes. Was that how Mom started?

I went back down to the living room to ask Helen to help think of rhymes. She was into the movie and I became caught up, too, and the next thing I knew it was morning and time for me to take Helen to the airport and pick up Adam and his wife Cindy and their little boy Eben. I thought Dad was going to go with me but he and Mom decided he should finish decorating the tree to have it all ready for Eben. So, as it worked out, Helen and I were alone in the car when I said, "I had a good talk with Henry during our run yesterday."

"That's nice."

"He seems just the same as ever."

"He's in his baker groove," she said.

"He asked if you were still mad at him."

"I was never mad at him."

"That's what I told him. I said, 'Henry, you are beneath Helen's contempt.'"

"Not beneath contempt—but beneath active anger, yes."

"Ah. A careful distinction."

"I don't need to be spiteful to Henry," she said. "I just don't want him to be a model for Denver."

"So, anyway, I just told him you weren't mad."

"Is he starting to think that there might be more to life than he finds down there in his man-cave?"

"No. He seems to think he has everything he needs."

"Wow."

"So, conversation over. He doesn't offer a look into his heart or his fears, and I don't pry."

"No," Helen said. "You shouldn't."

"And as far as I can tell, Mom and Dad can't, either. Or won't."

"Those personal boundaries are strong."

"Yes," I said. "I've been thinking that we have them, too."

"I suppose everyone does."

"Even happily married couples."

"That's probably part of what makes them happily married," Helen said.

"Their tacit agreement to avoid certain topics."

"Helps keep the peace."

"I suppose so," I said. "But it also keeps them at a certain distance, doesn't it?"

"Autonomy's a good thing," she said. "Is there something you want to talk about?"

"I think I should be in the loop on Denver's decision-making."

"You are in the loop," she said. "That's why you know he's thinking about staying with his dad."

"Doesn't Greg work anymore?"

"Of course he works," she snapped. "But he could be in touch from his office."

"What about Sally?" Greg had remarried.

"What about her?"

"Is she being consulted about all this?"

"That's Greg's problem," Helen said. She generally had precise views of problem ownership.

"Another thing we don't talk about is how much you are gone."

"My business is more important than ever now that you are in a looking phase."

"I see. You're going to France because I'm out of a job."

"I'm going to France because I'm being paid to do work there."

"But, see, fine, but you are skirting the basic issue of how much time we spend apart these days."

"Some time apart," she said, "and some time together. Wasn't last night nice?"

"Yes but I have no idea when our next night together will be."

"Sorry about that. Nature of the beast." She added, "I'll miss you."

"And I you," I said. "Do you think on the whole it's harder to be the one left behind?"

"You didn't have to stay behind. I said you could have come along."

"You said the words but you made it sound like I'd be in your way."

"Ike, what do you want for my life? What do you want me to say?"

"See what I mean about the boundary? I just want to communicate about it and you are snarling."

"And you aren't whining? We would have had more time for communication if you'd brought this up on the way to Ithaca instead of now." She was right about that because we were at the airport and I was taking her suitcase out of the trunk.

"The non-talk with Henry got me thinking about it."

"As I recall you listened to Christmas carols the whole way."

"They weren't all carols. I'm in contempt for enjoying Christmas music?"

"Why are you being defensive?"

A lady walking ahead of us looked back over her shoulder when she heard that, which forced a shift. "I hope you have a good time in Paris," I said.

We checked her suitcase and continued toward security. "And you have a good time with your family."

"Thank you," I said.

Helen let go of her carry-on and led us through a hug and kiss appropriate to spouses beginning a separation. "Don't forget to let

Susan know when you'll be going back home," she said. "She has your cell in case they have any problems."

I drew a blank. "Oh! The house sitters."

"Okay. Time to take off my shoes," she said.

"Merry Christmas, Helen. I love you." Maybe that sounded a little forced. I let her go.

She blew a kiss.

I left her there in line for security. I had some time to kill before Adam's flight arrived, so I found a place to sit that had a table, and began to work on my riddle.

I was penned by a scribe of old Concord.

What rhymes with Concord? Should I substitute a local pronunciation: *Concud?* What rhymes with that? Did Helen intentionally not respond that she loved me? Was she dodging or just preoccupied with starting her trip? Wasn't it trite to put my riddle into a limerick? Such a sing-song structure. Had Mom ever used it?

She researched old Abe

No, that was a give-away.

She researched the guy
Who was tall, who was shy

Was Lincoln shy? Not really. He told jokes. He ran for office. How could you be shy and run for office? And how sincere was I in telling Helen that I loved her? Was I just saying the formula of the human pair bond? She was attractive to me, sure, but how close did we feel? How much trust or affection did we have? Had we stayed together for the kids? Or, worse yet, had I stayed with her because I loved her kids? If I didn't love her, what should I do about it? Should I leave her? I couldn't if I wanted to—I *was* a kept man. I supposed I could move back to Ithaca and hang out with Henry and my parents and what an embarrassing thought that was—to return to adolescence.

My project ideas buoyed me up. Conversation—that topic continued to appeal. What credentials do you need to be a self-help author for talking? Was it good enough to have been host of a successful interview show? Did my twelve year run constitute success? I told myself to write the book proposal. That would be an active move toward an open door. Maybe I should start with a blog, which could lead to a book. Maybe Anna would do the show with me. *Talking the Talk*, she had called it.

I turned a page in my notebook. What was the basic structure for analyzing conversation? I needed a good metaphor. My eye was drawn to the airport television. The weather. Weather radar, color blobs moving west to east, flowing. A commercial showed a periodic table of the elements in the background. What were the elements of conversation? What were the elements of language? The real parts of speech.

I checked the flight status board. Adam's plane had arrived. Soon little Eben was regarding me with the interest small kids show people, relatives, whose names they hear regularly and whose face and voice are vaguely familiar. His mother looked on with the benign vigilance she gives all dependent beings—Cindy is at the other end of that spectrum from Helen. We chatted and felt happy to see each other and went home. Mom had made soup and Dad and I assembled ham sandwiches. Frothy family chatter dominated the soundtrack.

After lunch we went out for a stroll. I walked beside my dad. I was thinking that he could be a resource for my conversation project. He had taught all kinds of literature, attended a lifetime's worth of conferences, graded a trillion papers, and had long-term friendships with other English teachers.

"What's the best book you ever read about conversation?" I asked him.

"Conversation? About the subject of conversation? I don't know that I've read any. I never studied linguistics."

"I didn't mean scientific work. I mean, more, popular."

"Oh! Like, how-to?"

"Yeah, more like that."

"I haven't read one of those, either. They must have them, though. Why do you ask?"

"I'm thinking of writing one myself."

"It's about time we had an author in the family," he said. "Maybe that will take the pressure off of me. Your mother has never forgiven me for not having written a book. It must be nice to see yourself in a card catalogue."

"In a what?"

"Sorry—I guess libraries have been digital all your life."

"Oh, right, no, I do remember them. Dimly. I was talking to my former colleague Anna and we were brainstorming about dialogues in movies and plays. How they are models of conversations."

Dad leaned over and scooped Eben off his feet. "Getting tired, sonny-boy?" Eben collapsed in joy and trust on his grandfather's shoulder.

"So it occurs to me to ask you," I persisted, "to make me a list of great dialogues in literature."

"Put the old horse back in harness, eh?"

"Only if it would be fun for you."

He didn't reply because Cindy got his attention to report that Eben was looking forward to hearing Grandpa read *The Night Before Christmas*. Dad started right in from memory. Adam acted it out, playing the reindeer and Santa, as Dad narrated. The way the timing worked Adam laid his finger beside his nose and up the chimney he rose right through my parents' front door as we arrived back home. It was the sort of happy silly thing that gives holidays and families a good name.

That night Mom and Dad were wrapping presents. They never started before Christmas Eve and they did a sloppy, hasty, comical, job. Adam and Cindy were on the third floor with Eben the Excited, as they had dubbed him at supper. Henry and I were in the living room. Henry propped *Christmas Carols for Tenor Recorder* tenuously on the coffee table and began to play. He was no virtuoso, but the familiar melodies sounded nice on the sonorous instrument.

My gifts were wrapped but my poems were unwritten. I had barely begun and now it was the eleventh hour. I opened a new word-processing document on my computer and wondered how they were ever able to get "Word" as a brand name. *In the beginning was the Word, and the Word was with God and the Word was God.* What had John had been talking about? I've never understood it but it sounds great, the way those syllables march along. I wonder what Bill Gates thinks it means?

I typed a new beginning for Mom's riddle.

An author from Middlesex County

A text arrived from Denver. *Hey fish! Looking good. Hey Ike. Guess what? Sally does everyone's laundry. Yuck.* What an invasion of privacy that must have seemed to Denver, who had done all his own laundry since he was old enough to reach the washing machine. None of us could have imagined Helen touching our dirty clothes.

Merry Christmas, Denver, I replied through the phone.

"O Holy Night" stopped. The music had slumped and slid off the table. Did the fish notice the interruption? If so, they gave no sign. I asked Henry if he thought the black mollies had been listening.

"I hope so," he said.

"Maybe they think we believe the Christmas story. Are fish religious?"

"Those glass walls must give them a strange take on the universe."

Henry picked up his music and propped it up. It looked just as unstable as before. A consciousness came to me of sitting in the room with my bachelor brother. We were two odd ducks, me married with grown children who were with their real father while their mother arrived in Paris. A sense came to me of being awkwardly poised in life; of having mis-timed my passage. I wrote,

> *When she saw what he was*
> *She thought, why not, because*

Drivel. Was it time to give up on Mom's and try a different gift? Adam had invited us siblings to join with him in funding a one-year subscription to the online Oxford English Dictionary for Dad. All of us except Kate had signed up. Maybe a poem about that would come more easily? Would the OED website give inspiration? I took a quick look. Then I checked my email inbox. In a corner of the window was a place that showed availability for online chats. Helen's name had a green light beside it. Just as I clicked it, her light turned gray.

Marjie wasn't on my chat list so I entered her name in the search field. Up popped a green light. I typed, *Merry Christmas, Marjie.*

She responded, *Merry Christmas, Ike.*

Ready for tomorrow?

I think so.

I wondered if she was with Stephen. I assumed since they were engaged that they usually or invariably slept together. But I didn't know that—I really didn't know anything at all about their relationship or how they lived, and it felt a little tricky to inquire. I solved the problem by asking, *Have you and Stephen developed Christmas traditions?*

Yes, she replied. *He sings in a choir at a church. After his service we go out to dinner, then he goes home to start his shopping.*

?

He doesn't give regular presents. He prints out online gift cards and rolls them up and ties a ribbon around them.

Ah.

So after dinner I come home and write Christmas cards. That's my tradition.

Home as in your place, or home at your parents'?

Home at my parents'. I hang out here on Christmas. Mom and I cook, and Georgia and Lee come, and Grandfather, too—they're letting him out of rehab. How about you and Helen?

I, also, am with my parents. In Ithaca. Helen's flown to Paris on business.

Business? Over Christmas?

Specifically Christmas business to do with the art scene there.

Oh. Just a minute. Dad needs to confer.

Denver had texted, *Sean says HI.*

I sent Marjie an explanation of our gift-riddle tradition and my lack of success in composing a limerick.

"What are you doing?" Henry asked.

"Trying to write a poem for Mom."

"Let me know if you need any ammunition," he said. He began to play "It Came Upon a Midnight Clear."

I typed that word, *ammunition.* I meant to put it into the poem but it got sent to Marjie by mistake. Too much of Dad's merlot. When the border of Marjie's chat window changed colors, the words *I'm back,* appeared, and she continued, *Rhymes with ammunition: ambition repetition permission attrition.*

Competition, I typed. *The book is about how he recruited the guys who had been his best competition for president.*

So that's your last line.

What is?

He recruited his best competition.

Ah. The first two lines . . .

Have to rhyme with competition.

I typed, *A tall guy with lots of ambition.*
Used stories as strong ammunition.
When the election was done,
And this guy had won!!
Then your last line.

My second line is lame, Marijie wrote. *You'll have to fix it. Sorry, I have to go.*

I typed, *Good night*, but she was already offline.

"What's the matter, Bro?" Henry asked.

"Ah. Nothing. Do you ever feel like a leaf floating helter-skelter down a stream?"

"What do you think?"

"I suppose we all do sometimes."

Dad appeared in the doorway. "We all what?"

"We all don't necessarily feel like the pilots of our ships," I said. "Except you and Mom seem to. Have you been each other's constant happiness?"

"You don't have to answer that," Henry told Dad.

Dad looked thoughtful. "I'm tired of wrapping and came down to hear some music." He sat down.

Henry started "O Tannenbaum." My gaze fell on the fish, then moved to Henry, then to Dad.

"Henry's trying to work out how the fish see the world," I said.

"If ever I can't fall asleep," Dad said, "I occupy my brain with that conundrum. It paralyzes thought."

"After Christmas I want to identify the parts of speech of conversation," I said.

"I'm not sure I get what you mean."

"Well, I just mean, like, categories for sentences. Some sentences are a this, and others are a that." I finally realized that he just wanted to listen to Henry play the recorder, so I stopped talking. Dad silently mouthed the carol's words, in German.

When Henry finished playing, he looked at me and asked, "Any progress?"

"Yes."

"Can we hear it?"

I read what Marjie and I had come up with, and added, "I want to fix the second line."

The room was quiet for a beat before Henry said, "Read the first line again."

"A tall guy with lots of ambition."

"Believed there should be abolition."

"Thanks, Henry."

That left me sitting there thinking about how my parents had been able to create this place, this culture, where Henry and I could feel okay in spite of all the world's troubles and our own uncertain futures. Had Helen and I given that to Sean and Denver? Why had I hurried into a ready-made family? I remembered Denver, on our college tour, asking me about wanting kids of my own. Couldn't I have found someone to set up a family with, like Mom and Dad had? Could Marjie and I have done that? Why had Marjie left the chat so suddenly?

There was an incoming call on my cell—from an unknown number. I accepted it and said hello.

"Where's the fuse box?"

"I beg your pardon?"

"It's Susan. Camo and I can't find the fuse box."

"Who?"

"Camo. I'm Susan. Neither Camo nor I can find the fucking fuse box. Sorry."

"Oh! Susan. You're in the house."

"Right. And Camo's here too; your wife said that was okay. Could you please tell me where the electrical box is so we can, like, turn it back on?"

"What happened?"

"The lights went out. In the big room next to the kitchen; the family room or whatever you call it."

"Do you know what threw the breaker?"

"No. Maybe it was Camo's hotplates."

"Hotplates? What's wrong with the stove?"

"They're heavy-duty hot plates she uses in her work. You wouldn't want her doing it on the stove."

"What work?"

"She's making paper."

"It's a she? Camo?"

"Camille. So what?"

"The fuse box is in the basement in the cabinet next to the stationary bike."

"Okay."

"Maybe she better not use the heavy-duty hot plate."

"Or maybe fewer at the same time."

"Ah."

"Happy New Year," Susan said. "Or whatever."

"It's Christmas Eve."

"Oh right. Ho ho ho." She hung up.

"Merry Christmas, Susan," I said to nobody.

"I guess it's time to fill the stockings," Dad said.

Henry played "Good King Wenceslas."

My eyes closed. I was ready to call it a day.

Chapter 10

The morning after Christmas I sat down at my parents' kitchen table to start thinking about conversation. I had a yellow pad of paper and a pen, all ready to begin my excellent new project. Before I wrote anything, my mother came in. I volunteered to make supper.

"That would be nice," she said without hesitation.

"Do you have any suggestions about the menu?"

"Well, Henry is the only vegetarian."

"What? He ate ham yesterday. Didn't he?"

"It was Christmas. He takes holidays off from being a vegetarian but he makes up for it by being vegan on Sundays."

"Today's Boxing Day."

"Yes, well, you can discuss that with Henry but we are not in the United Kingdom and I don't think Boxing Day is on his list of approved flesh-eating holidays."

"Okay."

"On the other hand, Henry seems to be an unusually pragmatic vegetarian," Mother said. "Eggs and fish are fine. So is chicken if he's hungry. He's never objected to morsels of pork in his pea soup. You can check with him on guidelines if you want to. As for Kate, she thinks she's becoming gluten-intolerant."

"Really? What makes her think that?"

"One doesn't ask."

"No. Was Christmas dinner gluten-free?"

"She only took ham and green beans."

"I could stop by that gluten-free bakery."

"It went out of business," she said. "But there's plenty in the regular market now. And make sure there's dessert for Dad."

"Okay."

"Eben only eats peanut butter."

"Right." I had inferred that, because Adam and Cindy had not realized I was around the corner to hear what sounded like their hundredth conversation about Eben's diet. It went this way:

Adam: "Wouldn't it be better if Eben ate other foods?"

Cindy: "He likes peanut butter."

Adam: "He'd eat other stuff if he was hungry."

Cindy: (No audible reply.)

I never saw Eben put anything into his mouth except peanut butter and its cracker or celery vehicle during the whole visit. Unless you count Kate's dog's ears. Kate and Jones and Fievel had arrived just before Christmas dinner. Jones was glad to see we'd saved him the room with the television and Eben was delighted to see the dog.

My cell phone rang. "Who shovels the snow?" Susan asked.

"You do. You'll find shovels in the garage. A guy will plow the driveway."

"When do they pick up the trash?"

"Did Helen give you an information sheet about this stuff?"

"No. Wait. Camo, did we get information from the lady? About the house? No? No."

I said I'd send everything I could think of. She gave me her email address.

"Who was that?" my mother asked.

"The house-sitter. An art student. Her friend's there too. The friend goes by Camo."

"Camo?"

"Camille. She, also, is an artist, so I gather—"

"Do they want to bury something?"

"It snowed there, last night. I guess they hoped I'd run home and get it out of their way. They'll be my roommates for the rest of their winter vacations."

"It's good to have creative people around," she said. As she left the room she added, "Keeps you young."

I contemplated my notion of isolating and naming the elements of conversation. Kate appeared, followed by her dog. She let Fievel into the yard and made herself some tea. Eben and Cindy and Adam came down soon after, and then Dad, who started cooking bacon. The cheery food-talk-love holiday substance filled the room. We overuse that word *love*, don't we? We don't usually know what we mean by it. This was the kind of extended-family love that thrives in episodes of a few days that have been incubated by months of separation.

My sister accepted my invitation to collaborate on supper. We made a menu. My idea was to go right out to shop for everything we needed, but Kate wanted to scout the pantry and refrigerator and then inquire with Mom and then search again, to make sure we weren't going to buy something that was already on hand. This was sufficiently tedious but it merely foreshadowed the misery of being with her in the supermarket. Each actual physical item, when it had been located, seemed not-quite-right and called into question the whole menu, which Kate then had to reconsider. When the need for a substance was confirmed, the product in hand was evaluated for price, purity of ingredients, and expiration date, and compared with numerous similar possibilities. Being forced to stand by for these proceedings—well, the family holiday experience includes intervals of torture, doesn't it?

On the way home Kate said, "I'm worried about Henry."

"Why are you worried about Henry?"

"I wish he could get it together and have a life."

"He seems to be doing okay."

"Do you think he's gay?"

"I don't know. I've never heard of him going out with a guy."

"Then why doesn't he date women? He could get married if he wanted to."

"Well, exactly," I said. "There's no indication that he wants to. He saw that Michelle lady for a while."

"Divorced with kids," she snapped.

"Yeah?" I snarled.

"Sorry," she said. "But you know what I mean."

"No, I don't."

"Does he even have any friends?"

That was changing the subject but I let it go. I said, "Online, maybe. I don't know. I agree—I wish he had more friends." As we pulled into the driveway I added, "He used to be in a bowling league."

Kate talked baby-talk to Fievel while I put away the groceries.

When Henry came home from the bakery, he and I went for a jog. He laughed at my account of shopping with Kate. "She's a piece of work," he said. "I wish she were more grounded."

"That's funny," I ventured. "She wishes you'd find a girlfriend."

"That would be nice."

"So you would like that?"

"I would in theory," he said, as his feet picked up the pace. "In practice, there's a problem. They always want to fix me."

"Ah."

"Because I like my life the way it is I don't need ladies telling me I ought to do thus and so."

I didn't bother to construct a reply because I needed all my breath to keep up. I failed anyway, and barely had him in sight for the rest of the run.

After my shower it was time to start cooking. "How long are you guys staying?" I asked Kate, as I sliced mushrooms.

"Home tomorrow."

"So soon?"

"Yeah. Jones and Fievel do better at home. I like it here but, you know how it is, other needs come first. That's what it means to be married."

"Dad and I talked about that on our walk yesterday."

"About what?"

"About what it means to be married. I asked him whether he thought some couples stayed in love all their lives."

"Of course they do. What do you think? Look at you and Helen."

"But I mean not just in love but in that hot crushy phase."

"You have to work at it. You have to be committed."

"I'm not sure you can work at a feeling."

"Of course you can. Jones and I do. Besides, Mom makes it easy for Dad."

"What?"

126

"It's always the women who do most of the giving."

"I'm not sure we're talking about the same thing. Anyway, Dad's take was that, as infatuation fades, family makes up for it."

"Oh, I see. They're on my case to have kids. And you're helping."

"No they aren't. No I'm not."

"Obviously that's the point of the whole exercise."

"He and I were talking in general, not about you and Jones."

"If Jones and I decide to have kids, fine. Otherwise people don't need to worry about it."

"I didn't mean to upset you," I said. That's a certain kind of apology, isn't it? Where you don't claim to regret what you said or did—you're only sorry about unintended consequence. The person receiving the faux apology can continue to complain or she can take your response as though it really were an apology and move on. Kate chose the second path. After reprising her remarks about Henry she spoke of her dog and yoga and this new kind of canine yoga, which Fievel liked so much and did him so much good, and her own intricate practice and her experiences as a yoga instructor with commentaries on her students, some approving, some satirical. Just before we served the food we had prepared she revisited the question of whether we had chosen the right menu. As each of our offerings went into its serving dish she expressed doubts about the quality of its preparation. When the food was on the table I sat down at the other end from her, next to Eben, to let others listen to her worry.

After supper we played Pictionary. Then Henry headed downstairs to his computer and Jones went up to the television to provide his followers with commentary, via the Internet, on a basketball game. Dad put on water for his nightly herb tea, which he explained was to guarantee he had to get up early and often during the night. I followed Mom into the dining room, where she and Dad were about to play gin rummy. She took their ancient score pad and a deck of cards from a drawer in the sideboard, put them on the table, and left the room. I knew they kept a running score, which was now in its fourth decade. According to the sheet on top, Mom was three hundred points ahead. That was a surprisingly small difference—were they really so even after all these years? No. At the bottom of the pad was a cumulative page that showed Mom with a five-digit advantage. Whenever one of them got more than a thousand points ahead of the other, that thousand was transferred to this page. This had happened dozens of times in Mom's favor, but only three for Dad.

When my parents came in, I called for an audit, to make a joke of my surprise that Dad was a worse gin rummy player than Mom. Dad smiled and looked completely comfortable with his long-term defeat. Mom sniffed and smirked. As she shuffled the cards to start their game, I went to the adjacent room, the living room. Kate was doing some kind of stretching or meditation or something, but when I came in she jumped up and asked if I wanted to look at pictures.

"Okay," I said. She bent at the waist to take an album from beneath the coffee table. This raised her non-maternal, yoga-sculpted rear end to visual salience while her breasts, in passive obedience to gravity, multiplied their visible cleavage. It occurred to me that if the woman displaying these curves were anyone but my sister she would have my complete attention. Under the circumstances my observations were impersonal and vaguely disapproving, but I was reminded of my wiring. In the aquarium the male black molly followed the female. For the thousandth time I marveled that similar boy-girl reproductive behaviors applied to fish and squirrels and human beings. Have we no embarrassment at sharing the biological compulsions of our inferiors?

Kate sat down beside me on the couch and opened the album. Dad had made all of our albums the old-fashioned way—the pages were black paper with captions printed in silver ink. The photos were attached by triangular adhesive sleeves at each corner. There were four photos on each page. My eye fell on Kate dressed for her first day in kindergarten. She looked at the same picture and exclaimed, "Cute! I remember that top." On the front of the shirt was a strange-looking cartoon rabbit with a fake-happy expression on his face. "Bun McBunny! He was so cute. Don't you think I was cute, Ike? My first day of kindergarten you would have been starting, what, third grade? Right? Who did you have?"

"Ms. Williamson," I said, recalling only her name and the shrillness of her voice.

"I had her, too," Kate said. "She was funny. She was big on handwriting and spelling. She loved my handwriting. My spelling was awful. I guess I didn't study. Well, thank God for spell check, that's all I can say."

The dog looked in the doorway.

"Fievel! Want to see me on my first day of kindergarten?" He started across the room toward the sofa.

"Don't let him drool on those photographs," my father warned from the dining room.

"Hear that, Fievel?" Kate said. She pushed the album toward me to make more room on her lap for the dog. "No drooling! He hardly ever drools anymore, Daddy. I think that's something his yoga has really helped with."

"Kate, do you make that dog do yoga?" my mother asked. She had little patience with Kate's ditziness.

"Mom do you remember where we got this bunny blouse I wore to kindergarten? God it was cute. I wonder if it's still up there." She and Fievel dashed up the stairs.

"Did you know she has that dog do yoga?" my mother asked my father.

""Fievel shares Kate's interests," he said, in a tone of pleasant insincerity. "It seems natural enough to me."

"There's nothing natural about it. I knock with two."

"Ouch," my father said. I pictured him caught with a couple pairs of face cards. He was an optimist and played incautiously and paid the price.

If he announced the points he'd lost, I didn't hear, because Kate charged back into the room. "I found it!" she proclaimed. "You could really get cute kid's clothes back then." Did she truly think that conditions had deteriorated on that dimension? How reflexively, irrationally, people hearken back to imagined good old days.

"You could get good caramel apples, too," I said, to join in the spirit, having turned the album page and found photos from a Columbus Day trip to Vermont. It showed us at a certain farm where each year we stopped to purchase cider, maple syrup, and caramel apples. I called into the dining room, "Do you still go to Blessings Farm?"

"Yes," Dad said. "Want to go with us next year?"

"Sure," I said. I couldn't imagine why I'd never taken Sean and Denver there.

My cell phone rang. It was Greg. He sounded impatient. "Could we talk about Denver?"

"Sure." Realizing I didn't want an audience, I headed for my bedroom.

As I climbed the stairs, Greg said, "The whole point of him coming out here was for an independent software development project."

"Okay."

"Then Denver read that book you sent him about the CPR."

"Really?" No doubt I sounded more pleased to hear this than I meant to.

"Now he's announced that he wants to do his project about the construction technology used to build the railroad through the Sierra."

"Is that a problem?" His inflection had told me that it was, but I thought I'd check.

"Well, yeah. I mean, what has that got to do with anything?"

"It seems to me—"

"What has it got to do with MIT?"

"They don't do bridges?"

"Denver won't be studying civil engineering," Greg informed me.

"Oh? He's sure?"

"That is not even—"

"Or have other people made up his mind?"

"Okay, Ike. Anyway, that's not the worst of it."

"It gets even worse?"

"He says you taught him to play marbles."

I thought, *Uh oh*. I said, "I gave him some but he had natural ability."

"So he figures to go to Sacramento—this is the idea he's hatched from reading your book—to go to Sacramento to research the railroad and shoot marbles."

"Oh, right, there's a tournament out there in the winter."

"The tournament is for children," Greg said.

"Yeah, but they shoot opens after hours," I said. "Does Denver think he'll hustle?"

"That's what he thinks," Greg said. "I think he'd get hustled."

"Where would he stay?" I asked. "Do you know somebody over there?"

"We do have Sacramento friends but I haven't tried to set that up because I want him to stay here and build a game."

Denver's plan, it turned out, was to sleep on the street with homeless people. I didn't like that idea any more than Greg and Sally did. "What are you thinking I will do?" I asked.

"Sally and I are not going to give him permission to go," Greg said. "If he has to do the project on the railroad, we can drive him out there to the library or the museum or wherever." Greg wanted me to use my influence to talk Denver into sticking with the original program, the software project. After I agreed to call Denver, Greg tried to re-normalize the conversation by chatting about other family news. Sean had met a girl. He'd taken a job to keep himself busy, as he said, and, being Sean, he'd found a fancy restaurant where an efficient sharp-looking kid could make good money waiting tables. Sean liked to earn his own funds, which he invested with an uncanny prescience. The girl worked at the same place.

I mentioned my amusement that Sally did the laundry but the humor was lost on Greg. We didn't laugh at the same jokes but otherwise he and I had a decent relationship. We had met several times over the years. His attitude toward others was premised on his belief that he was smarter than they, and more powerful, but that it was shrewd for him to make nice. Because I was a collaborator in raising his sons, I often received an extra measure of heartiness. This exchange about marbles and railroads was the first time that his tone had taken me to task; before that he had always welcomed me as Chief Nurturing Officer of his biological start-up.

I sent Denver a text: *Good time to talk?*

He replied, *No.*

But ten minutes later he sent, *Now's okay,* so I called him. He guessed what was up; that Greg had asked me to check in. He said he wanted to do his independent study project about the construction of the Central Pacific Railroad not just because he liked the book (that was as close as he came to telling me that he did like it or to thanking me) but also because Sean's new girlfriend was Chinese and she had told him how men from China had come over to do the construction. He explained why he had to go to Sacramento to do the research.

I made no effort talk him out of the railroad idea, which I considered a laudable departure from the family obsession with ones and zeroes. I told him that Sally would drive him back and forth for day trips. He said, "Are you kidding? It's two hours away—not counting traffic."

That gave me pause. There weren't going to be many of those trips. "What if they got you a place to stay with their friends? You can't sleep on the street."

"They have friends there?"

"I think so."

"That would be okay I guess."

"If you go, leave your shooter at home. Do your project."

He didn't respond.

"Hear me?"

"Yeah, I hear you."

I decided that was the best I was going to get. "Okay. I'll see about a place for you to stay."

He made no objection.

I told him that I was glad he had found a subject for his project. "Let me know if there's any way I can help," I said.

"Okay."

"Okay. Well, I'll say good night. I love you."

"Yeah, you too."

I went back downstairs.

"What's going on?" my mother asked.

I explained. They made sympathetic remarks about lengthy duration of child rearing. I said I noticed they were still parenting after all these years. My mother made herself look blank, which I took to be tacit concurrence. Considering the relationship of *home* to *house*, I asked if they ever thought about selling their place.

"And moving to Florida?" Dad asked. It was hard to tell how much irony he intended. "Can't do that. Christina's duties on Public Works forbid it."

"That's not why," she said. "Your father thinks he has to keep an eye on the school." The school she referred to was Cornell University.

"True," he said. "My vigilance keeps them on the straight and narrow." He dealt the cards.

"Some couples down-size," I observed.

"Yeah but then what would we do about holidays?" he said.

The subject of their house reminded me that I had promised Susan Speeks a reference sheet. I left my parents to their game and went to work on my laptop trying to think what bits of information house sitters might need. The bullet list I sent Susan included short and medium term considerations. I wasn't sure how long I planned to stay in Ithaca, but I figured at least another week. Then I thought, with Kate and Jones leaving the next day, and Adam and Cindy the day after that, the holiday party would soon be over. How long would Helen be gone? I sent her a message asking when she'd be home.

It still seemed like a strange time for her to be off somewhere. The right response on my part would have been to make serious progress on my own work. Certainly there was a clear and present need, inasmuch as I was unemployed. I knew what I wanted to do and the hours were there, but, so far, it didn't seem to be happening. Originally I had imagined that my parent's house could be a sort of writer's retreat where I could work out my ideas for a new show or blog or whatever. But at this point I was feeling more like the visit was about the connection with my family and that once the holiday felt over I'd want to get back to my own space.

I glanced at my inbox. Marjie was online. I opened a chat box and typed, *Hey! Our poem was a hit.*

Hi Ike, she replied. *They liked it?*

Yes. It received the Martin Prize.

Best of the year?

If you don't count Mom's. She would always win so if anyone else does a creditable job, they get it.

Congratulations.

How was your Christmas?

Par for the course. Too much to eat and drink. Too much stuff. All our good old traditions were upheld. We should be creative like your family.

Riddles are the exception. Mostly we pig out like everyone else. Who's there?

I gave her a rundown on my siblings and short versions of their life situations and personalities. I satirized my shopping trip with Kate until I realized that for all I knew Marjie was the same way. I changed the subject and asked, *How's your grandfather?*

She told me that he was fine but that he and Stephen tended to find fault with the other.

Is Bill more socially appropriate than he was when I saw him?

For the most part. A few lapses. He's getting better.

How's Stephen doing with his play?

I haven't heard about that lately. I didn't mean to sound negative about Christmas. It's great. I have to sign off. Nice to talk with you.

Meanwhile a reply email had arrived from Susan, thanking me for the information and asking if we had any coolers.

Why do you need coolers?

For the beer. For the party.

What party?

New Year's Eve.

That helped me decide when I should head home. New Year's Eve was no big deal in Ithaca. My parents made a point of going to bed extra early that night. The few high school friends I was in touch with lived elsewhere. Henry did his own thing and my other siblings would be gone. I decided to greet the New Year at my house, to keep an eye on my stuff.

I emailed Helen again and asked her to call me. Which, in the morning, she did. After vague opening pleasantries I asked if she knew that Sean had a new girlfriend.

"Yeah, he told me."

"I wonder how Susan feels about that."

"Who?"

"Susan, his ex-girlfriend, currently occupying our house."

"Oh, right," Helen said. "They didn't seem all that attached."

"They shared his bedroom at Thanksgiving."

"Yeah."

"That wasn't long ago."

"They're kids. It's ancient history in kid time."

I pressed the point. "If she's upset maybe she'll take it out on our house."

"It's a risky world. Try to relax."

"They're already blowing fuses and stuff. Making paper."

"Susan's making paper?"

"Her friend is. Camo."

"Oh right. Camo's big in the City already," she said. "Julian thinks she's great."

I pictured Julian, in his ascot, crashing Denver's birthday party last fall. It was odd that he knew about this girl I'd never met who was staying at my house. "They are throwing a New Year's Eve party."

"Oh."

"How do they even know people to invite?"

"Camo's from Cambridge."

"Then why isn't she staying at home?" I asked.

"Why would she want to do that?"

"Some people like to be home for the holidays."

"Some people live in Currier and Ives but not everyone."

"And that's the difference between you and me, is that what you're saying?"

"Here's a cliché, Ike. If the shoe fits, wear it."

Oof. Was I sounding pathetic? I needed to get better about asserting my rights without whining.

Her tone changed. "That wasn't nice. I apologize."

I made some reply to the effect of that's okay but let's end this conversation and try again some other time—which was fine with her.

Mom had been listening from the next room. "That didn't sound very happy."

"It wasn't." I went into the kitchen.

Mom sat at the table with a newspaper. "Look! Ink! And paper! So Twentieth Century."

We were agreeing that it was easier to skim the old-fashioned pages when Kate and Jones came down the stairs with their luggage, with Fievel close on their heels. Mom and I went to the front hall to see them off. Jones took his bag outside but Kate stopped and turned to us. "Where's Dad?"

"He's upstairs with Eben," Mom said. "They had an appointment to play with blocks." She flicked the switch of the intercom and said, "Attention Floor Three. Kate is leaving."

Adam's voice said, "Bye, Kate."

Dad, in a rare display of paternal authority, said, "We'll be right down."

Jones returned for Kate's suitcase, took it to the car, and came in again. Kate, rooted to the spot, launched a review of the holiday visit. Jones took out his phone. He had been here before—the moment of Kate's parting from her kinfolk could be extremely long. When her body assumed this particular stance and her voice found its correspondingly motionless tone, her signal-to-noise ratio dropped even lower than usual. It appeared that she would and could linger in this transition, chatting tirelessly, until an asteroid nailed us or the sun burned out. Which couldn't happen soon enough—better to be blown up or flash-frozen rather than being stuck in that hallway, locked in an endless goodbye.

My parents were able to mirror Kate's posture with perfect parental affection or zen-like patience or both. I didn't exactly wish I could be like them—but I bore admiring witness. They weren't the cuddliest parents and they didn't always have your bed ready for you but there was something dear and reliable about them that made me glad I'd come home and readier to deal with whatever was going to come next.

Although I admired my parents' relaxed demeanor, there was no way my nervous system could put itself into suspended animation. I twitched restlessly and envied Jones's situation. He was able to excuse himself from common courtesy and play with his phone because he had inoculated himself. He had created a defensive perimeter of low expectations. No one would fault him for acting the way he always did. It went unnoticed and un-remarked on. Whereas any exhibition of impatience by me would constitute discourtesy to my sister and, by extension, disloyalty to my family.

Eben saved me. He remembered that today he had only been pushed on the swing for an hour. He wanted more and he took decisive action, heading for the back door muttering "woo, woo, woo"— the syllable his mother said each time she gave his little rump a propelling shove. I looked resignedly toward Cindy and grumbled, "My turn," with a counterfeit note of reluctant duty. I gave my sister a peck on her cheek and told Jones I'd catch him in the Bay State. He grunted and he might have glanced up but I don't know about that because I hurried after Eben, lest Kate find a way to block my retreat.

She tried, calling after me, "We'll have to have you guys over."

Too little, too late. "Good," I called back as I pursued the little boy through the kitchen into the mud room. We donned our winter jackets and burst outside into fresh, chilly, air. Sometimes it's great to be an uncle.

Chapter 11

When I arrived home I found what appeared to be Bill Trippy's van in my driveway exactly where I had parked it during the twenty-four hours I had owned it. I thought, *There could be many vans the same color.* I looked through a window and, yes, the back of the interior had a bed. It was a camper, just like Bill's. It *was* Bill's. It had returned.

A young man I had never seen before greeted me in my front hall.

"What's that smell?" I asked him.

"Camo's paper. It's cooked manure. Horse manure, I think."

The place reeked. Like a barn, only more concentrated. As I opened windows, I asked the kid, "Is that your van?"

"No, it's Camo's," he said. "Who are you?"

He had a slender build and a handsome face. His good looks were marred by irregular bleached patches in his dark hair and by his pallor. "I am Ike," I said. "This is my house."

"Hello, Ike. Thank you for letting us be here." He looked around. "It's a nice house."

"I'm glad you like it. Why are you taking down that picture?" An abstract acrylic by one of Helen's favorite artists had been removed from its hook and was at rest on the floor.

"Sorry! I would have waited to ask you but I didn't know you were coming. I didn't think I should just start putting nails in the walls and so I thought if I just kind of un-hung some work I could use the hooks without hurting anything if I was careful."

"What's your name?"

"My parents call me Peter. At school I have a nick-name."

"What's that?"

"Barbie's Ken. I think Camo started it."

"I look forward to making Camo's acquaintance."

"I think she's asleep. Maybe she's upstairs. I don't know where she is. She must be here because her van's here and if she was going somewhere she would have taken it."

"Did she purchase that van recently?"

"Yeah. It's wicked old but low mileage."

I turned down the thermostat, opened more windows, and gave myself a tour of the house. The fact that it smelled so awful suggested that the whole place would be a stinking mess. But it wasn't. In the family room, resting atop big hot plates, were large pots such as you would find in an institutional kitchen. Upstairs everything seemed okay. The door to my bedroom was closed. I started to knock, then, considering that I hadn't warned Susan that I was coming home, I decided not to reclaim my room on short notice. I went back downstairs.

"What are you planning to put on the wall?" I asked the kid. He had been looking at his phone.

"Did you know that there's a New Year's Eve party here tonight?"

"Yes, I'd heard that."

He looked relieved. "Oh, good. Well, you know, Susan and Camo and I are art students and my thing is video. I'm planning to film this party."

"Film it?"

"Yes, right, I mean not with actual film, you know"—at that point he made a series of quick gestures to indicate frames and sprocket holes and a coiled ribbon of celluloid—"it's actually digital video." He held up a small plastic item.

"What's that?"

"Basically its a camera and microphone. It's a security cam."

"And then, after, you go around and collect the memory cards?"

"No, no cards. It goes through the Wi-Fi to my laptop. I hope. It's kind of experimental with so many pickups."

"So basically everyone at the party will be getting spied on?"

"I'll sign 'em up as they arrive," said a woman coming down the stairs. She had thick brown hair, large liquid eyes, and a bright white smile. She wasn't Susan.

"Are you Camille?" I asked.

Her smile broadened. "People don't usually call me that," she said. "Only a few."

"You prefer Camo?"

"Whatever you like."

Turning to the guy, I asked, "And how about you? Are you Ken or Peter?"

Camo answered for him. "Never Ken." Her tone was cheerful but firm. "Barbie's Ken."

"Or Peter," he said, in deference to my advanced age. "Whatever."

I introduced myself to Camo. I had been prepared to be irritated with the person who had so thoroughly and irresponsibly stunk up my house. But her manner and appearance melted and dissipated my annoyance. All the severity I could muster was, "You know, it reeks in here."

"Sorry," she said, without sorrow.

"Is that your van?"

"Yes!"

"It's so strange because I owned it before—"

"Really? Did you have it a long time and never drive it?"

"No, that was the guy who bought it new."

"It's going to be perfect for my trips."

"Where do you go?"

"All over. To corporate headquarters. For my work."

"Are you a consultant?"

"No, I'm an artist."

"Ah. Listen, the smell is an issue."

"Sorry," she repeated.

"Do you think you could move it outside? Or at least to the garage?" Under the circumstances, I was absurdly meek. "You are making paper?"

She explained that she made horse manure into heavy paper that she used for greeting cards with thank you messages addressed to major corporations. The cards praised the companies' contributions to humanity and the environment. She delivered them in person to the actual chief executive officer and got him or, sometimes, her, to write something on the card and sign it. The executives didn't know what the cards were made out of nor how facetious the messages were. She took photos of the CEOs, their offices, and the corporate headquarters buildings, and mounted the pictures and the cards together for exhibition and sale.

"Very creative," I said. To me it seemed comic but rather pointless—but what did I know about art?

"How do you get into their offices?" Peter asked. "Don't you have to have a badge or something?"

"I forgot mine that day," Camo said. "If anybody asks. Usually they don't and I don't have to explain anything to anybody."

"It certainly is a novel commentary," I said. "But why cook the manure indoors?" It didn't seem like the house could ever be free of that smell.

"To reduce your carbon footprint!" she said. "Keep the heat in! And you have to admit it gives the place a country feel; a rural . . . something."

"Bouquet?" Peter suggested.

"Yes! That's the word I was looking for." When bathed in her smile he looked a little less pale.

"Thanks for considering our collective carbon footprint," I said. "Sustainability and all that. The garage will be a compromise. I'll buy some baking soda, a case of it, and maybe we can take the edge off a little."

Camo went over to her vats and looked down at them thoughtfully, speculatively. I realized this was her way of getting her boyfriend and me to do the lifting and carrying while she gathered up tools and supplies and played the artist, *the talent,* for whom others labored as a privilege. We complied.

"How many people are you expecting tonight?" I asked.

They both looked puzzled. The guy said, "No telling."

"It's impossible to predict," Camo said. "It's just, the word goes out, and we'll see who comes."

How do you know how much food you'll need, I wondered, then I realized how perfectly uptight, middle class, and old I could make myself sound and decided to produce as little evidence of that criminal guilt as I could, even if, on those counts, conviction by my youthful jury was inevitable. Instead I asked, "Where's Susan?"

"Here," she said. She was wearing one of my flannel shirts. "Hello Ike."

"Hello, Susan. Happy New Year."

"Yeah."

"I'd like to unpack into my bedroom."

"Sure if you want. I mean, it's your house. I've been sleeping there, because of my work, but you can have it back if you want."

"Your work?"

"Yeah, my mural project."

"In the master bedroom?"

"I hope you like it."

"Bugs?"

"I've moved on. Sort of."

I went up the stairs. My bed looked widely slept in. When I opened the curtains the room brightened more than it had in the past—the walls had been a dark red. Susan had followed me. "Didn't you find that burgundy oppressive?" she asked.

At first glance I thought she had put up wallpaper.

"This palette has kind of a spring look, don't you think?" she suggested. A background of pale cream had been decorated with figures in light green, light blue, yellow, and pink. The web was pearl gray—a giant spider web, or a web of webs. In style the drawings resembled what Susan had done on the jigsaw puzzle. In what they represented, the figures varied. Spiders preyed on football players. Generals were caught in the web, and weapons: missiles, airplanes, bombs. Pastel monsters tore powerless victims. Some of the victims might have resembled Sean.

"It's kind of ironic," I observed, "to see such angry images colored like tulips and daffodils."

"Does it make you think of wallpaper?" she asked. "At first glance?"

"How could you give yourself permission to do this?"

"If you don't like it I'll put it back just like it was," she said.

"It's a school project? How will you turn it in?"

At that point Peter came in the door holding another of his little cameras. "Mind if I hang this in here?" He used his eyes to signal that he wasn't sure who he should be asking. He looked back and forth between Susan and me. I thought his eyes spent longer on her than they did on me, which I took to mean he'd decided that I had less natural authority than she. But Susan defered to me—for once she held her peace.

I said, "Okay. How many are you putting up?"

"One in every room plus extras in the living room and kitchen."

"What are you after?"

"Life. Whatever happens."

The doorbell rang. It was Sgt. Decker, the policeman who had investigated Denver's accident. He greeted me with congratulations on having gotten a sticker for "that antique," meaning the van. I said I'd sold it but it had returned like a homing pigeon. Without attempting to make any sense of this, he explained why he had come. He was completing his paperwork for the year—he laughed that he had waited until the afternoon of its last day—and he had discovered that he needed some signatures and was Denver home?

After delivering the news that Denver was in California, I invited Sgt. Decker inside. He wrinkled his nose as he stepped through the door. "Whew!" He raised his eyebrows at the smell.

"Sorry. An art project got out of control. Can I sign for Denver?"

"An art project?"

"Our kids' friends are creative."

"Okay. Maybe you can sign. You're his father, right?"

We watched Peter walk into the living room with a burning stick of incense, which he thrust it into a houseplant's pot. When he went back into the kitchen, I said, "I'm his stepfather."

"Have you adopted him? Are you his legal parent?"

"No." I led him into the kitchen. "Sgt. Decker, this young man is my new friend Peter, who's hosting a party here tonight."

"Ah. Incense for air freshener," Sgt. Decker said. Looking closely at Peter's youthful face he added, "No alcohol, of course."

"I'm of age," Peter said as Camo entered, "and so are my friends."

Peter slid away while Camo offered Sgt. Decker a soda.

He declined and turned back to me. "I don't think you can sign for him. I guess I'm out of luck."

"Would it work if he faxed it?" I asked.

Sgt. Decker thought that would be okay, so he accepted the soda after all. I called Denver, explained the situation, and went upstairs. Peter was in the office, at Helen's desk, looking at the screen of his laptop. "I think my movie starts here," he said.

I looked over his shoulder. There was Sgt. Decker, taking a chair at the kitchen table, receiving a Mountain Dew from Camo. She explained her manure cards project to him as though she had every reason to assume that he, an American law enforcement professional, would fully share her attitude toward corporations.

I scanned the papers and emailed them to Denver. While waiting for him to print, sign, and send them back, I listened, through Peter's computer to Camo persuading the policeman to give permission to be in Peter's movie.

When I handed the documents to Sgt. Decker, I said, "Happy New Year."

He examined the papers and observed that one of them was signed in the wrong place but he thought it was close enough.

"The officer wants us to card the guests," Camo informed me. "I'll do it when they sign their release."

"Too many kids get killed," Sgt. Decker said. "Underage drinking. It's a plague." He stood up. "Thanks for your help. Get plenty of 7Up for tonight."

I showed him to the door. When I came back, Susan was there, telling Camo, "Ike thinks I ruined his walls."

"The policeman doesn't like the paper smell," Camo said. "And he's afraid there might be drinking at our party."

"Wow," Susan said. "Welcome to Copville."

No one was more surprised than I at what I found myself saying next. For no reason I can explain I told them that my mother said it was good to be around creative people and although Susan's mural was a bit of shock I was getting over it and Peter's video project was interesting and so were Camo's corporate visitations. I was happy to have imaginative companions for New Year's Eve but the place did stink and we had to make sure about the drinking thing because I'd seen enough of that policeman for one year. And what time did the party start?"

"Who knows?" Susan said. "Whenever. Maybe nobody will come. Maybe they'll find out we're in Copville."

Because I was going to need guidance as to whether to allow our boudoir to be honored as the permanent recipient of Susan's art, I went back upstairs, photographed the bedroom walls, texted the pictures to Helen, and fell asleep in a chair. When I woke up, about seven o'clock, the van had been replaced in the driveway by a car I did not recognize. Downstairs, a man was sitting by himself on the sofa. He looked up and said, "Hello, you're Helen's husband, aren't you? I'm her friend Julian. Remember me? We met briefly last fall."

Even without his ascot Julian was easy to recognize by his urbane smile, his glossy complexion, and perfect haircut. His sudden appearance in my living room was distinctly surprising.

"The ambient fragrance indicates the recent activities of Miss Camille," Julian said. "Wait—before I ask after her I must apologize for entering unannounced."

"Did you ring the bell?"

"No, I saw the note and let myself in. I hope that is permissible."

I opened the front door and found a sign that read, *Come In! Back soon! Party!*

"Aha."

"I gather that you did not authorize the notice. You have returned from your travels and yet your youthful housekeepers persist in occupation."

"They do—and I divine it is they you have come to visit."

His smile intensified in recognition of my mimicry. "You divine divinely, sir," he said. "Although I am pleased to see you as well. May I inquire as to the whereabouts of Miss Camille?"

"You may inquire but I am at present unable to inform you."

"Well. I was invited to this party and have decided to attend." He seemed tired.

"Julian, welcome." I tried to improve my attitude. "Did you just arrive from New York City?"

"Yes, sir, I did."

"How was the traffic?" I asked, and was he thirsty or hungry?

The traffic had been trying and, in candor, he was both thirsty and hungry. We established frozen pizza as the menu and beer as his drink. I thought, he's slumming, drinking beer, but that was wrong. He loved beer, made his own, appreciated New England microbrews, and settled himself at my kitchen table as a companionable guest.

I expressed surprise that he would choose this as his way of spending New Year's Eve.

"Many years ago," he explained, "I resolved that each New Year's Eve I would be in a different place with different people. It's a great holiday for me because I'm such a night person, an owl, truly a nocturnal beast." He boasted of overseas trips he'd made to carry out his resolution. He'd even gone on a cruise, "God help me," but he pronounced it memorable because it had been marketed to amateur magicians and they were very good. "The boundary between illusion and reality was fuzzy the whole four days and especially on New Year's Eve. At six o'clock they had you thinking it was midnight and then they revealed the deception and tricked you a hundred more times before midnight.

"This year I had nearly given up finding a new venue. I had resigned myself to returning to a loft that had an infamous party twenty-five years ago. I'm just getting over being scandalized," he claimed, with his eyebrows arching high, "and I thought I had no option but to return and see what might have changed over two and a half decades, when, lo and behold, Miss Camille extended this kind invitation so here I am. But we ask, we, her admiring public, ask: where *is* Miss Camille? Her fragrance is here, the very breath and air of her studio, but otherwise she is absent."

The front door opened. Two young guys entered the living room as I came from the kitchen to meet them. "Are we too early?" one of them asked.

"I only know what you saw on the sign," I told them. "It says, *soon*, but I'm not sure what that means."

"Okay, thanks," the other guy said. They sat down and took out their phones and began typing with their thumbs.

I returned to the kitchen. Julian was washing dishes the kids had left in the sink. "Company coming!" he said, cheerfully. "All must be in readiness." But company didn't come yet. After half an hour, the two guys left. When Julian heard them go, he said, "We seem once more to be alone. Would you care for some espresso?"

How did he plan to make good on this offer? When he travelled by car, he explained, there was plenty of room for his espresso-making apparatus. He brought it in and before long we were sipping doppios.

We hadn't finished them when Susan walked in. "Can I have some espresso? Where's Camo? Isn't she back yet? Are you Julian?"

"He stood up, bowed, and said, "Julian the Barista at your service. Single or double?"

"Triple," Susan said.

"Doppio it is," Julian said.

Susan sat down and looked at me. "Has anyone come yet?"

I told her that two guys had come and gone.

"What did they look like?"

"One guy had red hair; the other was African American."

"Oh. Them! I wonder where they went. I guess they'll be back."

"Will you be serving any food?" I asked. I couldn't help myself.

"Oh right, I told Camo I'd make brownies," she said. "I should get going."

That's what she said but she sat there looking befuddled. Observing her paralysis Julian used his wide experience of kitchens to locate a box of brownie mix, a mixing bowl, and a baking pan, without help from me, smoothly and quickly. With a few quiet cues he got her going. She was stirring the batter when the two guys came back.

"Hey Susan," the black guy said. "Need any help?"

"Oh crap I've lost count."

"Three more strokes," Julian said.

"You can grease the pan," Susan told the guy.

"Should I turn on the oven?" asked the redhead.

"Yeah," Susan said.

"It's on," Julian said. "Would you gentlemen care for espresso?" He had brought four little china cups, lovely things, in which to serve it. As soon as one was empty he washed and dried it and had it ready for his next customer.

My phone rang. It was Helen. "Happy New Year, Ike."

"Happy New Year to you, too, Helen."

"Where are you?" She asked.

"At our house." By then I was climbing the stairs, headed for the study.

"Are they having a party?"

"They say they will. Susan's making brownies. With support from her friends. She needs it. Is it midnight over there?"

"Yeah. It's already next year here. I'm calling from the future."

"When are you coming home?"

"Wednesday. Things are winding down. I looked at your pictures of Susan's mural."

"What do you think? Shall I let her leave it or make her put the room back the way it was?

"It's okay with me. She should have asked."

"She's clever but strange," I said.

"Does she seem mad about Sean?"

"It hasn't come up. Julian's here."

"Julian? What's he doing there?" She didn't sound happy about his unexpected appearance.

"He made a New Year's resolution about New Year's," I said, and explained.

"Well. Watch him. He's not trustworthy around the kids."

"You want me to chaperone?"

"I was just thinking out loud. Bad habit," she said. "Never mind. They're not really kids, are they? They can look out for themselves."

She changed the subject and described the style of painting she was seeing—the work of artists from all over Europe. Especially crazy young Russians.

As she was talking I realized how far past midnight it was in Paris.

"Yeah, it's late," she agreed. "I better go."

We ended the call, and I looked at Peter's computer. Through his video setup I saw that the party was getting under way. In the front hall, Camo said, "Sign here please," to an egregiously pierced young woman.

"Why?"

"It means you showed me your ID so you can drink," Camo told her. "And you can be in the movie."

"This place stinks," the girl said as she signed.

"Paper-making," Camo told her. "You'll get used to it. Olfactory fatigue."

Peter showed me how to use the computer to steer the cameras and how to switch from one to another.

"Is it recording only the one that's selected?" I asked.

"No, they're all being recorded. I hope." He encouraged me to point the cameras however I wanted. "You can get a credit on my film. Cinematography by Ike."

When he left, I went to the closet where I had stashed the Jack Daniels I'd removed from Bill's van. In a box of souvenirs I found a shot glass brought back from New Orleans. I poured myself a drink, sipped, reacted, sipped again, poured some more, and returned to Helen's desk with my glass.

The camera in the master bedroom showed a black-and-white image, which meant the room was dark. I couldn't see anyone. Then I heard the toilet flush. The bathroom door opened, spilling light across the bed. Susan came into the picture still adjusting her clothes. She turned on some lights and looked at the section of the wall, a corner that she hadn't finished. She took a marker out of her pocket and peered at the wall as though she was about to resume her drawing. Then she changed her mind and left.

I clicked to the next camera. At first I couldn't tell where it was. It showed the top of some people's heads and picked up a buzz of conversation. Using the arrow buttons on the keyboard I tilted the camera down. It was on the mantel in the living room. A woman on the couch, a person older than the others, noticed the motion and looked at the camera. It was Georgia Trippy! I went to greet her.

Georgia was as surprised to see me as I had been to see her. She stood up and hugged me and reintroduced me to her girlfriend.

Pointing to the camera I said, "I'm embarrassed to tell you, I saw you through that."

"You have the place under surveillance?" she asked, with some confusion. "But now you've blown your cover. What are you doing here?"

"It's my house."

"No! It is? Who are all these kids?"

After I explained the situation, Georgia decided to text Marjie to see if she and Stephen wanted to come over. While she did that I took her and Lee's empty wine glasses to the kitchen. Julian had stopped making espresso and was nowhere to be seen. A jug of cheap wine had appeared on the counter. In the refrigerator, hidden in the vegetable drawer, was a bottle of decent chardonnay. I opened it, refilled Lee's and Georgia's glasses, and put it back. Someone must have noticed me do that because it disappeared; the bottle turned up, empty, under Denver's bed.

Georgia was there through her girlfriend's acquaintances. Lee had friends in a rock band and one of the other musicians taught performance art—or something—I couldn't follow the chain of connection. More people kept arriving. Camo had left her station at the door. I heard her tell Peter that they had run out of releases. They laughed and fist-bumped.

When I turned back to Georgia, she pointed at the camera and said, "Is that a nanny-cam?"

"Sort of," I said. "They sell them, so I'm told, for home security. Peter—also known as Barbie's Ken—is using them to make a documentary about this party."

"Who?"

"Barbie's Ken." I pointed him out. "His real name is Peter." He was talking to Julian. They were sharing a joint. I reflected that marijuana smoke would improve the odor of the house—then I smelled the brownies burning. I heard someone open the oven door. Susan was fiddling with the stereo, plugging in her iPod. In a moment she had filled the room and most of the rest of the house with a pulsing chaotic sound. She began to dance. I leaned close to Georgia so I could speak into her ear. "The producer has appointed me cinematographer. Did you see your dad's van outside?"

"I thought you had sold it."

"I had, but Camo bought it."

"Who?"

"Camo. Barbie's Ken's girlfriend." I pointed her out as the girl emerging from the kitchen, looking mild and innocent, with Susan's oven-blackened brownies on a plate.

"Cute," was Georgia's assessment.

"It's noisy here," I said. "Want to see control central?"

She did, and she invited Lee, who declined, and we went upstairs, passing three twenty-somethings—I hoped they were that old—on the stairs, one above the other, looking at their phones. Were they calling in more troops, I wondered, or finding their next party?

"That looks good," Georgia said, when she saw the whisky where I'd left it on Helen's desk. I poured a couple of fingers of it into her empty wine glass. She sat down in front of the computer. The screen showed thumbnails of the image from each camera. Georgia clicked on them one after another. "A voyeur's dream come true!" she crowed. When she opened the camera of the master bedroom, there was Susan dancing with two other women. We couldn't make out what they were saying. Susan handed a marker to her friend, who drew on my wall while the other two continued to dance. There was motion at the edge of the frame. I showed Georgia how to steer the camera. We panned left far enough to see that the door to the balcony was open. Involuntarily I started to go close it when those same two guys, the early arrivals, came through it and slid it shut behind them. As they left the African-American guy said, "We'll do it from there." What were they up to?

We panned back to the girls, who had switched turns at drawing. Georgia clicked to the kitchen just in time to hear a crash at the sink. Camo said, "Damn! I think those were Julian's." She and some guy peered sorrowfully into the sink.

Georgia muttered, "Breakage," then looked up and said, "We're missing the party." Her phone made a noise. She glanced at it. "Marjie and Stephen can't come over but we're invited to her house for brunch tomorrow. Work for you?"

"I'm there."

We went downstairs just in time to receive five fluorescent yellow sticky dots from a woman I hadn't seen before, forty-ish, with curly hair. "Five votes for one or one vote for five or divide them however you want," she told us.

"What are we voting for?" Georgia asked.

"Best buns."

"Ah. Where is the polling place?"

The woman grinned. "Officially it's up around the shoulder blades. Don't say I told you any different."

Peter, halfway across the room, turned enough for us to see that the right hip of his jeans had three bright dots.

The music went dead. I looked at the stereo. There was Julian, replacing Susan's iPod with his. He cued up a playlist. *Thump thump, bum-bum-bum!* Mick Jagger could get no satisfaction. Everyone smiled and went with the rhythm.

"Man," Georgia said. "It was just the same forty years ago."

Chapter 12

Although music and dancing shook the living room and competed with loud conversation from the rest of the downstairs, a heavy hairy kid was able to make himself heard when he rose from the sofa and bellowed, "Sardines!" With a mad grin he said it again. "Sardines! I'm first fish; if you're playing, close your eyes and keep 'em closed for twenty-five."

I kept my eyes open and watched the burly guy go upstairs while others squinted and chanted the count in time with the music. "Twenty-five! First fish here we come!" They began searching under tables, opening closets, and climbing the stairs, dancing all the while.

People drifted upstairs and, one by one, became sardines around their hairy leader. The living room crowd thinned out. Georgia and Lee had joined the game. I looked into the kitchen and saw Julian explain to Peter that the shattered espresso cups were antiques purchased in

Italy for several hundred dollars on his honeymoon. In response to Peter's look of anguish, Julian changed his tone and said, "No, no, I'm pulling your leg. I picked them up in Chinatown for nothing—and I've never been married." Perhaps he leered just a little as he added, "I'm not, you know, not really the sort, not really the sort of chap who marries."

The house became quieter, as, one by one, the seekers located the first fish and packed themselves around him. When the round ended, people flooded back to the living room and the party resumed. The talk-buzz returned but in a different key. As midnight approached everyone put on coats and went out into the driveway. Without knowing what was up, I followed. It was snowing.

The two guys, the redhead and the black guy, were on the balcony of the master bedroom, holding glowing objects—miniature hot-air balloons. One after another the sky lanterns rose into the darkness, each in a dim umbra of light reflected from the snow. Someone started a countdown to midnight. Before it reached zero one of the lanterns began to flash and crack as a series of firecrackers exploded. The paper canopy ignited and made a fiery descent to the snow-covered ground.

"ZERO!"

Midnight. In quick succession the other lanterns erupted. We cheered and clapped. There was kissing and high-fiving and whooping. Blue lights flashed through the snow as a police cruiser came slowly down the street and stopped in front of us. I pushed through to meet it.

The officer who emerged was, of course, Sgt. Decker. "Happy New Year Mr. Martin," he said.

"Happy New Year to you, Sgt. Decker. That surprising occurrence was not completely kosher, I'm afraid." Although they are easily obtained in neighboring states, fireworks are illegal in Massachusetts.

"That would be correct, Mr. Martin," the policeman said. "I make some allowance for the holiday. But is it safe to assume you will permit no further attempts to ignite the neighborhood? Or disturbances of the peace?"

"Yes, we'll be going back indoors."

"And if any alcohol is being consumed, you are monitoring ages of persons served. May I have your assurance about that?"

"A system was put in place," I told him, with some discomfort.

"And for others, designated drivers, please."

From over my shoulder a girl called out in a helpful tone, "We youngsters can do all the driving!" I think she had a beer behind her back. I'm pretty sure she was over fifteen.

"Well, okay, then. Keep the noise under control. It's a quiet street, even on New Year's Eve," he said, addressing the multitude. "And maybe everybody doesn't like the Rolling Stones as much as we do."

Camo stepped forward, handed him another Mountain Dew, puckered, kissed him, and smiled. He tried not to look pleased as he got into his car and drove away.

Georgia and Lee pronounced themselves satisfied with their night's entertainment, and headed for their car.

Back inside, the big guy shouted, "Sardines! Peeled sardines!"

"No fucking way," a female voice responded. "Not with you ugly bastards."

Music pulsed as the party found a second life. Intending to make a Do Not Disturb notice for my bedroom door, I went to my desk. The video feeds on Peter's computer caught my eye. I found another glass—*Aloha from Maui*—and poured myself more head-clearing copper-colored fluid from the bottle that had come with the boomerang van—the bottle I was finishing for Helen and Bill. Then I sat down to observe unsuspecting strangers.

I flipped from one screen to another until I reached a guy standing close to the camera, wearing glasses, with studs in his lip, nose, and ears. He was talking about having been really sick when nobody knew it and he had been stuck in bed for days and his roommates ignored him—once they had yelled through the door to see if he was alive—and his girlfriend was mad because he hadn't responded to her texts and his phone had been dead because he'd left his charger in the library. Luckily they still had it when he went back.

Then he stopped because another person cut him off. A woman's voice described being in a sleeping bag in a tent by herself and she couldn't move and she felt awful and she thought she heard bears outside and wondered if a bear ate her would it catch whatever was wrong with her and then she woke up and it was a dream.

"Strange," the on-camera guy said. "Mine was no dream, though. I'd be sweating then shivering and dude, it was bad."

Then somebody else started talking to the person with the bear dream and the fellow who'd been sick pivoted and disappeared, revealing a guy across the room holding a beer, looking at the floor, standing still, not talking to anybody.

Another camera showed two people walking in the upstairs hall; a guy with with a girl in front of him, their backs to the camera. He put his hand on her shoulder and stepped up beside her. She had dark hair hanging over her shoulder blades. She stood still as he parted the hair behind her neck. I sipped from my glass and thought, maybe these two knew each other before tonight; maybe not. She let him kiss her neck, but didn't turn to him. For her it was a moment of decision. Did this guy appeal to her? Maybe she already knew whether or not she wished to have a relationship with him. Or maybe his attention was flattering and felt good and was fine with her but only because it was New Year's Eve. Maybe she was attached to someone else, some guy who wasn't here.

It struck me that this was really spying; that it crossed the line separating okay from not okay. They didn't think anyone could see this venturing of affection or lust on his part; this standing still for it on hers—and I shouldn't be watching. I decided to stop. He slowly slid across behind her and began to kiss her ear. She still didn't move. I switched cameras leaving them alone in that interval of excited possibility, of uncertainty, that no couple can ever return to. Too bad. Who wants to stop having those moments?

The next camera showed the dining room. No one was visible, just beer bottles and half-empty plastic cups. A mumble of voices spilled from adjacent rooms. Just as I was going to switch scenes the two guys who had launched the sky lanterns came in and passed through the frame. I panned and found them at the end of the table, leaning back in their chairs—expensive dining room chairs, not for rocking, but I stifled the impulse to run down and make them stop. Instead, I put a little more whisky into my mouth. The white guy said, "I suppose my parents will die some day—I mean, for sure they will—but I can't really believe it."

"They're so much in your face."

"Dude, if we'd been busted tonight for having fireworks and the cops had found my weed and I was like calling them from some police station outside Boston and they had to fly from Chicago to get me out or whatever they wouldn't get mad. They would just, like, say, *gosh son, oh well, youth,* and like take me out to dinner and to a concert or something or to a fucking museum or whatever like nothing had happened."

The other guy said, "Nothing *would* have happened, dude. You want them to give you a bunch of stuff over it, like to show they care or something?"

"Well, no, dude, but . . . I don't know."

I clicked to the kitchen. Chinese food had appeared. Some kids helped themselves to my dishes and silverware while others ate from the plastic tops of the take-out containers. "A kind word will keep someone warm for years," a woman said, then she laughed. It sounded like Susan. I panned the camera to the right. There was the big hairy guy who had started the sardines game, eating an egg roll. I went back to the left, to Susan unwrapping a fortune cookie. She broke it and read its slip of paper. "Keep true to the dreams of your youth."

"Nightmares!" someone said in the background.

Susan said, "These cookies think they're so smart." She unwrapped another and whispered into it, "Who have you got in there?" She laughed, crushed the cookie, and read, "Great works are performed not by strength, but by perseverance."

"How does it know?" a voice said.

"Anybody can be great if they try hard enough and stick to it," someone said. I panned to the speaker—the curly-haired woman who'd handed out the best-buns dots. She noticed the camera and said, "Does that thing move?"

"Apparently it does," the hairy guy said. "Hello, Barbie's Ken."

"I think he's out in the van," Susan said. "Maybe it's Ike. Is that you, Ike?"

"Who's Ike?" the curly-haired woman asked.

"The guy who lives here," Susan said.

"Your boyfriend's father."

"Something like that. Status unclear."

"The course of true love never did run smooth," the curly-haired woman pretended to read.

"Maybe false love runs smoother," Susan said.

The curly-haired woman looked into the camera, smiled, and said, "Drop dead."

"Yeah, go to bed, Ike," Susan said, "or whoever you are. Or come down and have some food."

That suggestion had merit and I went to the kitchen. I didn't get to eat, though, because big guy was curious to see the system. He and the curly-haired woman and I went back upstairs. When I showed them how you could tune in different cameras we found ourselves looking at the couple I'd seen in the hall. They were now in Sean's room and there was strong evidence the girl reciprocated the guy's interest. "I don't think they know there's a camera in there," I said.

"Why is it in black and white?" the woman asked.

"When it's dark the cameras switch to infrared," I said. I went down the hall and tapped on Sean's door. Without opening it, I said, "I just want to remind you that Barbie's Ken put security cameras in every room. For his movie."

"Thank you," a voice said.

As I passed by the door of the study the woman said, "Spoil sport," and chuckled.

"Sorry," I said. "Happy New Year." In my bedroom I examined the corner where Susan's friends had extended the faux wallpaper. They had used the same markers, the Easter-egg pastels, but their content was different than Susan's. They had left erotic graffiti. Tonight my house was full of sexual energy—but I didn't feel turned on. The curly-haired person seemed friendly and it was New Year's Eve and my wife was far away—but I hadn't been tempted. I felt like an observer, like a witness. What did I feel part of?

In bed I checked my email. There was a message from Helen: *Dear Ike, dear husband, good news! I'll be home Wednesday morning. Can you pick me up?*

As I drifted to sleep, I tried to believe that Helen really felt that I was her dear husband. I looked forward to having her home and to hearing her reaction to our new bedroom wall. Random noises made by young strangers, guests of my guests, reached for my attention but they couldn't hold it. I drifted off.

In the morning the house was silent and the bird feeder was empty. When I came in from filling it, I noticed the aroma. The stench of Camo's paper-making had been softened by incense then enriched with the smoke of tobacco and marijuana, burned brownies, and left-over beer. The sum was rich, lived in, and not unpleasant. I drank coffee and read the news online until it was time to get dressed and go to brunch at Marjie's.

I had never been to her apartment. She had one floor of a three-story house. Stephen opened the door and took my coat. As I came into the living room Georgia trumpeted, "Here he is! The host with the most! What a party he threw last night!"

Marjie presented herself for a courtesy hug. I calibrated my embrace to express as best I could the circumstances that had evolved since our first meeting—her engagement, our beach walk, her initial anger at my note, followed by oblique encouragement. And more; my relationship with her grandfather and her fiancé and having been fired by her dad. Over her shoulder I took stock of our audience: Mrs. Lu, Georgia, Lee, and Stephen.

When Georgia announced, "They voted on best buns; do you believe it?" Marjie released me. "Our own Lee was top vote-getter among the gals, I believe," Georgia continued.

Lee smiled and shook her head.

"And deservedly so," Georgia said. "And I believe Mr. Ike here must have found a dot or two on the back of his jeans when all was said and done. What about it, Ike?"

I think possibly the curly-haired lady had so honored me but I wasn't sure. Marjie looked disapproving. "Let me make it clear," I said, "that this event was neither produced nor directed by me."

"It wasn't your party?" Stephen asked.

"It was not," I said. "Helen invited house sitters. They took possession while I was with my family in Ithaca. They are young; they are artists; they did not request my input on the party games." I looked at Mrs. Lu and said, "Happy New Year to you."

"Happy Western New Year to you," she said. "Have you made resolutions?"

"No," I said. "Do you think it's too late?"

"It is never too late to be the one in charge of your own life," she said. "Like this party at your house, and you weren't even the boss. Why is that?"

There was accusation in her voice. Although the instance cited was unfair, I replied, "Mrs. Lu, I think you may have something there. I'll reflect upon it."

She looked satisfied.

"Do they make resolutions at Chinese New Year?"

"No. Not like Western. They check to see whether it will be a lucky year or not. If lucky, they feel happy. Otherwise, sad."

"It's not about self-improvement?"

"No. Most Chinese people think about luck. I think differently."

Lee had been listening. "Whoever really changes themselves anyway? It seems odd to us to emphasize luck—but there are many years of wisdom behind that way of thinking."

Mrs. Lu waved her hand. "Not years of wisdom. Years of superstition."

"Do they have fortune cookies in China?" I asked.

"No," Mrs. Lu said. "Fortune cookies are American."

Stephen handed me a tall, thin, glass containing a lower region of pink champagne that bubbled upwards through a zone of orange juice—a mimosa—the sunrise drink. Lee and Mrs. Lu each had one. Theirs remained nearly full, but mine didn't last long.

Georgia described the midnight release of the sky lanterns, the ignition of the firecrackers, the policeman, the sardines game, and the video recording. I surveyed the apartment. Marjie's commitment to teaching was on display. When she asked if I'd like another mimosa, I said, "Not yet, but how about a tour?"

"A tour of what?" she laughed. It wasn't a big apartment.

"This looks like the command center of your pedagogical operation."

"Yes but there's nothing much to see," she said, although her tone and posture expressed appreciation of my interest. Pointing to a device on her work table she said, "That's the scanner. The tour starts there. A whole lot of scannin' goin' on these days. Scan scan scan." She lifted a roll of tape. "This is the scotch tape. We still use tape. We're digital now but we still need tape. And sticky notes!"

"I'm writing my whole play on sticky notes," Stephen said, having appeared at her side.

"Ike requested a tour," Marjie explained.

"This lady is one dedicated teacher," Stephen said.

"What do you scan?" I asked Marjie.

"Kid's work, for one thing. Portfolio assessment! That's the buzz-word. Stephen, the man's glass is empty."

During my second drink I was required to explain my wife's absence and Julian's presence at the party, because Lee asked what such an old guy was doing among all those kids. When I told them about his resolution for non-repeating New Year's places and people, Georgia said, "Maybe *we* should make resolutions."

"Or fortunes," Lee said. "We could each write one on a slip and then draw one out of a hat. Except you can't keep the one you wrote."

We debated the rules and the time limit.

"This is great," Marjie said as she distributed writing instruments. "It's like the start of a new creative tradition like some families have." I recognized that she was referring to, but choosing not to mention, our collaboration on my Christmas riddle. Inwardly I signed up for a guilty pleasure—the conspiracy of a shared secret.

"Why isn't the rest of your family here?" Mrs. Lu asked Marjie. "Where are your father and mother?"

"Ev is busy!" Georgia said. "My ever-loving brother does the same thing every January first. He reconnects with his computer collection."

"He started with a Commodore 64" Marjie said.

"And he still has it," Georgia said, "It's from 1983 and he cranks it up every New Year's Day and runs some software on it."

"And he does the same for every computer he's ever owned," Marjie said. "By the time he's set each one up and run it, like played a game or something, and taken it apart and put it back in its eternal resting place in a cabinet, the day is over."

"He seems to find this satisfying," Georgia said, "or somehow necessary."

Marjie passed out slips of paper and pens and books for us to write on and brought in a kitchen timer. Georgia announced that any resolution mentioning weight loss was to be disqualified. Stephen said they weren't supposed to be resolutions anyway; they were supposed to be fortunes and could you mention death? How dire could your fortunes be? Marjie argued that the point of the whole thing was to challenge each other and you could do that with either fortunes or resolutions if we had constructive attitudes. She looked sideways toward Stephen.

If he got a resolution that called for him to improve his attitude, he told us, he would declare immediate failure.

Marjie started the timer. We each had four blank quarter-sheets of paper My strategy was to consider each person in the room. Lee was pretty. My fortune for her was: *You will be tempted to lead someone on.* Then I turned it into a resolution: *When I realize that someone finds* me attractive *I will flirt just enough to have fun, then clarify my non-availability.* Yuck, wordy. I put that slip into my pocket.

Georgia, seated next to Lee, looked honest and confident. I wrote her fortune: *You will provide strength and determination for those you love.* But what if Marjie drew this? If she had those qualities they were in a different form than Georgia's. Strength, though, could be camouflaged by tenderness.

Stephen should resolve: *I will not masquerade for new acquaintances.* And my take on his fortune: *You are luckier than you deserve.* But these were not on paper before I fell into a daydream about Bill and getting fired and the strange okayness of being here with the guy who'd replaced me, and time ran out. We folded our little papers and Marjie collected them. When all the slips were in her bag, we each drew one. Mine said: *When you begin to coast you're on the downgrade.* Neither a prophecy nor a resolution, this was another kind of fortune cookie message: a nugget of wisdom. Not one that felt timely for me.

Marjie read hers: *Balance care for the future with enjoyment of the present.* That was an admonition—a resolution the fortune-writer thinks everyone should make.

When everyone had had a turn Georgia said, "Now let's see the one Ike put in his pocket."

I just looked around.

Lee said, "Come on, Ike, out with it."

"He shouldn't have to read it if he doesn't want to," Marjie protested.

"It's not secret," I said. "I just didn't think it was very good."

"We'll be the judge," Georgia said.

I read, "You will be tempted to lead someone on."

"Wow," Georgia said. "What's great about that is the way it takes on different meanings according to the recipient."

"How?" Marjie asked.

"If Lee gets it," Georgia explained, "it refers to a guy hitting on her, which happens five to ten times every day."

"That's not true," Lee protested.

"Whereas if I got it," Georgia continued, "it would refer to the work setting because I might try to motivate somebody by creating a false hope that I would promote them."

"And if Stephen got it," I said, "it could mean that he would introduce himself to people as some character he'd made up."

Marjie called us to her dining room, where talk of fortunes was replaced by accounts of travel and book clubs and the insanity of the Republicans and we felt well-gathered and happy.

When I got home Julian was in the kitchen, in a silk dressing gown, poaching eggs. "There you are," he said. "No telling when the kids will appear. May I serve you an egg?"

I started to decline, having just come from brunch, but realized that the bowl of fruit and the half a waffle that I'd eaten at Marjie's left plenty of room for a poached egg. I sat down at the kitchen table.

"Allow me to wish our gracious host a good morning and a happy New Year," Julian said, "as we begin the second decade of the new century." He paused while he put English muffins in the toaster. "At least, it's still a new century to me but for these children, they don't remember much else, really. And for you, too, this is really your century, isn't it?"

"I feel like I spent plenty of time in the last one."

"Will you be having coffee or espresso with your egg?"

"Coffee will be fine," I said. "I'm afraid I witnessed the destruction of your little cups."

Julian's cheer dimmed. "Indeed. Regrettably, too true."

"I overheard you tell someone that they were not objects of value."

"I might have taken that line," he said, "last night, to let some young friend off the hook—not to burden his conscience with trivia. At times my devotion to good feelings overpowers my preference for strict veracity."

"Oh."

He brought me a tray with coffee, egg, fork, and napkin. "Do you take cream or sugar?" he asked.

I hadn't finished my egg when Peter appeared. Susan and Camo always called him Barbie's Ken as though taking the time to pronounce so many sounds was a luxury they had ample means to afford. In his smooth quiet way he went to work picking up the party mess. In remarkably few minutes he had all the cups and bottles in the recycling bins.

"Peter, how many eggs would you like?" Julian asked solicitously. "Poached often are preferred. Would that method be satisfactory? And do you take cream in your coffee, or milk?"

Peter wanted two eggs, poached was fine, and so was cream. He responded without looking at Julian—he just kept cleaning up. When his food was ready he took it and vanished, muttering, "Thank you," but strangely, noticeably, quiet.

Julian sat down at the kitchen table and peered at me anxiously. "One can't help wanting to serve these youngsters," he said. "They are not children, they are adults, but they are very young and my goodness, they have nature's highest gifts—they are so beautiful. Wouldn't you agree? Never mind. To a senior citizen like myself, you are barely past their age. And you must be tempted to think awful thoughts, like, *that old roué, that ancient soundrel.*"

"Helen warned me about you," I said. "But who am I to chaperone?"

"And who is Helen to be prim? One could ask. Well, you can answer that however you like; you are her husband, you pay your dues and deal with the membership and to all appearances deal with it very well."

"Membership?"

"In your marriage. Membership has costs, privileges, and responsibilities does it not? I wouldn't know. I've never signed up for that particular sort of club."

"What club?" Susan said as she came in, with tattooed skin exposed everywhere my favorite T-shirt didn't cover. The tattoos I had been curious about when I first met her—the ones that leaked out from beneath long sleeves and terminated on the backs of her hands—were visible. They were a vine-like tangle of flowers, hearts, eyes, and birds, in the same style as her drawings on the Thanksgiving jig-saw puzzle and her mural in my bedroom.

"The two-person club we call marriage," Julian said. "I employed a figure of speech."

"Were you a busy old goat last night, Mr. Jule-ee-an?" Susan asked, not expecting an answer. She went straight for the coffee, then sat down at the kitchen table. She put a cigarette into the corner of her mouth, where it bobbed as she looked at me and said, "So, is smoking permitted these days?"

"Do you mean, 'You didn't stop us last night so now there's a precedent?'"

"Yeah, plus you don't seem all that happy with Camo's horseshit smell so you could let me help."

"You always push the envelope, don't you?"

"That's my job," she replied. "And you always pull the envelope back, don't you?"

"What do you mean?"

"Like last night when Sam and whoever were about to have a fuck right in front of the camera until you warned them."

"Oh—that's pulling the envelop back? To tell an unsuspecting couple they were being watched?"

"They'd been warned," Susan said. "It would have been the best part of Barbie's Ken's movie—New Year sex. Except the cop part is going to be pretty funny."

"And this part right now will add a dimension," I said, nodding toward the silent camera.

Susan stood up, turned her back to the camera, and leaned far forward. Julian and I looked the other way.

"There. One more dimension," she said as she straightened. To the camera she added, "Barbie's Ken? Can you use that?" She laughed a crazy-sounding laugh. Then she looked at me and said, "When will the lady of the house be back?"

"The day after tomorrow," I replied.

"Ah. Getting her European affairs all wrapped up," she said, with a glance at Julian. "Back to Copville. Triumphant return. Was the cop pissed about those firecrackers?"

"He said he could wink on New Year's Eve but he wanted to make sure we weren't going to set fire to the town."

She lit her cigarette.

"God damn it Susan."

"All right, all right," she said, and she took her cigarette and her coffee outside.

Chapter 13

At some point that afternoon the van and the three kids disappeared. After serving breakfast and being to some degree called out on his nocturnal prowls, Julian kept a low profile. When he finally left his room he went out the front door and drove away. The house was empty and quiet for the first time since I'd returned from Ithaca.

It struck me that Denver might like to hear about the New Year's Eve party. I poured myself some Riesling, sat down at my computer, and began an email about coming home and being greeted by Barbie's Ken, a pleasant young man, fluid and considerate. As I wrote, I pictured Peter a little older, maybe thirty, in business school. Or managing a restaurant, a trendy place, with his friends' paintings on the walls.

And Camo? What might the future hold for her? Would her art success continue? Would she marry and have children? Or might her waltzes into corporate headquarters, on the passport of her white smile and perfect complexion, leave her locked behind her pretty mask, souring and alone? Perhaps she would grow tougher and more cynical while Susan mellowed and softened. It was funny to think—without evidence—just to entertain the possibility—that Susan would turn out to be the sweeter lady.

Helen, had she been there, would have had wry observations. Sardines. Peeled sardines. Oh brother. That train of thought reminded me that I was trying to write to Denver but before I got back to it the phone rang. Kate wondered if we'd like to stop by. I said that Helen wouldn't be home for a couple more days but that I could go, and I did. So instead of telling Denver about my New Year's Eve, I described it to Kate and Jones. I think it was the first time they'd ever listened to me. Something about that party interested them. Maybe it was the novelty of people whose lives did not revolve around jobs, pets, and television. Or it could have been the voyeurism of being a little older, settled into partnerships, watching the hot and uncoupled grope for each other.

For whatever reason, they paid attention. Jones snorted with the reflexive condescension of a person who defines normal as himself and not-normal as misguided. Nor was Kate prepared to condone unconventional behavior from anyone other than Jones, Fievel, or herself. She interjected disapproval. In her opinion, the policeman was too soft, too yielding. Julian made her sick "if he's as old as you say." Here was a rich supply of evidence that a once-wise world was in decline. "Peeled sardines!" she complained, as though they had actually taken off their clothes instead of having hooted down the suggestive phrase.

Jones seemed pleased to hear that while I had been lounging around Ithaca some college student had steamed the odor of horse manure into the interior of my house and its furnishings. The video surveillance of the party, by the party, under the direction of a guy called Barbie's Ken—this fixed his attention so strongly that I thought perhaps it would lead to an unprecedented interaction—a conversation. But that was not to be.

The image of the kids cracking fortune cookies to read their messages brought my narrative to Marjie's brunch. The shift from midnight revel to noon introspection punctured and deflated Jones's interest, and with his customary lack of ceremony he left the room. Kate didn't seem to notice his departure. Hearing of the tamer, more thoughtful group at Marjie's, she offered sympathetic attention. She wanted to know what I had written. I still had that slip I had put into my pocket, so I read it to her. "You will be tempted to lead someone on."

"What would I have written?" she asked herself out loud. "I'm not even sure we *can* change," she said, echoing Lee at the brunch. "Maybe we're just stuck with being ourselves who we are and we better get used to it. I wish I could be a good listener, like you always are. But I'm not, at least, I don't think I am,"—she looked to me to contradict her, which, lamely, belatedly, I did.

"I try to be," she resumed. "Maybe I'm getting better. I listen to Jones but I'm not necessarily really interested in what he has to say. So it's hard. It's too bad married people can't care about more of the same things. You and Helen do, though, don't you? Art and stuff. And getting her kids into college. You've been a big help to her, do you know that? How did we get onto this? Fortunes! I don't know. I guess I would have written one about staying hydrated or something. No, that would be a resolution. 'Become more considerate.' Is that a fortune? Or, 'You will care about someone.' How's that?"

We cleared the table but left the dirty dishes in the kitchen. It was Jones's job to rinse the dishes and load the dishwasher and wash the pots and pans and he always did his job, Kate assured me, but usually it happened in the middle of the night when sports were over and she was asleep. "So for me it's like the fairies did it."

I hugged her and said we should get together more often and she really was a good listener. She made me say goodbye to Fievel. I went home.

Peter was in the study, at his computer, looking at Susan's bottom. He was editing his movie. "It could end with Susan shooting the moon," he said. "As she bends, quick fade. Or I could roll the credits over her butt."

"Nice," I said.

"It begins with the policeman signing the release, talking to Camo," Peter said. "Then, chaos, dancing, talking, china gets broken, people make out. Thanks for warning those two in the bedroom."

"Susan was pissed."

"I would have felt bad, because they just didn't know. If they wanted to do it in front of everybody on purpose that would have been weird, but that would be one thing. But they just wanted an interval of sexual intercourse so it's good you told them."

"Did they stop?"

"No, he just put the camera into the hall. Anyway, the beginning, them making out, is hot and I can keep some of that. Nobody can see who they are."

He showed it to me. It *was* hot.

"I can't believe this is going to work," he said, speaking of his project as a whole. "It's going to be great."

My inbox showed a message from Denver. Its subject line was *construction technology*. He had written: *Did you know that Chinese men knew more about how to build a railroad through the mountains than the Americans did? Because of the Great Wall of China!* That revolved in my thoughts as I went to sleep—his comparison of the Great Wall with the Central Pacific Railroad. Which led to fortune cookies—I guess I was the last person to find out that they were American. An oral fortune cookie would be an oracle, which might be some kind of sea shell. Ms. Lu was Marjie's oracle and she was Chinese and why don't they get more credit for technology?

It's a self-centric universe, that's why, and there's a shortage of talented listeners. My wife could be counted among them, on a good day, which was one reason I was glad to have her back. On the way home from the airport, I told her all about my trip.

The morning after her return, I overheard Julian tell her, "Oh my dear, they are just candy, really, candy. That is something one shouldn't have too much of, I know, but a little can't hurt. I mean, why live, if you deny yourself everything?"

"Julian you are too old," Helen responded. "They might feel sorry for you at a weak moment but you are from a different world."

"I know, I know—a different world entirely. But, Helen, *feel sorry for me?* No! That is too harsh, and it's not true. They know I love them and they shine a little of it back my way, they reflect it, they have misgivings, perhaps, but they can't help it because my feeling for them is so bright, you see. A brilliant comet across a dark night sky. A wonderful shooting star."

Helen called out, "Ike!"

"Yes?" I responded, as I came around the corner.

"Make Julian leave the kids alone."

"Are you going to have him beat me up?" Julian said to Helen. "I don't think he'll do it, will you, Ike? We're old beer-drinking buddies."

"It's not easy to tell when to take you two seriously," I said.

"Julian thinks Peter and Camo adore him because he loves them so much."

"You love both of them?"

"Individually and as a couple," he said. Did you ever see anything in this world so beautiful? I rarely use that word; I ordinarily forswear it, but in this case—"

"Julian, get over them," Helen said. "I'm sure Camo is grateful for the attention you have brought to her work."

"That understates the case, doesn't it?" he said. "Where, without me, would she be?"

"Gratitude is not love," Helen insisted, "and neither of them loves you."

"Is this where things are at in the big city?" I asked. "Aging bachelors preying on juvenile couples?"

"Ike it sounds so sordid when you put it that way, so absolutely much lower than it is," Julian said. "Look at my personality! I'm fun! I might be aging a little but I am lively and I have a certain sensibility, wouldn't you agree, Helen? And these younger individuals can profit from contact with me."

"No they can't," Helen objected. "Not from the contact you have in mind. Max is a better partner for your sensibilities."

Julian wrinkled his nose. "*Max?*" He glanced my way and said, "Max is another good old beer-drinking buddy."

Helen lost patience. "Julian!"

He lowered his chin to peer at her, as though over spectacles.

"You should go back to the city," Helen continued. "New Year's Eve is over."

"I don't see why you are so high and mighty," Julian said. "Holier than others. Are we standing on our maiden purity?"

"Don't start with the *are we*'s, Julian, please. Not on me," Helen put an edge on her voice.

"*Aren't we* having a good time?" Julian replied, with a reptilian grin. "I know I am. What shall we do about lunch?" he asked, changing his expression from sarcasm to that of a forager. "All this having judgment passed on one does build the appetite. I find it to be so. Is anyone else hungry? Then again, of course, come to think of it, I'm the only one being judged. *Too loving.* Guilty, guilty, guilty! How do we wear each other out? Not that way; that is ever new. No. It's the worrying after each other. And the gone-ness of the dead. The separation from people you still need, and they just aren't there." He looked as though he was about to cry.

These two were hard to keep up with. As Helen decided whether to soften or to keep after him I felt ready for my run and I said so and headed out.

Jogging, I wondered whether Julian actually slept with either Camo or Peter or both of them, or had tried to, or whether it was all just talk. You can't really tell what other people are up to, can you? You guess, but your guesses are so colored by your own fantasies and fears that you can't take them seriously. You say *no one would do that* but you don't know whether they would or not. Even if they told you, you couldn't know what to believe.

Some people you credit as frank. I'd believe Susan. Because she was so out there. She could be annoying—she usually was annoying—but she inspired faith in her candor.

Helen had an interesting take on Susan's art. She liked Susan but wasn't interested in her work. She thought Susan was using art to process her feelings, like other people might do with a therapist.

I would have thought that art based on the authentic feelings of a talented person would be something to value. But Helen was in the art business, where sales to collectors was what mattered, and collectors wanted a distinct body of work. Almost like a brand. Helen's example was some guy who turns out one similar square canvas after another, painted a solid color with some small object added realistically, like a key or a raspberry. When people bought one of those they got more than just a single object; they bought into a circle of hip collectors who had this guy's paintings, which added meaning and value to owning one.

I could see the sense of that in her trade but it confirmed everyone's worst suspicions that the big-time art world was shallow and phony so you wouldn't think its representatives would admit it. To me the value of art is the experience it gives you; its effect on your thoughts and feelings, and Susan's enraged Easter-egg-colored wallpaper mural was stimulating to be surrounded by. You could feel caught within its ironies and resentments and experience her expression of where, in her life and head, she was at. Helen didn't care; she came to the whole thing through supply and demand. In that respect she was just like Greg but it was more acceptable in Greg's case because he and his employees made something utilitarian. Software's value was not based on what it caused you to think or feel; it was about what it could do for you. Helen's customers wanted art for the same reason, for what it could do for them, in status, in making a social impression, embedding them in a story they could tell their guests, or, more often, tell themselves. I have a such-and-such. The work didn't need to generate any emotional or intellectual effect; if it did, that was beside the point. To be fair to Helen she had always characterized her occupation in these terms. She was no hypocrite.

I felt sad for poor Susan, the innocent, who poured her actual self into authentic individual objects. But she was still a student. She had plenty of years before the futility and unlikelihood of her artwork achieving collectible status would become a definite and discouraging fact. Her life's validation would have to come from something else, which in time would become visible to her, ready for her to embrace— or so one could hope.

Camo, on the other hand, already had a viable art product. You might think that her facetious treatment of corporate capitalism would be off-putting to collectors whose capacity to hang original art was created by that system. Somehow, though, the affluent buyers of her pieces could claim to resent the wealth-generating engine or at least to regret its shortcomings. Julian's advocacy had made Camo's bullshit series a great success.

Suddenly a creature appeared a hundred feet in front of me—a cartoon figure come to life, a dog-sized oval with stick legs and a headless spaghetti neck. It was a turkey—a wild turkey. I had seen them from my car but had never encountered one while jogging. He stopped squarely in my path, then turned toward me. I came on. He took a few more steps, stopped, sized me up, and detoured into a patch of woods. By the time I reached the place he had been, he had vanished.

Does a turkey consider things from multiple points of view? Does it have more mental life than a fish or an acorn? It's hard to imagine any vertebrate existing as unconscious biological process when the animal I look out from the inside of is all nervous awareness, preoccupied with images of the past and the future. Our present is a boundary, having no width. Is the turkey trapped, unreflecting, inside that razor-thin zone of *now*?

When I jogged I did not usually think so much. I was in a funny mood. It struck me that Helen seemed out of place in our suburban house. She was polished to a perfect cosmopolitan luster. Helen of Paris and New York—and maybe of Boston, too, but not Helen of Westforest.

After my shower I found Susan and Helen in the living room. "How about a fire, Ike?" Helen said. "Wouldn't it be nice to have a fire?"

Agreeing, I began the process of building one. Procedures like starting a fire in the fireplace or making coffee in the morning have a ritual quality. The sequence of simple steps, frequently repeated, settle into muscle memory. I slid the glass doors apart, opened the flue, and scraped ashes off the grate, so that air could rise to the firewood. In our house only I knew the proper series of actions, the ones that secured the desired result. Meanwhile I listened to Susan and Helen. Susan was describing a recent conversation with her mother. "She complains about her husband."

"Your father?" Helen asked. "You mean, your father?"

"Yeah. I don't even know why they are married. They should give each other space like you guys do—but why get married if the point is to give each other space?"

"Not an easy question to answer," Helen said.

"I love my dad," Susan said. "What a corny thing to say."

"It's good to love your father," Helen said.

"Do you love yours?" Susan asked.

"We're not at all close," Helen said. "He tends to be inaccessible. He's on a golf course somewhere in Florida."

Inwardly I agreed that Helen's father was inaccessible to her—but so was she, to him. I had observed each of them, at different times, extend a hungry feeler toward the other. When either of them reached around Helen's tranquilized, checked-out, mother to invite father-daughter contact, the other always withdrew. They never wanted to get in touch at the same time, as though their relationship contained a prohibition against success.

I lit the fire. No one spoke while crumpled newspaper burned and ignited the kindling, which smoked, then brightened. Flames rose through the split oak, flickering, probing, becoming more confident.

"How do you do that?" Susan asked.

"What?"

"Get a fire going like that?"

"Remember from grade school—the triangle? Heat-fuel-oxygen? Or maybe it was Boy Scouts?" I offered a paragraph of talk on the art of fire building, balancing the theoretical with the practical. Helen looked at her phone. Susan stared at the flames.

"If I had lived in olden times," she said, "I could have been priestess of fire."

"Priestess would have been a natural calling for you," Helen said. Susan smiled.

I pictured her as a priestess. In profile, Egyptian style, with her chin parallel to her shoulders. It occurred to me to pose her that way for a photograph.

"It would have been up to me who got to use fire and who didn't," Susan said. "Rude to me; your ass freezes. Suck up to me, make sure I'm happy; you're good—you're toasty."

I recalled that Peter had deferred to Susan's natural authority over my status as man of the house and he hadn't found it difficult to choose. One of Susan's fortune cookies ought to have said, *You would have been an excellent priestess.*

"It must be cool to have power," Susan said.

"Isn't it better to have love?" I asked.

Both women looked at me.

"If you have power," Susan said, "then you get love. Right?"

"Or at least you get something that can feel like love," Helen said. "Or at least, feel good."

"I'd take power over love," Susan stood up. "I'd rather be able to make people do what I wanted them to. With love you have to be nice."

"Nice is overrated," Helen said.

"What would be a good name for a fire priestess?" Susan asked. "Amfieryatiti?"

I blurted out an ill-considered question: "Do priestesses have boyfriends?"

"Yes, like black widow spiders," Susan said. Dipping into her entomological knowledge, she added, "Or praying mantises. They let a guy get close then they kill 'em. I would have a cellar full of dead boyfriends. Their last thought was always, 'I'm her first boyfriend she hasn't killed.'"

We laughed. I pictured a *New Yorker* cartoon with a stack of dead Egyptian guys, each emanating a cut-off thought balloon that said, *I'm the first guy she hasn't killed!* while Susan smirked in the background.

"You could never marry," Helen said. "All the fiancés would be dead in the cellar."

"Priestesses don't have husbands," Susan said. "People think it's for religious reasons but it's not. Priestesses on the whole don't even do religion—they just want the power, and they like to snap off guys' heads."

"So they can never be a mother," I said.

The women looked at each other.

Susan said, "I could have all the children I wanted. They would never meet their fathers, unfortunately, because they had died soon after the you know. Too bad, no dad, but, being children of the high priestess would have . . . what do I want to say?"

"Compensations," Helen said. "You could give them each her own eunuch."

I thought that Susan appreciated, in Helen, a kindred spirit. Helen had power. Was I the eunuch Helen had given her children?

"Good idea," Susan said. "They could sing high. I'd keep a big supply."

"They could bathe and massage you, Helen said, "and do all the chores."

"Like stacking the dead ex-boyfriends," Susan said. "Oh, man, I knew I should have been a priestess."

"You were born for the part," I agreed.

"Okay," she said. "Gotta go. Me and the eunuchs are going bowling or something. No. We're going to annoy the Copville cops. Give them something to do."

When Susan had left I suggested to Helen that we go out for dinner. She accepted. I made a reservation. "Plenty of time before then," I said, patting the vacant space beside me on the couch. She came over but she brought her computer and kept it on her lap. "Here we are, alone in front of the fire," I said. "Romantic, huh?"

"Ike, we just did it last night," she said. "Aren't you feeling caught up in that department?"

"I guess you are," I said.

"Or maybe I just have some stuff I need to get done," she said. She tried to soften the effect by adding, "But it's nice to be with you."

"But *nice* is overrated, so I hear," I said.

"It's fun to play along with her, that's all," Helen said. "What a character she is."

"I might not be such a cooperative eunuch as you think," I said.

"What?"

"Give your kids a eunuch. That's me, isn't it?"

"Shouldn't you say, 'an eunuch?'"

"Make a joke out of it."

"You can't expect me to take you seriously."

I stopped to consider that I might be overreacting, and shifted my ground. "When are you going back to New York?"

"Monday."

"I'd like to go with you."

"Why?"

"We're supposedly married, but it isn't feeling like we're really a couple."

"We're a real couple in our own way. We don't have to be like everyone else. Do you need to be like all the little suburbanites around here?"

"Agreed we don't have to be like everyone else," I said. "It's not about conforming to anything but what we want."

"We already have what I want," Helen said. "I'm fine with the status quo."

"Are you saying you don't want me to come to New York?"

"No. That's a different subject. Why would you want to come to New York? I work twenty-four-seven when I'm there. Here there's the house and everything needs you. Who would fill the bird feeder? And keep these kids in line?"

"I could show Julian how to fill the bird feeder."

She scowled and gave her attention back to her computer.

I ruminated about her responses—her resistance to my going to New York. And her satisfaction with the way things were. Why was I *not* satisfied? If we were both comparing our marriage to that of our respective parents, I could see why we would feel differently. My parents had their gin rummy and their jokes and their not-empty nest. Her parents were emotionally separate. In comparison to them, Helen and I *were* close.

And what were my gripes? This time she'd kept her computer on her lap but usually she was reasonably responsive. Although I had noticed some attenuation in the eros department, I chalked that up to the nature of things, biologically. Helen didn't bother me about what I did with my time or limit my autonomy. So what was my problem? I watched the fire. It was at my favorite stage—underlain by a glowing prairie of orange coals—not the featureless steady orange of an electric heater but with a shimmering irregular fluctuation like a living thing. Above, in the fuel burning on the grate, flames danced in one region of the wood, leaped to the other side, then crept back toward the middle, healthy and ready, knowing their business, consuming the oak. Patient.

The problem with Helen was that she didn't need me—not in the heart's companion way of a loving partner. She had never needed me in that way. When I became involved with her and the boys they needed me for themselves and she needed me for them. That felt so good to me and Helen was so personally appealing, so sexy, that I bought in. Helen hadn't changed much—it was I who gradually had recognized that my marriage wasn't what I had envisioned for myself. It had a lot going for it—in many respects my situation was enviable—but for me there was a piece missing and as I sat here next to Helen, watching my fire, I was conscious of wishing for more. But would that have been the case if she had responded to my overtures and wrapped herself around me and sated my lust? Wouldn't her body have absorbed my dissatisfaction and deferred this whole train of thought? When I was happy that way I was happy every way.

I said to Helen, "We appreciate your willingness to participate in the our opinion survey." She looked up. "Which of the following best describes your attitude about your husband hanging out with you in New York City?" She sat back to listen. "A. What a great idea! B. I am concerned that he will have nothing to do because I will be working. C. That's a very sophisticated social scene and he won't fit in. D. I've got a boyfriend there and three's a crowd. E. I can't stand any more time with my husband than I already have to give him."

"F," Helen said. "None of the above. I choose F."

"In one or two sentences please describe your attitude toward Ike's suggestion."

"For many years now when I go to the city my mindset is to focus completely on my work. That would have to change if Ike came with me and I don't want it to change and I don't think my business could afford for it to change." She paused to put on an apologetic expression. "Sorry."

"Ah. No room for negotiation or even further discussion?"

"There can always be discussion. You asked me to describe my attitude and I did."

I put more wood on the fire.

"It's a free country," Helen said. "You can come if you want to, but I've told you how I feel about it. I've just got this tiny place down there and I've been going there for years by myself, and it's a pattern that works well for me. I'm sorry if it works less well for you."

The fireplace held my gaze.

"Ike, all you need is to get into something here, like a new show. Or some other kind of job. You'd be a great teacher. You should talk to that person—who is she?—Bill's granddaughter? Teaching would suit you very well."

Although I didn't want to become a teacher any more than I wanted to own a dog, Helen was right that I needed to re-engage with work. My dad had sent me the list of conversations from literature that I had requested. I could picture actors performing vignettes of dialogue followed by discussion that would help people learn and think about the art and science of talking. It was too academic, but I could work with it.

The blonde splits of oak I had added became surrounded by flames but they were neither as bright nor as cheerful as the earlier generation of flames from this same fire had been at the beginning, when we had shared the fantasy of Susan-as-priestess. "Yeah," I agreed. "Yeah."

Chapter 14

This isn't going well, was Denver's text to me.
What isn't? I replied.
CA.
Huh?
California.
What's wrong?
Sally won't take me to Sacramento. Dad's in China.
Shall I tell your mother to tell your father to make her take you?
No.
Can't you get enough information on the web?
No.
Is there some way I could help?
No.
I'll mention it to your mom.
No reply.

I went back to peeling apples until Susan came into the kitchen and asked if I could take her to the airport.

"You're leaving?"

"Yes and I need a ride to the airport."

"When?"

"Tomorrow night."

"I have Symphony."

"Crap."

"Do you think you'll always like your tattoos?" It seemed fair to be as random and plainspoken as she was.

"I don't know." She rolled down her sleeves. "It's nothing for you to worry about. Of that we may be certain."

"You are starting to sound like Julian. How about him?"

"What about him?"

"Maybe he could take you to the airport."

"No. He's a terrible driver. I won't ride with him. Maybe he could do the concert and you could take me to the airport."

"Where are you going?"

"Home. I'm homesick for Air-i-zone-uh."

"Where's Camo?"

"They left for Florida."

"In the van?"

"Yeah. How else?"

"Did she take her manure vats?"

"She said to tell you she'll get her stuff on her way back to school. They wrote you a note. Barbie's Ken gave me an envelope for you but I don't know what I did with it."

"Why did they go to Florida?"

"It's warm there. Camo likes Disney World. She wants to work there. Maybe things here were getting complicated."

"Heard some hints."

"Yeah, well." She turned and left the room.

It felt right for them to go. They'd had a rollicking camp-out in my house for the holidays but now it was January. The month for new places, new thoughts, new projects. *You need to get into something*, I had been admonished, and I agreed. I called Anna and left a message asking to talk about some of the ideas we'd had for a show about conversation.

Julian overheard me. He was not inhibited by privacy concerns from appraising my idea. "Ike, that would be great. You have a gift— you really do—and I think you ought to use it."

"What do you mean?"

"You have the touch for dealing with people. Just look at the way you managed things with the policeman on New Year's Eve. No one else could have done that."

"Thank you, Julian."

"No, I mean it. Plus, you should have me on your show."

"As a guest?"

"Yes. I look twenty or thirty years younger on television. It might sound immodest, but I believe my personality comes across."

"I can imagine that it would."

"You would bring it out like you bring out the best in everyone. Helen has always said so. She always says you've done wonders with those boys."

That reminded me of Denver's unhappy state of mind. I checked my laptop to see if he had emailed or was available to chat. He wasn't, but there was a surprising message from Stephen requesting my help with the Bill Trippy project. He made it sound like we'd each be doing a favor for the other because he thought he should concentrate on his play. He didn't offer to withdraw—the way he put it sounded more like I'd be his assistant—but it came at the time I needed to get something going. It was almost like Helen had talked Stephen into it, bribed him somehow, to get me off her case about going to New York.

In response I told Stephen that I would consider his offer but it was Bill who had originally hired me and I wanted to discuss it with him.

After rehab Bill had gone into an upscale assisted-living facility. I paid him a call. He was in his living room watching television— something about the Civil War. He paused the DVD and invited me to sit down. "I hate television except now you can get all the good shows on disk," he told me. "Ken Burns. And amazing nature programs. How do they even get some of those shots? Did you ever see those bowerbirds? Or the birds of paradise? Those guys must have patience. The photographers."

"I guess they must," I agreed. "In uncomfortable circumstances. Mosquitoes. Wet feet."

"Comfort is a fine thing," Bill said, "between adventures. I can't wait to get back to Yellowstone."

"Yellowstone? Next summer?"

"No! Right now! Next week or week after next, sometime soon; I can't keep track. Ev and Kathy are taking me out and Marjie's bringing me home. God I love that place. And winter is the best time there."

"How are you feeling?" I asked.

"Great," he said, dismissing the subject as boring. "I know how much people like to hear old guys go on about their health. Many years ago I decided that the day I couldn't find anything to talk about other than how I felt, I'd put myself to sleep. So to speak."

"You regard that as your right?"

"Sure—who could deny that? The problem is we're trapped in our consciousness at every individual moment. Your brain's like town meeting—this year can't pass an article that would bind next year from making a new decision."

"Things might look different when you come to the point—"

"Yeah. Now, if I hear some old fart complaining and being tedious and I think *that* life isn't worth living I make up my mind—why use up oxygen when it's time to draw down the curtain?"

"But—"

"Exactly! But when I myself am that old fart I might find, well, I'm still enjoying my vittles; I still like to look at a pretty woman. Or a sunflower. Maybe I'll change my mind. What the hell are you doing here?"

"I came to see if you want me back as your co-author."

"Of course I want you back for crying out loud, I never wanted you gone. What happened to the kid? That guy of Marjie's? When I came to after my stroke Ev said you were out and he was in."

"Yes, right, but today he, Marjie's guy, Stephen, asked if I'd help him out."

"Yeah? Are you going to?"

"I'm willing—but I thought I'd better check in with you first."

"Please remind me of your name."

"Ike Martin."

"Yes. Ike, you are the guy I picked for this job and I know you do good work."

"Thanks."

"There's just one thing."

"Yes?"

"You are married to a woman I kept company with for a while."

"Helen Marsh."

"Maybe you have it in for me. Maybe you want to make me look bad."

"Now that we both know the other knows, you can't really trust me. I'll tell Stephen it won't work."

"I think you're a reliable guy," Bill said. "A stand-up guy, as they said in the old movies. If you say we're good—then as far as I'm concerned we *are* good."

"Ah, Bill, we all have our pasts and who knows how many inter-- secting lines there have been. It's not, like, a once-and-forever world, is it?"

"Maybe for some people; I don't know," he said. "For others, we *do* have some intersections and sex is the root word and the tenses are past and future. I'm way in the past; you are the future."

"I don't see why I shouldn't ghost your book but promise me one thing."

"Yeah?"

"There won't be a photo of that old camper of yours on the dust jacket."

He laughed.

With things straight with Bill, I made an appointment to resume the conversation with Stephen. At the Black Horse Tavern. He showed up late but not too late. I asked why he wanted help. He said he needed to concentrate on his play and his teaching.

"How's your play coming along? Is it really all on sticky notes?"

"Yeah. The kid, hitchhiking, he's in the car with the lawyer, and the kid has the temerity to criticize the litigator for driving this big honking gas burner, one of those four-door luxury pickup trucks. So naturally the lawyer, whose name is Caligula Odds, doesn't have much patience for that—"

My phone rang. It was Greg. "Sorry, I have to take this," I told Stephen. Accepting the call, I said to Greg, "I thought you were in China."

"I am in China. I'm calling from Shenzhen," he said, with a deft pronunciation of the strange-sounding city.

I wondered how he could use his own phone there and what time it was for him and why he was calling. I said, "Hello."

"I hope I'm reaching you at an okay time, because there is a problem."

I stood up and said to Stephen, "Sorry, China calling." Walking toward an empty corner of the pub, I told Greg to go ahead.

"Denver has disappeared."

"Uh oh."

"It's a terrible time for me to break off this trip," he said, "and anyway it's hard to get a flight and I'm a long way from the United States."

Guessing that he was asking me to go to California to locate Denver, I offered to do that, and he accepted. He told me what he knew of the circumstances and that I could get more details from Sally, who was at home with their baby. "My take, best case, he's made friends online in Sacramento and he's staying with them. Worst case, he's making good on his threat to live with homeless people and he has no idea what he's getting into and we need to find him."

I told Greg I'd make some calls and if Denver hadn't surfaced I'd jump on a plane as soon as I could.

"Family crisis," I explained to Stephen. "Gotta run. I'll call you when I can and we'll pick up where we left off."

"No hurry," Stephen said. "Bill's flying to Bozeman with Ev and Kathy tomorrow. He wants one last look at Yellowstone."

"Tomorrow? He didn't know it was that soon."

"He's lost in time and space."

"Sorry I have to take off. That kid who knocked you off your bike has found another way to need assistance."

He saluted and said, "Go well."

Either from the expression on my face or the way I'd closed the door, Julian picked up that something was wrong. When I'd explained the situation he said, "You must go. At such times, on such a mission, is it not well to take a companion? As Holmes had his Watson? If you will permit me I will come along. To ride shotgun, as it were."

Perhaps my recoil from this suggestion was undetectable; I hope it was. I thanked him and said I could get help from Helen if it turned out I needed help—or from Sean—but that probably I wouldn't end up needing to make the trip. Up in the study, I called Helen's cell. No answer. "Hi. Greg called from China," I said to her voice mail. "They can't find Denver. I told him I'd go out. Want to meet me there?"

Next I called Sally. She had not heard from Denver. She was thinking she should call the police but she hadn't yet. Sean seemed a little strange on the subject, she told me, as though he knew more than he would say. She wished she could be more help but taking care of the baby tied her down. She wished Denver had settled on a computer project as his father had wanted him to. She was glad I was coming and probably I should take Denver back east with me when I found him, because it wasn't working out that well having him there because he got all of these ideas.

"Where's Sean?" I asked.

"He's at work."

I told her that I would call the Sacramento police.

A text arrived from Denver: *Ike, I'm okay. No worries.*

I called his phone but there was no answer.

The Sacramento police said that privacy rules prevented them from determining the location of a cell phone except in the case of a runaway juvenile or a disoriented senior. I said that Denver was under eighteen. They said that if he was over sixteen they weren't supposed to, but to hold on. When the lady came back she said, "Okay, I've got the phone's location and yes it is here in Sacramento. Let's see—its at the address of an REI—that's a store here for sporting goods, outdoor gear."

"Yes. Could one of your people go over there and find him and call me?"

"You have to fill out a missing person report. The form is online."

"Sure but do you have to wait until you get it? He might leave."

"We could still track the phone. You fill out the report and we'll see what we can do at this end."

At that point I wanted to simultaneously fill out the form, call Sean, and make a plane reservation. I called Sean. He didn't answer. I left a message asking him to call me because Denver's absence had everyone upset and I needed to know whatever he knew about it.

I found the Sacramento police website. Helen returned my call.

"Hello, Ike," she said.

"Greg called from China," I said. "Denver's gone missing."

"In California?"

"Yeah, Sally and he don't know where Denver is and if Sean knows, he's not saying."

"Okay," Helen said. "Don't forget, Greg always overreacts."

"What?"

"Greg's a drama queen," she said.

"Do you mean you are not concerned?" I asked. "Because I was planning to go out there and help find him."

"Why?"

"Because they want me to, for one thing. And because he'd had this plan to live with homeless people while he researched his school project. And the police say he's in an REI."

"He's probably going camping," Helen said. "He's a young guy. He should have some adventures. What do the cops have to do with it?"

"I'm reporting him missing."

"You're overreacting, too."

"He might be fine but how can we know that? He should communicate his plans to the people who care about him."

"Why? I sure didn't let my parents know where I was or what I was doing when I was that age. I think we should all just chill out a little."

"Okay," I said. "I better get off—I have other calls to make."

"Okay," Helen said. "Try to calm down."

When my mom heard Helen's attitude, she was furious. She had never cut Helen any slack—she regarded her as a manipulative cradle-robber. Not only did Mom think I should hurry out to California, like Julian she wanted someone to go with me. "Take Henry," she advised. "It will be good for him."

I called Henry. He didn't answer. I texted him, *Call me.*

I was halfway through filling out the missing person form when Henry phoned. I explained the situation and asked if he could take time off and go to California with me. At first I interpreted his hesitation to mean that he was puzzling about the logistics but as he enumerated difficulties related to his job, his volunteer commitments, and a video game conference, I realized that he was only figuring out how to tell me no. There was zero chance he was going.

That didn't matter, I thought, because the Sacramento Police had probably found Denver by now. Why didn't they call? I finished their form, scanned it, attached a picture of Denver, sent it to the email address on their website, then phoned them again. The woman remembered me and my problem but she didn't seem interested. She asked where I sent the missing person report.

"Have you found my son?"

"Sir, is he really your son? You have different last names."

"He's my stepson," I told her.

"Are you his legal guardian?" This was like the first time I had shown up for his parent-teacher conference.

"No, but I'm his actual guardian right now because his father, who he was visiting, who lives in Cupertino, is in China, and his mother, my wife, is also on a business trip and both of them have asked me to do whatever I can to find him. Was he at the REI?"

"No sir. The officer was able to locate his cell phone there. It was inside a sleeping bag."

That settled it. I was headed west.

I went to Julian. "The Sacramento cops are off the trail. I'm going out and my mother agrees with you that I should take someone. My brother is too busy. If you're still game, I accept your offer."

He was in earnest so we made a plan. He needed to go home to pack. He would drive to New York then fly to Sacramento. I would get out there as quickly as I could, rent a car, and we would find each other by cell phone when he arrived.

After emailing Sally, Greg, Sean, and Helen—and reminding Sean that I was waiting for him to call—I booked three flights: Boston to Philadelphia, Philadelphia to Dallas/Fort Worth, and from there to Sacramento. Tomorrow was going to be a long day. I rented a car and reserved a hotel room for Julian and me. It struck me as a little strange to sleep in the same room with a character whose nocturnal proclivities could raise the eyebrows of Susan and Helen, two non-puritanical individuals. But we were on a mission. I guessed he would behave himself.

In my bedroom I began to pack. This was a challenge because I didn't know how long I would be gone. It would take most of one day to get there. If the whole situation resolved itself while I travelled, as I half expected it would, I would just turn around and fly home. But who knew what Denver was up to or how clever he would be about it? I could be gone a week or more. As I placed a handful of underwear in my open suitcase, in walked Susan.

"Knock, knock." Eyeing my briefs, she added, "Handsome!"

"Thanks for knocking."

"Mr. Julian says he is meeting you in California."

"That's right. Do you want to come along?"

"If you need me I'll be in nearby Arizona," she said. "But how am I supposed to get to the airport? And why are both of you flying the coop?"

"Family emergency," I said. "Public transportation takes people to Logan every day."

My cell phone rang. It was Sean.

"Hey Ike."

"What's going on with Denver?"

"I don't know. He had the urge to travel. I wouldn't worry about it."

"But your Dad and your stepmother *are* worried about it, and I'm packing to come look for him."

"He'll be all right. I'll tell my dad to chill."

"Where is he? Denver, I mean."

"I don't know exactly but I'm sure he's okay. Why don't you call him on his phone?"

"The Sacramento police found his cell at an REI. In Sacramento. In a sleeping bag."

"Oh."

"So what can you tell me?"

"Nothing. Not really. Except he made friends with Nellie's brother and they might have been talking about a trip or something."

"Do you have the brother's phone number?"

"No."

"Who is the brother? Where does he live?"

"He's Luke and I guess he lives around here someplace."

"How old is he?"

"Eighteen I guess. Maybe nineteen. He's taking a year off before he starts college."

"Could I have Nellie's number, please?"

"She's at a concert. I'll talk to her and get Luke's number but it won't be until morning. Really, Ike, there's nothing to worry about. I'll call Dad. Stay home."

"Denver is younger than you—and he's more impulsive. I can see why your dad is worried." At that point I asked Sean about himself and how things were going, but it felt awkward because Susan just stood there listening. I ought to have shooed her out of the room to begin with.

Sean said everything was good with him and he'd send me Nellie's brother's phone number, tomorrow, and we ended the call.

"How's old Sean?" Susan chirped, with an aggressive edge to her voice.

"Working hard," I said. "Waiting tables."

"Gosh, I hope he saves some time for poor Nellie, whoever the fuck she is," Susan said. "What a corny, old-timey name."

"Yeah, well, everybody can't have a nice, safe, normal name like yours."

"I guess the little brother's gone off somewhere," Susan said.

"You guess right. He's probably okay."

"That makes this our last night."

"Um hmm." I muffled my surprise that she would put it that way.

"Because Sean's moved on and probably you won't be needing me to house-sit any more."

"Who knows?"

"Because I burn too many brownies and shoot moons and stuff."

"Never a dull moment—"

"Yeah. Well, seeing as there's nobody here but us and it's our last night, do you want to sleep with me?"

She caught me by surprise. After a beat I said, "That's flattering. But I'm married, you're too young for me, and we're not in a relationship."

"It would be for science."

"Science."

"I'm doing a study."

"Oh yeah?"

"Yeah. Compare and contrast. Fathers and sons."

The light dawned. To my shame, it had taken me this long to realize that she wanted to spite Sean. "He's not my son."

"Right. Well. Variation on the theme."

"Susan. Are you okay?"

"Don't start mothering me."

"How about if I uncle you a little?"

"My real uncle would not turn me down. That I know for a fact."

"But your fake uncle cares about you and wants good things for you and your life."

She just looked at me for a few seconds. Then she left the room and closed the door behind her.

I finished packing, set two alarms, and went to bed alone.

The airport people were still blinking early morning from their eyes while they checked my bag through to Sacramento. The line at security was just beginning to build. Untying my shoes, putting them into a plastic bin, I hated terrorism all over again. Because of having to take off my belt and the yuck of walking in a public space in only socks. My feet would resent it the rest of the day.

Something about my backpack disturbed the security people. They took me aside and made me unpack. In the front pocket was a zip-lock bag, a little first aid kit, with tubes of antibiotic ointment, toothpaste, and anti-itch cream.

"Sir, you were instructed to remove this from your carry-on and put it in the tray."

"Yes, ma'am. I forgot." I felt like my pants were about to fall down.

"Please try to remember that next time."

"Yes, ma'am."

"Have a good trip."

"Thank you." I put on my belt, then I repacked my bag. When my feet were once again safe within their shoes, I entered the local patch of the world known as *inside security*.

It was very early in the morning—still the middle of the night on the west coast—hours too early to expect to hear from Sean. Even in the East the morning rush hour had not begun but the airport was in full gear. I bought coffee and stood watching people walk by. They looked tired, preoccupied, defeated. Old.

I went to my gate. There, through the floor-to-ceiling windows, I saw the jets—the aluminum-sheathed pencils in which I and dozens of other innocents were about to strap ourselves into docile rows and be hurtled off the ground by engines far too powerful to have any place in the humdrum daily existence of guys like me who avoid roller coasters. I checked to make sure I was forming up with the right clot of people to get on the correct plane to be blasted into the sky. It seemed insane and obviously things could go terribly wrong and yet they so very seldom did. And how else was I to rip across North America between breakfast and bedtime?

This trip, I reflected, was neither for business nor for pleasure. I hoped it would be a needless exercise, the kind of thing that happens as the young birds flap away from the nest, beyond the sight of the parent who's in the habit of giving care. Maybe the fledgling has landed within view of a predator, a hawk, and is in urgent need of protection. Or perhaps he has precocious abilities and is ready to look out for himself. The parent has no way of knowing.

The weather was wet. Between the tubular gang-plank and the cylindrical vehicle there was just enough space to feel the freezing mist. When the plane was pushed away from the gate it taxied to a location where it could be sprayed with blue liquid to remove ice. They made it blue, I supposed, to remind you of windshield washer fluid, to make it seem familiar and reliable, to reinforce the illusion that it was rational to ride in a cold metal object through freezing rain in the hope of getting above the clouds before the ice-weight brought you down.

The flight attendant didn't seem concerned. She did this all day, every day, and experienced mostly tedium. If she could stand it I could, too, I supposed—but then she started talking. Her sing-song delivery made me cringe. She said everything in an odd cadence that emphasized the final syllable. "Regulations require your seatbelts to be securely fastened. You may be required to assist the crew in the event of an evacuation. Use caution when opening the overhead bins—" I thought she would drive me crazy. I decided to decline to help in the event of an evacuation if it was she who asked me but if it was someone else and they spoke in a normal voice, I would cooperate.

The plane trundled along until it made a long slow turn to face its runway. After a pause, the engine whirred, the aircraft accelerated, the wheels rumbled and then fell silent as the ground receded. I saw Boston's lights in the dim gray air, briefly, before the cloud curtain closed.

Five minutes later we shot into the sunlit blue, headed west.

Chapter 15

In Philadelphia, between planes, I called Helen, but she didn't answer. Instead of leaving a message, I sent her a text: *Any word from Denver?*

Her response came quickly: *No. Try to relax.*

Life would be easier if you knew for sure what to worry about. She might be right. Maybe I *was* overreacting.

My next flight was to Dallas. Mindful that it would take more than two hours, I stopped in the bookstore on the concourse. Should I buy a *New York Times* or a mystery? Neither. I needed to get something going. I boarded the flight with a new notebook, ready to organize my thoughts. *Conversation.* What is it? What are its component parts? I should do my thinking then bury it in my brain, forget about it, and concentrate on the show. How to connect with viewers? How to make it entertaining?

Actors could perform vignettes. Followed by discussion. Or I could show scenes from movies, or from television, and talk about them. The guests could be entertainer-psychologists—or garden-variety celebrities. I had to be careful about intellectuals—they had done me in last time. Actors would be safer. Some are dumb but most are lively and they're experts, in their way, on talk. They could repeat lines using different timings, different inflections, and we could see how the meaning had changed. Literary conversations from my dad's list could be mixed in sparingly—very sparingly. Just a little Shakespeare to add a whiff of class. Maybe some George Bernard Shaw—once a year.

These would have been fun ideas to think about if my mind hadn't kept reverting to my worries. Was Denver okay? Was he already back at Greg's? How foolish might I feel to be all the way to Texas when I find out I should have stayed home? And to have been told so, in advance, by my wife?

Or maybe Denver was *not* okay. That would be far worse. Maybe he was in the power of awful people, having destructive experiences—or maybe he was dead—and it was my fault. Except for my influence he would have done what his dad had wanted him to do—write software—and everything would have been fine. My unrequested

Christmas present—the book about the Central Pacific—would end up feeling like a disaster.

Probably Helen was right, I reminded myself. Denver was a capable young man on an adventure. That led to fretting about Helen, about her Christmas in Europe, about the way she no longer seemed appropriate to her own house. Had I lost my hold on her?

Next came self-reproach for allowing myself to be distracted. To get something going I needed to keep my focus. My credentials, such as they were, were about talk. I needed to build on my strength, otherwise I would never amount to anything. Maybe it was hopeless. Maybe I should teach school as Helen had suggested. A high calling or a sellout? That would depend on my attitude.

Such ruminations occupied my brain as the plane shot five miles above the states of Tennessee and Arkansas and Texas. As soon as we landed I turned on my phone. There was a text from Sean reminding me that Nellie's brother's name was Luke and providing his cell number.

I called Sally. Denver had not returned and she had not heard from him.

As soon as I could find a reasonably quiet corner of the terminal I called Luke's cell. No answer.

I looked around. The faces in Texas—were they different, as a group, from those in Boston? If you allowed for the cowboy hats and the tooled leather belts with heavy buckles and initials in the back?

My phone quacked the way it does when it gets a text. It was from Luke's number. It said, *Hey Ike.*

Denver?

Si.

Where are you?

CA where r u?

On my way to Sacramento.

Why?

To make sure you're ok.

Im fine.

I'm coming. I'm halfway there. He made no reply. I added, *Where will I find you?*

After two minutes he sent, *Tomorrow at noon. Bring sandwiches. Top of Summit Tunnel.*

I responded: *?*

Tunnel 6. At shaft top.

What do you mean? I wrote, but nothing came, so I called the phone but was dumped straight into voice mail as though the phone had been turned off. "Denver? Luke? Denver, I could use a little more information than that. Please call me."

He did not.

I took comfort, though, from this contact. I went to a restaurant, ordered a beer and enchiladas, and called Sean.

"Hi Ike."

"Hey. Could you put me in touch with Luke's parents?"

"Just a second." After a pause he said, "Here's Nellie."

"Mr. Martin?" a young woman said.

"Nellie? I'm Ike."

"Ike, my parents are on vacation in Hawaii. I can give you my dad's cell."

I wrote the name and number on a napkin. After a swallow of beer, I dialed it. "Mr. Wong?"

"Yes?"

"My name is Ike Martin. My stepson Sean Shields is a friend of your daughter Nellie."

"Yes?"

"I'm sorry to intrude on your vacation but I'm hoping you can help me."

"How can I help you?"

"My other stepson, Denver, seems to be travelling with your son Luke."

"I guess they like each other, eh? All get along well?"

"So it appears. But I'm trying to find Denver and I wonder if you know where they are."

I could hear him say something in Chinese, not into the phone. Then he told me, "No, we don't know where Luke is. He goes all over in his car. He has a good time. We don't know where he is. Sorry." Although he was polite, nothing in his way of speaking suggested that Mr. Wong would buy into my problem.

I thanked him and said goodbye.

Before my enchiladas came I had searched *summit tunnel* on my phone's browser. There was a Tunnel Number Six on the original Central Pacific Railroad route running through the crest of the

Sierra Nevada, at Donner Pass. By the time I boarded the flight for Sacramento I knew the tunnel had been built by Chinese workers drilling and blasting day and night, winter and summer. Because they could progress only inches per day, they bored in from both sides of the mountain and outward, in both directions, from the middle, which they reached by a shaft from above. The top of that shaft, I concluded, must be Denver's rendezvous. I was supposed to meet him there with sandwiches so that we could be swept down the mountain in an avalanche, frozen, not found until spring.

On the third flight I rested, half-dreaming of mountains and railroads and snow. In Sacramento, as I placed my suitcase into my rental car, Julian called. He had just landed. We met at his baggage carousel.

"Julian 'The Wolverine' Deftworth at your service, Captain Martin," was his greeting. "What are your instructions?"

"My instructions are to find your bag and follow me to the car."

"We've come a long way," he said. "But the safety of the young persons is paramount."

"I've had a text from the principal young person, the object of our search."

"Helen's youngest. Boulder."

"Denver. He has appointed a meeting for tomorrow. High noon."

"Among the homeless, I presume?" Julian said. "Behind a certain dumpster. Or within it. I'll keep watch, outside. I've brought all light-colored trousers, good for California but unsuitable for dumpsters, for their interiors, which so often are smudgy, bedaubed with substances liable to stain good fabric."

"He's not inside a dumpster."

"At the famous marbles tournament, then, I suppose," he sighed. "In the men's room. Imagine me at a marbles tournament."

"Marbles tournaments have unisex port-a-potties," I informed him.

"Gross. And cramped. Unless it's one of the handicapped ones. They are somewhat more capacious. Still—"

"We are not meeting him in a port-a-potty."

"Good."

"He's not even in Sacramento."

"Drat. Have we come all this way in error?"

"He's in the mountains."

"In the mountains?" His expression suggested that *in the mountains* was much more dreadful than in a dumpster or in a port-a-potty. This was self-parody on his part. He liked mountains.

As my phone guided us to our hotel I told Julian what I had learned about Tunnel Number Six. I could see why Denver had become so interested. Thousands of tough, hard-working men from China had driven the tunnel against four faces of granite, living under the snow, working under the mountain, sometimes killed by the cold or by errant blasts.

"What about mountain lions?" Julian asked.

"What about them?"

"Were they another cause of death to the Chinese?"

"I don't know. Wikipedia didn't mention them. I suppose they could have been."

"And even now. I suppose your Watson could follow his Holmes into the jaws of a catamount."

"I don't think that's likely," I guessed. "Anyway, bears will be hibernating."

"I hope that mountain lions also hibernate."

"I don't believe they do."

"It's called the Summit Tunnel?"

"That's right. It's also called Number Six."

"We are to tramp to the summit of this famous mountain in the middle of winter? We, who have never scaled Everest, only the Catskills."

"It's a pass—not a peak," I explained with phony confidence.

Julian looked back at his map. "I know where we'll have supper," he said. "Then, to our well-earned rest, preparing for the dangers of the morrow."

We dined at the place he had chosen online, and it was good. As we walked down the hall toward our hotel room my phone rang. "Ike, it's Marjie."

"Hi."

"Where are you?"

"In a hotel in Sacramento."

"Did you find your son?"

"No, we just got here." Julian opened the door to our room.

"You and Helen?"

"No. She's in New York. Julian's here." I took the phone into the bathroom.

"Julian?"

"A friend of the family. How did you know I was out here?"

"Stephen said you had to break off your meeting with him for a family crisis, which worried me so I stopped by after school and ended up taking that girl who was staying there—Cindy?—to the airport."

"Susan."

"Susan, right. She was vague about where you were but she knew that one of your sons was missing and you were going to look for him."

"I can't believe she got you to take her to the airport."

"She needed a grownup with a car and there I was."

"She's not shy about her needs."

"I think she kind of likes you."

"I wish her well."

"How are you going to locate Denver? Is he okay?"

"I think he is. On the way out here I got a text from him. He told me where to meet him for lunch tomorrow. We'll be at the rendezvous and see what happens and take it from there."

She asked about Denver's dad and stepmother so I explained the situation and added, "I hope I'm not being a helicopter parent. Helen thought I should stay home but Greg asked me to jump in, so here I am."

"You couldn't just sit there not knowing where he was."

"You are nice to call," I said. She didn't say anything. I added, "It's sweet of you."

"Well, we are friends, right?" Marjie said. "Friends have to look after each other a little, don't you think?"

"I do think, yes. How may I reciprocate?"

"What do you mean?"

"What kind of looking-after do you need from me?"

"Oh. I don't know. Just helping my grandfather with his memoir— I'm glad you are doing that. And when you came over on New Year's, I liked it that you were interested in my teaching. Even though I didn't find much to say about it."

After I promised to come sit in her garden next summer and drink coffee with her and Mrs. Lu, we said goodnight.

In the morning Julian and I went to the REI to buy clothes for the mountains and to see if they had Denver's telephone. The store was closed. Had we waited for it to open we wouldn't have had time to reach our rendezvous. We resorted to a nearby Walmart, then headed northeast into the Sierra, in sight of the famous train tracks. Soon we were in the foothills. As he studied the map, Julian wore a serious, determined look I had not yet seen. He announced the point at which he thought we should stop for sandwiches. "After that there isn't much until Truckee," he told me. "And that's past the tunnel."

Twenty minutes later, as we came over a rise of ground, the Sierras soared into view ahead of us. Julian said, "This reminds me of Herman's place, with the mountains so near."

"Herman?"

"Yes, his place in Austria. I've been there, which is how I know that I'll be okay with this altitude even though I'm an aging city boy."

"Altitude?"

"Yes. We'll be climbing all morning, obviously."

It *was* obvious, now that he mentioned it, but it had escaped my attention.

"Most people have to acclimate," Julian said. "Some never can. We aren't going that high, though."

"How high are we going?"

"About 7,000 feet. The range crests at 13,000 but of course they brought the trains through the lowest pass they could."

"How do you know all this?"

"I looked it up. You're in good condition. The altitude shouldn't cause you any trouble."

"Who is Herman?"

"Well . . . you know . . . Helen's Austrian friend."

"Oh, *that* Herman," I said. "Her European lover," I ventured.

"Well, if you put it that way, yes," Julian said. "Enviable he, of the square jaw, the brawny build, and the extreme wealth. We see him mostly in New York, but he has entertained me in his villa."

"He's the complete package, isn't he? It's a wonder she's stayed with me at all." It turned out I could improvise even with my heart stopped.

"Well, she likes you, obviously. And I think she deeply appreciates what a good stepfather you have been."

"But the boys are growing up," I said, "Wouldn't she really rather be married to a rich guy?"

"Herman Mann is rich and he is powerful and he has glamorous connections. But he's a family man. You have no worries. He'll never leave his wife."

"So you think Helen will stick with me?"

"Yes. You've made yourself a very practical husband and that's what she needs from marriage."

"And as for excitement and romance, she knows where to find that when she needs it."

He looked at me. "I suppose you have a little something going on the side, yourself."

"No. I'm her eunuch. She keeps me busy with the chores and the babysitting."

"You did know about Herman, right? I didn't mean to—"

"I know about him," I said. "The question is, what am I going to do about him? This car has satellite radio. Want to hear some music?"

Both of us were ready to end the conversation in which I had lied to learn. No wonder Helen had tried to get Julian out of the house. I had once suspected Julian of being a rival but I'd been barking up the wrong tree. I felt clubbed. Stunned.

But I didn't stay that way. As minutes went by I began to realize how much this explained that I'd never understood. The eunuch image was almost right—perhaps most eunuchs made fewer sexual demands, but Helen had never seemed to mind—that was a price she was happy to pay for a father for her children and a respectable front. Romance was elsewhere, safely isolated from reality. Memories of Helen's many absences brought painful imaginings.

The snow lining the highway became deeper and deeper.

Julian's phone rang. As he listened to whomever had called, I glanced at him. His expression was serious. "I will," he said. He became pale. "I can't," he said, then he listened. "Yes. As soon as I am able." Another pause. "I will, but I have something to do first." Finally he said, "Okay. Goodbye," and closed his phone.

"Is everything okay?" I asked.

"No. Trouble, with a capital T and a capital everything else."

"Personal or business?"

"Business. My presence is desired in the city, pretty damn quick, as they say."

"What do you want to do?"

"These towns must have something like a taxi service—someone who drives for hire."

"Want me to take you back to that last town?"

He considered. "No," he said uncertainly.

"Are you sure?"

"Let's find the kid."

"He's probably okay."

"Let's find him. Then I'll head on back."

We continued to the town Julian had chosen as the place we would stop for sandwiches, bought them in a small market, and proceeded into the National Forest until we reached the ranger station. Its parking lot was surrounded by a wall of snow. Inside, a uniformed Forest Service ranger looked up from his desk and said, "Good morning."

"Hello," I said. "I hope you can help me. I'm trying to locate my stepson, who might have been camping up here although it doesn't seem possible with the snow so deep."

"You'd be surprised," he said, standing up and coming to the counter. "We have sites in use all year round."

"I'm looking for a seventeen year-old-kid, five-ten, brown hair, named Denver Shields."

"I'd like to help you. But the Service has privacy policies. I'm not supposed to divulge our registrations."

"Yeah but this is a missing kid, last known to have been in the Sacramento REI and he wants me to meet him for lunch on top of the Summit Tunnel, wherever that is."

"If he's missing how can you have an appointment?"

"He sent me a text," I said. "Through his friend's phone. I haven't heard from him since then and I don't know whether he'll show up at noon or whether there is such a place or whether if there is whether he can get to it with all this snow or whether I can get there. And what about avalanches?"

"He and the other kid left their campsite about an hour ago," the ranger said. "I know that because I told them how to find the trail that goes up the old rail line. The skiers and snowshoers use it."

"Can you walk it in boots?"

"Not by a long shot. Not with this snow cover. You need skis or snowshoes and if you use skis, you better be good. No avalanches though, not here."

"Where's the campsite?"

He took a map from a stack of them they handed out to campers and marked, with practiced flourishes, the location of Denver's tent and the route from there to the railroad grade. "From the trailhead it's a mile up to the west entrance to the tunnel, which we had to block off. The trail goes up and over. The top of the shaft is covered with steel plates."

"Where can I get snowshoes?"

"If you're going to hike up before noon you'll have to borrow a pair of mine."

When I returned to the car with the ranger's snowshoes, Julian said "I gather that you plan to give chase on foot."

"Right," I said. "Should I have asked for a second pair for you? I assumed not."

"You assumed correctly. It's too cold. I'll see how close I can get with the car."

We turned into the campsite. I struggled into the snowshoes, found the trail, waved goodbye to Julian, and trudged off, uphill. It was not my first time on snowshoes but I was clumsy and I noticed the altitude right away. The chill was sharp. The trail led uphill. I stopped and filled my lungs. The snowshoes were heavy. I was well over a mile high and I had to go higher. Over my shoulder I watched Julian drive the rental car back the way we had come. With a start I realized that I had left the lunches in the car. Even if I was able to make it to the rendezvous I wouldn't have the sandwiches.

I started up the hill. Gradually I settled into a pace that I had the strength and wind to sustain—a rhythm of breathing and walking. Treetops protruded through the snow; the trees were mountain-stunted and the snow was deep. The sky was so blue it tinted my shadow. My chest hurt. The steady exertion concentrated my thoughts, and what they focused on was Helen and this tale of Julian's. The misery of my position, the humiliation, descended on me, then dissipated as I trudged uphill. Before long, all I felt was free. I perspired and drew in the thin air and forged ahead with all my strength and felt the gate swing open to the next era of my life.

My heart pounded in the stillness. The heels of the snowshoes shushed behind me. I was alone in mid-winter in the Sierra Nevada. The temperature was in single digits. Rugged peaks towered on either side of the trail. I reached the sealed-off entrance to Tunnel Number Six—only the top of it was visible above the drifted snow—and struck the steepest climb of all where the trail skirted the face of rock the tunnel had been cut into. The snowshoes' cleats prevented me from slipping backward. I took small steps and kept going.

Once above the tunnel my angle of climb diminished and I had a better view. In the distance I thought I could see people. Did they wave? Did one set out in my direction?

At first he was too far away for me to recognize his face but I kept hiking toward him, panting. He, coming downhill, closed the distance quickly. Presently I could make out Denver's smile. "Ike!" he shouted, "You're here!"

We hugged and I tried to catch my breath. "You're okay?"

"Yes. That old man brought the sandwiches. We didn't wait for you because Luke and I were hungry."

"What old man?"

"The man who says he came with you. Is he that friend of Mom's?"

"Julian? Julian found you?"

"Yeah. He drove up. There are roads all over the place. They've built a subdivision up there."

"You had lunch?" I was starting to catch my breath. Looking up, I could see two people at the summit.

"Yeah, sorry. We saved some for you, though."

I was excited and altitude-addled and wasn't able to process Denver's explanation. I couldn't make sense out of Julian getting there before me. But there he was, with his shiny cheerful face, standing beside a serious-looking lad at the center of a sheet of heavy steel. "One hundred twenty-four feet straight down, Ike," Julian told me. "Then the bottom of the tunnel stops you."

"I am extremely surprised to find you here."

Julian just smiled. He had driven back to the ranger station, requested automobile directions, and learned that he could drive all the way. He had parked in a nearby cul-de-sac and walked the short trail to the shaft—there was no snow accumulation atop the ridge; the wind swept it off.

Halfway through my sandwich I turned to Denver. "Do you know where your cell phone is?"

"I know where I put it."

"Where was that?"

"In a sleeping bag at REI."

"Why'd you do that?"

"Because I wanted to go on a trip without being pestered," he said.

"Is my being here in the pestering category?"

"I dunno, maybe, but I told you where to find us otherwise you wouldn't be here."

"True."

"I guess you wanted to go on a trip, too."

"I guess I did," I said.

"I guess I did, too," Julian said. "But now that the family's reunited I have a business need to get to the airport."

"Okay," I said, "What are we going to do about that?"

"The Sacramento airport?" Luke asked.

"Any airport with connections to New York," Julian said.

"I could take you to Sacramento," Luke said. "I ought to get home—I'm supposed to be watering the plants and taking care of the cat." He looked at Denver. "But you want to go to the Truckee Historical Society and library and everything and so if you want to stay with your dad, I mean, sorry—"

"That's okay," Denver and I said at the same time.

Luke and Julian drove the rental back to the campsite, where they left it for me, picked up Luke's gear, then headed back down the west slope of the Sierra in his car.

As soon as they were gone Denver started talking about the vertical shaft that we stood beside, blasted down through granite to the center of what would become the summit tunnel so that this longest, highest Central Pacific tunnel could be bored from four surfaces at once because time was money and the railroad couldn't build east across Nevada and the Great Basin until it could run trains through the Sierra. "They used that tunnel until the year I was born! They finally changed the route in 1993."

"When did they build it?"

"1866 and '67."

It was too cold to stand still in the wind for long. We started down the way we had come. Denver kept it up about constructing the railroad through the mountains, the engineering required, and the role of the Chinese. He was wondering out loud about how, without lasers, the civil engineers managed to make the tunnels meet each other, when we got back to the campsite. We struck the tent, returned the snowshoes, thanked the ranger, and headed for Truckee, which was a few miles and a slight drop to our east. My cell phone had a series of texts from Luke.

He says we could have been eaten by a mountain lion.

He says I would like somebody named Camo.

He says he can't wait to get back to New York.

He's singing: Start spreading the news—

Denver spent several hours taking notes and making photocopies at the library. I took a deep breath and called Helen. "You were right," I told her. "Denver's okay and there's no sign that he needed rescuing."

"I'm too good a girl to say I told you so."

"On the other hand we're having a great time and I'm really glad I came."

"Hooray."

"And when I get home I'll be moving out of your house."

After a beat of silence she asked, "Why?"

The hours I had had to prepare for this conversation had allowed me to realize that the why was not because of the Austrian who after all might turn out to be a figment of Julian's imagination.

"Because I'm ready."

"Are you serious?"

"Yes."

"We need to talk about this in person."

"Agreed."

It was pleasant to think about renouncing my eunuch status and seeking a life as a full-fledged adult man. Ruminating on the future filled the rest of the time at the library and all of the hour Denver worked at the local museum. When he was ready to leave we went out to the parking lot. "Cupertino?"

"I guess—"

We got in and drove away, but before we reached the interstate he said, "Or we could explore the rest of the Central Pacific Railroad route if you feel like driving to Utah."

Which I did. I skipped the I-80 West entrance, took East instead, and we descended into North America's Great Basin.

Chapter 16

Denver said he wasn't so sure about MIT after all. He was glad I'd made him apply to other colleges and maybe if they took him he'd go to Bowdoin and study history.

I tried not to look happy.

Although I wanted to tell him that I planned to get my own place, I did not, because I had promised to discuss it with Helen in person and it seemed neither fair nor prudent to say anything about it to Denver before I had looked into her pretty eyes and listened to her say whatever she had to say and then persisted in moving out. Who knows how she would respond? She might tell me that, yes, she had had an affair but it was over and I was her own true love. Or she might swear she had never looked at another man and throw dirt on Julian's credibility.

Denver told me that Sean's new friend Nellie planned to apply to medical school and was studying for the medical school admissions test. He said her brother Luke played the same video games he did and was pretty good but he had never shot marbles and he thought it was cool how well Denver could do that. Luke wanted to go to Berkeley and become a physicist but he wasn't sure he was good enough at math.

Denver pronounced Sally and her baby *okay* but on the whole he hadn't found Cupertino and its environs much to his liking. He had enjoyed the food Sean had brought home from the fancy restaurant where he and Nellie worked.

Denver's effusion of talk then reverted to the 1860s, to the eastward push by the Central Pacific Railroad, the invention of nitroglycerin, all the accidents it caused, and the other emerging technologies of the day. "It was all so new!" he said, speaking of steam-powered transportation and the telegraph and photography.

"The nineteenth century had its share of Bill Trippys."

"That's that guy you know, right?" Denver said.

"Yeah."

"How do you know him?"

"He was a guest on my show then he hired me for a while, until he had a stroke."

"Luke and Nellie were talking about him," Denver said. "I guess he's famous."

"It's funny—he and some of his family flew west the same day I did. Bill likes to visit Yellowstone Park in the winter."

"That's where the geyser is, right?"

"Some geysers and lots of wildlife."

"Maybe it stays warm there because of the steam?"

"I think it gets cold. It must be interesting. We should go there sometime."

"It was cold in these mountains that winter they were making the tunnel," Denver said. He resumed that theme with renewed fervor. I had never seen a young man more taken up by a subject than Denver was with the Central Pacific Railroad. He seemed riveted by every aspect—the snow tunnels, the blasting, the small physical size and reliable vigor of the workers. He was in the spell of having found something he wanted to learn everything about. My equivalent was the subject of talk, but at my stage of life such joys were less pure. They had to share attention with making a living and family and relationships and to-do lists.

When Denver stopped talking, I took my turn. I described the holidays with my family—Henry and my sister and my little nephew. And the artists at our house and the party they threw. And Mrs. Lu and fortune cookies and Susan's mural.

"Susan is an interesting person," Denver said.

"Yes," I agreed, and expressed my train of thought about Susan possibly becoming mild and home-motherly and, listening to myself, I realized that I was talking to Denver as to an adult friend, which had never happened before.

That was as we roared across Nevada in my rental. In Utah, we were still high on life and learning. Our destination was Promontory Summit, north of the Great Salt Lake, where they drove the golden spike at the place where the eastward-built Central Pacific met the Union Pacific, which had built west from the Missouri River. We spent the night in Tremonton assuming we would head back to Silicon Valley in the morning, but at breakfast I remembered that Bill Trippy was at Yellowstone, which was not that far away. I mentioned the possibility of driving up for a look.

"I have to write up my project," Denver said.

"Okay, I'll get you back to your dad's."

"I could work on it in the car. We could go."

So I called Sally—Greg still wasn't back from China—and told her our plan. She fussed a little but it didn't sound like she had any real objection; she was either naturally suspicious of spontaneity or she thought good form required her to quibble. We headed north for West Yellowstone, Montana, crossing the foot of Idaho to get there.

The west entrance and most of the park roads were closed for the winter. We drove up and around to the north entrance and into the park as far as the hotel at Mammoth Hot Springs. There we saw elk, which gave us the feeling of being in a different time and place.

The Trippys were not at Mammoth. They were near Old Faithful at a lodge that could not be reached, in winter, except over the snow. That lodge was full for the night, which didn't matter because we had already missed the last snowcoach. There was a room open for the next night, which I reserved.

That left the question of where to spend the present night. Although the hotel at Mammoth was technically full the clerk thought he could find a place for us. I said that I had noticed the campground was open and we had a tent. He said, okay, but the overnight forecast was for twenty below zero. We took the room.

In the morning Denver worked for an hour on his school project, then we explored Mammoth's hillside of hot springs and shopped for souvenirs. In the afternoon we boarded the snowcoach for the geyser basin—the complex of "thermal features" with Old Faithful as its centerpiece. A huge old inn serves visitors in the warm months but in the winter overnight guests are limited to the newer, smaller Snow Lodge, which we entered with our luggage. We encountered Ev Trippy in the lobby. He did a double take. "Hi Ev," I said. "This is Denver Shields, my stepson. We were in the neighborhood and thought we'd stop by."

Ev didn't seem particularly happy to see me. Maybe he'd always suspected me of being a leech and my unexpected appearance deep in Yellowstone National Park reinforced that view. "Dad's over there," he said, nodding toward a chair near the fireplace. "He says you are back on his case. I'll be interested to hear how that came about."

"Stephen asked for help," I hastened to explain. "I assumed that you—" then I stopped, because I sounded defensive to myself. I said, to Denver, "Let's say hello to Bill," then turned back to Ev and asked if they'd been having fun.

"We're headed for the Bay Area tomorrow—for a conference. Marjie and Stephen are coming later and they'll take Dad home."

I didn't see how that answered my question but then again I didn't really care whether Ev had been having fun.

Bill looked old and tired. He had a drink in his hand. I introduced Denver. As Bill squinted at him I added, "Denver is Helen's younger son."

"Whose?" Bill asked.

"My wife. Helen Marsh. You remember her."

"Oh—Helen—yes."

"Have you been here many times, Bill? In winter? This is amazing to see—the interplay of hot water and cold air."

"I brought my wife and kids when I was younger. We went everywhere on cross-country skis. Now the wolves are back and I come to see them."

"The wolves."

"The elk were getting out of hand. I think the wolves are helping. I'm not sure." He started looking around as though to find a park naturalist who could answer the question he had raised.

"You're probably wondering what we're doing here," I suggested, although he showed no evidence of surprise or curiosity.

"I think you are going to tell me."

"Denver's been researching a school project about the transcontinental railroad. The western part—" I looked at Denver. "What was it called?"

"Central Pacific," he said.

"The Central Pacific," I repeated. "And we followed the route to Promontory Summit, you know, in Utah, where they drove the golden spike, which isn't all that far from here and Denver had heard so much about you, and he had never been to Yellowstone and you'd told me you were coming, so we thought we'd look in."

Bill brightened. "What's the focus of your paper?" he asked Denver.

"At first it was the technology," Denver said, "like, the power of their locomotives."

"They weren't very powerful," Bill said. "Extremely inefficient."

"Now I want to find out how they surveyed the tunnel," Denver said. "How they could make it line up. And the workers from China— I'm interested in them."

"I have a Chinese friend at MIT," Bill said. "He's done amazing things. They built airplanes in caves during the war."

"Wow," Denver said.

"Seen the sights here yet?" Bill asked.

"I signed us up for the snowmobile safari in the morning," I said. "They go out early."

"Not all that early," Bill said. "That's the one bad thing about coming here in the winter. Short days. You can dress for the cold but there just aren't many hours of daylight. This far north. This time of year."

"Bill," I said, "Denver and I have a question for you. How would you compare the engineers of the present day to those who built the railroads way back when?"

"We have it easy," Bill said, "because we know what materials will do. Everything has been measured and tested and laid out in tables. In the old days, those guys had to have a feel for what would work. For example, railroad trestles. They had to go by their gut because they didn't have data."

"Almost by intuition," I said.

"Well, yes, I suppose," Bill said. "That's not the word I'd use. Maybe it's right. Then came the universities—the big state universities—they studied everything and laid it all out. Still, though, you have to be clever to solve a problem before somebody else does. Everything's a race."

Denver started to ask Bill a question but couldn't decide how to say it. I thought his awkwardness made Bill uncomfortable. Before Denver could stop stammering and express himself Bill told us he had some things he'd better do before supper, and, with difficulty, stood up. "Want an arm, Bill?" I offered mine. He waved me off.

In our rooms, we got on the wireless network. Denver put in earbuds and watched a television program on his iPad. I wrote an update about where we were and emailed it to Helen, Greg, Sean, and my mother.

Around the Old Faithful area walkways were cleared of snow. I decided to go out to stretch my legs and to breathe some fresh air. Denver preferred to stay put.

I thought ahead to my upcoming conversation with Helen. During my snowshoe hike at the Summit Tunnel I had formed a clear resolve—but with more oxygen in my brain I wondered what Helen would say when we talked it out in person. Could she convince me that the alleged European attachment was a spiteful ruse of Julian's? Would inertia, or soothing words and actions from Helen, dispel my intention? If not, if I continued my plan to move out, how would that affect the boys? It couldn't be a good time to disrupt home for Denver, just as he was poised to go to college. Could I deal with the guilt of letting him down at this sensitive point in his life?

That was the rub. How to balance the value of Denver's well-being with my own life choices? I thought that my perception of my needs was fallible and subject to change and so were my guesses as to what was best for Denver. How dare I shake things up? Then I remembered Julian's highly credible revelation of an Austrian man who wouldn't leave his family for his American girlfriend and again felt the humiliation of being her wedded au pair while her heart was in the pocket of a wealthy man's man.

That's where I was, mentally, when Old Faithful erupted. In bright moonlight its spout and plume of steam reached into the frigid sky. It had not quite subsided when I felt a tap on my shoulder and turned to find Stephen Pfeister—Marjie's Stephen. "We're here!" he informed me. "Are you going on the Sunrise Safari? We are. If you want to go you better hurry up and make a reservation. It's probably too late, though."

"Thanks for letting me know." I had booked two seats, on the phone from Mammoth. Why did he have to be so obnoxious?

"Marjie's visiting with her parents and grandfather. I thought I'd take a look around. They say you found the kid. Looks like you've lost him again already."

"Yeah, I'm not doing much right these days."

"Keep trying—you'll catch on. So, we're back to work on Bill?"

"Yes. Sorry I had to scurry out of the Black Horse that way. As soon as I get home I'll roll up my sleeves."

"When you can take an hour off from pleasuring those hot young artists you keep around the house."

"Right. I want to come get my stuff."

"What stuff?"

"My material about Bill. The notes and photos and clippings I gave you after he had the stroke."

"Okay. Man it's cold out here. I'm going in."

"All right. See you in the morning."

"At breakfast?"

"On the safari."

"Oh yeah. If you can get in. Good luck."

It wasn't time for our supper seating, so I could walk off some of my annoyance before I needed to collect Denver. I headed out one of the moonlit paths wondering why Stephen made himself so difficult. No one else was outside the lodge, so I thought, until I came upon a young couple.

"Would you take our picture?" the man asked. They were in a wide place in the boardwalk that, in season, allowed admiring crowds to gather in front of one of the colorful hot springs.

The woman's face was slender but her stomach bulged beneath her parka. "This is our last pre-baby adventure," she said. She was arm-in-arm with her husband. When he stepped forward to hand me his camera, she came with him. When they stood still and smiled they had an aura of serenity. After I took several pictures we huddled to look at them. The man, standing between me and his wife, removed his glove to operate his camera. He watched her as she viewed each exposure, as if to gauge her reaction.

"Want more?" I asked after they had seen the first batch.

"If you don't mind," the woman said. She hoped for a photo that matched the way she felt about them as a couple—that was my guess. She wanted them to look harmonious and supportive of each other—a trust-solid unit advancing to the next phase of their lives. As I took additional exposures I wondered whether she was realistic about what a couple, a marriage, could really be. I remembered my question to my father. Could these two be each other's constant joy? Would the minor irritations of daily life not erode their solidarity?

In the camera's flashes they looked healthy, content, and attractive. I envied them a little, but they cheered me and I lingered in their radiance until the man said, "Thank you," inflected to imply that I was once again a stranger—inviting me to resume a stranger's distance.

The woman had sounded both confident and vulnerable. In her voice I could hear, or imagine, her pride and pleasure at having married, not necessarily the boyfriend she most liked to remember, but the one she and her friends had agreed was the best husband material and now, in pregnancy, she relied on him. She felt that she had chosen well and was in good hands.

As I walked back toward the Snow Lodge I thought of my own marriage. Had Helen and I ever felt the way these two appeared to feel? I couldn't recall that we had. Then I remembered an evening in Florence, a champagne picnic on the roof of our hotel. She had seemed pleased with me—her mild-mannered nice guy, her volunteer daddy-man, not rich, unlikely to be powerful. She fed me cheese and kissed me and turned me on. If someone had taken our photo that evening would we have made the same impression as these two had tonight?

We had drawn apart since then. How much of the distance between us was my fault? Maybe I had pulled away, resenting, unconsciously, that we had no child of ours, or afraid of her glossy hyper-prettiness, or maybe her being five years older was more of a problem for me than I admitted to myself. I had to consider these possibilities.

Then too, I felt sorry for Helen because I didn't think she had ever been close to anyone. Probably when they handed baby Sean to her she had expected a wave of sentiment that never came. Instead he was, to her, a needy little bundle. She was like her parents—all three of them had lonely hearts. Helen had a low emotional valence whereas I bonded rather promiscuously. Not in the sexual sense—but my sympathies were easily attracted.

Which was how I had gotten myself a stepson to begin with. When I returned to the room, there he sat, still in earbuds, exactly where I had left him, staring at his iPad as though no time had passed. At supper he told me more about Greg and Sally and the fun he'd had with Luke, and I had to decide all over again how much to complain about his behavior. It struck me as age-appropriate and rather well done. I couldn't bring myself to give him a hard time.

The next morning it was dark and snowing as we boarded the snowcoach for the Sunrise Safari. Marjie and Stephen got on after we did, looking as sleepy as I felt. We exchanged waves and they sat down two rows in front of us. For five minutes, other reservation-holders straggled aboard. Then a member of the hotel staff appeared and said, "Marjory Trippy?"

Marjie held up her hand. The man spoke quietly to her, and she and Stephen followed him off the coach. Marjie cast a confused look back over her shoulder at me.

They had not returned when the snowcoach pulled out. By then there was a little light in the sky. As we moved away from the lodge, the world through the windows gained depth—a monochrome scene with a snow-covered foreground, a black band of trees, and a dark gray sky—an upside-down image blurred by falling snow. The guide's voice came over the intercom, friendly and wide awake, narrating the history of the park, the construction of the inn, and reporting bits of information about the nearest thermal feature.

A bison appeared, black against the white ground, its profile blurred by the mantle of snow on its back and head. More bison came into view, walking in the dim light. I traded seats with Denver so he would be next to the window. The guide told us about bison.

Half an hour out we stopped at an overlook. By then there was somewhat more light. The guide pointed to a dark spot in the valley below. It was a dead elk, she told us, and there was enough of it left to keep the wolves interested.

"It's hard to see them through this snow," she said, and we had no binoculars, but we could make out motions—comings and goings. We took our turn at the tripod-mounted telescope through which, sure enough, we saw wolves. Free-living wolves tearing meat from a carcass. Denver wore a big-eyed expression that made me glad we'd come to Yellowstone.

When we returned to the Snow Lodge an ambulance was backed up to the entrance. My heart sank because I associated it with Marjie and Stephen having been taken off the tour. As we entered the lobby a gurney turned the corner. It was Bill. His eyes were closed. His face was not covered but its extreme pallor, and the unhurried pace of the attendants, conveyed the worst. Ev and Kathy, red-eyed, walked behind the gurney, followed by Marjie and Stephen. Marjie was weeping. When she saw me she stepped over and put her arms around my neck. "Another stroke," she whispered. As I started to return her embrace, she pulled away and went to her mother, leaving Stephen by himself, wearing an expression I couldn't read.

Denver and I followed the family outside and watched the ambulance crew slide Bill and the gurney into the vehicle, respectfully, but with a detachment that suggested disappointment that there was no occasion for the life-saving skills they had labored to acquire. Their silent compliant burden was not at all like Bill. Bill would have made suggestions.

As the ambulance doors closed the couple I had photographed the previous night emerged from the lodge. Perhaps they'd heard it whispered, *a man died here last night. They're taking him now.* Or they knew nothing and only reacted to the emergency vehicle with natural interest. I don't think they recognized me. They moved on quickly—their courtesy overruled their curiosity.

The ambulance eased quietly away, without flashing lights. The family plus Stephen folded inward and followed Ev back inside. Marjie approached me again and said, "We are packing then following Grandfather to Bozeman."

I nodded.

By the time Denver and I had made up our minds to join the informal cortège the family had left. We checked out of the lodge without any plan other than to drive to Bozeman. In the car Denver retreated into music. I let him go and grieved for my friend Bill Trippy.

When we reached the city I realized that I had no idea where they had taken Bill or where the family was or what they were doing next. Out of sympathy and respect we had followed but we had nowhere to pay that respect. I could have texted Marjie but I decided to leave her alone. We were on our own. We found a motel and decided the next day we'd return to California. That evening we thought we'd see a movie, but it turned out there were competing cultural offerings, including a theatre that had seats available for that night's show. I reserved two tickets. After I emailed Helen the news of Bill's death, we went out to supper, then to the theater.

The production was a play with a small cast, no scenery, and few props. Its protagonist was portrayed at different ages, in philosophical conversations. His youthful idealism was challenged by questions from a jaded public defender named Caligula Odds. The protagonist resisted his cynicism, but in the course of the play he came to personify it. By the final scene the tables had turned completely, with the aging nonhero defending his self-centered materialism in dialogue with a kindly, thoughtful rabbi.

I might have been able to put all this down as a strange coincidence if Stephen had not so recently told me the name of his litigator. When the lights went on I examined my program. The playwright was not Stephen Pfeister. The author credit went to a man from Tennessee and the premiere had been ten years earlier. In spite of myself, in disregard of the program notes and all appearances, I wondered why Stephen pretended he had not finished his play when here it was already in production? And why had he used a pseudonym? But that was not my rational conclusion.

As we drove back to the motel, I told Denver that the man whose carelessness on his bicycle had forced him into a tree seemed to be a plagiarist.

"What do you mean?"

"He's always telling me that he's writing a play," I said, "and when he describes it, it's just like what we saw."

"Did he write it?"

"No, he claims to be writing it now."

"It was boring."

"Did you think so? I thought it was interesting, except I was distracted because of the Stephen thing."

"Why would he say he wrote that?"

"According to the program it's considered quite the distinguished contemporary drama."

"It's all talk. I guess I'm still in the action phase. Maybe I'll grow out of it."

"Not enough chase scenes?"

"Nothing blew up."

"Just relationships."

"It had heavy thoughts."

"And emotions."

"This is kind of random," Denver said. "I think Sean likes Nellie better than Susan."

"Susan is cool but she's awfully different than Sean. Did you like Nellie?"

"Yeah. And her brother. He hasn't grown out of the action phase either. He thinks he wants to study physics but he might be a philosopher."

"And yourself? Where are you?"

"I don't know. History is interesting. So is technology."

"There's such a thing as history of technology."

"Yeah. I could do that at MIT or somewhere else."

"MIT still looks good?"

"Kind of."

"But?"

"Geek central. I'm a geek myself but I might want non-geek influences. Are you going to tell his girlfriend?"

"Whose?"

"The phony guy's. She likes you, right?"

"Why do you think she likes me?"

"She hugged you."

"Oh. She was upset. They're engaged."

"Are you going to tell her?"

"I haven't been thinking about it—I've been talking with you."

"But, are you?"

"No. She must already know what he's like. It's not my place to rat him out. I don't think. What do you think?"

"I don't know."

"You thought it was boring?"

"Yeah. Why did Mr. Trippy die?"

"Marjie said he had another stroke.

"Does it make you sad?"

"Yes and no. It makes me sad in the way that all death makes everyone sad."

"Yeah."

"But he was old, he'd had a long rich life, and he didn't want a brainless lingering," I said. "He avoided that."

"Right."

"I'll miss him."

"Luke couldn't believe you knew him."

"He was a big deal."

"I guess."

"Your mother knew him, too."

"Did she?"

"Yes."

Chapter 17

Back in Boston, I took a shuttle to the satellite parking lot I always used. All the cars that had been left for more than one night were under eight inches of snow. I went to my approximate location and pressed the electronic key. Twenty feet away, my tail-lights flashed through the white.

Helen was supposed to be there when I got home—but she wasn't. Camo and Peter were in the driveway. I couldn't pull into the garage, because Bill's van was in the way. I lowered my window as Peter lifted one of the manure vats into the van. Camo came over to my car. "Hello, Ike. We're getting my stuff out of your way."

"Is my wife here?"

"Nobody answered the bell but it was not locked so we thought we'd just go ahead."

"That's fine." She had me pinned into the car. I was looking straight at her jacket where it bulged over her breasts.

"How have you been?" she asked, but rather than waiting for a reply she said, "Thank you for letting us stay here and have the party and all that. It was a good time. I got hired by Disney. They've cast me in several shows. You probably didn't know I could dance. And sing, some, although I have to work on that. I'll be getting back into voice."

"You're moving, then, to Florida?"

"Yes, I am but Peter's not—he's finishing school after he takes me down. We do okay—but we're too young, don't you think, to settle down, so we're going our separate ways for now."

Peter lifted the other vat and put it into the van.

"Won't Julian be sad when you're so far away?"

"I'll get up to the City from time to time."

"Will you still be making your corporate visitations?"

Peter jumped in. "I gave her the address of Disney Corporation. Wouldn't that be a good one?"

Camo backed away from my window enough to admit Peter into the conversational circle. "He wants me to bite the hand I want to feed me."

Peter smiled his friendly, mellow smile.

"What is your stage name? Does Disney call you Camo?"

"No, they use my real name."

"Camille?"

"Right. It's time for us to hit the road. Thanks again for everything." She gave me a quick, impersonal hug.

With warmer fellow-feeling, Peter and I shook hands. They got in Bill's van and drove away. I went into the house, where my wife was not waiting to have an important conversation.

After the night in Bozeman Denver and I felt that our trip was finished. We could have returned to Yellowstone but we decided that chapter, short though it had been, was over for us. Denver wanted to go to Greg's house to write up his project and then fly back home on the original schedule. Greg met us in Sacramento. Denver and I fist-bumped and he got into his dad's Lexus for the drive toward the coast.

At the airport, I proceeded to the rental car return. As the attendant checked the exterior, I searched the inside for stray possessions. Under the passenger seat I found an object with Denver's writing on it. It resembled a dumpling made of paper. I put it in my pocket and hurried into the airport. At security I emptied my pockets into a tray, for conveyance through the x-ray machine. When my tray had emerged from the dark tunnel, as I put on my belt, I read Denver's label: *Fortune Cookie for Ike*. It was taped shut. I borrowed a plastic knife from a food court restaurant, sawed through the tape, and unfolded what turned out to be a hotel coaster. Inside was a note on hotel stationery.

> Ike you rescue me whether I need it or not. Who rescues you? Thanks for the book and the trip. Sorry about Mr. Trippy. Your fortune: "Someone will ask you to edit his railroad project."

I thought, *Who rescues me? A kid.*

Flying west I had been preoccupied with Denver's whereabouts and safety. On the return trip I thought mostly of Helen's alleged long-term infidelity and what action I should take. Maybe she wasn't guilty. Taking into account the quality of Julian's information and the chances of his veracity to me, I put it between seventy-five and ninety-eight percent probability that there was a Herman Mann and that he was my wife's lover.

Intermittently I reproached myself for having let Denver off the hook too lightly. Shouldn't I have scolded him more for all the trouble he'd put me through? Maybe not. The whole point was to be absent without leave—otherwise it wasn't rebellion. There was no evidence, as far as I could see, that he and Luke had used poor judgment. Denver could have been sore at me for chasing him. He could have accused me of humiliating him in front of his new friend. But he didn't choose to; Julian and I just became part of what happened on his adventure— providers of sandwiches and trips to Yellowstone and hotel rooms.

After I arrived home and escaped being pinned in my car by Camo and she and Peter had departed, I went inside and found a note from Helen: *Shopping back soon.*

She hadn't appeared by the time I was unpacked. *Why should I leave?* I thought. I like it here. She could just stay in New York. But it was her house. Hers and Greg's. It had never been mine. If I wanted to split with Helen, I'd have to move.

My vest of many pockets, the Christmas present from Denver, was on a hanger in the closet in our study. I put the fortune cookie he had made into one of the pockets, then I turned on my computer. An email from Peter said *Here's my movie.* The hyperlink opened a file on YouTube. There sat Sgt. Decker in my kitchen. When I clicked *Play*, he started talking. "Oh, a Mountain Dew, thank you," he said, and then he said it exactly the same way four more times. Peter had repeated the clip. The next scene had people coming in the front door, looking around, taking off their coats, signing releases. But he didn't use the sound that went with that picture. Instead you heard excited breathing and erotic moans of the couple in the bedroom. Then Peter cut to Julian's espresso china getting broken, with its actual sound track.

I paused the video and checked to see whether Helen was home. She was not. I sent her a text: *I'm home. ?*

On edge, I returned to the party video. I had watched the next scene in real time—the couple alone in the upstairs hall, with their backs to the camera, as the guy began to kiss the girl's neck and ears, and to caress her hair with his fingers. Then it jumped to my bedroom with Susan and her friends dancing and drawing on the wall. A minute of that was followed by the big hairy guy hiding behind Denver's bed, then being found. In ones and twos, others piled on and beside him, giggling and making inaudible remarks.

From outside I heard a car door close—but it turned out to be the neighbors. On the screen, Julian addressed the camera. "Good evening ladies and gentlemen. My name is Julian Deftworth. Tonight is New Year's Eve. You join us not in Times Square but rather in a typical suburban domicile elsewhere in America." The picture belied Julian's claim that he looked younger on television. "Imagination, the creative spirit; these are at home everywhere," he continued. At this point, Peter cut to Susan and her friends dancing strangely, followed by the release of the sky lanterns, the still-dressed couple wrestling on the bed, and the curly-haired woman saying, "You can do anything."

I heard sounds downstairs. Helen had arrived. I went to greet her.

"Hello, Ike. Welcome home. I'm sorry I was so negative about you going out to find Denver. I was out of line about that."

"That's okay, no problem, really. What can you tell me about the Austrian guy Julian says you hang out with?"

Her face tightened. "He is my friend. His name is Herman."

Her admission that there was such a person made me believe that everything Julian had said was true.

"That's not why I'm leaving, though," I said. "At least, not directly."

"Far be it from you to be threatened by the competition."

"What a strange thing to say."

"You want us to be honest so there you have it."

"I don't remember saying I wanted us to be honest but I've always assumed that was a good idea. And now lately I hear you've had a big long-term secret."

"I didn't think you'd want to know about Herman. I've never been exactly the good little one-man story-book woman. I thought you were kind of aware of that, what with Bill and everything."

"I didn't find out about Bill until Thanksgiving. You've never given me any reason to believe you were playing around. You make it sound like it was right in front of me the whole time and it was my own fault if I didn't want to see it. Is that what you are saying?"

"No. Maybe. Jesus, Ike."

"Are you going to keep this place or sell it?"

"Ike, we have a good thing going. Why ruin it? I love you. Even if I have feelings for Herman I do love you. And it's not as though he has any visibility around here or with our family."

"Whether because your thoughts have long been elsewhere or because we weren't all that well suited to begin with, I don't know. Either way I've come to realize I don't love you—not in the hearts- · and-flowers way that I want to love a woman."

"If you don't love me why have you stayed around? Don't tell me it was for the boys."

"It's funny you should add that last part. Because it was for the boys you brought me in here to begin with, wasn't it?"

"No!"

"Yes. You wrapped your legs around me and fucked me until I couldn't see straight and that's how you made me their eunuch."

"Shut up, Ike. You're talking like a bastard."

"It wasn't for the boys, lately. Just for Denver."

"And now he's all grown up so you're ready to move on."

"Denver will be in my family all my life. Sean, too, if he wants to be."

We were in the living room. She sat down on the couch and started crying. Were these the same manipulative tears she would use to disarm a traffic cop? Or was she frightened and upset? Was there any possible way to tell the difference?

"I like having this house for our family," she said. "Herman's been a big help to us, you know."

"Is he rich?"

"Yes."

"Does he give you money?"

"He's a good client."

"Does he also give you money?"

"I sometimes dress beyond my means. Mainly he's been a huge help to my business as a client and an influential person. Other major clients have come my way because of Herman."

"He's rich and influential. Do you often get to Austria?"

"No. He's in New York a lot. And Paris. His family's in Austria—he's married with children and grandchildren and it's quite the family scene so I'm told. By Julian, who's been there."

"Yes. The California landscape reminded Julian of Herman's villa."

"And he told you so?"

"He made the remark assuming I knew all about it."

"Did he indeed?"

"He did. He thought I was happy to share you."

She had stopped crying. Her face looked like it always did. Her eyes had not puffed up. I pictured her as a child in conflict with her mother. Her father stayed aloof. By what age would Helen have established her dominance? Twelve? For sure. Was there a contest when she was ten? Maybe. Probably not. Imagining her at six I saw a little girl puzzled that her mother was so easily defeated. It was obvious who played what parts in the continuation of the drama—the Austrian was the distant father and I the subordinate service provider.

"Ike, I need you. Denver needs you," Helen said. "What if I promise to break off with Herman?"

"The way you need me isn't the way I want to be needed," I said. "It's time for me to go."

She cried. Her eyes reddened. "Ike, I don't blame you for being upset," she said. "You're a great guy and I've been a wayward wife—but only in that way. I've been good to you and good for you in other ways. Haven't I? Admit it—you're always fair. It's true, isn't it?"

"Yes in some ways but it's not the kind of relationship I want going forward and I need to move on."

"You are still angry and upset about Herman," she said. "And hurt. Of course you are. I'm sorry. You know better than to make any big decisions out of anger. I'll break with Herman. Give yourself a week. Okay?"

"The good news is I didn't feel angry when I made this decision," I said. "I wasn't thinking about your deceptions. I was in the mountains on snowshoes feeling light-headed from the altitude—and clarity came. Clarity!"

At that moment in her presence I felt just as free as I had in the Sierra. I was worried, though, because night would bring bedtime and she would do everything to please and to tempt. How would I react? She was lovely to look at and lovely to touch. I said, "If you want, we can give me a week to change my mind but meanwhile I'll be sleeping somewhere else. Tomorrow I'll be in and out as usual."

Helen just watched me.

I went to our study and closed the door and called my sister.

"Kate."

"Is something wrong?"

"Yes."

"Are you okay?"

"Yes, but I need a place to stay."

"Why?"

"May I come over?"

"Okay."

At her house, in her living room, Kate greeted me with news of Fievel's health and the consideration being given to acupuncture and her doubts as to whether the doggie yoga had been such a great idea. At first I thought she'd reached a new pitch of mutt preoccupation but then I noticed the tension in her face and decided that she was alarmed. Afraid of change. Her nerves had her chattering. She believed that Helen and I were a better couple than she and Jones; that we had more in common, more to talk about. That was true. She supposed this would give us more stability as a couple than she and Jones had—but of course there were other factors, dependencies that bind two individuals to a shared life that otherwise has little going for it. Perhaps I had been more timid than I should have been—but maybe in the end I was braver than my sister.

"So you and Helen are having a fight," Kate suggested.

"That's not how I would put it."

"If it's not a fight what is it? Jones and I don't fight much, like we don't yell at each other but they say fighting can be healthy for a relationship. That's what I've read. There's such a thing as good fighting. Probably Jones and I should try that but it doesn't seem to just happen, like, the distance isn't right. I hope you and Helen are having the good kind."

"Kate, I don't think I should go into it quite yet but I can say it's serious and I don't think it's good. It's not as though Helen and I are just working out some little misunderstanding. I'm still living there, basically, but I need a vacation from sleeping there for a few nights so if I could use your guest room that would be great."

"You might not like to sleep here though, because Fievel's kind of nocturnal and he paces up and down the hall all night. Not really all night but it seems like that because of how long the click-click-clicking can go on—you know—his toenails."

"I'll take a chance."

"And it's fine with me and Jones shouldn't have any problem with it but I better check because sometimes having people around makes him nervous."

"I could stay in a motel."

"No, we're family, we have a guest room. I'll check with Jones. It ought to be fine," she said. "But are you sure it's a good idea because sometimes, I don't know, in theory at least, sometimes the bedroom part can help couples through a rough patch—that's what they say— and it can kind of put everything else in a better light. For guys, at least. That's what I've read."

"That's the light I need not to see things in this week."

"A week. Okay. I thought you'd said a few days and that's what I was going to mention to Jones. But it's the week."

"I could stay in a motel."

"No, it's okay, I'll give you a key."

"It sounds like it would be better if I stayed somewhere else."

"I want you here. But Fievel might bark. He might snap at you once before he recognizes you. His protective instincts. He thinks he has to guard me. He might try to protect me from my own brother. I hope he doesn't keep you up."

She did give me a key and I left as soon as I could. I didn't know how or when she was going to check with Jones or how I would get her confirmation but it didn't matter. If she called and said *no go* I could get a motel room. I wished I'd done that to begin with rather than having applied through my sister to my brother-in-law to request a waiver of his presumed resistance. Why did they even have a guest room? I guess it would have been the kid's room if they had a kid but since they didn't they had to call it a guest room even if they didn't want any guests.

Driving back toward my house I passed the zoo. I decided to stop.

It was feeding time for the meerkats. What was I going to do about meals? Helen made us tiny carbohydrate-free suppers. Maybe I should offer to cook and make spaghetti with turkey meatballs—a menu served with broccoli, much favored by the boys and me. Helen pretended to approve and ate about one small meatball and two or three strands of spaghetti. What was normal supposed to look like if we

were too upset to sit down together to eat? I stood among my fellow
zoo-goers and watched the keeper describe individual differences
among emperor tamarins. Why had I told Helen that I would allow for
a week's cooling off? Thank goodness the boys weren't home. I felt
a wave of panic, like falling off a cliff. I tried to tune in to the keeper.
"Some are just amazingly patient," she said. "They might be males or
they might be females. It's just their temperament."

Maybe Mrs. Lu was here? I checked out everyone I could see. No
small Asian women. What would I have said to Mrs. Lu had she been
there? As little as possible, I guess, but I would have been glad to see
her anyway. Why was that?

My nerves swirled until I steered my thoughts back to my climb on
the snowshoes. I had just begun to calm down when my phone rang.

"Ike? It's Julian."

"Hello, Julian."

"Am I reaching you at a good time?"

I headed for an empty part of the building. "Yes, go ahead."

"I am surprised and confused and I wanted to check in with you.
But first of all, how was the rest of the trip for you and the young
man?"

"It was eventful. We went up to Yellowstone. Our friend William
Trippy was there, too, but he had a second stroke and died."

"How shocking. I am so sorry to hear it."

"Thank you. He was old. Otherwise we had a good time. And
you—how did your crisis pan out?"

"Satisfactorily, I am happy to say. As had been hoped, once on the
scene I was able to pour oil on troubled waters."

"I'm glad."

"Listen, Ike, I had a call from Helen. According to her you had not
been aware of her friend Herman prior to our conversation."

"Yes, that is correct," I said.

"Somehow when we discussed it I formed the impression that you
already knew about him."

"Conversation can be so confusing."

"Perhaps I made an unjustified assumption."

"Perhaps I was somewhat misleading."

"Ah." He paused. "Well, as you can imagine, Helen is furious with
me."

"And, as *you* can imagine, I don't care much about that one way or the other."

"Help me with this. The late gentleman, the one who passed at the geyser park, was he not also a friend of Helen's?"

"He had been, yes."

"And you were okay about that?"

"I was able to regard it as history."

"Whereas you learned from me or from me you formed the impression that her connection with the Austrian gentleman was ongoing?"

"Yes. That impression Helen did not see fit to correct." At this point a keeper brought food into the enclosure at my shoulder. Its resident, a macaw, screamed in excitement, drawing spectators my way. I walked around them to a calmer place. Next to the sloth.

"Helen tells me you are threatening to leave her. She is considering breaking off with Herman if it would keep you. She is very reluctant to lose you."

"Is she? Well, that would be a heavy price to pay, to stop cheating on me, because doesn't everyone have the right to a little romance in their lives?"

"Your anger shows through when you put it that way. She's upset at me and you are put out with her. I am sorry to have been the cause of such turmoil."

"You must find it entertaining."

"I prefer tranquility and I value the happiness of all my friends, among whom I count you. I hope that you will, in the long run, reciprocate, although that's of no consequence to you at present."

"Julian, after you told me about the situation with Helen I hiked up the mountain."

"Yes."

"Wearing snowshoes."

"Yes."

"I hadn't adjusted to the altitude."

"No."

"I felt hurt and humiliated at first but then I had a sense of enlightenment. By the time I reached Denver—"

"He went down to meet you—"

"I was clear and resolved."

"But mist and fog roll back," Julian said. "Be open to changing your mind. You have to recognize one thing about Helen."

"What's that?"

"She's an A-list lady. *A* for attractive. In the extreme."

"So?"

"A-list individuals are subject to temptations the rest of us don't experience."

"Okay."

"If you want to affiliate yourself with an A-list person you have to recognize that. I thought you did understand that, which, added to being misled, is why I spoke openly about Herman."

"Julian."

"Yes?"

"I'm not saying she's good or bad—I'm just saying it's not what I want. Maybe I was naive about the reality you refer to as A-list."

"Think it over," he told me. "Herman's a world-class guy."

"While I'm Joe Schmo."

"You and I are wonderful interesting talented people. But Herman's in a different category. Ike, heads of state return Herman's calls. He was an Olympic skier in his day. His resources know no bounds. It's just too much for her."

"Okay Julian. Time for me to go. Be well." I hung up.

Across from the sloths the tamarins were grooming each other. I looked around again for Mrs. Lu but she wasn't there. No one was there. I was alone with the animals.

I called Helen's cell.

"Where are you?" she asked.

"I'm at the zoo. I'm going to stay at Kate's tonight. I'll see you in the morning."

"I miss you," she said.

"I don't know what to say," I said.

That annoyed her. "Goodnight. Just say goodnight."

I did, and ended the call.

While I was having supper at a supermarket, from its hot bar, a text arrived from Kate. *Jones says ok.*

I went to a movie, then I let myself into Kate's and went to bed without seeing anyone. Maybe I'd make my peace with the reality of having an A-list wife and think how to balance the account. Then I considered, *No, here I am, away from her at night. This was the hardest part; I made it this far.* I fell asleep and rested well. Maybe Fievel clicked back and forth the whole time but I didn't hear him.

In the morning when I drove up to my house Helen's car was gone. I was glad because that meant I could settle into some work in the study before she returned from whatever she was doing. It didn't pan out that way, though, because she pulled into the driveway right behind me. When her car stopped, three doors opened. Sean and Denver emerged onto the pavement looking tired and put-upon.

"They took the red-eye," Helen announced. "I just picked them up."

"I thought you weren't coming home for another week," I said to Sean.

"We weren't," he said, "but Mom said you were having some kind of mid-life crisis or something and needed us here."

"Oh she said that, did she?"

"Yeah, what's going on?" Denver asked. "You seemed okay two days ago. Is it because your friend died?"

"I was okay and I still am," I said.

We all looked at Helen.

"He wants to move out," she announced. "I don't call that okay."

Sean seemed stunned; Denver looked hyper-alert.

"Let's go inside," I suggested.

The wheels of their suitcases sounded loud on the concrete driveway. We went to the living room and took the places we always sat in for family conferences.

The serious expression Sean had worn in the driveway was changing—he was melting down. He began to cry. Helen started crying, too, more to keep Sean company, I thought, than because she herself was upset. After all, she had me where she wanted me, face-to-face with the guys I loved, accused of intending to desert.

"Is it true?" Denver asked.

"Yes, that's what I'm thinking about. If I do, it's not about you guys. I love you both very much. But I don't think things have been going well for your mother and me as a couple."

"Couldn't you work on it?" Sean asked. "Get some counseling?"

"That's what I was thinking," Helen said. No lie-detector in the world would have let her get away with that. She wasn't the type to seek counseling. I was, and had suggested it about five years before, and been flatly turned down. "Shall we get counseling, Ike?" Helen asked.

I thought this was a stall so she could have time to get me sleeping at home and convince me that her affair was over and when I had been subdued she'd head back to New York and do exactly as she chose and I'd be just as much in the dark about her life as ever. Still, it wouldn't have been reasonable to refuse to go to counseling. All four of us knew that I was a reasonable guy. I had no choice but to agree.

Chapter 18

A therapist at the Three Rivers Counseling Center was available to meet with us the next morning at eight o'clock. I was in their parking lot at seven-fifty-five when a woman arrived and opened the office. I went into the waiting room and took a seat. At eight o'clock the therapist opened her door. "Mr. Martin? Is your wife coming, too?"

"Yes, but she's not here yet."

"Let's give her five minutes." She went back to her desk but left her door open.

Four minutes later I called Helen's cell. She didn't answer. I left a message: "We're hoping you are almost here."

The therapist rose and turned to me. "I'm Judy. We only have this hour. Do you think your wife will be here soon?"

"I hope so. She made the appointment. I haven't seen her yet this morning."

"Why don't you come in? You can start bringing me up to speed about what's been going on."

When I had settled into one of the chairs in her office she asked, "How long have you been married?"

"We've lived together nine years and have been married for eight."

"Your wife's name is Helen?"

"Yes. Helen Marsh."

"Do you have children?"

"Helen had two sons when we got together."

"How old are they now?"

"Denver is seventeen and Sean is nearly twenty."

"Do they live with you?"

"Denver does. He's a senior in high school. Sean's at college."

"Do they spend time with their biological father?"

When I had finished telling her about Greg and his business and Sally and their baby and the boys' holiday visit, Helen still hadn't arrived.

"Tell me about yourself," Judy said. "Is this your first marriage?"

She made notes as I gave her an overview of my childhood, my parents and siblings, my career in television, and the beginning of my relationship with Helen. I did my best to represent her fairly. It felt awkward that she wasn't there. I offered to try her phone again—but we agreed that one call was enough.

When I described my role in raising Denver and Sean, Judy stopped taking notes and just looked at me. She started writing again as I told about Helen's trips to New York. When I described the end of *Hubcaps*—Judy said she had often watched—and mentioned Bill Trippy, it became natural to allude to his relationship with Helen. "I learned about that last fall," I explained, "and I accepted the story that she broke off with him because of me." Judy looked up from her notepad again. "But last week Helen's friend Julian happened to disclose that about that time she met a rich, handsome, powerful, married, art-loving Austrian guy and she's been carrying on with him ever since."

"How did you feel about hearing this from her friend?"

"It was painful."

"That's your reaction to it? Pain?"

"Yes, but at the same time it is kind of liberating."

She nodded. "What did Helen have to say about this reported relationship?"

"She confirmed the relationship and offered to end it."

"What do her sons know about all this?"

That's when we heard the building door open. As Judy went to greet Helen I glanced at the clock. Eight-forty.

Helen entered the room talking. "I am sorry—have you started? Couldn't you have waited ten minutes?"

"The appointment was for eight," Judy told her.

"I thought it was eight-thirty," Helen said.

"Our sessions always begin on the hour and run fifty minutes. I wish, because this is an intake, that I could give you additional time this morning. But I have other appointments and we will have to stop at eight-fifty."

"All right," Helen said crossly.

Looking at Helen, Judy said, "Ike has been describing the history of your marriage from his point of view. I gather that things have reached a crisis, and that's why you are here today."

"Yes. We promised our sons we'd get help to work this out," Helen said.

"And just before you came in Ike was saying that the crisis was precipitated by a conversation, a disclosure, of a relationship of yours outside the marriage."

"I haven't been a perfect wife in every respect—but I'm willing to improve." Helen drummed her fingers on the arm of her chair. "That's why I'm here."

"Why don't you tell me about the beginning of your relationship with Ike," Judy suggested.

"I first met him on television. He had a little local talk show—did you know that?"

Judy nodded.

"My husband had moved to California and even before that he was too preoccupied with his start-up to be very present for his sons."

"You had an opening for a dad?"

"I did," Helen agreed.

"And here's this nice single guy on TV—"

"And cute, in his way, and when I happened to meet him in person he made a good impression. But none of that would have meant anything if he hadn't liked me and my guys."

"But he did like you and your sons and you became a couple."

"That's right," Helen said. I wondered if she knew how all this sounded. It was surprising but soothing, somehow, that she agreed, in the court of therapy, to these stipulations.

"And at that time and since that time you maintained other relationships with men."

Helen looked uncomfortable.

"But we're not going to be able to go into that," Judy said, "because we're out of time."

"We have two minutes left," Helen complained.

"Yes. I left time to tell you that I will have to refer you to another therapist and to explain why."

Helen sat back and scowled.

"The appointment was in your name," she said to Helen. "If Ike Martin had been mentioned, I never would have seen you to begin with. As we've been talking I have realized that I have to, in essence, recuse myself from working with you because I was a fairly regular viewer of Ike's show. I'm too much like a fan to work with you as a couple."

"I wish you had told us earlier," Helen complained. "Can you refer us to someone else?"

Judy could and did, and we stood up to end the session. As Helen and I started for the door Judy said, "One more minute with you, please, Ike." She shook hands with Helen and watched her out the door of her office and the waiting room. Then she came back inside and closed the door. We both sat down.

"I can't work with you as a couple," she said. "But I could see you as an individual if you want."

"Do you think I need that?"

"That's up to you. But while you decide I'll give you one question to think about." We heard someone enter the waiting room. "I'm just wondering why in the world you have been wasting your time in this marriage. That's my next client. We'll have to stop; please telephone if you want an appointment."

I called Sean from the parking lot. "Could I take you and Denver out to lunch?" I asked. He checked with Denver. They were agreeable. We set a time to meet at a fish place where we liked the chowder and coconut shrimp.

Before we hung up Sean asked, "How was the counseling?"

"Not such a great start," I reported. "Our appointment was for eight. Mom thought it was eight-thirty. And she was late for that."

"Ah," Sean said.

"See you later," I said.

I thought about what to do next. I decided to phone my *Hubcaps* collaborator, Anna McKnight.

"Ike!" she said. "What's going on?"

"Hard to know where to begin. I'm just back from the West Coast."

"Business or pleasure?"

"Family business that turned out to be a pleasure. What's doing with you?"

"Not a whole lot. Same old same old. Everybody misses you at IVB."

"Tell them hello for me. Listen, on the plane I started organizing my thoughts about that idea for a new show."

"What was that?"

"You called it *Taking the Talk*. Remember? About conversation. For entertainment and learning. Can we get together to discuss it?"

"It would be good to see you."

"So how about—"

"But first, before we spend more time on it let me check with some people."

"Okay. But wouldn't it be good to be able to sketch out an approach?"

"You know how it is," she said. "In the end they'll tell us what the approach would be. Let me run the basic concept by some people and then we'll see where we are."

"So you don't want to meet quite yet?"

"Give me a couple of weeks."

"Okay."

"The ball's in my court. I'll get back to you."

"Okay."

That was that. I needed to get something going and I had an idea, but my producer—if she still thought of herself as my producer—told me to chill. I was supposed to wait for the phone to ring.

The rest of the morning I spent at the gym, thinking about my experience at Three Rivers Counseling. Judy had impressed me as a person who was sympathetic but businesslike. *Why in the world have you been wasting your time in this marriage?* Was it professional for her to say that? I kind of liked it, though. I wondered whether Helen had made an appointment with the person Judy had referred us to. I might have to show up somewhere for that later in the day. I checked my phone. No text or voice messages from Helen. Why shouldn't I start looking for a place?

I considered telling my mother what was going on—but I decided not to call her yet.

Sean and Denver were waiting for me at the restaurant. We ordered chowder and coconut shrimp. Usually, as a nod to good nutrition, we all had side salads. Today, though, I asked if they wanted onion rings. They did.

When the waitress left to get our drinks I said, "I'm sorry you guys came home early."

"Don't worry," Sean said. "We get it."

"What do you mean?"

"Why she made us come home."

"Because she knows I love you," I suggested, "and she thought if I was having a hard time it would help me to see you guys."

"Are you having a hard time?" Sean asked.

"It's a challenging situation. I'm sorry if it upsets you," I said, looking at Sean.

"But are you feeling crazy?" Sean persisted.

"Not really. No."

"You just want to get your own place?" Denver asked.

"Right," I said.

"And get divorced?" Sean introduced the D-word.

"Probably," I said, trying not to sound like I was admitting to criminal intent.

"But Mom doesn't want you to move out?" Denver asked.

"She says she likes things the way they are."

"We talked it over last night," Sean said. "We think she brought us home to make it harder for you to get your own place."

I didn't know what to say to that. Were they accusing their mother of being manipulative; of using those around her to obtain her preferred result? I couldn't look them in the eye and plead her innocence. Fortunately the onion rings arrived and I got busy trying, and failing, to shake ketchup out of the glass bottle. Why didn't they all use squeeze bottles? I requested a bowl of ketchup. And extra tartar sauce. When all these matters were resolved I said to the guys, "I'm sorry that your time with your dad was cut short."

They glanced at each other and took more onion rings.

"If I get another place what do you think it should be like?"

"Whatever you want," Denver said.

"I want room for you guys," I said.

"Then you need a sixty-inch TV," Sean said.

"At least," his brother added.

After lunch we went to the house and made ourselves busy. Denver worked on his school project. Sean watched television on the Internet and chatted online with Nellie. I caught up with my email—that didn't take long— and read. We all tried to act normal. So did Helen, who succeeded by sitting on the couch with her laptop. She didn't look her best. The area under her eyes was showing some age.

Helen said she had called the number Judy had given us and left a message with the answering service, but she hadn't heard back yet.

Late in the afternoon we watched an old movie together. It was *The Big Sleep*, which we all loved. Denver and I made supper. At the table they got me talking about the New Year's Eve party. Sean asked for the link to Peter's video. I wondered whether or not Sean had noticed the resemblance between himself and the victims in Susan's cartoon mural.

When we had cleaned up the kitchen, Denver and Sean went up to Sean's room. I followed and said I'd see them in the morning.

"Want to go to the gym?" Sean asked. "All three of us? Before breakfast?"

Trying not to sound as grateful as I felt, I accepted this proposal. I gave a quick squeeze to each of their shoulders and left for Kate's.

The next day, after working out with the guys at the gym, I was ready to start looking for a place to live. I took my laptop to a coffee shop that offered free Wi-Fi. I had two new emails; one from Greg and one from Georgia. Georgia's told me the time and place of Bill's memorial service. It was the following Saturday.

Greg's message said that Helen had told him I was deserting the boys. *What's she talking about?* he asked. *Thanks again for finding Denver.*

I wrote back that I was probably separating from Helen but added that I hoped Sean and Denver would always be part of my life.

A few minutes later Greg answered, *Could I pay Helen's child support directly to you?* Looking back over the years I decided that I had liked Greg a tiny bit more every time I'd interacted with him.

I started checking out rental properties. That was time consuming. It helped the days pass and led to the future. Mornings the guys and I went to the gym. We had supper together. Helen didn't mention whether she had ever heard from the couples counselor, and I didn't ask. On Friday Sean returned to college, which was clearly a welcome escape from the tension in his home. The next day was Bill's service. Because Denver planned to go with us, he and I went shopping. We bought him a navy blazer, a white shirt, and his first tie.

The service was in a Unitarian church. I got us there early, which is why we were able to be inside the sanctuary instead of being diverted to an adjacent hall with the overflow crowd, to sit on folding chairs and watch the proceedings on television.

In the pew Denver took out his phone. I looked at Helen, who nodded. Denver had been willing to be here with us and to wear his tie. It was enough to ask of him.

There was plenty of time before the service to think about the strangeness of the circumstance and our relationships with the deceased. Would people be invited to share their memories of Bill? On such occasions only the mildest of sins are recalled out loud. I imagined Helen taking the microphone to say, *I had an affair with Bill. He was quite a guy!*

There was a measure of bitterness in this fantasy, but humor also. Yes I had some anger but it did not possess me. Helen had tried to insulate me from her secret life. Her infidelity had never, as far as I could see, been motivated by a wish to hurt me or to humble me or bring me down. I had no reason to think she had been promiscuous in her disloyalty. I didn't need to make excuses for her—but as Julian had pointed out, her combination of attractive qualities—her savoir-faire, wit, and beauty, gave her a lot of options. And her time away from home had provided ample opportunity. Why had I stood for it?

Sitting in the pew between my wife and her younger son, I realized that I was free of lust toward Helen. This week, for the first time, she seemed too old for me. I asked myself if I felt sorry for her. She had received thin love from her parents and had limited emotional bonds with anyone. She needed people around her. She took interest in them—I thought of her welcoming Susan at Thanksgiving—and she could charm. She had feelings but they didn't seem to be strong feelings. She had been a perfect fit into a chilly family. Was that sad? If your emotional needs are low, surely it's easier to feel happy.

In the pew in front of us an auburn-haired man sat with a red-haired teenager. When the organ started she turned to look up toward the choir loft. She had the prettiness of green eyes, healthy, wavy red hair, and a smooth, slightly freckled complexion. When her eyes dropped from the balcony to the dark-haired boy seated behind her, she smiled. Denver looked up from his phone. She turned back to face the front.

Denver gazed at the back of her head for a few seconds before returning his attention to his little screen. Because the music had begun I pointed to his phone and shook my head. He turned it off and put it into a pocket.

Listening to the organist labor at her Bach, I thought about where I was in life. I had belonged to two families: my parents' and Helen's. Why did I think of it as Helen's rather than as ours? Her kids, her house, and, mostly, her money. Or Greg's money, depending on how you wanted to look at it. I had contributed but certainly I was not the *provider* as the now-archaic-sounding term expressed that family role. Had I been important in the raising of Sean and Denver? Yes. In many respects, I had been the family's leader. The boys cared for me, and I for them. And yet in one way they had never been and never could be mine. We were not of the same blood. Why should that matter after so many transactions of care-and-be-cared-for? It shouldn't. I felt that it did matter, anyway.

Where, in time, was I? No longer young but not yet middle-aged. I was a person in the midst of life. Even if I broke with Helen there was no prospect of a fresh start. My past would exert a heavy influence on my future. And my future would end on an occasion like this—with my days of action over, my self, my personhood, perpetuated, for a while, in the hearts of those who loved me. And by the usefulness of what I had made—if I ever made anything that was useful.

The service began. The minister set a pleasant, upbeat tone. This church intended to be a supportive community for the living. It didn't promise much for the dead. Neither the reading nor the hymn mentioned God, and the phrase *eternal life* didn't come up. The forms of the service and the architecture of the venue were Protestant Christian—but none of the words would have annoyed a person skeptical of conventional Christianity.

Georgia offered an appreciation of Bill as a father without exaggerating his virtues. She appeared to have Ev's proxy for eulogizing their dad. I supposed it might have been easier to be a daughter of Bill's than to be his son. Perhaps Bill's love for Ev had seemed more conditional than his love for Georgia.

A surviving college classmate recalled Bill's creativity, determination, and leadership of pranks. He gave the example of the time the dean decided to use the campus radio station for a series of broadcasts. The first program found fault with the student body on every conceivable parameter. Their poor intellectual application. Their lax morals. Their neglected physical fitness. As the second of the series began, the dean warmed to the same theme until one of Bill's confederates threw a switch that diverted the broadcast feed. Instead of the Dean, listeners heard Bill playing his tenor saxophone. At first he sounded gassy, "shall we say, flatulent?" which Bill gradually segued into the excellent jazz he played, at that time, in clubs. It was easy to picture young Bill serene in the confidence that he could persuade anyone of the correctness of his point of view or of any point of view he chose to adopt.

After the remembrances, a string quartet played Beethoven. Probably Bill stipulated that professionals be paid to perform at his service. I wondered, was he still trying to impress people? That seemed harsh. If you have the means why not make your funeral what you want it to be? The quartet filled the church with soothing, complex, lovely music.

After the service Denver could have left with his mother, who didn't know Bill's family and wanted to hurry back to her work. But Denver chose to stay with me for the reception. As we entered the large room under the sanctuary I was greeted by the auburn-haired man who had sat in front of us. "Aren't you Ike Martin from *Hubcaps*?"

"Yes," I replied. "Host of the show formerly known as *Hubcaps*."

The tall, pleasant-looking man introduced himself as Sam Bostrup, a nephew of Bill's. "My mom was a younger sister," he explained, "but I didn't see much of Uncle Bill. I think Dad found Bill hard to be around. He might have been a little much for Dad." The red-haired girl appeared with a paper cup in her hand. "This is my daughter Kelly."

"The lemonade's pretty good," Kelly told us.

I introduced Denver.

"We were sitting behind you," he informed her.

"Mr. Martin was the host of an excellent television program," Sam said. "What are you doing now?" he asked me.

"I'm floating the concept of a new show. It's about talk." He looked interested, so I described my idea. While I explained the concept Kelly moved closer to Denver and seemed to ask him something. As he responded they drifted a step farther from us. Was that why Denver stayed?

Sam liked my idea. His response to it exceeded any encouragement I'd received about anything in a long time. When he told me that he worked in radio, it finally clicked that I'd heard of him. He was a senior producer at our public radio station, which created local and national programming. Sam asked if I'd consider developing the concept for radio instead of television. "It might be a better fit for you."

"That makes sense. My siblings always advised me to wear a bag over my head when I was on camera."

He laughed and explained that radio was a safer environment for intellectual content, "Except for public affairs." He gave me his card and asked me to send him a paragraph describing my concept. "I've always wanted to produce a show called *Earshot*," he said. "Maybe this is it."

I promised to supply the paragraph and expressed pleasure at making his acquaintance.

Georgia's partner Lee appeared at my elbow. "Is it true that you were out there when he died?"

"Yes, because of the oddest circumstances."

"What were they?"

Before I answered, I located Denver. He was at the refreshment table. I explained that my stepson had taken an unauthorized expedition and I'd gone west to round him up.

"It's so strange for Bill to have died way out there in the mountains in winter."

Georgia came up. I congratulated her on her remarks. "It couldn't have been easy to strike all the balances the occasion required."

"Thank you. We will miss him."

Lee took her hand. Georgia turned to her embrace.

I went to Marjie and Stephen, who were talking with Sam's daughter. "Hello again," Kelly said. "This is my cousin Marjie—I guess we're cousins—is that right?"

"Something like that," Marjie said. She asked Kelly, "Do you know Ike?"

"We only met today," Kelly explained. "I need a lemonade refill." She headed for the beverage table.

I said, "Hello, Marjie."

"Hello, Ike. I'm sorry we didn't have a chance to talk out west."

"I'm so sorry about your grandfather."

"I guess that's the end of our project," Stephen said.

It occurred to me to remind him that I wanted my materials back but it didn't seem like the right time. Instead I said, "The family might need something pulled together," and immediately wished I hadn't. It sounded like I was promoting my services right here at the memorial service.

"How are you, Ike?" Marjie asked, looking hard at me. Was I showing signs of stress from the personal transition I was attempting to negotiate? "How is Denver? I haven't even gotten to hear how you found him."

"It was all about a school project. Perfectly innocent except he went off on his own without permission. He really caught fire about his research. It might change where he goes to college and what he wants to study."

"Is that okay with you?" Marjie asked me.

Stephen looked around the room. "Is your wife here?"

"She was here for the service. She had to leave. Any progress on your play?" I only mentioned it to needle him. Rather than pause for him to respond, I said to Marjie, "Yes, I'm fine with that. Never underestimate the power of a school project. I sure appreciated your phone call." Stephen looked at her. "It was very kind. Also, thank you for taking Susan to the airport. She is so funny, to have the nerve to impose on a complete stranger."

"Georgia remembered Susan from the New Year's Eve party we've all heard so much about," Marjie said. "There was something about a mural in the bedroom? And over-baked brownies?"

"Susan was one of the co-conspirators," I said. "Georgia fit right in. I thought she did a great job this morning."

"I did, too," Marjie said.

"Would you like some coffee?" Stephen asked her. "I'll get you some coffee."

As he walked away, Marjie whispered, "That means *he* wants some coffee."

I glanced around the room. Mrs. Lu was headed our way. Denver was talking with Kelly. Marjie embraced Mrs. Lu.

After their hug, Mrs. Lu stepped back and said, "Hello, Ike Martin. I am so sad that my friend Marjory has lost her wonderful grandfather."

"Yes," I said.

"I know he was old but it doesn't matter," Mrs. Lu continued. "We want the people we love to stay with us forever." She looked at Marjie. "Life is always renewed. That's why we live in the garden. There is always new life. Autumn comes and there is death but spring will come again."

Marjie smiled and cried. My eyes, too, felt warm.

"Who knows the future?" Mrs. Lu continued. "Spring returns, and seeds, and growth, and fruit."

Marjie took her hand and tried to smile.

"You will see," Mrs. Lu whispered, looking up into Marjie's eyes. "Time will tell."

As Stephen handed Marjie a styrofoam cup, Denver appeared at my side. Introducing him, I read in his face that he was ready to leave. After goodbyes we went to my car.

"That was fun," Denver said.

I did not blurt, *It was a memorial service!* Instead I reflected for two beats, then agreed, "Yes. It was. A certain kind of fun."

I started the car. Denver took out his phone. He looked pleased.

Chapter 19

As usual, unless it was too wet, Denver rode to my house after school on his bicycle. It was Monday. Over the weekend he had slept at Helen's, but now he was back with me for the school week.

"I stopped at home and picked up the mail," were his first words as he came in the door.

"Any news?" It was the season for colleges to send out their admissions decisions.

"I'm in at Bowdoin."

"Hey. Excellent."

"Yeah. So now I have to decide where to go." He reached into his pack and extracted sheets of paper. "I printed some of our data. For easy reference. Bowdoin. Dorkiness of student body. Five point six. WiFi coverage. Four point three. Nachos at student center. One. Availability of squash courts—"

"I don't recall us evaluating the athletic facilities there or anywhere."

"I didn't keep you in the loop on every dimension."

"No?"

"No."

"Since when do you care about squash?"

"I always liked it. The white walls. The little racquet."

"Okay. So where do you think you'll go?"

"That's a big decision. It deserves thought."

"True."

"Remember how you said that Mrs. Lu was somebody's oracle?"

"Yes."

"I have an oracle, too."

"Kelly?"

"She goes by Kelly in daily life but as an oracle she's known as Red."

"Has she rendered an opinion on this matter of your post-secondary education?"

"It's in process."

"How does that work?" I asked.

After he took a can of root beer from my refrigerator and slid it into an insulating sleeve, Denver zeroed in on the Zone of Snacks—a particular cabinet. Before I moved in with Helen I had lived with housemates. I had never before had sole management of a kitchen. It was enjoyable to organize everything to suit myself, with Denver's input on the few topics of interest to him—such as the Zone of Snacks—from which he extracted a bag of cheese-coated popcorn. He put it on the counter and took out his phone. "*Black must soon his college choose*," he read. "That started it."

"Started what?"

"The process. A text from me to her."

"Who's Black?"

"Me. As an oracle."

"You're also an oracle?"

"Red says so. She calls me Black." I had always thought of Denver's hair as brown but it had become darker in his teenage years.

"Red replied, *Set your course without taboos.* Then, Black: *Engineering brings the dough.*"

"These are text messages?"

"Right. *But what is it you want to know?*"

"The oracle is Red and Red is Kelly?"

"Yeah. Why are you having so much trouble with this?"

"I'm not. I'm with you. Go on."

"Black responded—"

"Wait a minute. When was all this?"

"On my way over here."

"Just now?"

"Yeah."

"You were on your bike."

"So was she. At least, she might have been."

"That can't be safe."

"We text from our bikes all the time."

"Denver."

"It's okay. When we're stopped. Usually."

"Nobody can text and ride a bike."

"Sure they can. One hand for the bike, one for the phone."

I looked at him over my glasses—the universal signal of condescending disapproval.

"Black wrote: *The where, the when, the why, the how.* And Red: *If how's the thing, to Cambridge swing.*"

"What?"

"MIT. Black: *If what is stuff, but what if what is us?*"

"What if what is us?"

"Yeah."

"What did she say to that?"

"She hasn't responded yet." He shook his phone as if he were trying to shake out something that might be stuck within it. "She probably had to do something. Isn't that that guy?" He was looking at the television I kept in the kitchen. The picture was on but the sound was off.

"What guy?" I looked at the screen. "Oh. It's Stephen." I turned on the sound.

"Bill Trippy was the Twentieth Century's Thomas Edison," Stephen said.

The host was a professional rival of mine when I'd been in the Boston-area talk show world—a take-no-prisoners competitor named Shirley Banks. She said, "Your biography has been rushed into print since Professor Trippy's death in January."

"Yes, which is possible only because I had been working with Bill and his family for a year before his passing. Most people don't yet realize how much his work changed the terms of everyday life."

That sounded familiar. Had I written it?

"Could you give us an example?"

"Well, for one thing, we don't spend much time worrying about World War III. That's because Bill Trippy won the Cold War."

My cell phone rang. I was going to decline the call until I saw it was Ev. "Turn on your television," he ordered.

"We're watching." The program went to a commercial.

"Did you see him claim to be the authorized biographer?"

"We didn't have the sound on until just now."

"How could he do this? I don't know where he got the manuscript. Marjie thinks it might be yours."

"He had my stuff. I'd asked him to return it."

"As soon as Dad died he got a deal with this publisher."

"Is Marjie okay with it?"

"No she's not okay with it. She broke up with him a month ago when she found out what he was doing. We're evaluating our legal options. But my lawyer, goddamn it, is taking too long to get the thing squashed and now they're already on television."

The program resumed. Denver said, "Isn't that the guy I hit with your car?"

"Yeah," I said, folding my hand around my phone. "The guy who didn't write the play we saw in Bozeman."

"Ike," I heard my phone say, "I'll call you later." Ev hung up.

"Tell us more," Shirley prompted, "about how Professor Trippy won the Cold War for the United States."

Stephen tried to make himself sound like an expert. Pretending he'd been on television so much that he was bored but he was trying to be nice about it. I'd watched plenty of shallow conceited guests act the same way.

"The oracle currently known as Red has weighed in," Denver said.

Stephen made a rambling speech about MIT's role in defense technology. I couldn't really listen because Denver was reading the text from Kelly. "*The who! If that's for you, then Institutes won't do.* Yeah. I guess she means that if *what* is technology I'm good at MIT but if *what* is more about people or history then maybe Bowdoin would be better. I knew that already."

My cell rang. It was my sister. I wanted to decline the call but I hit the screen the wrong way and accepted it by accident. "Kate," I began, "this isn't—"

"Ike! Turn on your TV!"

"It's on."

"Congratulations! Your guy is famous. There's going to be a book about him. I didn't know he was so famous. This is about your guy, right?"

"Yes, and—"

"Maybe *you* can write a book about him, too!"

"Let's talk later. I want to hear this."

"Okay," she said. "Call me."

The call ended—and so did Stephen's interview.

I decided I shouldn't dwell on how outrageous Stephen was. He must have been trying to set a record for obnoxiousness. What did I care? Would I have preferred to be him? A phony in the spotlight, instead of an honest guy in obscurity? No. Besides, I finally had something going. Or maybe I did. I was scheduled for my third meeting with Sam Bostrup about hosting a show with that name he liked—*Earshot*. Starting local but with the goal of having it picked up nationally. Having that hope in mind made it easier to stop thinking about Stephen and his theft of my material. After all, Bill had paid me to write it. In his own way Stephen was giving Bill what he wanted—keeping him famous. I looked at Denver and congratulated him again about getting into Bowdoin.

"Thanks," he said. "Guess who showed up at Mom's yesterday?"

"I give."

"Susan. And a guy—the guy who made the video on New Year's Eve."

"Peter?"

"Susan calls him B.K."

"Barbie's Ken," I explained. "He reminds his friends of the Ken doll, if Ken frosted his hair."

"He's there, too."

"With Camo?"

"Who?"

"A girl named Camille?"

"No, just him and Susan. Mom's letting her paint the whole inside of the house. And the guy is taking a cooking course."

Mentally I went back to Ev saying that Marjie had broken up with Stephen.

"That old guy, what's-his-name?"

"Julian?"

"Yeah—Mom says he's going to make some kind of big deal about the house being an installation in the suburbs. What's an installation?"

"I don't know. It's when an artist puts something somewhere. Or something."

"Kelly thinks it's all so cool."

"Do you think it's cool? For the house you grew up in?"

"If Kelly thinks it's cool, I'm good."

"Right."

"I better text her back. What should I say?"

"What was her last send?"

"The who? If that's for you, the institute won't do."

"Read the whole thing."

"Okay. *Black must soon his college choose. Set your course without taboos. Engineering brings the dough. But what is it you want to know? The where, the what, the why, the how. If how's the thing, to Cambridge swing. If what is stuff, but what if what is us? The who? If that's for you—"*

"It's nice to have a friend," I said.

He started typing.

"What are you writing?"

"What you said."

"I didn't mean that was the next line."

"No. But it's what I want to say."

Chapter 20

As Mrs. Lu entered the garden plot she asked, "Where's Marjory?"

"She'll be here soon," I said. "You and I are early." Morning sun sparkled on the dewy foliage.

"Did you know I am invited to the party?"

Denver's graduation was to be celebrated that afternoon and Mrs. Lu had been invited. "I am glad. Will you attend?"

"I look forward to visiting the famous place."

"It gives a whole new meaning to the phrase *bedroom community*." That had become my standard line because as Susan had converted Helen's house into a work of art she had made each room into a bedroom. Julian had kept the media informed about Susan's project; they had taken it up as a story, and everyone seemed to know about the house I used to live in.

Mrs. Lu placed the contents of her wicker basket onto the little table in the center of Marjie's plot. She didn't share Marjie's and my appreciation of coffee. She brought tea for herself in a thermal carafe and a beautiful china service, carefully padded in her basket.

"I'm a little worried," I said, "that the artists will distract attention from Denver."

"You must make sure that he is in the spotlight," Mrs. Lu declared. "You can make a speech about him. Maybe he can make a speech, too."

Marjie was within hearing before we noticed her. "I hope Denver will speak. He has an interesting way of looking at things."

"Greg and Sally will be there," I said. "Maybe Greg will offer a toast."

Marjie sat down, took my hand in hers, and asked if I had coffee for her.

With my free hand I handed her a travel mug. We were too shy for a hello kiss in front of Mrs. Lu. This was kind of silly because Mrs. Lu had helped us get together. After I heard, during my strange phone call with Ev, that Marjie had broken up with Stephen, I did some thinking. We could be right for each other but if we came together on the rebound it might not work. It might ruin everything. My conclusion was to give us both a year. I could complete my divorce and let Marjie get over Stephen and the death of her grandfather and then sometime next winter—not necessarily a full year, but most of one—call her.

That seemed like a good plan, and prudent. Meanwhile I was busy preparing to record the pilot of my new show. Sam had suggested that instead of using actors my guests could be storytellers. Our material could come from their stories and from literature and from emails sent by members of our audience. The weekend slot Sam had in mind was just before a popular quiz show. I had a good feeling about the whole thing. The storyteller to be featured on the pilot was truly gifted. To prepare for working with him I had borrowed his recordings from the library. I'd been in my living room listening to him portray a girl's attempts to persuade her brother that human beings are animals, making notes, when my doorbell rang. It was Mrs. Lu.

Her smallness made my couch look large. I offered her tea but she, in her oracular way, cut to the chase.

"You are no longer married?"

"Legally I am but I live here now and Helen and I are getting a divorce."

"Why haven't you called Marjory? Don't you like her?"

"I do like her but it hasn't been very long since she broke up with Stephen and I thought I'd better give her some time."

"Why?"

"Wouldn't that be better? To give her some time?"

"No."

"No? You don't agree?"

"No. She was never heart-close with that man."

"No?"

"Never. Why did she stay with him so long? Do you wonder that?"

"I could ask myself the same question about my marriage."

"What would your answer be?"

"Love comes in many flavors. We had some."

"If you loved that woman why did you move out?"

"I want a different life."

"You want a real wife."

"That's one way to put it."

"Don't you think Marjory wants a real husband?"

"Does she?"

"Of course she does." Her expression relaxed for the first time since she arrived. In a softer voice she repeated, "Of course she does."

"It seems a little soon for me to be trying out for the part when I'm so recently single. I've only lived here a few months."

Mrs. Lu responded silently, with a derisive grimace.

"You think that's long enough?"

"Georgia called me. You know, Georgia, Marjory's aunt?"

"Yes. What did Georgia have to say?"

"I will tell you what she said. She said, 'What's the matter with Ike? What is he waiting for?'"

There was silence while I observed my responding thoughts and feelings. Finally I asked, "What do you think I should do?" What's the point of having an oracle around if you aren't going to seek advice?

"Take her some coffee."

So I did. Our first visit was friendly but guarded. I think Marjie shared my worry about timing. We spent an evening together, then another, and the next time I had the impulse to reach for her hand, I did not suppress the urge. She responded encouragingly, and these few weeks later on the morning of Denver's graduation party I felt that I was hers. My worries about going too fast seemed over-cautious, too old-Ike. New Ike was a little bolder. And yet, is it not wise to avoid errors?

"What are you thinking about?" Marjie asked.

"Precipitous behavior leading to error."

"Try not to worry," she said. "This is good coffee."

I spied, in the distance, a fluorescent orange spot moving in our direction. "I wonder where he got that helmet?"

Marjie followed my gaze. "It gives him good visibility."

It was Denver, on his bicycle, wearing his day-glo helmet.

"Can he really text and bike at the same time?" Marjie asked.

"I don't know. He claims that he can and that Kelly does it, too."

"It can't be safe," Marjie said.

"No," I agreed. "Good morning, Denver."

"Peter needs broccoli," Denver said.

Marjie gave him a knife. "You may cut it yourself."

"Who is Peter?" Mrs. Lu asked.

"Peter is a recent art graduate who has taken up cooking," I said. "He's helping with Denver's party."

"Is he your roommate?" Mrs. Lu asked Denver.

"He's with Susan," Denver said. "The girl who paints the walls."

"Is he *with* Susan?" Marjie asked. "I thought he was *with* Camo."

"You should see Camo on YouTube," Denver said, "in her Daisy Duck costume. She dances. She sings."

"Denver and I make no attempt to sort out the *with*-ness of these particular friends," I said. "We take them in whatever affiliations we find them. How are Susan and Nellie getting along?" I asked Denver.

"Susan calls her *Belly*," Denver said, "which is pretty funny considering how thin Nellie is."

"How does Nellie react," Marjie asked, "to being called Belly?"

"She ignores it. Julian tells Susan to stop."

"Julian's around?" I knew he was invited to the party but I didn't realize he was already on the scene.

"Yes. He keeps showing people through the rooms Susan's painted. He tells them he's the keeper—or whatever."

"Curator?"

"Right—curator."

Half curator, half house parent, I thought. We've entrusted the morals of our youth to Julian Deftworth. "Has Kelly met Julian?" I asked Denver, who had nearly filled his ziplock bag with Marjie's broccoli.

"Yes. She says it's amazing the way he can be phony and real at the same time."

Georgia arrived with a box of scones and offered one to Denver. Around his first buttery mouthful Denver added, "Julian told Kelly his theory that, by natural law, red haired people can only be so smart."

"How did that go over with Kelly?"

"She said she had a theory that perverted old men were full of crap."

"I didn't realize that the term 'perverted' was politically correct," Marjie said.

"Redheads, when aroused, are excused," Georgia said. "By natural law."

"Susan is helping Peter with the cooking," Denver said. "They are making all the meals. Kelly thinks Susan is in love with Peter."

"In love!" Georgia shouted. "Cupid found Susan? Susan the brownie-burner? She's back?"

"She's our artist-in-residence," Denver said, as he got on his bike. He rode away with his broccoli. His orange helmet receded in the distance.

"When you were at the party, did you see that mural she'd made?" I asked Georgia. "Helen's letting her spread it all over the house. As you might have seen on *Chronicle*."

"I didn't go in there during the party," Georgia said, "but I watched them on that kid's video. Susan was on *Chronicle?*"

"Last week," I said. "The young videographer also has returned. The lad they used to call Barbie's Ken. He's catering the party! He's going into the business. Susan the Brownie Burner is Peter's sous chef or understudy or girlfriend. Or something. Who knows?"

My phone rang. It was Helen. Taking the call, I walked away from Marjie's garden.

"Hello Ike." She sounded upset. "I was supposed to be landing at Logan right now but I'm still in Florida."

"What's the matter?"

"Mom's taken a turn for the worse. They don't think she'll last much longer."

"I'm sorry."

"It's frustrating. She might go tonight or she might last for weeks. What do you think I should do?"

"I guess you should stay down there. At this point you don't really have time to make it here for the party, anyway."

"And Greg will be there, right? Will you explain to Denver?"

"No! If you aren't coming you have to call Denver yourself."

"Julian's there. You and he are better mothers than I ever was."

"You flatter us. I hear he's brought Max with him this time. Do you know Max? Maybe he'll turn out to be the best mother of all."

"Max is perfect. You'll talk to Denver for me?"

"No, you have to call him."

When I got back to Marjie's plot, everyone was gone except her. She and I sat in the sun of summer's first morning, sipped our tepid coffee, and talked, cautiously, about future possibilities.

We arrived at Denver's party early to help with the final preparations. The first person we saw was Susan, in a shortness of sleeve and skirt that maximized exposure of her body art. She presented herself with a tah-dah and a slightly self-conscious expression.

We had brought extra chairs, which we carried through the garage into the back yard. There by the pool sat a young woman who fit Nellie's description. She looked up at me from her iPad. Sean was using a long-handled skimmer to remove a dead frog from the pool.

"Are there more chairs?" Nellie asked. "May I help?"

We introduced ourselves.

"I've heard so much about you," Nellie said to me. "I guess we sort of talked on the phone a few months ago."

"Yes, through an intermediary. It's nice to meet you in person. Where's Denver?" I asked Sean.

"He and Kelly are upstairs finishing their puppet show."

"Puppet show?"

"The Education of Denver Shields."

"A puppet show?"

"Kind of a multi-media thing, so we gather," Nellie said.

I left Marjie talking with Sean and Nellie and went into the house. It was the first time I'd been inside it since I'd moved out. Today its smell was dominated by Susan's art supplies and Peter's cooking. Possibly the fragrance of Camo's paper-making could be detected underneath—but that might have been my imagination.

Susan and Peter were in the kitchen. "Hi guys," I said.

"Hey Ike," Peter said.

Susan fluttered her eyelids at me and kept working. Whatever she meant by that gesture, it didn't seem unfriendly.

The only furniture in the living room was a queen-sized bed in the middle. The walls were covered in graffiti-like drawings that resembled Susan's tattoos and the decoration she had added to the Thanksgiving jig-saw puzzle. The bed itself—the headboard and footboard—had also served her as canvas. At a distance her cartooning merged into abstraction, like a floral pattern in an oriental carpet, but when you looked closer you saw that every figure was something that was related to something else. Either one thing was transforming into another, as for example a monkey's arm that elongated into a reticulated snake—or the figure was engaged in a transaction with its neighbor—eating it, mating with it, doing it bodily injury. Some were gross, some violent, some just funny—a girl in a tutu danced in the spout of a whale. The whale appeared to be defecating a guy. Or giving birth to him. Susan always provided something to react to.

I went up to the study. Denver and Kelly, side by side, peered at computer screens, whispering back and forth. Denver looked up. "Go away, Ike, we're not finished yet."

"He can see; it doesn't matter," Kelly told him.

"I don't mean to interrupt and I don't need to see. You are giving a puppet show?"

"Sort of," Kelly said.

"Are there puppets?"

"Kind of," Denver said.

"Okay. You don't have to stay up here during the party, do you?"

"No. We'll be down," Kelly said.

"Good because I want to be on your volleyball team." I looked at Denver. "Did you hear from Mom?"

"Yeah," he said.

"I know it seems typical. But this time she really can't help it."

"Dad's coming, though," Denver said. "Is he here yet?"

"No. When I see him shall I send him up?"

"We're almost finished," Kelly said. "We'll be right down."

People began to arrive. Julian and Max brought homemade beer. Max turned out to be one of the most comical individuals I'd ever had the pleasure of hearing tell jokes. Teenagers—friends of Denver's, plus some of Kelly's—arrived in small groups. Sam came with a banjo. Greg and Sally smiled and looked at everything through their west coast eyes. If you wanted to, you could guess they were thinking they'd seen better in the Bay Area—or you could cut them a little slack and think that they were relaxing and enjoying themselves on a perfect June afternoon here at the other end of the country—in the Bay *State*. Georgia asked me how *Earshot* was going and I told her, fine, except I'd convinced Sam to change the name to *Talk Talk Talk*. It was testing well with audiences.

Georgia paid extra attention to Denver and his friends. When Susan and Peter presented appetizers, Georgia served the kids and fussed at them about sunscreen and hydration and asked about their plans for the following year and acted impressed with every one of them.

Julian was master of ceremonies. He prompted us to applaud the chef, Peter, whose dark hair had been growing out. At this point, only the outer fourth of his hair was partly yellow. When Susan distributed business cards for BK Catering, Julian, in an ironic but kindly tone, encouraged everyone to support small businesses and entrepreneurs. When the dinner was ready he managed the traffic flow. The young and ravenous he sent first to the buffet.

After the meal Sam got everyone's attention by playing reveille on his banjo. Julian said, "Ladies and gentlemen, please step into the Shields Puppet Studio—it resembles a garage but do not be deceived—and—special seating tonight—take your chairs with you."

People carried their chairs into the garage.

Denver and Kelly were on a platform behind a large flat-screen television. Their faces were painted like mimes, but gray instead of white. When we were all seated Julian clapped his hands for attention and announced, "Tonight's production is entitled, 'The Education of Denver Shields.'"

A picture appeared on the television. I recognized the scene: one of the campuses Denver and I had visited. Holding sticks representing marionette control rods, Kelly pretended to walk a puppet onto the stage. As she did so an animated figure slid onto the TV screen; a cut-out of a woman. "I can't wait until the new students get here so I can share my wisdom with them," Kelly muttered, as though she was that woman talking to herself. "They are going to be so happy to learn from me."

Using his control sticks, Denver mimed walking a marionette from the opposite side of the stage. The "puppet" appeared on the screen—a picture of him. Because both Denver and Kelly wore headsets plugged into an amplifier, their mumbled dialogue was audible. "Here I am on campus," Denver said. "Another shallow, materialistic high school student."

We laughed.

Kelly's lady moved nearer to Denver's picture and said, "Here's an ignorant-looking young man."

"Of course I'm ignorant" Denver responded. "All I've done since puberty is play video games." The picture cut to a scene from the game demo movie that Sean and Denver had assembled at Thanksgiving. The two young puppeteers waved their hands and sticks above the screen as though their manipulations were causing vehicles to fly, shoot, and blow up.

"Here is my opportunity to impart some wisdom," Kelly said, as the professor-cutout returned to the screen. "Young man, you should take my course on philosophy of poetry. So you can get over being shallow."

"Uh, okay, but how can I get rich?"

"Meaning is better than money."

Denver said, "I'd trade money *and* meaning for a girlfriend." The scene changed to actual video of Denver crouched, playing marbles. "Don't think," Denver said to himself. "Just shoot." He made the shot. People clapped. I supposed Luke took this video at the California tournament. "You're cool," Denver congratulated himself. "So cool. Denver you da man."

The picture cut to Peter's New Year's Eve video. There was Susan, opening fortune cookies in the kitchen with the big hairy guy. Kelly mimed bringing out another puppet, a red translucent glow that stopped over Susan. "Hello everybody, I'm Red," Kelly said.

"Oh, oh, here comes Black," Denver said, pretending to bring out a black circle, a ring, that stopped over the face of a guy. "Red, what's my fortune?"

"It's bad, Black," Kelly said, "Bad stuff is going down."

As the picture went white, we were all startled by a loud crash from the sound system. Whiteness dissolved into my car wrapped around that tree.

"Damn, you're right," Denver said. "Way to go, Red."

A crash test dummy hit an airbag. The shot looped, repeating faster and faster.

Suddenly there stood Julian in a still picture, on the steel plate that covered the shaft in the Sierra. "Who's that, Black?" Kelly asked.

"Some guy," Denver said. "Out west."

Then came a series of stills of me climbing toward the camera on snowshoes. "Another guy?" Kelly asked.

"That's Ike," Denver said. The picture cut to snow-covered bison. Kelly hummed a jazzy version of "Home on the Range." We saw elk among ice-draped hot springs, which dissolved to black. Kelly stopped humming. A photo of Denver slid onto the screen. His hair had been photoshopped to look white.

"Now you're old," Kelly said. "Black is gray."

"Old but wise," Denver said. "Life's lessons learned."

"What are they?" she asked. "What are life's lessons?"

"Still to come," he said, as his picture faded out. "We'll find out."

Kelly and Denver put down their control sticks and bowed. When the applause ended, the party was over. In a complicated way, I felt good. I felt as though, just then, I had nothing to worry about.

Made in the USA
Middletown, DE
12 March 2015